Dead Man's Hand

Mark Lock

Published by Accent Press Ltd 2016

ISBN 9781783758142

For Z

About the author

Mark Lock is a lecturer in mathematics in South Wales, where he lives with his young family and more animals than you can shake a wonky stick at. *Dead Man's Hand* is his first novel.

Part One: Ceremony

Chapter One

His head was thumping like fuck as he tried to open his eyes. He must have been sleeping. His sight was blurry and he tried to turn his head to see where he was. As he turned, the thing on his neck dug further in and he cried out in pain. He was still in his own room – the man hadn't moved him. Thank God the man hadn't moved him. He felt a tiny twitch of relief that he was still on his own territory, that he had at least a fighting chance if he knew he was at home.

His eyes were beginning to regain their focus now, and he could see all of his things dotted around the room. Above the gas fireplace, the *Abbey Road* poster. Stripes of black and white going up and down. Below that, on the mantelpiece, the Southern Comfort bottle with an old candle stuck in the neck, dried wax dribbling over the sides. On the floor in front of him, about two feet from where he lay, was the home-made bong he'd been using for the last couple of weeks – a crumpled two-litre bottle of Coke with a small length of hose. Just behind that he could make out the shoes that his mother had bought for his last court appearance. The shoes that he refused to wear even though she said that it would make a good impression on the board. 'A good clean pair of shoes could make all the difference,' she'd said, and the thought of it now made his eyes well up with heavy tears. How could he find himself in such a position? Lying here utterly helpless while this man moved about his flat.

The man. Where was he? Danny tried to twist around to see if he was standing behind him but the strap around his neck made him wince once again so he remained still and listened to the light *phut phut phut* that seemed to come from somewhere nearby. What was that? What was it?

Why did he feel this weak? All he could do was lie there. Why couldn't he just get up and walk out of the room and knock on the door of one of the other flats and tell them there was a psychopath trying to kill him on his floor and, if they'd be so kind, could they call the police please, thank you. Not that he'd ever met one of his neighbours before. A brief brush past someone in the hallway a few months back, music coming from some of the rooms late at night.

1

That's all the evidence he had to suggest that other people lived in the building. Not exactly a great deal of –

The door opened and the man walked back in carrying two large navy blue holdalls. Danny's heart thumped into life again. His stomach flipped over and he felt his legs tense. The man set the bags down near Danny's head before leaning over him once more.

'Sorry about leaving you alone there for a bit, Danny,' he said. 'Had to pick these up.'

The bags looked heavy and Danny worried about what exactly they contained.

'Now. Shall we try again?'

The man reached up on to the nearby table and brought down the dictaphone that he'd used earlier. In his other hand was the piece of card. Shiny. Laminated perhaps. It reminded Danny of his school timetable. The teachers always made the kids write them out on thin pieces of card and then cover them with strips of sellotape to prevent them from getting soggy.

Squatting over his body, the man thrust both the dictaphone and the card into Danny's face.

'Just read the words. That's all I ask of you. Just say them nice and slowly into the tape recorder here. Where you see the asterisk, just say your name.'

Danny stared hard at the card but his eyes were still blurred and his head still thumped. He could see that they were typed, not hand-written. But that was about all. The words themselves were nothing more than smears.

'Please, Danny. I'm parked on a double yellow outside and I don't want to get clamped, so let's hurry up and get it over with, eh? There's a good boy.'

Danny's mind slipped to the traffic wardens who strolled up the road. They could help him. They could stop this man. They were like police. How could he get to them? Could he shout out and be heard? Surely they would hear him? Unfortunately his room looked out over the back of the property. An unkempt tuft of scrubby garden that backed on to another unkempt tuft of scrubby garden. No one would hear him. Anyway, he'd already tried that when the man first went out. His body and his throat were weak for some reason and he could barely manage a useless croak. Shouting was no good. Nor was reading at the moment. His eyes were starting to water, or was he crying? He didn't know. Couldn't tell.

'Come on, Danny,' the voice was a little less patient sounding now. 'Let's get it over with. Please. I need you to do this.'

The floor around Danny's neck and head felt warm, wet, and sticky. His hair was clinging to his scalp and he wanted to scratch at it. Loosen it up. He needed to wash it – that was the truth. He needed to get a good shampoo and conditioner from the shop around the corner and clean himself off. He would definitely need both shampoo and conditioner. Those shampoos that were also conditioners at the same time were rubbish. Left your hair feeling half washed. No, he needed both for this particular job. In fact, it was probably a good idea to go somewhere in town to buy the stuff. The shop around the corner probably only sold cheapo nonsense. Go to a proper chemist like Boots or something. Or even a salon. They sold the best stuff in hairdressers these days. That would be –

'Look! Just READ THE BLOODY CARD, WILL YOU? Just read the bloody thing! *Jesus!*'

The man got up from Danny and stormed to the window shaking his head. Danny got the impression that he was trying to compose himself. Calm himself down. He was looking outside. Probably thinking that the lawn (if there was one under all the mess and growth) needed some serious TLC.

'Look, Danny.' The voice was softer again. 'You're dying. It's unavoidable. You're lying there bleeding to death. It could take ages. You could be rolling around there for hours, which isn't nice, and I don't want that, trust me. I *really* don't want that for you. Read the card for me and I will speed it up. We'll get to the end a lot quicker.' The man turned away from the window to look at Danny. On his face was a smile. Not a cruel, malicious smile. Not even a vaguely sarcastic one. But a pleasant smile. Friendly. 'OK?'

The man walked over to one of the blue holdalls and, after unzipping it, pulled out the biggest saw that Danny had ever seen in his short life.

His head was thumping like fuck as he tried to open his eyes. He must have been sleeping. His sight was blurry and he tried to turn his head to see where he was. The orange glow from the bedside clock made him realise that he was at home. Untypically. Whenever he awoke with a bad head he was usually in somebody else's bed. Embarrassed, he'd scurry his clothes together, garble an excuse, and head for the door. This morning, though, he was at home. Which was convenient in many ways, but also inconvenient in that he had to somehow get rid of the person lying next to him. He found being tactful difficult when hungover and tired. He turned in the sheets and looked up at the white-emulsioned ceiling. A fly was *zzz*-ing around the lightshade, momentarily stopping now and then to rub its legs together. It was late spring and the flies were becoming more apparent in the slowly warming air of south London. A few more weeks and they would be a pest, getting themselves caught indoors or tetching about your head while you were walking through the park. Hal wished he had a rolled-up newspaper to hand so that he could finish this particular buzzing bugger off. He'd have to pick its squashed carcass off the ceiling, but it was a price worth paying to prevent it from dive-bombing his ears later in the day.

His latest lover gave a short sharp snort. Dear God, thought Hal, a snorer. The last time he'd drunkenly slept with a snorer he got virtually no sleep and spent the entire night flicking through their collection of photograph albums. Beautifully annotated, by the time dawn came around Hal could have told you anything you needed to know about that person and their family, from their first boyfriend to their inter-railing holiday with friends during university. For Christ's sake, he even knew that the family had once had a pet rabbit called Bertrand Russell.

The clock said 7.09 and Hal tutted at himself for not having had the presence of mind to set the alarm for 6.30. He'd been too out of it. Too horny. He got up out of bed, slipped on some boxers and a T-shirt, and headed down to the kitchen.

In the fridge, Hal considered the Free Trade Organic Decaffeinated Coffee, but decided that today was a Hot Lava Java (Strength 5) sort of day. Flicking the wall-mounted TV on, he prepared the cafetière and popped some bread in the toaster. The BBC news was a litany of disaster and despair as usual. Plane crash in Colombia – 170 dead. Villages flooded in Pakistan – thousands lost, suspected dead. Car bomb in Iraq – five killed. The only story not guaranteed to make you slash your wrists was an item on the latest Pixar film, and even that left a slightly stale taste in the mouth after all that misery. Sitting down at the breakfast bar to nibble his toast, Hal nudged the rubber buttons on the remote control. A kiddies' cartoon on BBC2. *Daybreak* interviewing some minor actor from some minor soap opera (about to launch a minor pop career, no doubt). Some mindless, talentless boy band yobbos bouncing around to their latest single on Channel Four. Irritating, squeaky-voiced children's presenter on Five. Hal turned the television off.

In the first floor bathroom, he showered. At six foot four, he needed the showerhead high. He twisted the nozzle and the water shot out in a single powerful jet. He liked the feeling of water hitting his skin hard, and turned the temperature up so that it was as hot as he could take it. The bathroom was thick with steam as he rubbed the soap over his completely shaven head and rinsed it off.

Stepping out of the cubicle he patted himself dry with a towel that was slightly too damp and too overused to be totally effective. His body was still as strong as it always had been, but his visits to the gym had become less frequent in the last few months, and the onset of middle-aged spread meant that he was losing his muscle tone. Not greatly. Not yet. But the rot was beginning to set in. He was all too aware of that. Of course, excesses like the previous night's didn't help. Left you feeling shit and bloated. He was drinking too much again. Doing too much in the evenings, like a stupid first year university student, overexcited at having left home for the first time and the freedom that entailed. Unfortunately, Hal thought, he wasn't eighteen any more. He wasn't even eighteen times two any more. At thirty-nine years old he felt as though he should have known better.

But he didn't.

Downstairs, with a towel still wrapped around his waist, he checked the post. Nothing but bills. And junk mail. Bills and bilge, as he liked to call it. Suddenly a high-pitched beeping came from the sitting room. Hal sighed and wandered in, picking up the pager that sat on top of the stereo. He pressed a button and read the message before carrying it upstairs with him.

Back in the bedroom, last night's shag was stirring. Hal went to the wardrobe and pulled out a shirt and an immaculately pressed light cotton suit.

'Nice suit.'

'Eh? Oh. Yeah. Sleep well?'

'Wonderfully. Eventually.' The twinkle in the eye made Hal feel uneasy. He pulled on his trousers then went to work on the shirt buttons, popping them through each little eyelet.

'I've got to go to work. Had a message.' He waved the pager in the air, as if it explained everything. 'Urgent.'

'What do you do exactly? You never told me last night.'

'Er ...' Hal stumbled. 'Accountant.'

'Must be a very important accountant if you're summoned out of bed at twenty to eight in the morning. Must be an important account you're dealing with.'

'Yeah. Something like that.'

A pause. The sort of thing that happens when two strangers are trapped in a room together.

'Do you want me to get dressed and go?'

'No, no,' Hal lied. 'As long as you just pull the front door behind you when you do go. Take as long as you need to get ready.' He slipped his shoes over each foot. 'There's food and coffee in the kitchen. Help yourself.'

'I prefer tea.'

'I think I might have some tea in one of the cupboards down there. It'll be quite old but it might be all right. Main bathroom's downstairs on the first floor.'

'Thanks.'

'Sorry I have to shoot off like this,' he lied again. 'Work.'

'That's OK. I understand.'

Hal pulled on his jacket and started heading for the bedroom door.

'Hey, before you go ... I'm sorry, but I've forgotten your name – inherited my father's inability to remember names, I'm afraid. What is it?'

Hal turned back. 'It's Harry. Harry Luchewski.' Feeling somewhat obliged, he asked, 'And yours?'

'It's Steven,' replied the man in Hal's bed. 'Steven Denyer.'

Chapter Two

Detective Inspector Harry Luchewski closed the front door of his three-storey Victorian townhouse, and walked down the steps to the hard standing where his black Audi TT awaited him. He *peep-peeped* the locks open with the key and clambered into the driving seat. Everyone told him that a TT wasn't a suitable car for someone of his height, but he liked it so much that he chose to ignore them. His seat was set as far back as possible, but still his knees kept bashing the dashboard – especially when he changed gear. He knew it would be sensible to swap it soon. Change it to something bigger and more practical. Like a VW. Or a Volvo.

'Ach!' Hal shuddered to himself as he turned right off the forecourt, up Maple Road towards Penge High Street. 'Volvos. Ach!'

On a normal day, he would take a right at the junction down towards Beckenham, where the team were based. Today however he went left, up through Crystal Palace towards West Norwood and one of the streets around Gipsy Hill Station. Singh had paged him with the address. No other details.

Driving up the hill towards Crystal Palace, Hal got trapped behind a bus dragging seventy or so bleary-eyed souls to their place of work. It pulled in to let some more on and Hal dropped the car to second and roared past it. The traffic was relatively light for that time in the morning and, notwithstanding a few minutes consulting the *London A-to-Z* on the passenger seat (the TT's 'as standard' GPS having never been turned on once in its lifetime), he managed to arrive surprisingly quickly. He could see Singh talking to the Good Professor on the doorstep of the house. Noticing his car pull up, she broke off and strolled over to meet him.

'What's up?' Hal *peep-peeped* the locks shut again, coming round the front of the car to where she stood.

'Come and see for yourself, sir,' replied DS Priti Singh. Her hand beckoned him up the path to where the Good Professor was now taking pictures of something on the doorstep.

'Morning Hal,' the Good Professor greeted Harry without stopping his photographic session. 'Funny bloody thing this.'

'Old lady who lives in one of the flats found it this morning. She lets her little dog out at six to go wee-wees.' Singh popped a Polo mint into her mouth. 'Thought a drunk had left it so she peered in.'

On the doorstep sat a McDonald's bag.

'Open it up.' The Good Professor nodded at Hal.

'Margaret and the boys OK?' Hal asked, prising the sides of the bag open.

'Very good. She's away this week. Up in Sheffield on a –'

'Jesus!' Inside the bag was another bag. A clear plastic bag. Hal recognised it as a freezer bag. A small thing with a popper device across the top to stop food getting contaminated in the freezer. Inside *that* was a fleshy, bloody mess. 'What is it?'

'Look closer.'

Hal brought his head down closer to the wrapper. His eyes could just make out some sausage-shaped things hidden amongst the blood and gore.

'It's a hand.'

'Yep. Left hand. Male Caucasian, I'd say at first glance, but I can't be sure until I get it to the lab. Severed just below the wrist by the looks of it.'

Hal straightened up. 'What's it doing here?'

'Don't ask me. That's your job.'

'Who was first on the scene?'

'Locals sent a young bobby round to check,' Singh interjected. 'He's in the hallway. He's pretty shaken up.'

'Milking it a little, if you ask me.' The Good Professor was packing his camera away now. 'Making the most of it by trying to wing the rest of the day off. My lad's in there now trying to calm him down. He should be out here with me. That's why I'm taking the shots.'

'Is that digital? Or do you still use film?' Hal's mind slipped off on a tangent and pointed at the camera in its case.

'We still tend to use film. Harder to fiddle with film. If you alter a digital photo it can look pretty convincing. If you alter a real photo, it's usually quite easy to spot. Besides which there's no fun in taking digital pictures. Anyone can do it.'

'Who lives here?' Hal asked turning to Singh.

'Flats. Bedsits. Six or seven of them. Looks like only three or four are occupied. House is owned by a Mr Rabin – he's in there now with the old lady. He's divorced. Owns a couple of other houses in the area which he rents out. Drives a Mercedes.' She pointed to a car parked further up the road. 'Takes good care of his tenants according to the old lady. Doesn't strike me as the sort of bloke to have too many enemies.'

Singh was always very thorough. Very, very thorough. And very, very ambitious.

'We'd better go up and have a word. See what this is all about. John …' The Good Professor looked up momentarily. 'This hand. The person who …' he stumbled for the right word but settled on quite the wrong one instead, '… owned it. Dead or alive?'

'Dead.' His eyes didn't even flicker away from the back of the camera case with which he was still fidgeting. 'Unquestionably dead. Impossible to survive such an injury. Unless they were practically standing in the foyer of a hospital when it occurred and managed to get it dealt with straight away. But …' his voice trailed away. 'Not that I'm here to tell you your job – but I would have thought that the fact that it has been put on somebody's doorstep, presumably by somebody else, means that you are looking at a murder enquiry here.'

'Yeah. I know.'

'I'll get it packed away, whip it off to the lab and print it before I do anything else. Just in case some poor sod *is* suffering somewhere. But I very much doubt it.'

'Cheers.' Hal and Singh went inside the house where Dr Good's assistant (a ruddy-faced, ginger-haired boy called Spud or Sponge or something – Hal could never remember) was sat chatting to an even younger, uniformed officer. The copper looked wide-eyed and shaky.

'Good work,' acknowledged Hal as both he and Singh started climbing the stairs.

'This is the man I was telling you about, Doris.'

Singh's voice seemed to get louder as she walked through the door to the flat. Actually, flat was far too generous a word. It was a fairly large single room with a tiny bed tucked to one side, a wardrobe, a table in front of a grimy window, and a small kitchen area with a cooker, fridge, and sink in the corner nearest the door. The walls were all painted a shiny off-white colour which appeared to be flaking off in places, revealing pink plasterwork underneath. The carpet was dark with dirt and had numerous threadbare patches. On a weedy-looking sofa with wooden armrests, an old woman and an olive-skinned man in his fifties were drinking cups of tea. The woman had a slight tremor to her hand as she lifted the cup to her lips. They both turned as Hal and Singh entered the room.

9

'This is Inspector Luchewski. He'll be in charge of the investigation. He'll be the one trying to find out who left this thing on your doorstep.' Then, to Hal, 'This is Doris Thompson.' A yap pricked at Hal's ears and a dog ran out at him from under the bed. It was one of those miniature things, all fluff and noise. Hal didn't know exactly what type of dog it was – he couldn't understand dogs and cats. Didn't know anything about them. Couldn't bear pets of any variety, in fact. He'd had a Yorkshire terrier when he was a boy. Sammy. But it went and died on him, which rather put him off animals altogether. 'And this is Archie.' Hal twisted around to meet the man, but suddenly realised that Singh meant the dog. It yapped again and she crouched down on her knees to tickle it.

'He loves strangers. He always gets excited whenever there's anybody new around. You see, we don't do much these days so if somebody new comes into the flat he's all over them.' Hal detected traces of an upper-class accent, gradually worn away by years of struggle and hardship. He also noticed that contrary to the volume level projected by Singh, the woman wasn't as old as he'd previously imagined.

'He gets very excitable.'

Too excitable, thought Hal as he watched Singh desperately try to avoid getting her nose knocked by the bouncing canine, its tongue flicking saliva all over the place. Bloody thing should be put down.

'He's lovely,' said Hal drily before turning his attention to Doris herself. 'How are you feeling, Mrs Thompson? Must have been a bit of a shock finding that on your front doorstep.'

'I tell you, Inspector, it wasn't very nice. Not very nice at all. I'm glad that doesn't happen very often. I mean, I trained as a nurse so I'm used to seeing blood and … other things. But to be caught off guard at six in the morning like that … Oh dear.' She took a quick sip of her tea. 'Would you like some tea, Inspector? This young lady didn't want any but that young officer downstairs did. Poor boy. His face when he saw it.'

'No. No tea, thank you, Mrs Thompson.' Hal looked up and saw several photographs on the wall. A black and white wedding picture with a pretty girl and a tough-looking, bumpy-faced man arm in arm. Mr Thompson, no doubt. Another picture of the bumpy-faced man standing in a garden, resting his elbow on a water butt. In this one, the man was smiling and squinting slightly, as if the sun was shining directly into his eyes. Alongside this was a picture – colour this time – of a large detached house with a tree in the front garden.

'Could you tell me exactly what happened this morning, Mrs

Thompson? Go through it minute by minute if you like. Tell me what you did.'

'Go on, Doris.' The man sitting next to Doris Thompson spoke for the first time, and Hal took an immediate and irrational dislike to him. 'Tell him everything.'

'Well, it was like this.' She set her tea on the floor by her feet and sat up straight. Hal knew that secretly she was loving the attention. She was revelling in the fuss and excitement that the day was bringing. This little incident would probably keep her going for months down at the Derby and Joan club. All the other old dears would be sick of it soon, but she'd keep banging on about it ad infinitum, winding them all up and exaggerating her role. Still. If it kept her going.

'Go on,' the little man piped in again. Shut up, thought Hal.

'I always get up at 5.30. Have done for the last two years now, since my Pete died. I don't really know why, but when I wake up and look at my clock it always says 5.29. Funny that. Regular thing the body, you know. Keeps time better than any clock. Anyway, Archie was in his basket. He was awake too. Or was he? Was that yesterday? No. No, he was definitely awake this morning. There's no doubt about it. Anyway, I got up and put the kettle on for a cup of tea and put some food in Archie's bowl. I then went down the hallway to the bathroom and had my wash for the day. When I got back, Archie's bowl had been licked clean – he loves his food you see. So I got myself dressed ... same clothes as yesterday, I'm afraid ... cuts down on the laundry. Hard work carrying a big black bin liner down the road. I'm not young any more.'

'No.'

'So, after I got dressed, I took Archie downstairs to do his business in the front garden. I do that every morning. After his breakfast. Otherwise he'll soil the carpet again and that's not very nice to clean up, I'm sure you will agree.'

'Mmm.'

'We went down the stairs and I opened the door to let him out. I didn't notice it at first. Archie normally runs off when I let him out, you see. Gets excited and scampers off round the garden – it's difficult to get him back in sometimes. This morning though, he didn't. Just sat at my feet sniffing at something. So I looked down and ... there it was.' She took another sip of her tea. 'Just sitting there. I assumed it was rubbish. You know, somebody arriving home drunk had put it there not realising there was a big green wheelie bin at the end of the drive.'

11

'What did you do next?' Hal asked, listening more intently now that the story had eventually arrived at the important bit. He hoped she hadn't noticed that the thing inside the McDonald's wrapper was a hand. It was information they would try to hold back from the press if the investigation kicked off.

'Well. I looked inside. I thought that perhaps there were some leftovers for Archie's lunch in there. Save a few pennies. But there wasn't. Only that thing. Tell me, Inspector, is it human? I assume it must be if the police are so involved.'

'We don't know yet,' Hal answered, sighing inwardly. 'The lab needs to check it out. Please, Mrs Thompson. Carry on.'

'Oh, very well. I'm afraid I dropped it, Inspector. I picked up the bag and dropped it and it fell onto its side. I know you police like your evidence as fresh and untampered with as possible, but I'm afraid I did move it from its original position. Will that be a problem? I've watched *CSI: Miami*.'

'I doubt it,' Singh chipped in, overloud of course. The dog had quietened down now and was lying across Singh's legs, licking her hand.

'After I dropped it, I ran back into the hallway and phoned Mr Rabin here – I thought it best to let him know first.' She looked at the man sitting next to her. 'He told me to stay inside and to call the local police station – which I did. Then Mr Rabin turned up, just before the police officer. We've been drinking tea ever since, haven't we?'

'We have, Doris.'

'Tell me, Doris. When you were in the doorway letting Archie out, did you see anybody? Anyone behaving suspiciously or walking away from the house?'

'Let me think … No. No, I don't think so. Of course, I saw Mr Phillips across the road standing in his front window. But then he does that all the time. Hasn't worked for years, you know. Incapacity benefit. Went a bit mental after the accident and goes around collecting old crisp packets or some such nonsense. Think his wife left him, you see.'

'But nothing else that strikes you as a bit odd?'

'No. Nothing I can think of. My memory isn't as good as it used to be. I'll try and think harder if you like.'

'Well if you do remember anything, let us know.' Hal gave her a smile. 'Mr Rabin, could I have a word in private.'

'Yes.'

Hal indicated the door, and Mr Rabin got up off the sofa and followed him out onto the landing. Mr Rabin was a very short man, even by normal standards. Five foot five at a push. He was quite thin and wiry, with stubby fingers and dirty nails. His hair was thick and velvety and was brushed back from his head into a semi-quiff. A twitchy moustache floated around in the middle of his face.

'Can you think of any reason why someone would leave this on your doorstep, sir?'

'Why do you think it was left for me?' His voiced squeaked indignantly, his English slightly fractured, his eyes wide with horror. 'Isn't it more likely that somebody put it there to frighten one of my tenants? Shouldn't you be talking to them? I don't want no bloody psychos living in my house. This is a good, well-respected house. All of my houses are.'

'We'll talk to your tenants in due course, sir. But we need to consider all possibilities. Can you think of anyone who might do this to you?''

'I am a businessman, Inspector. I always have enemies. But nobody crazy enough to leave a human hand in my house.'

Bugger, thought Hal. He'd looked inside the bag. That's that piece of restricted evidence gone for a Burton.

'What sort of business do you run, Mr Rabin?' asked Hal. The man shifted from one foot to the other.

'I own this house. I have two more in Streatham. I run them well. We never have any trouble until now. I also have two shops – one in Norwood and one in Streatham. You might know them. Rabin Mini-Mart?'

'Oh, right.' Hal didn't have a clue.

'They're good businesses. Good money. My son runs the Norwood shop. I try to run the Streatham one. I live near, you see.'

Hal looked at the man closely. His clothes were smart and crisp. A lilac shirt tucked into his black trousers, around which a wide brown leather belt was looped. The shoes looked expensive and shone as if he'd spent hours polishing them up. On his fingers, a number of chunky gold rings clunked together as Mr Rabin gesticulated.

'My sergeant tells me you're divorced, Mr Rabin. You don't think –'

'No, Inspector. Bloody woman wouldn't have anything to do with this. She sucks blood and money from me but … No. She couldn't have anything to do with this.' He tapped the side of his head with his index finger. 'Too bloody simple-minded.'

Hal smiled and looked around the landing. The stairs ran past

Doris's door and curled up to a second floor where Hal could see more doors to other flats. The whole area looked seedy and unkempt, as if every surface was covered in either a layer of dust or grease. The white paint on the banister felt sticky and grubby and Hal recoiled, automatically wiping his hand across the top of his trouser leg.

'It must be difficult being a landlord. Keeping all of your tenants in check.'

Mr Rabin looked suspiciously at Hal. 'Like I said, Inspector, we never had any trouble here before. I make sure all of my tenants are good people.' He straightened himself up and tried to look proud. 'Nobody here – in this house – has missed a rent payment. Ever. I respect them and they respect me. I leave them alone and they pay me on time. Respect, Inspector. It is what my father taught me.'

'How long have you owned the house?'

'Four years now. Yes. Four years this July. It's a good building this, yes? A doctor owned it before me.'

Hal scratched the top of his head. Just being in the place made him feel as if he was riddled with fleas. He wondered what terrible turn of events had left poor old Doris Thompson with no other option than to live in this pit.

'Mrs Thompson is a good tenant?'

'Doris? She's an excellent tenant. She always keeps an eye on the place for me. Tells me if somebody is making too much noise or leaving the rubbish out or something. I let her keep the dog. I don't let nobody else keep an animal. Too much mess normally. But Doris – I let her keep the dog.'

'We're going to need a list of your other tenants. Who they are, where they work – that sort of thing. We'll also need to talk to them.' Hal walked slowly back into the room where Singh was now carrying the empty tea cups to the sink. Doris, sitting on the edge of her chair, was tickling Archie's belly. 'Sergeant Singh will ask you about all that.'

'Yes.'

'Again, if you think of anything … well … you know. Please let us know.'

'Yes.'

Hal turned his attention to Singh. 'Singh.'

'Yessir?'

'Downstairs a moment.'

In the wide hallway, Spud (or Sponge, he could never remember) and the copper had disappeared. Hal and Singh stood near the opened door.

'Get him to open up each of the flats. Just in case it's one of the poor bastards who live here. Find out who does live here, and chat to them if you can. If not, we'll have to chase it up later. Check the neighbours. I'll go to the station and ring round the local hospitals.'

'Yessir.'

Hal looked up at the brown-stained ceiling and the damp paper curling off the wall.

'Have you ever lived in a place like this, Singh?'

'What? You mean a place as *awful* as this? Yes. I remember at university having to smash a rat with a saucepan once. Left a terrible mark on the carpet. Landlord refused to give us our deposit back that year, I think.'

'I'll see you later, Singh.'

'Don't forget the Four Bells at twelve. Morrison's leaving do.'

'Oh Christ, yes.' Bloody Old Man Morrison and his leaving do. Hal sighed and walked out of the door into bright sunlight – exactly what his hangover didn't need at that moment.

John Good had packed away his equipment and was waiting for Hal at the end of the garden. The package on the doorstep was gone, sitting in a cold box in the back of Good's large white transit van.

'You look rough.' His eyes scanned Hal up and down.

'I always look rough. How're Margaret and the boys?'

'You already asked me that.'

'Did I?'

'Mmm. Margaret's away in Sheffield on a course this week. I'm looking after the boys on my own. We're going to spend the weekend living off frozen lasagne and Chinese takeaways.' John Good ran his fingers through his thick greying hair. It was the sort of hair you'd hope to have at the age of fifty-two. No little areas where people could see the top of your scalp. No widow's peak eating away at the front. Just pure luxuriant, thick hair which, if it were tighter and curlier, would look like a little woolly hat on the top of your head. Hal patted the top of his shaven head in response. He suddenly felt that he looked like a big pink watermelon alongside Good.

'You been drinking again?' Good continued.

'Last night.'

'It's no good for you, you know. Just messes up your liver and gives you free radicals and broken veins. I don't drink any more.'

15

Then, more sadly: 'Never have the chance. What with work and two teenage boys running riot all the time, I don't even think about it. To be perfectly honest, I don't miss it.' He sounded anything other than perfectly honest.

Hal didn't want to talk about his drinking so he rapidly changed the subject. 'How quickly can you get me the prints?'

'I'll fax them over early this afternoon.'

'Good.'

'That's me.'

Hal unlocked the car and strolled up to it.

'Still driving the TT then. It's far too small for you.'

'I know. Everybody tells me.'

'You look like a daddy-long-legs stuck in a matchbox.'

'Thanks.' And with that, Hal started up the engine and drove off.

Chapter Three

The car park in Beckenham seemed to be getting smaller by the day. Hal could see already that he was going to have difficulty finding a space. He leant out of the window and ran his magnetic strip card through the slot. The barrier arced upwards and came to a jerky stop, allowing him through like a silent snooty doorman in a posh hotel. Fridays were always busy first thing in the morning – too many people desperate to get the working day over with and start their weekend in earnest. By two o'clock, you could take your pick of parking spaces – straddle your car over three if you wanted to (and if your car was long enough).

Hal drove slowly to the Metropolitan Police parking area and blocked at least two cars in. Rooting about in the glove compartment, he found the piece of card with his name and extension number on and left it in clear view on his dashboard. He got out, locked up, and went up the stairs.

Hartshorn House was a four-storey office block with a flat roof. A dreadful glass construction from the sixties, it had the look of a building that should have been condemned years ago. In any other European city it would have been. Knocked down to make way for something more vibrant and attractive which, in due course, would also be knocked down to make way for something more vibrant and attractive. However, London had a knack of clinging to its dead, holding on, refusing to give up. And so, in the late nineties, Hartshorn House was refurbished and given the kiss of life. The Metropolitan Police Force took over the two top floors, using it as a base for one of the area Major Investigation Teams. The first floor was inhabited by a national insurance company and the ground floor used every Tuesday and Friday night by the Beckenham Model Railway Enthusiasts Club. A bizarre combination, Hal always thought. Geeks, con men, and coppers.

The Met's offices in Hartshorn House were essentially that – offices. The MIT team were based there, but they usually used the cells and interview rooms of nearby Croydon or Lewisham police stations. Hartshorn house was equipped with a holding cell and an interview room but Hal could not remember the last time that either were used. If ever.

Hal flicked open the flimsy door frosted with the Met's logo. The front of the station was much like any other in London with a couple of uniformed desk sergeants on loan from the Beckenham station milling around behind a security screen.

'Morning, sir.' One of them beamed at Hal. 'Beautiful day.'

'Mmm.'

The sergeant pressed the button situated on the top of his desk. 'Though they do say it's going to rain later.'

'Do they?'

A loud buzz.

'Afraid so.'

Hal pushed the security door and walked into the main office at Hartshorn. It was a large, soulless place with desks evenly spaced around the room. In the corner nearest the door through which Hal had just walked, a handful of uniformed officers were chatting on seats in the coffee area. One, a pretty girl in her mid-twenties with long, blonde hair pulled back into a ponytail, was laughing uncontrollably at something somebody had just said. A constable with particularly bushy eyebrows pulled his chair closer to her and said something else that made the girl spill her drink through laughter. Hal looked to the centre of the room and saw Burlock talking to his sergeant. He was sitting perched on the edge of the sergeant's desk, demonstrating something with his hands. The sergeant looked as though he was desperately trying to show an interest in what the big man was saying, a nervous smile fixed rigidly to his face. His fingers twiddled with his tie, twisting the bottom end around so the pointy end disappeared. Hal wandered over.

'What are you boring the poor bugger with now?'

Detective Inspector Freddie Burlock looked up and grinned at Hal. 'Boring? I'm not boring you, am I, Green?'

'Er … no … er …'

'I'm telling Green here the best way to catch a rainbow trout. How you need to use a good, well-splayed fly. He's very interested, aren't you, Green?'

'Er … well … yes.'

Burlock shifted his weight from one buttock to the other, a frown creeping down his face. 'You don't *sound* very interested, I must say.' His Yorkshire intonation made him come across like an old schoolmaster admonishing a pupil.

'You're boring him.' Hal smiled. 'Like you bore every other

poor bastard in this nick with your fishing stories.'

'You all love my fishing stories! None of you can wait 'til Monday mornings when I fill you in with all of the weekend's fishing exploits.' He gave Green a wink. The sergeant suddenly relaxed his shoulders, as if he'd been released from purgatory. You could almost see him loosening his tie and undoing the top button through relief.

'I suppose you'd all rather talk about football or who you banged on Saturday night. You'd rather sit around discussing last night's episode of *EastEnders* or something.'

'I'd prefer talking about the ins and outs of a cat's arse to one of your bloody fishing bollocks.'

'Now cats' arses I can talk about. The number of cats we've had over the years I can honestly say that I am practically an expert on the feline derrière.'

'Why doesn't that surprise me?'

'One cat we had used to shit on the carpet in the hallway. Bloody thing.' Archie momentarily bounced back into Hal's head. 'I used to come down first thing in the morning and be greeted by a watery turd under the hatstand. Always did it under the bloody hatstand. She was quite old by this time. Died quite quickly, thank God. I'd have done it meself otherwise. Run the bath, dunk it under. Job done.' Burlock got up from the desk. He was fifty-five years old and kept a record of the number of pay days left before his retirement. There weren't many. He was fat and always wore a suit that looked as though it had shrunk in the wash, the sleeves riding tightly up his arms. His nose was ruddy and he had a shock of white hair which seemed to travel all the way around his face to the prominent beard underneath. He looked like Father Christmas. Everybody thought so. He even played Santa at the South London Met's Christmas party every year. Hal thought he'd frighten the kids with his gruff Yorkshire ways, but he never did. Despite his tough, northern, I-take-no-nonsense-me attitude, he was as soft as a kitten with a ball of wool. All the women in and around the office loved him. All the men respected him. (All the men except Baldwin, anyway, but then Baldwin respected no one but his own pompous, ambitious self). He was likeable, good-natured and fair – despite his tendency to wind up inexperienced new sergeants. Hal always thought that it must have something to do with living in a house full of women. One wife and four daughters. Enough to make even the most masculine of men become fluffy and caring. Burlock once admitted over a pint that he'd cried when ET's heart stopped glowing and he was zipped up in the clear body bag.

'Heard you found a nice little package this morning.' Burlock walked slowly towards the back of the office with Hal. At the far end were the DI's individual offices in alphabetical order: Baldwin, Burlock, and Luchewski. Next to them were the stairs to the top floor, where the DCI's office, the unused holding cell, and interview room were to be found. 'Probably Triads or some other gang warfare thing going down in da 'hood.' Burlock flicked his fingers in a funky homeboy fashion, before continuing in a mock-Jamaican Yardie accent, 'I b'ain't be taking no shit on ma patch. You's gonna be losing some fingers if you's not watchful, boy.'

'I didn't realise you were a racist, Freddie.'

Burlock looked chastised, an ashamed lop-sided grin appearing in the middle of his beard. 'Sorry.'

Hal smiled at him and stood at the entrance to his office. 'We've got his hand. We just need the rest of him now.'

Burlock nodded his hairy head. 'Well. Good luck.' He turned aside and started to head for his own office next door. 'Oh, don't forget Morrison's leaving do at twelve.'

'I won't,' said Hal entering the relative calm of his office.

By ten o'clock Luchewski had established that no London hospital had recently given help to a person who had just lost a left hand. One hospital near Watford had had to treat a man whose hand had come off in a farming accident, but the hand had been salvaged and was currently in the process of being stitched back on. Hal had also had difficulty trying to get through to an appropriate person at one hospital in Richmond. In the end he'd been misdirected through the switchboard to the kitchens, where an irate Irish woman berated him for being misdirected through the switchboard to the kitchens.

Sitting at his desk and staring at the phone, Hal hoped that Singh was having better luck with the tenants and the neighbours. He rubbed his eyes and felt his head throb again. He'd never discovered a suitable cure for a hangover. He'd done the usual nonsense of drinking a pint of water before going to bed and then drinking a pint of water in the morning. He'd taken large doses of vitamin C and aspirin. He'd even once tried a herbal remedy that an old gypsy had made up for him (her brother had murdered her son and hidden the body, and she was very grateful when Hal eventually discovered its whereabouts), but nothing ever seemed to work. His head continued to pound numbly.

Hal suddenly remembered the guy in his house. What was it

again? Steve or Simon or something. He picked up the receiver and punched in his home number. It rang. And rang. Finally it cut to voicemail and he put the phone back in its cradle. Thankfully, Hal told himself, it looked as though he'd left. The last thing he needed right now was an obsessive gay guy rifling through his belongings. Hal lowered the back of his chair and instantly started to doze off to sleep.

By the time the phone rang, Stevie Denyer was working his way through the wardrobe in Hal's bedroom. He'd already looked around downstairs. A Bang and Olufsen stereo system. A forty-two inch, Sony plasma screen television on a stand, beneath which was set a Sony DVD recorder. The computer in the corner was a good-quality Dell with TFT screen, and the printer a Hewlett-Packard all-in-one. The kitchen was equally well equipped, with NEFF appliances and an enormous silver fridge-freezer sitting next to the window which overlooked the long, manicured garden. Now Stevie was checking out the guy's suits. Silk-linen mixes for the summer and heavier woollen suits for the winter. And there were lots of them. Stevie counted twelve or thirteen. Black suits, navy suits, brown suits, sand-coloured suits, even green suits. He whistled and shut the wardrobe door. This Luchewski man was rich. Very rich. Even the carpet beneath his bare feet felt as if it had been woven by hand in a Turkish sweatshop. The whole place smacked of money. He must be mad, thought Stevie, to let someone he barely knew hang around this Aladdin's cave. It would be easy to walk off with something expensive and pawn it – the guy had so much stuff he probably wouldn't even notice it had gone missing. He was either very stupid, very naïve, or very fucked up.

Luckily for him, Stevie was not a thief. In fact, he had never stolen anything in his life. He rubbed his eyes and wandered through to the other room on the top floor of the house. The house itself could probably be put on the market for between six and seven hundred thousand, he thought as the door creaked open. Three-storey Victorian semi in good condition with lots of original fea –

Stevie stopped in his tracks.

The room was empty. Almost. There were no pictures or photos on the walls. There were no curtains or blinds. Not even a light shade over the bare bulb. The only piece of furniture was a ladderback chair placed exactly in the centre of the room, making it look like a South American torture chamber. Against the three walls facing the chair were three large chests, each one made of what

21

seemed to be ebony, with intricate colourful carvings of flowers and trees across their sides, and heavy-looking lids. Stevie thought they looked Japanese. Nothing else was in the room.

He wandered in and sat on the chair. The chests had been positioned exactly. Almost reverently. One in the middle of the back wall, the other two in the middle of the walls to each side. They hadn't just been dumped there out of the way. This Luchewski guy had taken great care to place them here. Whatever they contained was something very special to him.

Stevie got up and kneeled down in front of the chest immediately before him. He tried pushing up the lid, but it was locked. He fingered the big brass keyhole and looked around the room, scanning the floor and walls to see if there were keys kept here, but he could see nothing. He tried the two other chests, but they too were locked. This frustrated Stevie's journalist mind. He desperately wanted to find out what made this man tick, and he felt that the answers were here in these caskets. He momentarily toyed with the idea of smashing one up to get inside, but his common sense restrained him. Sighing, he got up and walked out of the room, closing the enigma behind him.

In the kitchen, he abandoned any hope of finding the tea and settled for a coffee instead. He picked up a pen and a note pad from the man's table and scribbled his telephone number. He was interested, and would definitely like to see him again. He hoped the other guy felt the same way and that last night wasn't just a one-night stand. He'd seen him around the Clapham clubs before, and felt drawn to him. Stevie always felt drawn to seemingly vulnerable straight-acting gay guys.

Finding his shoes in the top bedroom, he got his belongings together and left the house. He had a meeting with his editor at twelve – never a good thing – and getting across London on the train was always tricky.

DS Singh was having a busy morning. She was happy about that. She would much rather have a busy morning than sit around in the office, filling out backdated paperwork and listening to the male detectives scratching themselves and stroking their egos. She was the only female detective in the team. The other women around the office were either secretary types like Yvonne or uniformed constables, and it made her feel slightly uneasy to think that she was the most senior woman in the South team. Uneasy, and yet thrilled. Thrilled to have done so well. Her parents were proud. Her fiancé admired her. Friends were, if not quite jealous, appreciative. Singh was a success, but she wasn't going to stop there. She fully intended to go all the way. Inspector wouldn't be too far away now, and then after that was DCI. It might take another thirteen to fifteen years, but she was going to do it. Let's face it, she thought, the competition wasn't up to much. A bunch of bloated beery blokes laughing at their own jokes and picking their noses. Men in scruffy crumpled suits with ketchup on their ties who could belch the national anthem and who still thought that any woman should be overcome with joy at the offer of a shag. She'd had that a couple of times. As if. Wankers.

Singh had done a lot of legwork this morning. One of the tenants had worked quite nearby, so she had strolled down to West Norwood absorbing the early morning sun. Now she was back on Chester Row, knocking on neighbours' doors. So far, nobody had seen a thing. Unsurprising really. It would take a few seconds for somebody to leave a package on a doorstep. Unlikely that anyone would be looking at that precise moment in time. Still, that's what Luchewski wanted her to do. He was her boss, and she was a good girl.

She left number thirty till last. It was the house directly across the road from where the hand was found. If anyone was in a good position to see anything, it was the person who lived here. The front garden had been laid as a patio. Some time ago, by the looks of it. Moss was bulging out between the dirt-stained slabs, and masses of dandelions had taken root. A large black bin liner was slumped to one side of the front door. Singh pushed the antiquated doorbell and could hear a shrill and aggressive buzz in response coming from somewhere inside the house. She waited a few seconds before again hitting the doorbell. Nothing. It looked as if there was nobody in. Singh sighed. It would mean she'd have to come back at some other time and try again, and she really didn't want to have to do that. Please God, make someone answer the door.

She knocked on the wooden door – good and loud – and peered through the letterbox. It was very dark inside and all she could really make out was a hat and a coat hanging over the banister rail at the bottom of the stairs. She moved to the bay window next to the door and tried to see in. Again, it was very dark and she could just about identify some pieces of furniture. A coffee table, a small sofa. Was that a picture on the wall above the fireplace? Looking closer at the fireplace, she could see a thin orange line, glowing weakly. It was an electric fire and someone had left a bar on. Which meant that there was someone in the house. Thank God.

Suddenly the curtain to the right of her twitched. Not hugely. Just a tiny, insignificant little jerk that an untrained eye would probably not even notice. Singh turned to look. She could see nothing – the curtains were too thick – but she could feel him. Standing not more than two feet away from her, the other side of the window. Holding his breath trying not to be seen. A man. She assumed it was a man. He was watching her, she knew. Watching her breath steam up the outside of the pane as she stared in. He wasn't moving, at all, but she knew he was there. Could feel the warm radiation of his body as his eyes danced over her. A shiver ran up Singh's spine and she suddenly felt alone and at risk. She backed away from the window and, turning on her heels, opened the little wrought iron gate and walked back down the street to where her car sat. Her legs shook nervously as she climbed into the driver's seat. Composing herself, she started the engine and drove off.

Luchewski could deal with that one, she thought.

Chapter Four

The Four Bells was heaving with fuzz. Both uniformed and plain clothes. Anyone desperately trying to sell on some stolen goods or score smack would have been advised to do so in another pub that lunchtime. Not that the Four Bells was that sort of pub. Situated on good old-fashioned, leafy, middle-class Beckenham High Street, it was a respectable and well-established joint frequented by good old-fashioned, leafy, middle-class people. Between twelve and two, solicitors and accountants from the many nearby offices were usually to be seen nibbling on the microwaved panini or vegetarian lasagnes, washed down by glasses of cold orange juice (with ice) or Evian. Today though, it was fuzz that predominated.

By the time Hal walked in, the air was so full of bad language and noise that he wished he hadn't come.

'Harry! How are you, me old mucker?'

Shit. Harry waved back at the dreary old cockney who'd spotted him. There was no escape now. He pushed his way to the bar, and tried to get the barmaid's attention. She was busy checking out her appearance in the mirror behind the optics. Hal didn't know why. She might as well give up, he thought. Years of working in a smoky environment had obviously taken its toll on her skin. He waggled his ten pound note in her direction. To no avail. Her sight had obviously been affected too. Hal suddenly felt a tap on his shoulder. Turning, he saw Singh reaching out over some burly constables.

'Got you a drink here, sir' she shouted over the noise, jerking her head in the direction of one of the tables. He followed her back through the crowd, watching some of the men eyeing her up as she went.

'You took your bloody time.' Burlock barely even looked up as Hal positioned himself on the small stool. Burlock's new sergeant gave a twitchy little smile. 'Thought you'd gone to sleep in your office.'

'I did.' Hal sipped the pint of bitter that Singh had kept back for him. 'Good morning, Singh?'

Singh supped her orange juice like it was being rationed. 'So-so. I'll write it up for you this afternoon, if you like.'

'Anything major to report?'

'No.'

'Then don't bother yourself.' Hal looked around the pub. There was an extraordinary number of uniformed officers getting quite seriously drunk. He could hear strains of vomiting coming from the distant corner and a couple of people trying, and failing – thankfully – to get a bawdy sing-song going. Hal wondered if there was anyone left on duty at the main Beckenham police station at the other end of the town.

'You've missed all the fun.' Burlock folded his arms across his chest and gave his Sergeant another wink.

'Fun?'

'The stripper. Old Morrison practically had a heart attack. Especially when she got him to put his head between her tits. Poor bugger thought he was back on holiday sailing up the Norwegian fjords. Bit of a slapper though, if you ask me.'

'You're only jealous.'

'Aye. Fair enough.' A wink to Hal now, 'Young Green here couldn't take his eyes off her, could you Green?'

'Well ... er ...'

When Hal thought about it, he realised that in the two weeks that Green had been Burlock's sergeant, the only words he'd ever heard him speak were 'Er', 'Um', and 'Well'. Burlock could have that affect. Hal wondered if the poor sod was regretting his move to AMIT.

Singh looked at Green over the top of her glass. 'Ignore him,' she said warmly. 'He does this to everyone.'

'Does what?' Green added two more words to his vocabulary.

'Wind them up. Just ignore him. I do.'

Burlock gave a great big hearty laugh. 'Aye. That you do, young lady. That you do.' Then, to Hal, 'No respect these youngsters today, you know.' Hal slightly resented being bunched together with the oldies like that – he was nearer Singh and Green's ages than he was Burlock's. He should still be seen as an up-and-coming thrusting young thing, not some jaded old dog waiting to be put out of its misery. Though, he had to admit, in recent months he'd been feeling more like the latter. He rubbed his tired eyes.

'No joy with the hospitals then?' Singh asked Hal while fiddling with her beer mat.

'Nope. We're basically waiting on the prints and Forensics to do their job. Take it from there. We'll see if –'

Suddenly, Singh leapt up from her stool almost spilling her drink

26

in the process. 'Oh, here's Nick.' Without saying any more she left the table and headed for the door where a tall, dark-haired man had just come in and was scanning the pub looking for someone. Hal recognised him as Singh's fiancé. Nick. A dentist working in a private practice in Clapham, he had the air of someone who had landed himself a cushy number. Drove a silver Merc SLK. Large house in Blackheath. Hal had first met him at last year's Christmas meal and had found him to be pleasant in a superficial way. Dig deeper and Hal felt that he probably wouldn't really like him.

'Boyfriend?' Green was getting verbally adventurous this lunchtime.

'Yep.' Hal noticed Green's face drop ever so slightly.

Burlock gently punched his Sergeant on the arm. 'Never mind, boy. There are plenty of good-looking uniformed girls around. You get to meet them in this job. It's one of the perks.' He gave Hal a smile, and Hal smiled back. Turning around, Hal saw that Singh and her beau had left. Gone to find somewhere a bit more quiet and civilised to have lunch, no doubt. He couldn't blame them.

'Harry, me old son.' He felt two hands come to rest on his shoulders. 'How're you doing, me old mucker?' The dreary old cockney had zoomed in on him. He brought his head down next to Hal's ear. The smell of beer and fags was overwhelming. 'Funny old day, eh? Funny old day. Retiring. Never thought I'd see the day. Thought they'd have to drag me out. Screaming and kicking. "I ain't gonna go, yer cunts. I ain't gonna go". But here I am, retiring.'

'Well, congratulations. Time to do things you've always wanted to do now.' Hal forced pleasantries.

'Have I ever told you,' the voice in his ear dropped to a whisper, 'have I ever told you what an ugly bastard you are. Ugly great bastard, you are. Ugly as fuck, with your bald head and your big sticky-out ears. Fuckin' hell! You know what people call you, doncha? You know what people call you.' Hal knew exactly what people called him. It always amused him. 'Vulcan, they call you. Or Klingon, is it? I can't remember I'm so pissed. One of those anyway. One of those things from Star Trek.' It's Vulcan, Hal thought. They call me Vulcan. 'That's what they call you because you're such an ugly fucker. You look like a fuckin' alien. What are you, nine foot tall or summat?'

'Leave it out, Morrison,' chided Burlock, 'you dozy old pisshead.'

'You can shut yer fuckin' mouth an' all, yer boring Yorkshire twat!' Morrison's voice got louder and more abrasive. 'Droning on and on with yer fuckin' Yorkshire ways. Fuckin' idiot!' He gave a short belch before continuing. 'I mean, the fuckin' people I've had to put up with all these years. Thank fuck I don't have to work with them any more. Bunch of cunts. Make me fuckin' sick.'

'Come on, Morrison. Let's get you some fresh air.' One of the burly constables grabbed him by the shoulders and manoeuvred him towards the door. 'You've had a bit too much to drink, haven't you?'

'I ain't drunk enough yet, yer cunt.'

They disappeared through the door. Hal picked up his pint and gulped a good bit down before smiling at Burlock.

'Promise me something, Freddie.'

'What's that?'

'If I ever start to turn into an embittered old prick like that –'

'I'll cut your throat open. Spare us all the bloody misery. But only if you promise to do the same for me.'

'Oh it's far too late for you to be saved. You've gone beyond the embittered old prick stage.'

'Cheers.' Burlock folded his arms in a pretend defensive way. 'What stage am I at now then?'

'The dribbling, gibbering, strait-jacket stage. The couldn't be arsed about anything stage. The "Fuck everyone, I'm going fishing" stage.'

'Sounds about right.' Then, with a wink, 'You ugly great bastard.'

Chapter Five

By the time Hal got back to the office, Singh had written up and deposited on his desk the report that he'd told her not to bother writing. Typical Singh. Doing everything properly. In a war, she'd be adhering firmly to the Geneva Conventions, polishing people off in a legitimate manner and reporting those that didn't. Taking his jacket and hanging it over the back of his chair, he sat back and read the thin document.

Briefing of interviews carried out by Detective Sergeant Priti Singh (AMIT 6) on Friday June 5th (a.m.)

On the orders of Detective Inspector Luchewski (AMIT 6), I inspected the rooms for rent at 33 Chester Row, Norwood. There are six rentable rooms in the property owned by Mr Mehrzad Rabin. The current occupancy is as follows:

Flat 1 (Ground Floor): Mr Graham Parke [Age 49]
Flat 2 (Ground Floor): Mr Nathan Marchant [Age 27]
Flat 3 (First Floor): Unoccupied
Flat 4 (First Floor): Mrs Doris Thompson [Age 68]
Flat 5 (First Floor): Mr Neville Willett [Age 35]
Flat 6 (Second Floor): Unoccupied

There was nothing obvious in any of the rooms to show that the severed hand had come from one of the occupants. I then interviewed as many of the tenants as I possibly could, starting with Nathan Marchant who was still asleep in bed upon mine and Mr Rabin's entrance. He claims not to have seen or heard anything out of the ordinary that previous night. He spent the evening with friends in pubs around West Norwood and got back to the house at around midnight. He cannot remember anything being left on the doorstep at this time. Mr Marchant is unemployed.

Mr Graham Parke works in a bank on Norwood High Street. He has lived at 33 Chester Row for the last eighteen years. His room faces the rear aspect of the property and so would not have been able to see anyone placing the package on the doorstep. Mr Parke retired to bed at nine thirty and left for work at six o'clock – he always has breakfast at the Bella Café on the High Street before arriving for work at around eight. He remembers stepping over the bag on the doorstep, but thought nothing of it. By this time, Mrs Doris Thompson had already disturbed the package and had called Mr Rabin and the police.

Mrs Doris Thompson was interviewed earlier in the morning by DI Luchewski and myself. Please consult DI Luchewski's report for the details.

Fuck, thought Hal. That meant he had to write the bloody thing now. Typical bloody Singh. He continued reading:

According to Mr Rabin, Mr Neville Willett is very rarely at home. He appears to work as a roadie and is regularly away travelling with different musical groups. He has not been seen by any of the other tenants for a few weeks now.

After interviewing the tenants of 33 Chester Row, I carried out a quick door-to-door enquiry of the immediate neighbours. None of them claimed to have seen anything out of the ordinary, although a Mrs Turner of number 28 Chester Row did hear a car stop for a few seconds as she was lying in bed at around three thirty.

There was no answer at number 30.

Brief and to the point. Hal let the sheet of paper drift down onto his desk. There was nothing much he could do yet. He hated being dependent on Forensics. They always took so bloody long and even then their results came with a disclaimer. Nothing ever seemed to be guaranteed in the world of forensics. There was always a 0.001% or something chance of being incorrect. A 0.001% chance seemed like nothing to Hal, so why didn't they just ignore it? Just forget all about it? It wasn't really all that important, was it? But still they clung to their little opt-out clause. If science is so fucking wonderful, thought Hal, why can't they do something and be certain of it?

As Hal jiggled the mouse to wake up his computer screen, the phone rang. He picked it up and logged on at the same time.

'DI Luchewski.'

'Hi, Harry,' Hal recognised Trudy's voice. That meant a meeting with the big man. Shit. 'It's Trudy. How are you?'

'OK. Yourself?'

'Fine. DCI Woode would like to see you in his office.'

'Sure. When?'

'Now if you can manage it.'

'OK. See you in a minute.'

Hal put the phone down and watched the monitor as the 'welcome' screen flickered to life. Ah well. At least he could put off writing that interview report for a few minutes. He picked his coat off the back of his chair and left the office.

Trudy was rummaging around in a filing cabinet as Hal reached the top of the stairs. Hearing his footsteps, she stopped what she was doing and turned round to see him. She smoothed down the sides of her A-line skirt and smiled broadly. The very top buttons on her blouse were undone and Hal could see the crease of her bosom.

'Hi, Harry. Lovely day for it.' Hal felt that there was too much emphasis on that 'it'. 'Although they say it's going to rain later.'

'So I've heard.'

Trudy put her hands on her hips, thrusting her breasts forward and up. The blouse strained to keep them in place.

'Been busy?'

'Well, you know.' Hal shuffled from foot to foot. 'Paperwork mostly.'

'Hah,' she threw her head back and pointed to the cabinet. 'Tell me about it. I spend all day moving pieces of paper from one place to another. Then a week later I get orders to move them back again. Madness. I'll be pleased when all of the trees in the world have been used up and I can stick to keeping stuff on my computer. They say it's a paperless revolution, but I'm not so sure. Not yet anyway.'

'Yes.' Hal nodded in the direction of Woode's office. 'He in?'

Trudy suddenly looked like a young girl who realised that she'd been talking too much. She gave a little cough and reined herself in. 'Mmm. Go straight in. He's expecting you.'

Hal walked up to the office door and knocked on the glass. A voice behind mumbled, 'Come in,' and Hal started to push the door open. Before stepping into the room, Hal turned back to Trudy. She was shoving her hand deep into the filing cabinet, trying to tease out a document with her manicured nails.

'Oh, by the way, Trudy.'

'Yes?'

'That blouse. The colour really suits you.'

She beamed. 'Do you think so?'

'I do. Yes.'

Her cheeks flushed ever so slightly as Hal walked into the office.

DCI Woode's desk was more of a shrine to his wife and kids than a desk. Everyone always wondered how he could do any work on it, the damn thing was so cluttered with photographs of a middle-aged woman and her three grinning sprogs. Hal imagined him sitting on the chair with his work on his lap, trying not to accidentally shove his pen through the paper into the top of his leg.

The walls of the office were covered in certificates. Woode liked to display his qualifications and achievements with pride. He framed and exhibited even the most petty and irrelevant certificates. Hal had gone on a one-day Health and Safety course with him two years ago. At the end of the day everyone was given a diploma to show that they had been through the process. Hal had thrown his straight into the bin that same evening. Woode, on the other hand, had bought a lacquered oak frame and had positioned it in between his Police Driving Competency certificate and his Handgun Handling award on the wall next to his computer.

'This hand business,' Woode started, his square-shaped head wobbling like a Weeble. 'Murder enquiry?'

'John Good seems to think so. I tend to trust his judgement on such matters.' Hal was sitting in the seat set before Woode's desk. 'We're just waiting on some results.'

'Mmm.' Woode stared at his pen, clicking it out and in repeatedly. 'He knows his stuff. Hopefully, we can get moving on it quite soon. Have you put the river police on standby? Is it possible that the rest of this person is floating down the Thames?'

'I felt it best to wait for Dr Good to clarify things before we went down that route. If the body *has* been dumped, then there's not a great deal we can do to save it. It will probably turn up eventually. I don't think that a river search will do anything other than waste money and man hours.' Always mention money and man hours, thought Hal. It's what the top brass always want to hear.

Woode got up from behind his desk. 'How are you feeling, Harry?' The question came left of centre and caught Hal unawares.

'Er … fine, sir.'

'Really?' Woode's reply had a slightly doubtful tone about it. 'You're fine?'

'Yes, sir. I'm fine.'

'Look Harry. The police force is not what it once was, you know. People with problems aren't vilified or kicked out any more.' Hal picked up on the sympathetic undercurrent in Woode's voice. 'The Met has come a long way in the last ten or twenty years. We recognise the need to be understanding and patient, and to offer help to those who need it most.'

Hal sat there dumfounded. He didn't know what was going on. What *was* this man on about?

Woode continued. 'A number of your colleagues have expressed a concern. A concern about you, Harry. A concern about your drinking.'

'My drinking?'

'Yes. Your drinking. They think you're putting it away a little too much when you leave work at night. They think that it could start affecting the work you do.'

'My colleagues?' Hal shook his head. 'You mean Baldwin. Look, sir, Baldwin has never liked me – and to be perfectly honest with you, I've never liked him. He's desperate to try and get something over me. Ask Burlock. He can't stand Baldwin either. The man's a –'

'I'm not at liberty to discuss the individuals involved, Harry.' Woode sternly interjected. 'Suffice to say that we are talking more than one complaint here.'

Hal's mind raced. Baldwin was a certainty. He'd shag his own grandmother for a step up the ladder. But who else would have gone to Woode to sneak on him? The only person he could think of was Singh. Singh must have done it. His own sergeant, running to his boss behind his back. Hal felt a cold, bilious trickle in his chest. Bloody Singh.

'Look, sir –' But Woode held his hand out to stop him.

'Harry. I'm not judging you. I don't want you to get too worried by this. The people who've brought this to my attention have done so out of concern for you.' Yeah right, thought Hal. 'But I need you to know that I am here for you should you need to talk. It's an issue that needs addressing, I'm sure you'll agree. You're a good copper, Harry. I'd hate to see you waste your talents. Don't go pissing them up the wall, OK?'

Hal nodded, stunned into silence. He didn't think that his drinking was a problem, but obviously people were starting to notice it now. For Christ's sake, he had worse things to resolve than the fucking drinking. Anyway, Singh bought him a drink at lunchtime, so what was her fucking problem? Bloody hypocrite. His head raced and he felt more than a little hurt. Hurt at being grassed up like a naughty schoolboy, but also hurt at being talked gently to by this solid block of a man in front of him. Hal didn't need people's sympathy. He could manage perfectly well on his own. Always had done really. He couldn't bear people cooing and fussing over him, taking him under their wing and keeping a special eye on him. He hated all that stuff. He hated being criticised and he hated being praised. Hal was happiest when left alone to do his own thing.

'This is a dreadful profession, Harry.' Woode sat down on his chair again, the black leather squeaking as he did so. 'I've seen so many marriages fail, so many nervous breakdowns, I've lost count. Drink is endemic in the police force. We see so much pain and loss it's bound to affect us in the end.' Hal wondered if Woode had a recent certificate for counselling somewhere on the wall. 'The boys over in vice. Some of them have to sit through videos of children being abused. Kiddie porn. Try to identify them. It's not healthy. I've seen so many of them turn to drink. Trying to forget the things they've seen. The job usually kills them in the end. It's the same for us. We deal with death. The only people we really get involved with have been killed. Horribly sometimes. The killed and the killers. That's our lot. We find the killed, then we find the killers ...' Woode paused, his staccato speech stumbling to an end. 'Sometimes I wish I was a traffic warden.'

'Oh, I don't know, sir.' Hal mumbled. 'I think I'd rather deal with a baseball bat-wielding crackhead psycho than an irate middle-aged Volvo driver parked on a double yellow. At least you can talk sense to someone off their face on ketamine.'

Woode smiled. 'Just talk to me, Harry. That's all I ask. The Met has an excellent counselling service now. Let me know and I'll put you in touch with someone.'

'OK, sir.' Hal got up, half-smiled in Woode's direction, and pushed the door open. 'Thanks.'

Corrie was standing halfway up the stairs waiting for him. She was a short round woman with thick cat's eyes specs and a mound of boyishly tight blonde hair perched on top of her head. She was out of shape, and Hal could almost hear her puffing, having exerted herself a little more than usual by climbing eight stairs. Too much time spent in front of her computer, accessing the HOLMES 2 system and stuffing cream splits down her throat, Hal believed. Luckily for the unit she was an expert at using the Met's databases and she could find information infinitely more quickly than a technophobe constable with clumsy slow-witted fingers. She held something out to him as he came down to her.

'Dr Good sent the prints over,' she exhaled. 'I've run them through the system and we've got a match.' Hal took the file off her. 'We know him, Hal. We know the owner of the severed hand.'

Stevie Denyer was walking up Oxford Street. He'd bunked off work a couple of hours early and was busy undertaking some retail therapy. So far he'd bought eight CDs in HMV (old stuff mostly), three hardback books in Waterstones (the latest Stephen King, a travel book about India and Bangladesh, a Jordan biography), two pairs of shoes, a short-sleeved shirt, a pair of three-quarter-length combat trousers, an *Absolutely Fabulous* DVD, a new colour cartridge for his printer, a luminescent lime green Swatch, five magazines (two music, two film, one gay) and some Porky Pig socks. The old Mastercard was being hit so hard it didn't know what was happening. Struggling up past the large Topshop on Oxford Circus, Steven sipped his white chocolate mocha from Starbucks.

His editor had been vicious, as he'd expected. This was his last warning. Find a decent story or get another job. Stop pilfering watered down stories from the locals that nobody outside of those areas wanted to read about. Find something big. Or, at least, something interesting.

For the last two years he'd basically been supplying Polyfilla stories (the editor's term). Stories that filled the small gaps in the paper. Columns on the edges of columns. The problem was that he was getting lazy and had essentially started regurgitating the quirky and funny stories he found in the local press. A recent and unfortunate incident involving the possibility of legal action by the *Brighton and Hove Herald* had brought it all to a head. If he really wanted a career in journalism, his editor had warned, he'd really, *really* need to step up his act.

Crossing the road, laden down by bags, Stevie headed for the tube station. He'd find a story. A bloody good one. He'd make that editor eat his words.

Chapter Six

The drive to Catford was virtually silent. Singh pushed the pedals and spun the wheel while Hal read the file that Corrie had given them. Two uniforms in a police car followed.

Daniel Wiseman had spent some time at the Granton Young Offender Institution in Mitcham. He was a dying breed – an accomplished pickpocket. One of Fagin's army. Repeat offending meant that, aged sixteen, he was whisked away from his parents' home in Redhill to enjoy some time (nine months, in fact) at Her Majesty's pleasure. His father had practically disowned him, according to the file, and upon his release he lived in a series of B&Bs before landing a job at a garden centre in Bellingham. A small indiscretion with a lady's handbag six months ago resulted in a trip to the local nick and a formal warning. Hence the prints. Probation gave his most recent address as Flat 1, 67 Hale Road, Catford.

'Here we are.' Singh pulled over onto the double yellows and the woodentops behind followed suit.

67 Hale Road was a fish and chip shop, above which were two or three storeys of flats. Inside the dimly lit shop, a man in white overalls shifted a large bucket of sliced potatoes from a back room into the frying area. The 'Closed' sign on the door was in the shape of a fat-lipped fish leaping out of some water.

To the left of the chip shop was a frosted double-glazed glass door. A series of doorbells to each of the flats sat on the wall next to it. Singh and Hal got out of the silver Peugeot with blacked-out rear windows (Hal never understood why Singh wanted a car with blacked-out windows) and walked up to the door.

'You stay in the car,' Hal shouted back at the uniforms. 'I'll let you know if we need you.' One of the officers gave a thumbs up sign and wound down the window, letting some air in.

Hal looked up. Clouds were thickening in the once blue sky. It suddenly looked as though it could rain. No. More than rain, in fact. It suddenly looked as though there might be a storm on its way. It was warm and sticky, and the back of Hal's neck felt wet.

Singh pressed the doorbell to number one. Nobody came so

she tried the glass door. It opened and they both walked into a tiny hallway, cramped on either side by an oppressively dark painted wall. Some mail was stacked to one side on the floor. Hal noticed that the top envelope – a mail order catalogue – was addressed to Daniel Wiseman. The steep, narrow little staircase ahead of them led up and round to the right. They trudged up in single file and found number one directly in front of them. The stairs themselves continued on up to the other flats in the block. This time Hal knocked. Again, there was no answer.

'Mr Wiseman. This is the police.' Hal crouched on his knees and tried to peer through the keyhole. All he could see was some light coming from a window somewhere inside. He tried the door but it was locked. 'OK Singh, stand back.' He gently pushed her back towards the top of the stairs.

'What are you doing, sir?'

'I'm kicking the door in.'

'Shouldn't we get a warrant before we do that?'

'Normally, yes. But put your ear down to the keyhole and listen.'

Singh kneeled down and squashed her ear next to the small hole. A buzzing noise tickled her eardrum and she retracted quickly.

'Flies?'

'Mmm.' Hal nodded.

'Dear God.' She stood back and Hal positioned his foot at the same height as the lock. He bent his knee and then straightened it quickly, smashing it into the wood. The door buckled slightly, the lock still intact. He tried it again, and again it stayed shut. On the third attempt, the frame splintered and the door gave way, arcing open. Hal pushed in, Singh close behind.

The flat was awash with flies. They zipped around Hal's head, landing on his scalp and tickling his skin. That wasn't the thing that bothered him most, though. What bothered him most was the smell. A smell he had come across many times before. He was hardened to it, it was true, but every time he smelled it his heart sank. It was the smell of death. Pain, jealousy, anger, and death.

'Don't touch anything,' he shouted at Singh. He saw her retching from the corner of his eye. She wasn't so used to the stench of rotting flesh. 'And don't fucking puke, whatever you do!' Singh ran back out into the corridor and vomited on the stairs. 'Fuck's sake!' Hal mumbled to himself as he edged himself into the room opposite.

A bedsit. His second one today. This one seemed a little classier, though – he'd noticed a separate kitchen area, and that it had its own bathroom. The main room however – the one he was now entering – was still, to all intents and purposes, a bedsit. A small sitting area, with a wardrobe and bed to one side. In the bed lay a young man with spiky brown hair and a long ski-jump nose. Hal recognised him from the picture in the file. He lay motionless, his head resting on a pillow. Sheets were pulled over him and you might think that he was having a deep, late afternoon rest. Initially, that is. Until your eyes took in the fact that the sheets were soaked through with blood, a dark crimson stain that had smothered out their true colour. Hal had never seen so much blood. A small puddle had formed beside the bed where the drenched sheets had dripped onto the carpet.

The flies continued to zip around Hal's sweating brow. He shooed them away with his hand. He turned to take in the rest of the scene. In front of the fireplace sat a cream-coloured plastic bucket. The sort of squat bucket that people do their washing up in. Hal looked over the sofa at it, trying hard not to touch anything. The bucket was approximately a third full with dirty water. No, hold on. Hal rubbed his eyes. That wasn't water. It was too thick and viscous-looking for water. It was blood. Somebody had filled the bucket with blood.

'Fuck!' Hal backed away from the scene. It was his duty to leave the room as uncontaminated as possible. Out in the hallway, he pulled the door to. 'Get those uniforms to seal the front door off. I don't want anyone coming in.' He side-stepped Singh's puke. 'You, knock on the doors and make sure that if there is anyone else in the building, they stay in their rooms for the time being.'

'Yessir.' She looked a little embarrassed.

'I'm going to call the unit.'

The rain was hard. Passers-by were caught between their desire to stop and see what was going on, and their desire to get home and dry themselves off. Cars slowed as they passed. The evening rush hour was becoming more of an evening snail's pace in Catford. The police had sealed off the whole pavement area around 67 Hale Road, and men in white protective overalls trekked in and out of the front door carrying cameras and boxes, their big vans dominating the street. Hal and Singh were both sitting in the back of DCI Woode's car. Woode was smoking one of his foul-smelling cigarillos. 'A bucket, did you say?'

'Full of blood.'

'What the hell is all that about? Devil worship? Don't they use pig's blood or chicken blood for devil worship? Sacrifice a virgin, and all that.' Woode obviously felt that he'd hit upon something. 'Might be worth finding out if that boy was a virgin or not.'

'Mmm. Afraid that's not very easy with a bloke, sir.' Hal was watching the Good Professor make his way over to the car. Woode hadn't noticed and when Good tapped on the window he jumped slightly, ash from his cigarillo flaking off onto his lap. He wound the window down.

'We'll be getting ready to move him soon.' Hal was pleased that Good referred to the body as 'him' and not 'it', which other forensics officers did. 'Do you want to come up and see the scene before we do it?'

'We've done a fingertip of the hallway and stairs, so once we've got him out of the way you can allow the other residents to come and go as they please.' Good led Hal and Woode up the stairs, all of them wearing protective white suits with slip-on covers over their shoes. 'We'll start a fingertip of the room itself soon.' Then, passing the pool of vomit, 'This sort of thing doesn't help much, I'm afraid. You must make sure your officers control themselves at situations like this, Inspector Woode. Can make life tricky for us, otherwise.' He opened the door and the three of them walked into the room. Spud, or Sponge or whatever the hell his name was, was standing in the kitchen area, looking through the wall cupboards. 'Give us a few minutes will you, Spound.' Spound. That was it, thought Hal. Spound. Must remember that. The young man left and the three of them were alone in the flat.

The room was smaller than the image Hal's memory had filed away somewhere in his brain. Smaller and darker – although the darkness could be attributed to the dimming light outside. Hal noticed that the ceiling had been artexed. Amateurish swirls swept overhead, smudging themselves until all that was left was a blobby mess with dried drips dangling down. Hal wondered if it would be possible, just by looking at which swirls overrode which swirls, to work out where the brush was initially placed on the ceiling. He shook his head and emptied the stupid idea out of it.

Danny Wiseman lay in exactly the same position that Hal had found him, peacefully oblivious to the fuss going on in his flat. The bloodied sheet was still draped over his body. Turning around, Hal saw that the bucket was still sitting in front of the sofa. Good noticed him looking.

'Yes. If you look just next to it …' Hal looked and saw that there was a large circular bloodstain just to the right of it. 'Obviously, something had gone on just there. My guess – and I hasten to add that it is only a guess at this stage – my guess is that he was killed on the floor, and was moved to the bed afterwards.'

'The bucket?' Hal enquired.

Good shrugged. 'Don't know yet. I'll let you know asap.'

They picked their way over to the body. 'Any idea how long he's been like this?' Woode rested his hands on his hips and Hal thought he suddenly looked quite gay.

'Insect activity would suggest longer than twenty-four hours. Although, in this warm weather, that becomes increasingly unreliable. I can tell you one thing for certain, though ...' He reached out and grabbed the top of the sheet with both hands. 'It's going to be impossible to do a rectal temperature check.' He pulled back hard to reveal Danny Wiseman's body. Or at least, what was left of Danny Wiseman's body.

Both Hal and Woode gasped at what they saw. The upper torso was virtually intact. The left hand was missing, obviously, but otherwise everything was fine. The feet and legs beneath the knees were also whole. Bloodied but whole. The thing that shocked Hal and Woode was that a large piece of the body was missing. From below the stomach area to just above the knees was a large gap. Whoever had murdered Danny Wiseman had cut off his middle section leaving him to spill his intestines all over the bed.

'Jesus Kid Jensen!' Woode's jaw dropped.

'Left hand missing,' Good continued, 'we found that this morning. Trunk also missing.' He looked at Hal. 'When and where is that going to turn up, I wonder.'

'It's not in the flat?'

'Not so far as we've been able to see. The murderer took it with him, along with the hand.' Hal pictured the scene when he first came through the door to see Danny Wiseman's body. It was something he hadn't really taken in at the time. Probably too concerned with Singh puking. Now though he realised that the sheet over the body had sagged far too low in the middle. It was not consistent with the normal shape of a normal body.

'How heavy would the trunk have been?' Woode could not take his eyes off the mess on the bed. 'I mean, how would he have got it out of here?'

'Suitcase. Large bag. He could have wrapped it in a couple of bin liners and carried it out like that. Wouldn't have attracted too much attention, I'm sure.'

Hal looked around. He could see an old coke bottle on the floor near the bed. On the wall above the fireplace was a Beatles poster. *Abbey Road*. Hal had never been too keen on *Abbey Road* – he was a big *White Album* fan. The *White Album* and *Rubber Soul*. He made a mental note to dig them both out the next time he had an opportunity to listen to them.

'There is one more thing I think you should see.' Good walked over to the brown, scratched wardrobe. 'One of my boys stumbled across it earlier on. When we do the fingertip later on, we'll check to see if there are any more in the flat.' He flipped one of the wardrobe doors open with the tip of his gloved index finger. On the inside of the door was pinned a piece of A4-sized paper. Printed in large letters (in what Hal thought was Times New Roman) were the words:

THE PERSON WHO MURDERED ME WAS A WHITE MALE
IN HIS THIRTIES OR FORTIES.
GOD BLESS MY TARNISHED SOUL.

'What the hell …' Woode's jaw dropped for the second time in three minutes. Good gave a small smile and shrugged his shoulders.

'We'll pack them away carefully – the paper and the drawing pin, that is. You never know. Might have a print or two.'

Outside, the rain had let up for a few minutes. Standing on the pavement, Hal filled Singh in on everything.

'Could Wiseman have written it himself?' she asked.

'So, hold on. Let me get this. A man comes in and tells Wiseman that he's going to kill him. The man conveniently leaves to let Wiseman power up his computer, log on, open a Word document, and type a statement describing his killer. He prints it off, sticks it to the inside of his wardrobe door and patiently waits for the man to return. Come to think of it, I don't remember seeing a computer up there. So Wiseman must have left the house, taken a quick stroll over to the nearest internet café or library, paid his fifty pee for an hour's hire and printed it off there before wandering back to his flat to be brutally slaughtered. Sorry, Singh, I don't see it myself.'

'No. What I mean is, if he felt at risk – like he realised somebody had been following him – he might have put it there as a precaution. Just in case.'

'If I was worried that someone was going to murder me, I think I'd do a lot more than put some bloody stupid cryptic nonsense on my wardrobe door. Wouldn't you?'

'The guy had form. He probably didn't want to deal with the police.'

'The guy was a kid, Singh. Nineteen years old. The murderer put it there.' Sometimes Singh could be incredibly bloody stupid, thought Hal.

'Why would he do it?' Woode came up behind them. He'd been finalising details with the forensics team, making sure that the coroner got a wriggle on with this one. 'Do you think it's true? Is the murderer in his thirties or forties?'

Hal frowned. 'I don't know. He could be putting us off the scent. Confusing us. On the other hand, for some sick reason – he's definitely a sicko, you saw his handiwork up there – for some sick reason he might actually be trying to help us. Trying to get caught. The man's – I'm assuming it's a man – the man's a psychopath so you can't trust a thing he says or writes. Ignore it and hope that Forensics give us some good data.'

'Hmm.' Woode reached into his jacket pocket, fishing out one of his cigarillos. 'Well, the parents have been informed. I think the mum's going to come up and identify the body. The top half anyway. You'd best have a chat with her, Harry. See if she can shed any light. Who owns this place?' His head jerked in the direction of the flats.

Singh pulled out her notebook. 'Mr Thurley – runs the chip shop.' She nodded over to a man standing with his arms crossed in the doorway of the Greasy Palace. An unusually honest name for a chip shop, thought Hal. The sign in the window still read 'Closed'. He'd obviously given up any hope of selling chips that evening. 'Says Wiseman was a good tenant. Always paid his rent on time. Hadn't seen him around the last couple of days, but didn't think anything of it. He hasn't seen anything or anybody acting suspicious at all recently.' She flipped the notebook shut.

Suddenly a large estate screeched to a halt in the middle of the road, blocking the entire street. Out of the car zipped three people, two men and a woman. One of the men held a camera over his shoulder, the other opened the boot and pulled out a long microphone with a furry end. Boom, thought Hal. Boom. The woman was youngish and dressed in a smart grey skirt suit. She brushed down her long dark hair with the palm of her hand as she approached the pavement. Hal thought that she looked vaguely familiar. The two men kept close behind her, and Hal saw a logo printed on the side of the chunky camera: 'LONDON NEWS

CHANNEL.' One of those many satellite things.

'Oh, no.' Woode sighed and started towards them.

'Inspector. Inspector.' Her eyes scanned the area trying to seek out the most senior officer. 'Inspector.' Her eyes saw Woode approach. 'Is it true you've found a dead body at this address?'

'You're a bit quick off the mark, aren't you?'

'And is it true that you're treating the death as suspicious?'

'Now hold on.' Woode held his hand out to slow the woman down. 'I'm not at liberty to discuss anything yet. There'll be a press conference in due course, you know that. I'll speak to you then.'

'A young boy's body has been found, has it not, Inspector …?'

'Woode. I can't say anything to you that may interfere with our investigations. Now please leave.' He tapped her on the arm and she hastily withdrew it. 'I'm not saying any more. Goodbye.'

She took a step backwards and nearly bumped into the man holding the microphone. 'Wanker!'

'What did you say?'

'I said wanker.' She flicked the Vs at Woode before the three of them crossed to the other side of the road to do some more filming at further distance.

'Did you hear that?' Woode sounded a little hurt as he walked back to Hal and Singh. 'Bloody woman. No need for it. I'm just doing my job.'

'And she's probably thinks she's just doing hers,' smiled Hal.

'I'm pretty sure her job description doesn't involved hurling abuse at the constabulary. Bloody cheek.'

Hal felt some droplets of water hit the top of his head. The rain was starting up once again.

Stevie Denyer was on his fourth glass of red. He put the phone down and turned back to the book he was reading. That Luchewski guy wasn't answering his phone. He'd left him a message earlier in the evening, along with his number but he hadn't bothered to get back. Perhaps he was just a bang-and-run merchant. Stevie had had his fill of bang-and-run merchants. Even the sensitive guys who looked as though they might burst into tears for no particular reason at any time, usually turned out to be uninterested after a night of lustful shagging. London, it seemed, was full of promiscuous gay men.

He was on page twenty-eight of the new Stephen King, but his mind wasn't really taking it in. So he put the book down and turned the television on. He absently flicked from one channel to another.

It was Friday night and he should have been out on the town, shaking his ass and getting down and dirty with friends. But he felt low. Depressed. It made him sick to think of how much money he'd spent today in a futile attempt to make himself feel better. He couldn't afford it. He was constantly over his overdraft limit and was close to maxing out his current credit cards. He could barely cope with paying the modest – for London – mortgage on his two-bedroom flat in Deptford, and the second half of every month was always fraught with concern over where the money for next week's food was coming from.

He tried to wipe his fiscal difficulties from his mind. If you thought too much about it you'd go off your trogger. Something will come up. That's what he always told himself. Something will come up.

Hal could still smell last night's conquest as he walked through the door. He was so used to the way his house smelt that he could easily detect any tiny inconsistencies in odour. The boy had gone but Hal could sense him. Dumping his keys on the hallway table, he headed for the kitchen.

It was just after ten o'clock. DCI Woode was going to hold a briefing at eight the following morning and Hal needed to be there. Photos of the crime scene would be back from Good by then, so everyone could get a feel for what exactly had gone on at Hale Road. He picked some bread out of the bread bin and made himself a ham sandwich. He hadn't eaten since lunchtime, and even then all he'd had was a pint and a packet of crisps. He put it on a small plate and carried it out into the sitting room where he sat on a chair and devoured it.

His eyes glanced over to where the spirits were kept. He kept the cabinet pretty well stocked up. If something was running low, he'd quickly replace it with a bottle bought at the off licence just at the end of the road. He wasn't particularly snobbish about the quality of the whiskey, vodka or gin. As long as it tasted OK, that was all that mattered. He got up off the chair and sauntered over to the cupboard. Opening it, he pulled out the whiskey – a bog-standard bottle of Bell's. He unscrewed the top and sniffed the rich aroma. His taste buds tingled in anticipation, fully aware of what was to follow. Woode's sympathetic goon face jumped into his head and he poured the whiskey straight into a tumbler and downed it in one gulp. Drink problem! He didn't have a drink problem. He had many other problems but drinking wasn't one of them. The drinking was entirely under control. He wasn't like some hopeless alcoholic who wakes up needing to swallow the best part of a bottle of vodka before midday. He'd never been like that. Never would be. And, as if to make the point, he screwed the top back on the bottle and returned it to its home in the cabinet.

Undoing his tie, he started up the stairs to the bathroom. He needed to feel warm and wet – wash the shit of the day off himself. The image of the mutilated body of a nineteen-year-old boy pestered him as he got undressed, and he hit the DAB radio's 'on' button before climbing in to the bath. Distraction came via BBC 6 Music, and 'Monkey Gone to Heaven' by the Pixies. He sighed and eased himself in. The phone start to ring downstairs. Hal didn't budge. Whoever it was could leave a message. He might listen to it later if he was in the mood.

Glass number five was being filled. It was a particularly large receptacle, so glass number five was actually being filled from bottle number two. Stevie took a big mouthful. He felt very, very drunk.

That editor. Simpson. Looked like a member of the bloody cartoon family, what with his dopey eyes and fat lips. Silly old turd. Wanted something bigger, did he? Well, Stevie boy was going to get him something bigger. That'd show him. That'd show him that Stevie boy wasn't some useless tool to be shoved around. He'd be a real name on the *London Chronicle*. Have his own office and everything. Have Simpson's office. That'd be good. Get the googly-eyed pillwit kicked out. Yeah.

He continued flicking through the satellite channels. Auction channels trying to palm off some naff looking jewellery and a diamond encrusted globe ('Look at how major world cities are indicated by a 24-carat diamond. Not 9-carat. Not even 18-carat but …'). A never-ending live game show where dial-up contestants had to name a type of vegetable or tree ('That's not the answer on my card, I'm afraid'). Bottom of the barrel reality things with people prepared to virtually empty their bowels live on air in exchange for a tiny dose of fame ('Britain's Toughest Jailbird – vote now to keep your favourite hardman in jail'). News channels with their bitchy-looking female reporters.

Stevie sat up.

The London News Channel was on. He'd nicked stories off them in the past. On the screen was that reporter with the long dark hair that looked as if she could do some damage in a catfight. Nasty piece of work, Stevie always thought. Laurie Frasier. That was her name. She was standing in a street. Behind her, across the road, was a lot of police activity. The thing that grabbed his attention was one of the men milling around in the background. He looked exactly like Luchewski. Tall and bald, but slightly out of focus so Stevie couldn't be sure.

Suddenly, the article cut to a shot of another police officer being interviewed by Frasier.

'Inspector. Is it true you've found a dead body at this address?'

'You're a bit quick off the mark, aren't you?'

'And is it true that you're treating the death as suspicious?'

'I'm not at liberty to discuss anything yet. There'll be a press conference in due course, you know that. I'll speak to you then.'

'A young boy's body has been found, has it not, Inspector…?'

'I can't say anything to you that may interfere with our investigations.'

Stevie clapped his hands in delight. The camera had swayed during the exchange and had caught a few glimpses of the tall bald man. It was definitely Luchewski. No doubt about it. Standing next to a short Indian woman. Stevie squealed.

So Luchewski wasn't an accountant after all. He was a copper. The lying git. This was much more interesting. He must have been a murder detective if what the reporter said was true. What was it? A boy found dead? 'Catford Murder' the caption across the bottom of the screen had read. This was brilliant. It was what Stevie was looking for.

Simpson could well get a bigger story after all.

The clock *pinged* eleven. He was still sitting at his table, screwdrivers and small ratchets cluttering the place up. The main light in the room was off – a powerful table lamp giving him all the light he needed to work by.

The pump hadn't worked. At least, it hadn't worked very well. For a start, it took a couple of attempts to get it in the right place. Then, when he had inserted it into the boy's neck, the tube kept slipping out. In the end, he'd had to use some duct tape to keep it in place. The suction was too strong too. Danny had winced when he had first switched it on. That's what he was adjusting now. The box was opened up and he twisted screws and played with the inner workings, his fingers oily and gritty. The plug was on too short a lead as well. An extension cord would have been useful, and he made a mental note to put one in the holdall that he kept the pump in.

He wasn't going to need the pump for the next one, but for the one after that he would. So it needed to be ready. Just in case he had no time between Two and Three.

Chapter Seven

The main room at Hartshorn House was full of DCs, DSs, and DIs. Woode had just filled them all in on the case. 'So, unusually, we have one body and two crime scenes. DI Luchewski is in charge, so he'll boss you around from now on – I'm going to be up at the Old Bailey later this morning and probably most of next week with Inspector Baldwin. Giving evidence in the Dawson case.' Baldwin had already been at the Old Bailey for the last week, watching proceedings and preparing to give evidence. Hal was glad that he was going to be away for another week, the slimy toad. 'Any questions?' A hand went up – an earnest young man with a red tie.

'Was there any evidence of a forced entry at Hale Road?'

'You mean *before* Inspector Luchewski's?' Woode gave Hal a look that pretty much amounted to a gentle reprimand.

'Sir.' Hal stepped forward. 'No. Both Sergeant Singh and myself can testify to the fact that the door was shut and there was no sign of a disturbance. In fact, the door was locked, which suggests that the killer had locked it on the way out. Which in turn suggests that the killer had his own key or took Wiseman's with him. We need to check if Wiseman's key has gone. We also need to check with the landlord. See if all the other keys are accounted for.' Behind him, on a board, were the photographs that Good had had sent over first thing that morning. Grisly, garish, uncompromising pictures of a bloodied room and body. The bucket, the note, the stains on the floor all meticulously snapped and immortalised. 'There are a number of things that we need to do today – yes, I know it's a Saturday, Evans, and your beloved Arsenal are playing at home, but I need door-to-doors in both Catford and Norwood. Sergeant Singh did a quick run-through in Norwood yesterday, but they need double-checking.' Singh glanced in Hal's direction. 'Not all households in the area were accounted for, and those that were need some extra pressure to try and remember anything out of the ordinary.' He could see Singh out of the corner of his eye, shaking her head. He wasn't trying to get at her. He wasn't being petty – it was standard procedure. 'Try and find out who Wiseman's friends were. What he did in the evenings. Did he drink in the local? Did he play pool, or go stock car racing, or play bridge, or dance naked at the Wah-Wah Club? Whatever. Just see what you can pick up. We also need to know why the hand was left on the doorstep of 33 Chester Row. See what you can find out about the residents and, more importantly, find out what you can about the landlord, Mehrzad Rabin. It was left there for a reason, I'm sure of it. It wasn't just some random drop. Rabin, or one of the residents, must have some idea. Also check out the landlord and residents of Hale Road. Someone out there knows something. We've just got to squeeze them and find out ourselves.'

Another hand went up. 'Yes?'

'The note, sir. What's all that about?'

Hal gave Woode a look. 'Ignore it. It might be true, it might not. Who cares. Whatever reason this nutbag's got for leaving it there is irrelevant. We are not necessarily looking for a white male in his thirties or forties. Bear that in mind, please. Or rather, should I say, *don't* bear it in mind. At all.'

'What about his work, sir? Shouldn't we be checking that out?'

Hal nodded. 'Sergeant Singh and I are going to take a run out to Bellingham this morning. Talk to the manager of Blossom Hill Garden Centre. Any more questions? We're waiting for the coroner to do his bit. And Dr Good and his forensics team.' A long silence. 'OK then. Let's get going. Oh, and before you go,' he put on a mock American accent, 'let's be careful out there.' The joke had been done too many times before, and nobody even smiled as they got up off their chairs.

It was a short drive from Hartshorn House to Bellingham. Skirting around Beckenham High Street and sweeping up past Beckenham Place Park, Singh's Peugeot quickly found the Blossom Hill Garden Centre. They pulled in to the large car park with generously sized parking spaces, got out, and walked over to the main entrance.

Most garden centres in Britain are little more than nurseries, where a diversifying farmer grows a few scrappy looking annuals and tries to sell them on to the public at an EU subsidy-enhancing cost. This garden centre though was obviously a big concern. In front of the main building was an area half the size of a small football pitch that seemed to be dedicated to fake Grecian urns and gnomes shaped like celebrities. Hal wondered what sort of person would have a eighteen-inch high model of Sharon Osbourne sitting in his garden. Possibly the same sort of person who would install a water feature as hideous as the one to the right of the main entrance (clumsy metal frog jumping up to catch a clumsy metal fly, water draining like vomit out of the frog's mouth).

The automatic doors swished apart and the two coppers sauntered in like a married couple on the lookout for a new strimmer. Hal's nostrils were attacked by the unmistakable smell of birdseed and rodent bedding, and he nearly fell over a small display of shiny garden windmills. A young man with acne stopped his brushing to watch them. Pulling his card out of his jacket pocket, Hal approached the boy. He flipped it open and shut quickly before placing it back into his pocket.

'Police. Is the manager in?'

'He's out the back. In the office.' The boy made no obvious attempt to take them there and stared down at his brush. He looked knackered. Must have been overdoing it the night before, thought Hal. Some of the spots on his face looked as though they were on the verge of exploding. Just a tiny touch and, pop! Pus and blood all over the place.

'Could we see him, please?' Singh leant forward.

'Oh. Yeah. Sure.' He started shuffling away.

It was the hanging basket time of the year. Old women and middle-aged men with baseball caps on were checking out the sweet peas, impatiens, petunias, and violas that sat in polystyrene cartons in the outside flower section of Blossom Hill. Ready-made baskets containing lobelia and surfina were hung from stands above big wooden barrels overflowing with mimulus. Pots of tulips, already past the flowering stage and now withered, were plastered with 'Half Price!' stickers. Singh stopped momentarily to look at a display of multi-headed purple verbena, before catching up with Hal's long strides.

The boy led them to a large blue Portakabin at the rear of the site. Inside was a small hallway with three doors leading off in different directions.

'You better wait here,' the boy mumbled incoherently. He knocked on one of the doors and walked in before anyone could reply.

'I bet he drinks Carling Black Label,' Hal turned to Singh raising his eyebrows.

'What? Old pointillism-features? Mmm.'

'Bit lifeless, don't you think? Like a piece of lettuce on a kebab shop floor.'

Singh smiled at the absurd imagery. 'Mmm. Needs a kick up the backside to get him going in the morning, I'll bet.'

'His mum must rue the day she –' The door reopened and the boy appeared with a goatee-bearded man aged about fifty standing behind him.

'Thank you, Paul.' The boy passed them without even looking up. 'Come in, come in. Take a seat.' The two detectives entered closing the door behind them before sitting down in the chairs provided. The man worked his way around the IKEA-style desk to his own chair. 'How can I help you?' He looked a little worried.

'Well, Mr …?'

'Judd. Alexander Judd.' He gave a brief nervous twitch of a smile.

'We're here to talk to you about one of your employees. Daniel Wiseman.'

'Daniel, yes? Why? What's happened?'

'How well do you know Mr Wiseman?' Hal was careful to use the present tense.

'As well as I know any of my staff, I suppose. Which is to say, probably not very well at all. He's worked here for about two years now – I could check exactly, if you'd like. He works well. Never had any complaints about him. There was that business with the handbag a while back, of course. But that occurred outside of work and I'm always willing to give people a second chance. If it had happened here, I'd've had to let him go. But, like I said, he always works well. Gets on with the rest of the staff – we're quite a small organisation – mixes well.' A small pause. 'Not a great deal to say, really. Why? Is he in trouble again? I don't think he's here at the moment. A week's holiday, I think.'

'There's nobody you can think of who bears a grudge or who harbours any animosity towards Mr Wiseman?'

'No. Why? What's going on? Has he –'

'Mr Judd, I'm afraid that Daniel Wiseman has been found dead and –'

'What?'

'– and at this stage we suspect foul play.'

'Dead?' Judd shook his head. 'Foul play? You mean murdered. He's been murdered? Good Lord.'

Outside the door, Paul Norris was eavesdropping, his ear fixed to the keyhole.

'Jesus!' He straightened up, a shiver running down his spine. Danny was dead. Murdered, they'd said. Fuck! Who the fuck would kill Danny? He quickly put his head back down to continue listening.

'Mr Judd, I'm sorry to be the bearer of such bad news, but I need you to think back to the last time you saw Mr Wiseman. Was he behaving strangely? Was he worried about something? Anything at all. Any information you can give us would be much appreciated.'

'Well … I suppose the last time I saw him would have been on Saturday – last Saturday, that is. Just before he started his week off. He seemed all right to me. I can't think of anything strange happening. I remember him saying that he was just going to chill. Not do too much. Just chill. Oh, yes of course. That's right, he said an old friend was going to visit him. At his flat, I suppose.'

Hal and Singh looked at each other.

'A friend?'

'Yes. That's what he said.' Judd's face dropped. 'You don't think …?'

'He didn't say any more about this friend, did he, sir?' Singh enquired.

'No. No he wouldn't have done. Not to me. He might have done to somebody else on the staff, but not to me. Perhaps you'd better speak to the rest of the staff and find out.'

'We'll send a small team out later to interview them, sir. If that's OK? It's probably best if you call your staff together beforehand and explain the terrible circumstances. Make them aware. We'd also like a copy of any work record or file that you have on Mr Wiseman.'

'Of course. Of course. I really can't believe this.'

'Something else I want to ask you, sir,' Hal opened the file that he had brought in with him. 'According to the probation service, you promised Mr Wiseman a job here before he'd completed his time at Granton Young Offender Institution. Why is that? Did you know him before he came here?'

Judd sat up in his chair and stroked his beard. 'Sergeant –'

'Inspector,' Hal corrected him.

'Inspector, if you contact the probation service and ask them, you'll find out that I've done the same thing for a number of the boys from Granton. Not just Daniel Wiseman. Part of the pleasure of being in business is to be had in helping those less blessed than oneself.' Hal noticed for the first time the tiny silver cross hanging around Judd's neck. 'Some of those poor boys have had an awful time of it. Drugs, abuse, violence. You name it they've seen it. It's no wonder they end up in a place like Granton. It's a slippery slope to self-destruction, believe me. The only way up and out of the mire is to claw back some self-respect with hard work. Inspector ...?'

'Luchewski.'

'Inspector Luchewski. We live in an age of laziness and despondency.' Hal felt that he'd found Alexander Judd's bugbear. 'We are promised so much by the media and the world that we've wrapped around ourselves, that we are disappointed when these things don't come to pass. And with disappointment comes anger. Anger at the world and also, more destructive, anger at ourselves. I try to make these boys realise that life is a slog. You have to work at it to get what you want. Wouldn't you agree, Inspector Luchewski?'

Hal ignored the question. 'So, do you have any Granton boys working for you now?'

'Two. Paul you've already met. And Denzil. Denzil tends to do a lot of work in the flower section. He's really caught the gardening bug, has Denzil. He's always going on at me about how he can't wait to have a garden of his own. Grow some stuff. Always asking about the conditions required to grow this or that.' His face lit up. 'It's the sort of thing that makes life feel really worthwhile.'

'I'd like to speak to both of them if I could.'

'Dead?' Paul was sitting on Singh's chair. Singh was standing against the wall watching Hal conduct the interview. 'Dead?' Paul Norris was a very poor actor. Hal realised immediately that he must have been listening in on the conversation with Judd. 'Fucking hell. Who would want to murder Danny?'

'I didn't say anything about him being murdered, Paul. Why? Is there something you want to tell us? Did *you* murder Danny Wiseman?'

'Fucking hell, no!'

'How did you know he'd been murdered then? If I didn't say anything about him being murdered.' Hal toyed with him. 'Seems a bit of a coincidence to me. Wouldn't you agree?'

'I didn't fucking kill him, did I!'

'Didn't you?'

'No I fucking didn't.' His eyes widened with fear that he'd put himself in this position.

'How did you know then?'

'I fucking listened in, didn't I. When you were talking to Mr Judd. I was fucking listening in through the keyhole.'

'Mmm. I know. I wonder what Mr Judd would think about that. Think I'd better tell him, Sergeant?'

Paul's head swept around to take in Singh. 'Fucking hell, no. Don't do that. He's religious. He don't like things like that.'

'Doesn't he?'

'No. He don't. He hates things that ain't proper.'

'Does he? But he doesn't mind the fact that you spent time in Granton. What were you in Granton for, Paul.'

Paul shuffled in his chair, his face twisting into a wince like he was suffering from piles. 'I knifed someone, didn't I. It was an accident, I kept telling them that. I didn't mean to do it but this bastard was having a go at my bird, saying she was ugly an' that.'

'Where was this?'

'Up west. We were out havin' a laugh, clubbin' it, when this geezer comes up and says something like, 'She's an old bitch. Where'd you fucking pick her up then? Fucking Battersea Dogs' Home or something?' I always used to carry a knife back then. He kept on an' I lost it. Woomph! I rammed it straight into his ribs.' Paul suddenly became quite animated, his hands illustrating the action of sticking a knife into the chest of a fellow human being. He smiled at the memory. 'Fucking shut him up, I can tell you. Nearly fucking died, though. That's what did for me. Eighteen fucking months in Granton. Fucking hellhole.'

'So it wasn't really an accident then, like you said? You deliberately stabbed this other guy?'

'Well, yeah.' His lanky shoulders shifted uncomfortably. 'But it was a fucking accident that he came along when he did and started givin' it all tha'. Fucking twat.'

'Eighteen months? Did you know Danny when you were at Granton?'

'No. He was there earlier than me. He'd left before I got banged up. We were both in the same wing, though. C wing. Same as Denzil – he works here too. He was in C wing. D wing was the bad one. Fucking riots all the time in D wing. Didn't wanna be in fucking D wing if you could help it. Bunch of psychos.'

Hal relaxed back into his chair, the flimsy back giving way slightly due to his size. 'Do you enjoy working here, Paul?'

The boy shrugged his shoulders. 'S'all right. Brings a few quid in. Job innit?'

'What do you do exactly?'

'Cleaner. Keep things clean, don't I. I brush up all the mess the customers make. Some of the people who come in here make a load of fucking mess. They empty out the earth from the pots an' tha'. Fussy bloody bunch. Making sure they've got a good plant and stuff. Checking its roots.'

'And Mr Judd is a good boss, is he?'

'Yeah. S'all right. Bit religious but all right. Fair enough, know what I mean.'

'Paul, according to Mr Judd, Danny was going to have an old friend visit him during his week off. Did he tell you about this?'

'No. No, he didn't say anything to me.'

'Is there anything about Danny that you think we should know about? I know you've probably had a bad experience with the police in the past –'

'Too fucking right.'

'– but this time, Paul, we're the good guys. We're just trying to find the person who killed your friend.'

'Yeah. I know.' His head drooped and he stared at the floor.

'So can you think of anything? Did you socialise with him much?'

'Went out for a coupla drinks a coupla times. Wasn't like he was me best mate in the whole world or nuthin'. Didn't tell me much about himself, know what I mean. Just knew each other at work really.'

'Anyone at work he didn't get on with?' Hal watched the boy's face carefully.

'No. Not really. He wasn't Mr Hopkins' favourite, but then none of us Granton boys are.'

'Mr Hopkins?'

'Shrub and tree manager. He's nice to everyone else but us. Keeps telling us we're wasting vital fucking breathing space and jobs being here. Says we don't deserve our fucking jobs. He's a fat twat. He's the only one I can think of. Doesn't speak to us most of the time.'

'Do you think Mr Hopkins is capable of killing someone?'

'Fuck, no!' He chuckled. 'He's just a useless fat nonce. Talks big but ain't got the guts to do something like that. We just fucking ignore him.'

'Paul. If you can think of anything else we should know give me a ring.' He handed him his card. 'That's my office number and my mobile number. Please. Anything at all. Anything. No matter how small. OK?'

The boy mumbled something that might have been a response.

Denzil McKenzie was a much more laid-back individual altogether. A young black lad aged in his early twenties, he slouched backwards in the chair until his head was virtually at the same height as his knees. He wore a beanie hat and his hand occasionally reached up to adjust its position. Hal had asked him the same questions as Paul Norris and he had got more or less the same answers. No, he didn't know anything about the friend coming to visit. No, he couldn't think of anyone who didn't get on with Danny (except Mr Hopkins, that is). No, *(big grin)* he didn't believe that Mr Hopkins could be capable of killing someone. However, there was one question that did elicit a different response.

'Did you know Danny in Granton, Denzil?'

'A bit.' His eyes glanced over to Singh. He rotated back and forth in the chair and smiled at her. 'He was in C wing too. A few cells down from me but we used to play pool sometimes in the rec hall. I always used to beat him, of course. He wasn't too hot. Kept potting my balls for me. Didn't really know how to hold a cue.'

'Was there anyone in Granton who had a grudge against him? Any other inmates or any warders?'

He shook his head slowly. 'I can't think of anyone. He was a nice guy really. A bit gay sometimes but all right.'

'Gay? Was Danny gay?'

Denzil's eyes looked up and to the right. Hal remembered reading somewhere that that was an indication that the person was lying. Or was that up and to the left? Dammit. 'Don't know. Couldn't tell you.' The eyes came back down and focused sheepishly on a point just to the left of Hal.

He was definitely lying. Danny Wiseman was gay.

'What were you in Granton for, Denzil?' Hal asked.

'Shouldn't you be calling me Mr McKenzie? Aren't the police supposed to be courteous and respectful to the general public?' He winked at Singh.

'Very well. What were you in Granton for, Mr McKenzie?'

'That's better. Much more like it. You'll go far, my man.'

Hal felt like leaning across and giving the lad a smack on the hooter. 'Come on, Denzil, what did you do?'

'Providing a service. I got put away for merely providing a vital service to the community.'

'You were pushing?'

'I much prefer the phrase "providing a service". Doesn't sound so aggressive. Wouldn't you agree?'

Judd saw them out of the Portakabin when they had finished. The sky was black and, somewhere to the east, a storm was bubbling up.

'More rain on the way,' observed Judd. 'Ah well, good for the plants.'

'You've a Mr Hopkins that works for you?'

'Barry, yes.'

'Is he here?'

'Sorry no. He's up in Lancashire or Yorkshire this week. Mother's been taken poorly, I'm afraid. Mercy dash. I don't think she's likely to survive by the sound of it. Heart's given out.'

Judd reached out and shook their hands.

'I'll send a couple of officers around this afternoon to interview the rest of your staff, Mr Judd. Thank you for your time.' They turned to leave.

'Oh, before you go, Inspector. Luchewski. That's a very unusual name. Wasn't Victor Liddle's real surname Luchewski? You're not related by any chance?'

'No, sir,' Hal lied. 'No relation.'

The parents looked a little taken aback when they found out that the children's entertainer they had hired had come by bus. They rather expected a van with 'Booboo the Clown' emblazoned in colourful lettering on the side. That's what they normally have, don't they? Instead, a shambling man with carrier bags had knocked on the door and announced that he was Booboo the Clown and did they have a bedroom he could get dressed in. The party was getting under way in the kitchen with Sophie squealing away like an excited gerbil at the presents her friends had brought for her eighth birthday, so the mother escorted him upstairs to one of the back bedrooms. Leaving the door slightly ajar, Booboo could hear the mother giving the dad a quiet bollocking for trying to do things on the cheap. If he'd looked harder he could have got someone more professional, not some fat office worker trying to earn a few extra quid at the weekend.

The Creep unpacked his things on the bed and started to change into his costume. He was getting around by public transport these days because he couldn't get the tax for his car. He couldn't get the tax for his car because he couldn't get his car through the MOT. He couldn't get his car through the MOT because the rear axle needed changing. He couldn't change the rear axle because he couldn't afford it. Money. Ultimately, it always came down to money.

Not that he really needed money. He was, of course, above such things.

Clothes on, he settled down in front of the mirror to apply his make-up. He enjoyed putting on the make-up. He always wondered if this was the way a slut felt, dressing up her face, making herself look all tarted up in the hope of a late-night back alley fuck. He ran the lipstick over his wet mouth and the feeling sparked his loins once again. Bitches. All women were bitches. All women were desperate to be fucked. Just look at them walking along the street. All of them teasing cocks, knowing exactly what they were doing. They were asking for it. Some of them didn't realise it, but they were definitely all asking for it. It was a fact of life that was rarely spoken in these dark politically correct days, but women fantasised about being raped. Women and some men. Everyone knew that.

The door to the landing pushed open slowly and the Creep swivelled around to see what was going on. A tiny little girl of about nine stood there, a look of confusion on her face. Her hair was tied back in pigtails and she wore a top that said 'Barbie Girl' in big pink lettering. A purple velveteen skirt covered her stick-like legs and a pair of spangly shoes peeked out from beneath.

'Oh. Sorry. I was looking for the bathroom.' He could see big gaps of missing teeth in her mouth. 'Sorry.'

'That's all right, my dear.' His hand beckoned her in. 'Come in. Come in. Let me show you a trick.'

Chapter Eight

The pathologist had completed his inspection of the body parts so John Good had given Hal a call. They arranged to meet outside the coroner's offices in Brixton.

'He was quick,' Hal said to Good as he approached him on the pavement. Good was wearing a long grey raincoat.

'Don't think he was very happy to be working on a Saturday though – he's missing a golfing tournament in Surrey.'

'Do all pathologists play golf, then?' Hal enquired. It seemed to him that every time a pathologist had to do some work it was at the expense of a day on the links. 'Is there a little tick box on the application form which says "Do you play golf?" or something?' Singh stood alongside Hal, her pony-tailed hair swinging as she turned from one to the other.

'He rushed the boy through. Was here first thing this morning, apparently. So you be thankful. Also be thankful that my team and I were up all of last night preparing this for you.' In his hands was a thick file. 'I'll go through it with you once Dr Price has filled us in.'

They turned and went inside the building.

'I hope you realise I'm missing some golf because of this. Had a bloody good chance of winning it too.'

Dr Price was a short rotund man with delicate gold-framed spectacles perched on the end of his nose. The top of his head was completely free of hair, but the sides of his head made up for it. Fluffy white clouds of the stuff billowed up over his ears and the back of his neck. He looked a little like that stripy-jumpered man from *Time Team*, thought Hal as he, Singh, and Good took up the chairs in Price's dusty office.

'Didn't win it last year. Came close but didn't win it. No, I've been preparing all year for this. Typical, eh?'

Singh smiled gently at Price. 'Perhaps you'll win it next year.'

Price peered over the top of his specs and scowled. 'Huh! Something else'll probably ruin it. Bound to. That's the sort of luck I've been having recently. Anyway ...' He moved some of the mess on his desk around. 'Where did I put it? It was here somewhere ...'

He got up and, standing on tiptoe, tried to see what was on top of a metal filing cabinet. 'Ah. There it is.' He pulled down a file. 'Knew I'd left it somewhere.' He sat down in his seat and opened up the file. 'OK. So, yesterday afternoon we took receipt of a human hand and then in the evening we were given a cadaver in three separate parts – the majority of a torso and two legs severed just above the knee joint. You'll be relieved to know that they all belong to the same individual. The body was obviously cut up with a large-toothed saw – probably the sort of thing used for chopping hefty branches off trees, I'd've thought. But a large-toothed saw of some sort, anyway.'

'A handsaw, you think? Not some kind of electric saw?' Hal enquired.

'Handsaw. Definitely. A close look at the saw marks on the limbs and on the spinal column would definitely indicate a handsaw. Very jagged marks. Not smooth.' His arm made a sawing motion. 'Quite hard work cutting through the bone, you know. The flesh is easy. Bloody messy but a doddle, really. No, he had a bit of trouble getting through the bone. More difficult than he'd thought, I'd imagine. Anyway, where was I?' He flicked a few pages through the file. 'Ah. Yes. He was dead before the dismembering began. Luckily. Actual cause of death was, I believe, due to blood loss. His heart packed in.'

'Blood loss? So, how did he lose so much blood if the sawing started after his death?'

'The puncture wounds.'

'Puncture wounds?'

'To the neck. Hold on … Here.' Price picked out a photograph and threw it across the table at Hal. Hal held it up and looked at it. 'At some point while he was alive, the killer stabbed an implement into the poor boy's neck. Three times. I think he was trying to hit the major artery.' The picture was a close-up shot of a bloodied neck. In the flesh were three slits, one of which was more open than the other two. 'He got it eventually.'

Singh leant over to see the photograph and then backed off quickly. 'Was Wiseman drugged? How did the killer manage to do this without him struggling?'

'No sign of any drug in the system – other than some minor cannabis traces, that is. No, I think the person who killed Mr Wiseman firstly knocked him out – there is some slight damage to the back of the cranium. Not enough of a knock to kill him, but enough to render him unconscious for a few minutes. Quite difficult to judge precisely, I should think.' He threw another photograph across to Hal. It showed the back of Wiseman's head, matted with dried blood. 'So, he knocks him out. While unconscious he straps him up with duct tape – sticky traces were found around both hands and both feet – before stabbing the neck, trying to find the major artery. Then he did a very strange thing indeed.'

'What's that?' Hal looked up from the photograph.

'He sucked the blood out of Mr Wiseman's neck.'

'Sucked the blood …?'

'Or should I say, pumped, it out of his neck. The major artery was slightly collapsed and bruised. After cutting it open he inserted something – a tube of some sort – and pumped blood out of the neck. Quite unsuccessfully, I'd've thought. Then once he was dead he chopped him up.' Price smiled across at the three of them. 'Cup of tea?'

Hal, Singh, and Good sat at a table in a greasy spoon just off Electric Avenue. It was fairly quiet and the waitress was showing more interest in her celebrity magazine than her customers. Hal squinted, trying to read the front page: 'Celebs and Their Tracksuits. Haute Couture Workouts with the Stars!'

'The blood in the bucket was Mr Wiseman's,' said Good, stirring his tea. 'Or should I say it exactly matches Mr Wiseman's.'

'So he tries to draw the blood from Wiseman into the bucket. Why? Vampire killer? Someone who fantasises about being Dracula?' Hal opened the file from Dr Price. The post-mortem photos spilled out over the table. Pictures of arms, legs and various body parts, bloody and meaty, distributed all over the Formica tabletop. Nobody in the café noticed.

'Woode might have been right about it being a sort of devil worship thing.' Singh joined in. 'Using the blood for some ceremony or other.'

'But he left the blood there. He didn't take it with him so what was the point in collecting it up?'

'Could have carried out the ceremony in the room. Anyway, he *did* take a big part of the body,' Singh returned. 'What has he done with that?'

Hal shook his head. 'I've no idea.' He tried sipping his unbearably hot coffee, but it was still the temperature of molten lava. His tongue went numb with the heat. 'I've no idea.' He turned to face Good. 'Keys?'

'Oh yes. No. There was no key in that flat that fitted the lock.

Not as far as we could see.'

'So he took Wiseman's with him and locked the door behind himself. Rather scotches the idea that he left the note in a bid to get caught. If he wanted to get caught why lock the door? Why not leave it wide open for the whole world to see?'

'What about the hand?' Singh tapped the table with her finger. 'He left that as a clue, surely? If he hadn't left that at Chester Row we probably still wouldn't have found Wiseman's body yet. He must have known that we'd have the prints on file.'

'No. I still don't buy that. I'm sure he left it there for a purpose. Why single out that particular house? It was done as a threat or a warning to someone in that house. Probably Rabin.'

'The amount of blood on the carpet strongly suggests he was killed on the floor. The dissection probably happened there too.' Good was flicking through the file that he was about to hand over to Hal. 'He was moved to the bed after death.'

'Prints?'

Good nodded. 'Lots of them. Unfortunately, nothing on the note. That is completely clear. However, I'll fax through the ones we have found on the walls etc. You can ask Corrie to run them through the system. I wouldn't be too hopeful, though. It's a bedsit and loads of people come and go through bedsits. It doesn't necessarily mean anything. I've seen it before. Police getting overexcited at a print found on a wall and it turning out to be from someone who lived there six years previously.'

'Anything else I need to know?'

Good indicated the file. 'It's all in there. Oh, yes. It might interest you to know that we found a hardcore gay magazine under the bed. Looks like Mr Wiseman was ... how shall I put it? ... not playing with a straight cue.'

'No surprise there.'

Good got up. 'Now if you'll excuse me Harry,' he turned to Singh, 'Priti, I have to get back and pick up the boys. They've been at my sister-in-law's all last night and this morning. A bit cheesed off with me, I'm afraid – we *were* meant to be going bowling. I'm going to have to try and make it up somehow.' He started to leave but twisted around to see Hal. 'Perhaps the fact that the penis and anus have been taken away has something to do with Mr Wiseman's sexuality? Just an idea. Bye.'

The old woman sitting at the next table looked up in horror at Good's parting shot. 'This country,' she tutted, putting down her mug. 'Whatever happened to this country?'

The laptop glowed in the gloomy kitchen. Outside it was pissing it down. Again. The rain pitter-pattered heavily against the window, and streaking water obscured the partial view of the Thames that Stevie 'enjoyed' from his first floor flat on Princess Street in Deptford.

He'd left Luchewski another message – his answer phone must be filling up quickly. Obviously he didn't expect him to be home. A murder enquiry must take up most of a copper's time, but he left a message nevertheless. He wanted to talk to him. Wanted to see him.

Stevie waited for Google to load before typing in 'Luchewski' and hitting return. It took a good few seconds for the screen to change but the results page popped up eventually. Stevie quickly scanned through but each of the results was about some dodgy old entertainers in the seventies – Liddle and Moore. Stevie had never heard of them. Sounded like something his mum would like. He needed to refine his search. Scrolling back to the top of the page he added 'Metropolitan Police' to the criteria. He clicked 'search' and waited again.

This time he hit gold. Seven results. The first from BBC News. He double clicked and waited for the page to load up. It was a story about The Headmaster – that guy who'd murdered those women the previous year. Stevie remembered it being the lead story for a couple of weeks before disappearing into the ether. He read it through carefully:

Wednesday May 7th. London.

A man who kidnapped, tortured, and eventually murdered two prostitutes in his Surbiton garage has been jailed for life at the High Court today. Arnold Richards – known commonly in the press as The Headmaster or the Butcher of Suburbia – was given two life sentences to run concurrently by Lord Justice Frome. Speaking in court, Frome called Richards 'a despicable blight on the face of humanity' and 'a coward who acted in the most deplorable way imaginable, snatching away the lives of two poor and desperate women for your own depraved pleasures.'

Richards, 62, a former headmaster of Farnham Green Grammar School for Boys, is said to have picked up 17-year-old prostitute and heroin addict Stacey Graham from the red light district near King's Cross station on June 17th last year. After drugging the girl he drove *across South London to his five-bedroomed detached house on the outskirts of Surbiton before subjecting her to six days of sexual abuse and torture.*

On June 20th, three days after the first abduction, Richards kidnapped 28-year-old former model Cassandra Shoneye. Both girls were gagged and tied to hooks fixed into the garage wall. During the trial, Richards admitted using a blowtorch and a garden strimmer to torture the two unfortunate young women. They were fed Mars bars during the ordeal and Richards had placed a television set in the garage 'to stop them getting bored. I didn't want them to get bored. I'd come in and change the channel occasionally. Put on EastEnders or some such programme.' At the time, Richards' wife Moira was away visiting an elderly relative in Scotland.

On June 25th, binmen found Graham's remains in a green dustcart in Richards' garden. Her body had been dismembered in order to fit into the receptacle. Police later found Shoneye's body still handcuffed to the wall in the garage. Both girls had died from severe head injuries.

A plea of diminished responsibility from the defence team was thrown out of court by Lord Justice Frome. Frome summed up by saying to Richards, 'You are a highly intelligent man who knew exactly what you were doing. You used your wife's absence to indulge the base and sick desires that you had probably kept hidden from the world for most of your life. I believe you to be a clever and manipulative individual and for that reason I cannot accept any suggestion of a sense of diminished responsibility.'

After sentencing, while being led away, Richards shouted out to the courtroom, 'In the end they both begged me to do it. They begged me to take their pathetic little lives. I enjoyed taking them.' Scuffles broke out in the crowd and a mobile phone was thrown at Richards before he was escorted out.

Speaking outside the courtroom, Senior Investigating Officer Harry Luchewski of the Metropolitan Police said that Richards, 'was, and always will be, a monster. He fully deserves to be locked away forever for what he did to those two poor women. Having seen first-hand the mayhem and the despair that this awful incident has

*caused to the families of the dead girls, I seriously mean it when I
say that I hope he chokes!'*

Stevie sat back in his chair. Luchewski didn't mince his words.
He probably got into trouble for that 'hope he chokes' remark. So a
bit of a rogue officer then?

He clicked on another search result. This one was a case
involving a group of travellers. One of them had killed the fourteen-
year-old son of his sister, after his sexual advances were rejected by
the boy. The murderer, Pat O'Donnell, had tried to dispose of the
body by breaking into someone's garden one night and stuffing it
down below the large metal sewerage access cover. The man from
Dyno-Rod got quite a shock, it seems, when he was called out a few
days later. Stevie thought how awful it must be to be a binman or a
drain clearer-type bloke. All the bodies and limbs and things you
must keep coming across! Again Luchewski was in charge of the
investigation, successfully sending O'Connell down for fifteen
years.

Stevie got up from the computer and walked to the window. The
tiny bend of the Thames that he could see from the flat looked
murky and still. A small boat was fighting its way upstream and
another, a long flatbed transporter devoid of anything to transport,
started to push its way past the smaller vessel, on its way out to sea.
The small boat bobbed up and down violently in its wake.

He knew the basics of his story. Knew the angle he was going to
take. So what if Luchewski got hurt in the process? That was his
hard luck and would teach him a lesson for being a one-night
standing bastard anyway. It meant swallowing a bit of pride and
quite a lot of personal integrity, but it was something that he just had
to do. He kind of loved his job and he certainly wanted to keep it.
Didn't want to lose it just yet. And if it meant sacrificing
Luchewski's professional comfort, then so be it. He'd show the
world he could be ruthless too.

Chapter Nine

Chief Manager Hurley's secretary was sitting on a chair to the side of the large desk, tapping his pen nervously on his black ring binder. They were waiting for Hurley to appear. That was the problem with a female governor, thought Hal in as sexist a way as his usually fairly liberal brain could handle. Probably doing her face in the loo. Might even be choosing a new outfit for the meeting. A nice chiffon blouse with some linen slacks perhaps.

'She came in specially for this meeting,' the secretary piped up. 'She doesn't usually work on Saturdays.' His face looked as though he was chewing on a particularly sour sherbet lemon. 'Neither for that matter do I.'

The door opened and in walked a woman aged around fifty wearing a dark grey skirt suit. Her hair was cut extremely short with tight little blonde curls sticking to the sides of her head. Her face was thin and sharp, to the extent of looking rather hard. Her long skinny nose pointed like a knife. To Hal she looked like a cross between an elfin princess and a leather-clad Harley-riding dyke.

'Sorry, I'm late, Inspector.' The voice was a good semitone lower than one might have imagined. She shook Hal's hand before taking up her position behind the desk. 'I hope Simon here has been taking care of you.' Hal tried to smile at her. 'Now, you tell me that one of our old residents has been found dead. That is dreadful, of course. But how can I help you?'

'Mr Wiseman's death is being treated as suspicious, I'm afraid.' *Being treated as suspicious!* thought Hal, remembering the crime scene. *I should fucking say it's being treated as suspicious.* 'I would just like any information or files that you've kept on his time in Granton. I would also like to talk to any guards that were around during the time Mr Wiseman was here. Just a quick chat.'

'We only have one C wing guard left from that period,' the secretary was consulting his file. 'Robert Francombe. Not in today. Now works on D wing. Everybody else has either left or been let go.'

Chief Manager Hurley shifted in her seat. 'You see, Inspector, we have had quite a turnover in staff in recent years. After the scandal involving the previous Chief Manager, I was brought in to straighten the place out. A new broom and all that.' Hal remembered reading about it in the papers. It was front page in the tabloids for a good few days. The governor had been embezzling funds, using them to buy a large house, nice car, and foreign holidays for himself and his wife. In the end, it was discovered that several hundred thousand pounds had been secreted away during the years he was in charge of the place. Before it all came to court, however, the governor strapped a hosepipe to his exhaust, fed the other end through his car window, and gassed himself in a wood somewhere in Kent – a nice quick way out of a financial black hole, and saving the taxpayer millions in court costs.

'The scandal had seriously damaged the institution,' Hurley went on. 'What with that and the Feltham murder enquiry, young offender institutions were starting to become something of a dubious proposition.' Hal looked up on the wall behind her. Along the entire length of it were the official photographic portraits of the governors since the place had opened up in 1984. Hal noticed that even the embezzling governor was still in place, his hard face stern and unsmiling. In retrospect, it was pretty obvious to see that the man was capable of stealing thousands of pounds. He had an old-fashioned face that seemed to glare at the photographer and a slightly shifty, unsettling look in his eye. Beneath the picture was a small insignificant little plaque that read '*Peter Burgess 1997-2012*'. Hal looked back at the other portraits: '*Frederick Masterson OBE 1984-1987*', '*Lionel Numan 1987-1991*', '*Sir Randolph Peach 1991-1996*' and '*Neal O'Donnelly 1996-1997*'.

'Over the last few years, I've done my damnedest to ensure that this institution's reputation has improved. We've tightened up on the drugs, fully trained our staff, and tried to make the environment as harmonious and conducive to rehabilitation as possible. If there *was* any corruption before, it no longer exists here at Granton.'

'You sound like a lady who doth protest too much, Ms Hurley.' Hal smiled at the Governor. To his surprise she smiled back.

'You're a police officer. You know what these places are like. Some people are only too willing to exploit others to make some extra cash. Yes, I think that Granton has had more than its fair share of corruption in the past. Some guards were definitely on the take, so to speak.'

'But no more?'

She shook her head. 'No. No more. All of our staff are fully vetted nowadays. They have a much greater sense of community and of vocation.'

'I'd be grateful to have a list of all the members of staff – even the sacked ones – that Mr Wiseman could have come into contact with. I'd also like a list of every C wing inmate from Wiseman's period of incarceration.'

She nodded. 'Simon will get on to it right away. Won't you, Simon?'

'Yes, ma'am. I'll have them faxed over to you asap, Inspector.'

'Cheers.'

As they got up to leave, Hurley tapped Hal on the arm. 'You used the word "incarceration" just then, Inspector Luchewski.'

'Am I not allowed to do that?'

'Best not.'

'I'll try to bear it in mind.'

Denzil McKenzie drove a souped-up W-reg Ford Fiesta that he loved more than even his own mother. More than any of the women in his life in fact. Larissa, Naomi, Polly. None of them were anywhere near as important to him as his Fiesta. He'd recently had alloys put on – they had eaten up nearly all of his savings – and the strobe light along the bumper was a relatively new addition too. The original front seats had been ripped out and replaced by some second-hand hard-backed racing ones, kindly donated by a neighbour. Denzil's neighbour had upgraded to a white 52-reg BMW and obviously didn't need them any more. The windows on Denzil's Fiesta were tinted and the dashboard lovingly polished up.

Denzil sang along as Eminem whinged about his motherfucking ex-wife one more time. He'd finished work at midday and had taken a drive over to his partner's house. His partner wasn't there, the wife had said, rolling her eyes. 'He's working on that fuckin' car of his'. His partner loved cars almost as much as he did. At the moment, he was working on a 1973 Capri. Fucking thing wasn't much more than a rustbucket, but he'd put a 'new' engine in and was currently doing something to the front axle. Denzil didn't know much about how cars worked. Didn't know anything about fixing them. Not like his partner. His partner could make anything move. It was one of the few things that Denzil admired about the bloke. So Denzil had gone to the lock-up where the car was being kept. He needed an address. His partner had nodded and told him that he couldn't remember whether it was number thirty or thirty-one, but the street name was definitely right.

Denzil wound down the window. The rain had stopped and it

was beginning to feel decidedly muggy. He indicated left before turning onto the street. A little further along and he could see that thirty and thirty-one were right next to each other. He pulled over and switched off the engine. The houses were dingy-looking, and Denzil had second thoughts about what he was about to do. Steeling himself, he got out of the car and walked up the path to number thirty.

Denzil knew exactly who had killed Daniel Wiseman. Knew exactly *why* he had killed Daniel Wiseman. And now, here he was, standing on the killer's doorstep. *I must be fucking mad*, he thought.

Pulling the beanie hat hard down onto his head, Denzil rang the doorbell.

Paul Norris was knackered. His whole body seemed to throb from exhaustion and it took all of his strength to keep himself upright at the bus stop. Someone at work had given him a lift to the green in Elmer's End, and he was waiting for the number 60 to the New Addington estate. He yawned as two buses to Croydon flew past.

The reason he was so knackered these days was all down to his two-year-old son. Levi. Energetic Levi. Energetic and Unwilling to Go to Bed Before Midnight Little Levi. Paul couldn't understand where the boy got his energy from. Tracey took him to playgroups in the morning where, apparently, he'd run his tiny little socks off and bounce up and down on the miniature trampolines until he was virtually sick. In the evening, Paul always took him out onto the scruffy patch of waste ground that stood in for a local park and kicked the football as far as he could so that the little bastard had to run for it, but still the boy kept them up until around midnight. They'd tried sleep-training him in the early days. Someone had told them that if they left him to cry in his cot he'd eventually fall asleep. 'It might take a week or so before he settles,' they had said, 'but eventually he'll associate being put in his cot at a particular time with going to sleep.' Paul knew what a load of shit that was. After six weeks of continual crying, with neither Paul nor Tracey getting more than a couple of hours kip a night, they abandoned the training and just let him go off to sleep in his own time. Unfortunately, that was usually midnight. Some kids didn't seem to have much energy at all. He'd seen them in the parks with their dads. They'd jump about a bit for half an hour and then went off to sleep at seven o'clock, waking up about seven the following morning. Those dads didn't know they were born. Even when they were awake, the kids seemed to be able to occupy themselves, playing with their toys and stuff. Little Levi always wanted your attention. If you weren't in the room with him, he'd kick up a bloody fuss, stomping his feet and screaming. And then, of course, you had to watch the boy's DVDs. Bob the bloody Builder, Fireman Sam, and the frigging Wiggles. Paul seemed to spend most of his evenings nowadays deciding which of the Wiggles he'd most like to twat. Definitely the fucker with the teeth. Definitely. He needed a fucking good kicking. Paul wouldn't have minded if he could watch *new* episodes, but the boy always wanted to watch the same one over and over again. He felt like his head would explode if he had to endure another session of *Bob's Pizza*. He knew the script off by heart. Could probably recite it word for word if he sat down and tried. Thankfully he didn't have the energy.

It was hard enough dragging himself into work most mornings, shuffling through the day and then bearing little Levi's antics until some God-awful hour. These days, Paul's only relief was in falling asleep. He more or less lived for that moment when his head hit the pillow and he would think about things he used to do in the old days when he was free. He would mentally walk up streets he knew as a kid, or recall a fight he had with a friend or a Chelsea supporter somewhere. Then, before he'd even got started on the reminiscing, unconsciousness would overwhelm him and he'd start snoring away (or, at least, that's what Tracey always told him he did.) Having a toddler was a fucking amazing way of curing insomnia. You get so bloody tired that you can't do *anything* other than fall asleep.

Another bus to Croydon pulled in, dropping several people off and whisking several more away. Paul started thinking about that copper and what he'd said. Poor fucking Danny. Murdered. He was a funny little fucker but he didn't deserve to be murdered. He stuck his hand in his pocket and pulled out the business card that the copper had given him. '*Detective Inspector Harry Luchewski – Metropolitan Police.*' Funny fucking name. Funny-looking fucker too, come to think of it. What did he say? 'Anything. Anything at all.'

At long last the 60 pulled in and Paul clambered on, flashing his weekly ticket to the driver. Taking his seat, he wiped a circle out of the condensation on the window. Perhaps he should have told that copper with the funny name about The Club. Danny had mentioned it a few weeks back. Said he could earn some cash. It wasn't hard. Danny had earned quite a bit of money from The Club apparently. But then …

Paul was always desperate for money – with a girlfriend and

child to support – but he wasn't going to go down that route. Not yet, anyway. That was a last resort.

The results of the house to house enquiries were complete, and Singh was relieved to find out that there was nothing she had missed at Chester Row. No extra piece of vital information had been unearthed, no new sightings, nothing. Zilch. Nada. Eat that, Luchewski, she had thought after reading the report, and had taken a self-congratulatory gulp of decaffeinated instant coffee, the jar of which she kept in her desk. Eat that, Luchewski.

She didn't know why he was being so petty with her. He'd tried to keep it hidden, be professional, but she knew that he was pissed with her for some reason. He tried to make jokes but she could still detect it. Women's intuition, perhaps? Which was a shame, because she liked the guy. He was one of the few officers in the department that she respected. He could be an arsehole like all of the others, but she always found herself coming back to the concept of him being a good cop. Moral, even. All right, some mornings recently he smelled like an explosion at a brewery, but ultimately he was a man doing things for the right reasons. Which made his attitude today all the more peculiar and irritating. She'd been going to say something to him when they got back to the office, but before she'd had the chance to do so he'd snatched up his copy of the report and strolled back out to his car, waving goodbye to the dwindling numbers on the third floor. Maybe tomorrow instead.

The report lay wide open on the top of her desk. Still no answer at number thirty then, she thought, remembering the previous day's encounter (or rather, non-encounter). Grabbing a notepad, Singh scribbled a note to herself to find out who lived at number thirty. Corrie could probably run it through one of her databases.

She looked at her watch. 5.23. She was meant to be at Nicky's by six. He was cooking her a meal. He was an excellent cook – much better than she was. She'd never really inherited the cooking gene from her mother. Her mother would make the most incredible curries and breads, supplemented with homemade chutneys and sauces, and she was equally good when cooking traditional British food such as meat pies and roasts. Lamb joints drizzled with honey and crushed rosemary were one of Singh's favourites.

Just the thought of food made Priti Singh's mouth start tingling with saliva, and she hurried her desk clearing and left the building, heading for the car and a decent home-cooked meal.

71

The results of the house to house enquiries were complete. Singh had missed nothing at Chester Row. Hal felt a sense of relief. He'd been pretty mean to the poor girl today – ignoring her a little too much, dismissing what she'd said out of hand, questioning her ability. He knew that he could be a nit-picking wanker sometimes, but there was no need to drag other people into it. She was only doing her job. Even reporting him to Woode was probably done out of a sense of propriety. She was young and had a lot to learn, and she wasn't going to learn anything with him being a class one tossbucket.

He put down the report on the oak coffee table and loosened his tie. It could all wait until tomorrow. He'd have to go in for a few hours in the morning and stand around the office, writing reports and putting things straight in his head. Put various pieces of paper in order and then write up some more pieces of paper to explain the order in which the other pieces of paper had been put. The usual convoluted, red tape bullshit.

Hal got up and pressed the button on his answerphone. *You have five new messages*, the Stephen Hawking-style voice barked at him. *First new message… Beep*

'Oh, hello, Hal … This is a message for Hal Luchewski … Hi. This is Stevie Denyer … Stevie from the other night at Dickie's Bar. Hi. I tried leaving messages last night so I hope your machine is working. Anyway, I thought I'd try again, so here goes. Just wondering really if you'd like to meet up for a drink sometime soon. No ties, just a drink and a chat. If you like. My mobile is –' he spat out a number way too fast to be caught on first hearing, 'I enjoyed our night together and… well…. I'd like to see you to have a chat and a laugh really. If you'd like to get back in touch with then feel free – I'll be in all night tonight – otherwise… er… well, don't worry too much, I'll see you around. Bye.'

The message ended. *Second new message… Beep*

'Hi. Looks as though you're still not in. I'll try again later. Bye.' *Third new message…*

'OK. Still not there. Hope this machine is working.' Jesus, Hal thought. He's persistent.

Fourth new message…

'Hello, Harold. This is Elizabeth. Wonder if you could get back to me at some point. It's to do with that book that's coming out about Dad – I don't know if you got the letter – but the publishers are happy for us to look at it before it goes to the presses. Think we should get our heads together over this one. Speak to you soon.' His sister's voice was cold, efficient, and abrupt. Not a droplet of warmth contaminating the iciness. She still blamed him, even after all this time. Still wanted as little to do with him as she could possibly get away with. Hal couldn't remember the last time he'd seen his niece and his nephew. Three years, was it? Four?

Fifth new message...

'Hi. I'm probably beginning to sound a bit like an obsessive psycho here now. Sorry. I'm not, honestly. No need to hide your pet bunny and your big saucepan quite yet.' Hal smiled. 'And I haven't got my mother stuffed and sitting in a chair in the basement either, so don't worry. Just wondered if you were there. I'd really like to speak to you. Like I said, no ties. Just a chat and a drink. That's all. Speak to you soon – hopefully. Bye.'

Hal thought back to Thursday night and the boy he'd picked up from Dickie's. He seemed sane enough. Fairly bright and quick-witted, in the taxi back to the house he'd made Hal laugh out loud with a story about shellfish and a well-known pop star from the seventies. The punchline was too rude to be true and Hal had filed it away in the joke section of his brain for later use. The boy was pleasant enough, slightly bitchy perhaps but then most of the guys who hung around Dickie's were. If anything, Hal decided, there was something sad about him. Lonely, possibly. Someone who had lots of acquaintances but very few actual friends. He was delicate, like a house of cards. Flittering to the ground with a breeze. Hal's stomach sank and, with some residue of the guilt he felt over Singh still clinging to his sense of decency, he picked up a pen and hit the 'Replay' button.

Nicholas Gardener had just finished setting the table for dinner. He hadn't cooked anything particularly special tonight. A simple beef and green lentil casserole sat bubbling away in the oven alongside some homemade herb focaccia. He had yet to prepare the vegetables – new potatoes and organic asparagus tips with a pepper sauce – but thought it better to wait for Priti to arrive, lest they be spoiled.

The dining room looked out over the garden, French windows opening out on to the patio. Stepping outside for a few seconds into the humid air, Nicholas noticed that the tiny white flowers of the cherry blossom were starting to drop, hundreds of them already covering the ground around the base of the tree. They never seemed to last long. A couple of weeks and it would be completely bare. That was the problem with most plants and trees, you spend most of the year staring at woody stumps willing something to happen then, come spring and early summer, *whoosh* – a flurry of colour before quickly slipping back to the dead wood stage. Nicholas sometimes wondered if it was all really worth it. Or rather, he wondered if paying someone eight pounds an hour to deal with it all was really worth it.

Further down towards the rear of the garden, the eucalyptus was going berserk once again. Every time he looked at it, it seemed to have grown another three feet or so. He'd have to ask Dave to hack it back a bit. Otherwise the neighbours might complain like they did last year. Silly buggers.

Back inside the house, Nicholas put on some Satie. He fast-forwarded to tracks 26, 27, and 28 – the 'Trois Gymnopedies'. He'd always loved the Gymnopedies. They made him feel terribly sad yet strangely joyous at the same time. The fragile piano pieces followed him down the hallway as he made his way to the kitchen to check on the bread. On the way, he checked himself out in the mirror. He'd showered earlier that afternoon, so his hair looked full and fresh. The pink-striped Boden shirt he'd ironed looked crisp tucked into his chino trousers, and his new suede loafers rounded the look off. He gave himself a cocky little wink and carried on.

The bread had fluffed itself up and looked ready. Grabbing a pair of Jane Asher oven gloves from the hook near the sink, Nicholas pulled the bread tin out and set it aside, dusting a number of stray crumbs into the Brabantia bin with a drying up cloth. In the distance, beyond the strains of gently tinkling piano, he could hear the front door being unlocked.

'Hi, Nicky.'

'Hello. In here.' He called back. 'In the kitchen.'

His fiancée – the woman he loved more than anything, or anyone, in the entire world – had arrived. He smiled to himself before putting the potatoes on.

'I saw you on television last night.'

'Television? What do you mean?'

The bar was filling up quickly – most bars in central London did on a Saturday evening. From shopgirls and Modern Apprenticeship car mechanics to older middle-class couples spilling into and out of theatres. From Japanese businessmen looking for cheap thrills to pushers and pimps plying their sacred wares. From rich, besuited playboys, to designer-scruffy undercover policemen. In an area bounded by Oxford Street, Charing Cross Road, The Strand, and

Regent Street, the whole world collided in a kaleidoscope of drunken noise and colour. Hal and Stevie Denyer were sitting at a back table in a small pub just on the edge of Soho. It seemed relatively quiet initially, but now a band of girls on a hen night were screeching through the door, each of them wearing a set of deely-boppers on their badly bleached heads.

'You were on the news.'

Shit, thought Hal. 'Was I?'

'Yes. You're not an accountant after all, are you? You're a policeman.' Stevie took a surprisingly large gulp of his Campari and soda. Hal sipped his vodka slowly. 'You're investigating some murder, aren't you? In Catford. I saw you in the background on the news.'

Hal couldn't deny it. In fact he didn't want to deny it. 'Yes. I am. Sorry I lied.'

'That's all right. Your name *is* Luchewski, isn't it? You didn't lie about that, did you?'

'No. No, I didn't. Look, Steven –'

'Stevie, please. I prefer to be called Stevie. Everyone does it. Even my mum.'

'Look, Stevie, I wanted to meet up with you to say that –'

'So tell me all about this murder then.'

'What?'

'Tell me all about this gruesome murder that you're investigating.'

'I can't, I'm afraid.'

'Oh go on. Give me all the juicy details. Brutal, was it?'

Christ, thought Hal. Perhaps he was a nutter after all. 'Look, Stevie –'

'Who was killed? On the news they said it was a young boy. How young?'

'He was about nineteen. That's all I can really say.'

'It must be great being a detective, investigating serial killers and stuff. Hard work though, I bet.'

Hal undid another of the buttons on his grandfather shirt. 'Well, it is hard work. Not much fun, though.'

'No, well, that's right,' Stevie tried to sound more serious. His head was light and he felt quite drunk already. 'No. It must be horrible seeing all that death and stuff. Depressing as well. Must make you miserable, sometimes.'

'Oh, you'll never know,' Hal said sadly. 'You'll never know.'

The girls at the bar were laughing loudly at something the

barman had just said. They'd obviously been pissing it up all afternoon, and one or two of them looked a little the worse for wear. 'Show us yer bum,' one of the fatter ones insisted, and the barman blushed as a response. 'Go on! Show us yer bum!'

'So, tell me about yourself,' Stevie grinned at Hal, putting his empty glass down on the table.

'What?' Hal was snapped away from watching the scene at the bar.

'Tell me about yourself. What you like to do, where you like to go. Your family. Tell me about your family.'

'Look, Stevie. The reason I asked you to come here tonight was to apologise for behaving so badly the other night. I shouldn't have –'

'Apologise? No need to apologise.'

'I shouldn't have led you on like that. I've been feeling a bit down recently and I shouldn't have taken out my frustrations on you.'

'I don't understand.'

'I shouldn't have taken you home with me. It was wrong of me.'

'But we had a good time together. Didn't we?'

'Yes, but ...' Hal's voice trailed off. 'We just shouldn't have done. Sorry.' He knew he was looking sheepish. The angle his head was tilted at was definitely a sheepish one. He twisted his glass around on the cardboard coaster on the table. 'It was all my fault.'

'Ah, well. Never mind.' The boy sounded either nonchalant about the whole thing or badly hurt, depending on how you viewed it. 'Tell me about yourself. How old are you for a start?'

'Eh?' Hal was caught off guard. 'I'm thirty-nine. Thirty-nine years old.'

'Thirty-nine. I'm twenty-nine, so you're ten years older than me. When's your birthday?'

'July 27th. Why?'

'July 27th. That makes you a Leo. Good leaders, Leos. Excellent leaders, in fact. But vain and aggressive. Love to be the centre of attention, I'm afraid. My birthday's September 3rd. I'm a Virgo. Virgos are well-organised and efficient. However, they can be petty and over-fussy about things.'

'Can they?'

'Mmm. You live in an expensive house, don't you? How can a policeman afford to live in such an expensive house? You on the take? You one of these corrupt officers we're always hearing about on the news?'

The questions caught Hal unaware and he started to answer honestly. 'Er ... I inherited a lot of money.'

'Really?'

'Yeah. Look, what's with all these questions?'

'I'm just interested, that's all. After what you've just told me – about leading me on and that – I think it's the least you could do. Don't you?'

'Well ... What about you? Are you going to answer questions about yourself? Where do you live, for example? I don't know anything about you.'

'My name is Steven Peter Denyer. I am twenty-nine years old. I own a small flat in Deptford. I work as an assistant clerk at the gas board. My mother's name is Wendy. My father's name is Frank. I have one brother and one sister. My brother Robert is an engineer in Brighton. My sister, Sarah, is an optician in Ipswich. She's married to a fellow optician called Marco, and they recently had a baby daughter who they've decided to call Petronella. I studied English at London University before dropping out in the second year. Growing up, I always wanted to be an English teacher – you know, a bit like Robin Williams in *Dead Poets Society*. Instead I'm an assistant clerk at the gas board. I was fifteen when I discovered I was gay. I have slept with seven people in total – one woman and six men. My favourite television programme is *Embarrassing Bodies* – gross but fab – although I am partial to a little *Pingu* of a morning. My favourite book is *The Catcher In The Rye* by J. D. Salinger. My favourite song of all time is *Believe* by Cher – absolutely awesome. I love lemon meringue pie and Ben and Jerry's ice cream – but not at the same time. When I was nineteen, I went inter-railing with friends but got lost in Turin. I had to come back home on my own. I once spent a summer teaching English to ski instructors in La Plagne. I own a laptop computer but not a vacuum cleaner. Last Christmas I got arrested for urinating in the street – if you must know it was Trafalgar Square. I was let off with a caution. I buy a lottery ticket every Saturday with the numbers 3, 8, 15, 19, 20, and 30. I own eight pairs of shoes. And I have a Blue Peter badge. Anything else you'd like to know?' Apart from the one lie about the gas board, everything Stevie had said was true.

'No. I think you've more or less covered it.'

Suddenly a shrill *brrr-brrr* split the air. Hal jerked around and pulled a mobile phone out of the pocket of the jacket hanging on the back of his chair. *Brrr-brrr*. He stared at the screen for a few seconds before slowly getting up from his seat.

'You need a better ringtone,' Stevie sniped, tapping the side of the empty glass.

'Excuse me a second.' Hal looked back at the screen. 'I'd better take this outside. It's my daughter.'

After they had finished supper and loaded the dishwasher with what seemed like far too many plates for two people, Singh and her fiancé sprawled out on the large leather sofa, kicked off their shoes, pulled a large woollen blanket over themselves, and tuned into Netflix. Pigging out on season three of *Orange Is The New Black*, Singh lay back in the arms of Gardener, softly stroking the back of his hand with her nails.

'You know,' Gardener started as episode four came to an end, 'if you ended up in prison –'

'Oh, thanks a lot! I see you've got confidence in your future wife's ability to stay on the straight and narrow.'

He smiled. 'If you ended up in prison, I'd come and break you out.'

'Really? How would you do that then? Rip down the walls with your bulging biceps? Buy a tank? Helicopter me out?'

'I'd find a way. I'm very resourceful, you know.' He brought up his hand and ran his fingers through her hair. 'I'd probably smuggle in a rope ladder.'

'A rope ladder?'

'Mmm. No, no. A *silk* ladder. Yes, that's it. A silk ladder. It'd be easier to get past security.'

'Yeah, but,' she twisted to see his face, 'stuffing a silk ladder down your trousers wouldn't be any good. You'd need grappling hooks on the end of it.'

'True.'

'And I'm sure a large metal grappling hook down each leg might just – *just* – get noticed.'

'True.'

'Not to mention being rather uncomfortable.'

Gardener gave a pretend wince.

'Breaking me out of prison's all very well, but not if you have to castrate yourself in the process.'

He laughed and kissed her neck.

'Anyway, I'm a copper. Someone with an unfaltering belief in the concept of justice. If I ended up in prison, there's a massive chance that I'm guilty, so it'd be where I belonged. So I'd actually be very annoyed if you tried to break me out. If I'm guilty then I deserve everything I get.'

'Are you sure you're not Catholic? Only some of the things you say are very, *very* Catholic.'

She snorted. 'Better not say that to my mum. Don't think you get too many Indian Catholics round these parts. They'd be constantly confessing to the sins of wanting their daughters to marry good men and for their sons to become well-respected chiropodists.'

'Does your mum think I'm a good man?' he asked quietly.

'She's seen your car, she's seen this house, and she's seen that you wash behind your ears. That's all she needs to know. Oh, and she thinks you're marvellous.

She kissed him on the mouth.

'Early night?' Gardener raised an eyebrow.

'Why not?' Singh raised both eyebrows. 'Early night it is.'

After fighting his way back into the pub – during which he had to nudge a few slurring bridesmaids-to-be out of the way with his elbow – Hal slipped back into the seat he'd recently left. The glasses on the table had been replenished and Stevie was already close to having fully drained his.

'So. You've got a daughter?'

Hal nodded. 'Yes. Lily. She's just turned twelve.'

'No problem, I hope.'

'What? Oh. No. No. Just some silly tiff between Lily and her mother. Lily wanted to go to some party and Jackie –'

'Jackie? Your wife?'

'*Ex*-wife,' Hal emphasised. 'Jackie, my ex-wife, said she couldn't go because there weren't going to be any parents to supervise.'

'So Lily was phoning to see if she could play you both off against each other, yes? "Daddy, Daddy, Mummy says this and I want to do that", yes?'

'Basically, yes.'

'Typical teenager.' Stevie smiled. 'So how long were you with Jackie?'

Hal sighed. He never really talked about his failed marriage with anyone. Never really wanted to. Not many people at his work knew he had even been married. Freddie Burlock at the station, Woode obviously knew, and Dr John Good were all that he could really think of. Other than that, it just wasn't something that came up often. Now it had, though, and Hal felt that the boy needed an explanation. Something more substantial than a mere apology. He took a mouthful of his vodka and started to speak.

'I met Jackie at University. In Exeter. She was studying History, and I was trying to struggle through the first year of a law degree. She was bright and bubbly and was, for some peculiar reason, attracted to me. So we started going out together. When I decided that I wasn't going to be a successful lawyer, but a copper instead, she came up to Hendon with me and we both trained on the fast track officer course.'

'So she's a policeman ... sorry, policewoman too? Sorry, you know what I mean.'

'Used to be. For a short while. We eventually got married, bought a house in Muswell Hill, and then along came little Lily.'

'Then you discovered you were gay and it all fell apart, right?'

Hal's face darkened, his eyes becoming cold and angry. 'I'm not gay.'

'What?'

'I said I'm not gay.'

'Well, excuse me, but the other night when you were banging away it seemed as if you were very much batting for the queer team!'

'I'm not fucking gay!'

Stevie shook his head. 'Well if you're not gay, what the fuck are you? Bisexual? What?'

Hal started playing with his glass again. A moment passed in silence before he looked up. 'I don't know.'

'You don't know? You're thirty-nine years old and you don't know? How can you get to be thirty-nine years old and not know whether you're gay or straight? You're in denial.'

'Huh?'

'You're gay. You're just in denial. Lots of guys are, you know.'

'I am not!'

'You are. For some reason you can't bring yourself to admit it. It's usually to do with parents. Look at George Michael. He couldn't come out until his mother had died. Are you waiting for your parents to die before you come out?'

'Both of my parents are already dead!'

'Oh, sorry to hear that. So it's nothing to do with that then. Must be your work. There probably aren't that many gay cops, are there? Must be difficult to admit in such a male dominated environment. Yes. That must be it.'

'No, it's not! Look, can we talk about something else please?'

'I'm only trying to help, you know. It's best to talk about these things. Help you resolve the issue.'

'Not now. Talk about something else. Please.' Hal looked sad again and Stevie realised that changing the subject was probably the best thing to do right now.

'Tell me about the Headmaster.'

Hal's head sprang up. 'How do you know about the Headmaster? I mean, how do you know I was involved in the Headmaster case?'

'A wonderful invention, the internet.'

'You looked me up on the internet?' Hal was amused by the idea. 'It's a wonder you could spell my name correctly.'

'Oh, Luchewski's not that hard. I'm not stupid, you know.'

'No.' One of the hen party had started up the jukebox. Queen's *Don't Stop Me Now.* As the song approached the chorus, the band of women started singing along, waving their arms in the air and causing havoc with all the other drinkers. 'Bloody noisy buggers.'

'Don't worry about them,' Stevie leaned in closer over the table. 'Tell me about the Headmaster. You put him away, didn't you?'

'Not for long enough, I'm afraid.'

'What do you mean?'

'He'd killed others. There just wasn't enough evidence to link him to the murders, though. In the end, we had to settle on the two that he'd obviously done. They found them in his garage.'

'Well, they found one in his garage. The other was in his wheelie bin.'

'A wonderful invention, the internet!' Hal winked.

'Mmm. So how many do you think he really killed?' Stevie seemed to be practically salivating.

'Five. Possibly six.'

'Six!' Stevie seemed to squeal at this news. 'Six! Really? Who were they?'

'Do you remember the murder of Deborah Reed? About … oh … nine years ago now? She was found in a pub car park. In Surrey. Strangled with her own tights.'

'I vaguely remember. I dunno really, it's a long time ago.'

'Then there were Lisa and Suzie Wilson – mother and daughter. Found murdered in the same bed, both naked. Both had had some implement rammed inside them. Suzie was fifteen years old. Arnold Richards was tutoring her for her GCSE Geography exam.'

'God! That's five. What about the sixth?'

Hal leant back in his chair and sighed. 'In 1965, Richards' little sister disappeared from the family home in Cambridgeshire. She was never seen again. A tiny bloodstain was found on the floor in the kitchen of the house, and the parents were brought in for questioning. Neither of them were charged, but I get the impression that nobody really believed them. The dad hanged himself about four years later.'

'You think the Headmaster killed her?'

Hal nodded. 'He was thirteen at the time.'

They both sat in silence for a while, listening to the screeching banshees near the bar. One of them had climbed onto a table and was teasing the crowd with the possibility of a striptease. She was at least forty years old and fourteen stone in weight, and the table buckled slightly beneath her.

'You can't do that,' a balding man ran out from behind the bar. 'Come on, get down. You'll break it. Besides, if you fall and hurt somebody, health and safety won't cover us. So, come on …'

She paid no attention to the man and lifted her top a little to reveal a loose and flabby stomach hanging over her too tight trousers. Hal couldn't think of a less erotic scene.

'So who did you inherit your money off?' Stevie enquired eventually. 'Your father? Was he a rich banker or something? You're not posh, are you? You don't sound posh.'

Hal gulped down some more of his drink. 'You tell me. You're so good on the internet, you tell me where I got my money from?'

Stevie shrugged. 'I don't know.'

'Then that's your homework for tonight. Find out how Harry Luchewski got to be so rich.' Hal looked up at precisely the wrong moment to see a pair of large, floppy, cellulite-pocked breasts being wobbled from side to side. 'Dear God! Look at that. That's going to put me off solids for the next month.'

Chapter Ten

Despite having taken four of his prescribed sleeping tablets (no more than four in any twenty-four hour period, it said on the label), Trevor Phillips still couldn't sleep. Couldn't rest at all, in fact. He kicked the flimsy, worn sheets off himself and turned onto his side, clutching the stained pillow to his ear.

The police were knocking on his door. *Bang, bang, bang*. Why didn't they stop? *Bang, bang, bang*. First that girl. The black one. She rang the bell. *Buzz, buzz, buzz*. He'd ignored her, stood still. Watched her go back to the door. Saw her peering in. *Buzz, buzz, buzz, buzz, buzz, buzz* … She probably saw him. He didn't care. Didn't give a tinker's cuss any more. About anything. Nothing. Nothing. Then they came back today. Two big men in suits. Scruffy suits. They were young. All the police were young these days. Young. With short hair and muscles. He hid in the cupboard until they'd gone. They'd knocked the door. Could have damaged it.

BANG, BANG, BANG, BUZZ, BUZZ, BUZZ, BANG, BANG…

Trevor sat bolt upright. He couldn't sleep again. It was no good. He couldn't sleep nowadays. The pills never helped. Just made his brain feel foggy.

He got up out of the bed and scooped up the keys that sat on the bedside table. Walking out of the room across the landing to the second bedroom, he picked out the one key that he needed. *I know why the police are coming for me*, he thought. *I know why*. He slipped the key into the large Chubb and turned it. The lock sprung open.

It was all to do with his special collection. They were after his special collection. Especially after today.

Hal had used the work excuse to escape from the pub and from the boy. At first, Stevie had found it difficult to comprehend having to go into work on a Sunday. 'I could never work on a Sunday,' he'd said. 'It would feel like opening a nice bottle of wine and then having to pour it down the sink.' Hal agreed, wished him well and left.

The time was 10.49, and Hal had decided to listen to some

music. Standing in front of the rows and rows of CDs in the sitting room, holding a glass of Bell's in his hand, he contemplated the choice.

Hal was essentially an eighties indie kid with New Order being the very first group that ever actually said something to him. Through New Order he'd got into bands he'd been too young to enjoy first time around. Bands like The Smiths and Joy Division. His fingers traced across the rack to *Closer*, but Hal decided that, even though his mood had a tinge of despair to it, *Closer* wasn't the right album for this particular moment.

From then on, the teenage Luchewski followed the standard route of cool, intelligent bands that eschewed the cheesy bubblegum pop values of the usual chart fare: The Pixies, Nirvana, Radiohead. More recently, artists like Django Django, Everything Everything, and John Grant had worked their way on to his iPod. Classic, left-of-centre, unconventional pop.

Hal's fingers tickled over the CDs. He felt very drunk, and the inebriation added to his indecision. Finally his hand fell back onto Radiohead's *The Bends* – in Hal's opinion the greatest album of the nineties. He popped the case open and inserted the disc. He sat himself in his chair and scanned the CD cover before flicking the remote to track four, 'Fake Plastic Trees'. As the acoustic guitar part strummed in, Hal knocked back what was left of his drink and poured himself a neat whiskey from the bottle on the floor. He downed the drink in one mouthful and proceeded to pour himself another. His eyes were tired and he rubbed them one by one, listening to the music.

The boy didn't understand, of course. Nobody did. He didn't expect the boy to understand. He was too young. Well, no. That wasn't the case. He wasn't too young. He just didn't understand. How could he? DI Harry Luchewski of the Metropolitan Police never opened himself up to anyone. Not these days. The last time he opened himself up he ripped a family apart, so why bother now?

He loved his daughter. Almost more than life itself. She meant everything to him, but seeing her for just a few days twice a month was tearing him up. Not that he'd be able to cope with much more, however. He hadn't proved to be a very good father, had he? Presents here, the occasional holiday there. Doesn't add up to much, does it? She barely saw him. Barely knew him really. He was probably little more than a stranger to her. He didn't know much about her friends, what she did, where she went after school. He didn't even know about her favourite bands, her favourite TV programmes, her favourite colour. His work had been part of the problem, of course. He could give it up and just live off his father's capital, but his job was, to an extent, his life. As much as he loathed it – and, dear Christ, did he loathe it sometimes – it was all that he really had to call his own. Nobody had handed it to him on a plate. He worked hard to be where he was. It was all down to Harry Luchewski. Nobody else. Just Harry Luchewski.

The song finished and 'Bones' kicked in.

Hal yawned. Here he was again on a Saturday night, pissed off his tits listening to music from his past. Desperately trying to reclaim something that never actually existed in the first place. A wave of self-disgust washed over him, and he got up to switch the music off. However, instead of hitting the off button, he changed the CD for Simon and Garfunkel's *Greatest Hits* and flick-forwarded to 'I Am A Rock'.

After Luchewski had left the pub, Stevie Denyer had bumped into a couple of friends on their way to Heaven, where a Cher lookalike was performing. Stevie tagged along for an hour before making his way back home via taxi. He had too much on his mind to really enjoy himself. Even if she was belting out 'Believe' like her lungs depended on it.

Hitching his laptop to the phone socket once again, Stevie logged on. He desperately wanted to know how Luchewski had inherited his money. Calling up Google, Stevie typed in Luchewski. In a flash, the results he'd previously dismissed appeared on the screen. *Liddle and Moore*. He clicked on what seemed to be a fanboy entertainment guide. At the top of the screen was a shot of two middle-aged men in awful Seventies style suits with awful Seventies-style haircuts. One was tall and blond with big bulbous eyes; the other short, rotund with an excessive amount of dark curly hair. Stevie started reading.

Victor Liddle and Barry Moore

TV Programmes:
The Liddle and Moore Show (BBC) 1971-1978
Liddle and Moore (Thames) 1979-1980

The BBC's golden boys of the mid-seventies. Two knockabout magicians with a flair for the absurd, Liddle and Moore were the epitome of Sunday evening family entertainment. Attracting as many as fifteen million viewers at their peak, Victor Liddle (real name Luchewski) and Barry Moore were, for a time, household names, earning more than Morecambe and Wise and Little and Large combined!

After winning the BBC talent show Stars Of The Future *in 1970, Liddle and Moore's brand of inept magic tricks (basically a Tommy Cooper rip-off) and zany humour won them their own television series,* The Liddle and Moore Show. *Liddle (tall, blond, and sophisticated) was usually the straight man to Moore's bumbling jokey clown, although on some occasions the roles were reversed. At the 1972 British Television Awards,* The Liddle and Moore Show *won Best Light Entertainment Programme. They also scooped the same award in 1974 and 1975.*

However, in 1976 a change in writers meant a change in style. Coupled with Moore's increasingly dependent use of alcohol, the show started to lose its edge and was beginning to feel rather flabby and irrelevant, with some of the sketches from the later shows being just plain weird. In 1978, the BBC released them from their ten-year contract.

In 1979, they made a series for ITV, but it wasn't a success and they were dropped from the schedules after just eight shows.

After television, the boys toured the world for three years with a stage show that managed to recapture some of the glory of the early days. (For some reason, Liddle and Moore were extremely popular in both Japan and Australia and their shows are still transmitted in those countries to this day. In fact, it is said that not a day goes by in Australia without some satellite channel showing an episode of The Liddle and Moore Show*!)*

In 2004, talk of a reunion tour was cut short when, while on holiday in Monte Carlo, Victor Liddle crashed his car down a ravine, killing both himself and Mary, his wife of thirty-five years. The inquest declared that they were accidental deaths.

Barry Moore, meanwhile, lives in semi-retirement somewhere in the Vale of Glamorgan, South Wales. In 2006, he entered and eventually won the Channel Four reality show Celebrity House Arrest. *After being crowned King Of The House, Moore dedicated his win to the memory of his comedy partner. He has been married three times and divorced three times!*

DVDs available: The Best Of Liddle And Moore *(BBC, 2000)*

Stevie went back to the results page and clicked on another site. This one said much the same thing, but there were more pictures. Lots of them, in fact. Most of them were shots taken from the television programmes, with captions that said things like *Series 2, Show 5: The pirate sketch. Liddle's leg comes a cropper* and *Series 1, Show 2: The infamous gardening sketch. Any artichokes going spare?* A couple of pages along however and the photographs became more personal. A black and white one of Moore standing next to a homely looking woman in spectacles: *Moore with his first wife Elsie in 1968.* A shot of Liddle and his wife standing next to a large burgundy car: *Victor buys his first Rolls-Royce, 1974. Moore with his second wife Joan. Blackpool Summer Season 1973'* – wife number two was obviously an improvement on the first, tall and elegant with some serious diamante earrings. Finally, Stevie found what he was looking for. A picture of Liddle in the garden of a large house on a beautiful summer's day. Alongside him were two children, a boy and a girl. The girl was pretty and looked about ten. She wore her hair long with an Alice band, and her dress was both garish and drab at the same time, the way that seventies and eighties clothes generally were. The boy was a little younger, with a floppy blond basin cut. His eyes looked angry, as if he wasn't at all keen to have his photo taken, and his mouth was fixed into a sullen straight line. Stevie recognised him straight away. The caption beneath read, *Victor with his children Elizabeth and Harold outside their Weybridge home in 1983.*

Stevie sat back in his chair and folded his arms. So, when Luchewski had said that his parents were dead he wasn't kidding. He whistled to himself. Crashed down a cliff in Monte Carlo. Shit. That must have been rough.

Still. Never mind. He'd established how the guy had inherited his money. It was getting better by the second. Stevie could almost feel his luck changing. A copper in charge of a murder investigation. Who happens to be gay. But denies it. With an estranged wife and kid. And a famous dead dad. It was perfect. Enough meat in there for two or three stories, probably, but one really good one was all he was after. He could see it now. One of the more senior writers would be despatched to cover the actual murder. They'd write that. And his story would be the back-up. A human interest addendum to the main thing. A nice little column alongside. Fan-fucking-tastic!

Stevie felt like wanking.

Approximately five minutes after Stevie turned off his bedroom light, Goughy Gough was puking all over his shoes. Tezzer watched him as he continued to dry-retch.

'That's it, man. Get it all out. Get it all out.'

Goughy straightened up and wiped the sides of his mouth. 'Awwww. Fucking hell, man. Did you fucking see that?' He doubled up and retched one more time. 'Fucking hell.'

'Come on. Don't hang around here. Let's get fucking going. Get out of this fucking place before anybody catches us.'

'Shouldn't we call the police.'

'Fuck the fucking police, man. They'll just think it was us. Fucking police'll look at our records and think it was fucking us what done it. Come on!' Tezzer started marching away from the area outside the lock-up, but Goughy stayed put.

'I think we'd better call the police, man. I mean, he's dead in there. He's a fucking mess. Poor cunt.'

'Fucker probably had it coming. Now come on!' Tezzer walked another three yards before stopping and turning around. 'Fucking come on, will you!'

But Goughy still stayed put.

'No. Not yet.' He reached inside his coat and pulled out his mobile. 'I'm going to make an anonymous phone call.' He pressed a button on the phone.

'Don't use your fucking mobile then, you twat. They'll be able to trace you.'

'Oh, yeah. That's true.'

Tezzer sighed. Why did he have to put up with this sort of shit? All he wanted was a good night out. A few drinks and a couple of totes before hitting the clubs. Then a kebab and a wander through the deserted streets home to sleep it all off. Not too much to fucking ask, was it? It wasn't like he was asking to win the fucking lottery or nothing. It was Goughy who'd spotted the door flapping open. A lock-up garage with its door flapping open. And no one around. They couldn't believe their luck. There could have been anything in there, and it would have served the owner right if it all got nicked. Tezzer had known blokes keep stereos and jewellery and stuff like that in their lock-ups. It would have taught the cunt a lesson.

Unfortunately, it looked as though somebody else had taught the owner a lesson before they'd even got there.

'There's a fucking phone box around the corner from here. Phone the pigs from there.'

'I think we should. Don't you?'

Tezzer noticed a trail of orange puke on Goughy's white shirt. 'No. I don't. I think we should just leave it alone and let some other cunt find it.'

'No. I'm going to phone the police. I won't leave my name. I'll just give them the address.'

'Fine.' Tezzer stormed off impatiently, Goughy trotting in his wake.

Chapter Eleven

The first members of the AMIT team on the scene were DI Burlock and Sergeant Green. The local uniforms had secured the site – a tiny lock-up garage built into one of the arches of a railway viaduct in Peckham. The road outside it was a scruffy track which looked as though it had last been tarmacked in about 1982, and one of the two street lamps that badly lit the whole length of the lane was spluttering and stuttering to a slow death.

It was Sunday morning, and Burlock was pleased as punch to be getting out of his wife's monthly visit to church. It was something he'd always hated but persevered with for the sake of the girls' moral wellbeing. Though now that three of them had flown the nest, he was much more reluctant to enter into the spirit of the thing, trying every month to think of reasons why they shouldn't bother going along to the happy-clappy, self-sacrificing 'oh-we're-not-worthy' service with its shaking-hands-with-strangers ideas of a common humanity. He much preferred the thought of staying in bed late and reading the paper.

Today, though, he had the perfect ready-made excuse for not going.

'It's not very nice, sir,' the officer guarding the garage door said as Burlock pushed it open with the tip of his finger. 'Mind your foot, sir.' Green nearly stepped in the pool of sick behind him.

Peering into the dimly lit workshop, Burlock could see a car up on blocks with its tyres removed. It looked like an old Capri with a faux soft-top roof. As his eyes adjusted to the gloominess, he could see that there was something sitting on top of the roof. It was the size and shape of a football. Except that this football had eye sockets, ears, a nose and a mouth. Somebody had decapitated the man and placed his head on top of the car.

'Bloody hell.'

'Oh, my.'

In the corner, near a large unit for holding tools, was slumped the rest of the body – badly knocked about with an axe by the looks of it. An arm seemed to be attached to the torso by the slightest of threads. A puddle of blood covered the whole of the floor.

'Good God. Good bloody God.'

'I did warn you, sir.' The copper behind them seemed to gloat as he said it. 'I did warn you.'

Burlock and Green sat in Burlock's car while Forensics went about their nit-picking business. Green sat in the passenger seat rubbing his eyes, while Burlock started the *Sunday Telegraph* crossword.

'What about this one, then? "Scared domesticated animal badly fired about one." Nine letters. That's an easy one.'

'Is it?' Green yawned.

A long pause.

'Come on then, Green. What's the answer?'

'I don't know, sir. I'm no good at crosswords. I can do general knowledge crosswords but not these cryptic ones, I'm afraid.'

'Well, you want to practise. Keeps your brain alert. Look at you yawning there. Good cold shower in the morning, that's what you need. Wakes you up, I can tell you.'

Green wasn't really listening. 'Sir.'

Another pause.

'Petrified.'

'Hmm?'

'Petrified. That's the answer. '"Domesticated animal" – that's a pet. "Badly fired about one" means rearrange the letters in the word fired and bung an i into it – i looks like a one, you see – that gives you the "rified" part. Hence "petrified".'

'Oh. How do you know the answer's petrified?'

Burlock sighed. 'It's scared, you see. Scared. "Scared domesticated animal badly fired about one." Scared is the word you're trying to replace.'

'Oh.'

'Not a flicker of interest, is there? Not a single spark of curiosity. I'm trying to educate you here, boy. And all you can do is sit there yawning and stare at your watch.'

'I'm sorry, sir. I'm not very good first thing in the morning.'

'That's an understatement.' Burlock flicked his paper angrily and turned back to his crossword. 'Now, look at this one. Even you will be able to get this one, Green. Any old moron can get this one. "Girl's smart item of clothing sounds hairy." Seven letters.'

'Oh look, sir.' Green was pleased that Dr Good had come out of the lock-up at that particular moment. He couldn't bear another damned crossword clue. 'Looks like he might be finished.'

'That was bloody quick.' They got out of the car. 'You

finished?' Burlock shouted to Good.

'You are kidding, aren't you?' Good removed his silicon gloves and deposited them into a bag in the back of his van. 'We'll be all day at this. He's in a terrible mess. Any idea who he is yet?'

'Council rent the lock-up to someone called Raymond Larby. Lives somewhere on the Brixton side of Peckham. Any chance of you rummaging through his wallet to confirm if it's him or not?'

'Hold on.' Good stood in the doorway and shouted to one of his team. 'Spound. See if you can get his wallet without disturbing anything.' He turned back to Burlock and Green. 'We'll find out now.' Good looked up at the blue sky. 'This is a fine way to spend a Sunday morning, isn't it? How are your girls, Freddie? Deborah still at university, is she?'

'Still at home, you mean. Travelling into college every day from home. Desperate to suck every ounce of hospitality from us before launching herself onto the real world, to make a mint more than likely. Margaret keeping well?'

'Yes. She's away on a course all this week.'

'Is she?'

Spound came out and handed the wallet to the Good Professor. 'Thank you, Spound.' Good undid the latch on the leather wallet and pushed one of the gold-coloured credit cards up a little to see the name. 'Yes. Card belongs to Raymond Larby.' He pushed the card back in and put the entire wallet into one of the little plastic evidence bags before depositing it in the van.

'Anything to do with the murder down in Catford?'

'I don't know. That's your job. Detection. I just analyse stuff for you.'

'Come on, John. Don't give me that bullshit. Any connection do you think?'

'Probably. Although this one looks as though he was hacked with an axe – not sawn into pieces with a big saw.'

'Changed his MO. Realised that using the saw took a bit of time. Wanted to be quicker this time around.'

'I suppose.'

'He didn't take any part of the body with him, did he?' Green nervously proffered. 'Like the last one?'

'No. As far as I can tell everything is there. The head's been removed, but not taken.'

'Dead long?' Burlock's fingers twiddled with his beard.

'Seems fairly fresh to me. We're not talking days here. Yesterday sometime. Last night. Something of that order. Oh, and the head's been damaged.'

'What do you mean, "the head's been damaged"?'

'The murderer found time to stab the eyes out, stab the ears, and sew the lips together.'

'Sew the lips together! What do –'

'With some sort of coarse thread.' Good puckered up his lips and wriggled his index finger in front of them. 'Stitched together.'

Hal had got the message at around eight that morning. After downing a couple of Alka-Seltzers and forcing down a piece of toast, he drove to the office. He was due to see Daniel Wiseman's mother at ten thirty and needed to be vaguely presentable by then. Waiting at the office for Singh to arrive, Hal checked his email. Clicking his mouse, he opened up the list that he'd asked for from the secretary at Granton. Settling back in his chair, Hal started reading:

To: Detective Inspector Luchewski (MPF)
From: Simon Thurston @ Granton Young Offender Institution

Inspector,

Find attached the list of former residents and employees that you asked us to supply earlier today. Hope it helps.

<u>C wing Residents</u>

Steven Ableman (theft)
Robert Aston (theft)
Gregory Carman (aggravated assault)
Samuel Davies (theft)
Winston Degauge (sexual assault)
Stephen Durham (supplying drugs)
Justin Eddy (theft)
Ian Francis (aggravated assault)
Klaus Geissler (aggravated assault)
Patrick Glover (supplying drugs)
Nigel Green (theft)
Richard Green (criminal damage)
David Keene (supplying drugs)
Andre Khan (supplying drugs)
Warren McCabe (sexual assault)

Denzil McKenzie (supplying drugs)
Christopher Passmore (theft)
Bijal Patel (criminal damage)
Derrick Polzmann (sexual assault)
Ian Rich (supplying drugs)
Jacob Robinson-Price (rape)
Wilber Skoçzek (aggravated assault)
Andrew Stevens (theft)
Christopher Storey (theft)
Leslie Teale (aggravated assault)
Simon Thayer (aggravated assault)
Jason Thickett (theft)
Neil Thorne (sexual assault)
Christopher Trueman (theft)
David Vaughn (theft)
Richard Vincent (criminal damage)
William Walstow (supplying drugs)
Keith Watson (theft)
Martin Wigley-Jones (theft)
John Willoughby (theft)
Daniel Wiseman (theft)
Kim Sang Wong (aggravated assault)
Aaron Young (aggravated assault)
San Yu (theft)

Hal noticed that the secretary had stupidly left Wiseman's name on the list. He tutted at the insensitivity of it and continued reading.

I generalise with the 'theft' category. Many of the boys had taken cars, others had shoplifted repeatedly, etc.

I have last known contact addresses for all of the above names. I left them off because I thought that it might be too much info at once. Let me know if you need an address and I'll get it to you.

C wing Guards

Anthony Beaton (left – personal reasons)
Thomas Dagwood (retired)
Robert Francombe (still with us)
Keith Humphreys (let go)
Christopher Hunt (let go)

Peter Killmore (resigned)
Raymond Larby (let go)

Hal leaned forward onto his desk, and quickly scrabbled about for the piece of paper that he'd written the name on. Burlock's body. He'd written it down and – ah, there it was. *Raymond Larby*.

Shit.

The list went on, but Hal couldn't read it. All he could think was Raymond Larby. *Raymond Larby. Raymond Larby. Raymond Larby…*

Shit.

'So, we've got some nutcase going around doing in Granton inmates and warders alike. Why?' Burlock was throwing peanuts into the back of his mouth. 'Why would they do that? Must be another of the inmates, surely. Or one of the guards even. That's what it sounds like to me. Someone with an axe to grind.'

'Wiseman was at Granton during Larby's stint in C wing. We need to interview everyone on the list. Prisoners and guards. See if anyone can give us a connection between the two of them.' Hal spoke to the whole room. 'I'm having last known addresses faxed over. As soon as they arrive, I need you to get to work on it. Find out as much as you can about Granton and the situation there. Raymond Larby was sacked because he was supplying drugs to the inmates. Drug paraphernalia was found at Wiseman's flat, so it might well be that drugs are the connection. But keep an open mind. Just find out what you can.'

'Are we sure it's the same killer, sir?' Green suggested, his shaky hand in the air. 'I mean, Wiseman's murderer took a part of the body away with him. I don't think that he did the same with the body we found this morning.'

'Officially, no,' said Hal. We cannot be certain it's the same killer. Until the forensics confirm it, that's what we tell the world. But, on the other hand … Yes, of course it's the same killer. I'm 110% certain of it.'

Singh coughed. 'Sir. If someone is murdering the people on that list, shouldn't we warn the others that they might be a potential target?'

'No.' A long pause. 'Not yet, Sergeant. Don't alarm them. As far as we know the killer might have finished what he wanted to do. He might not kill any others. Until we've got a better feel for what's going on here, I don't think we should go broadcasting that we've got a serial killer on the loose. Especially to the press.' The official press statement about Wiseman's murder had been released that morning, although many of the papers were already running with a half-baked story about a murder in Catford. 'Just play it close to your chests and see what you can find.'

Chapter Twelve

Susan Wiseman was probably in her late forties but looked ten years younger. Her blonde hair was cut into a gentle bob – a slight wave to it giving a greater impression of thickness – and her clothes were respectfully sombre but fashionably relaxed. Her fingers were long, thin, and artistic-looking, with a number of delicate rings wrapped around them. She sipped the last of her tea before placing the cup and saucer on the floor between her and the sofa on which sat Luchewski and Singh. The relatives with whom she was staying had sensibly retired to the kitchen to get out of the way.

'I'm afraid my husband never really forgave Daniel,' she said, brushing biscuit crumbs off her dark velveteen skirt.

'For the pickpocketing incident or for being gay?' Hal asked gently.

'Oh, both. He could never forgive him for either of those things. In fact, I can't recall the last time Daniel spoke to his father. He usually just went through me.'

'So you kept regular contact with Daniel?'

'I did.'

'Tell me, Mrs Wiseman, when was the last time you spoke to Daniel?'

'That would have been Wednesday evening. I telephoned him.'

'And what did you talk about?'

'Oh nothing very much really.' She tapped her knee with the tips of her fingers. 'His work. Life in general. Frightfully dull things. You know how it is with someone you know very well. You don't need to talk too much sometimes. You get a feel for how they are.'

'And how did he feel that night, Mrs Wiseman?' Singh piped in.

'Slightly disappointed, I'm afraid.'

'Disappointed?'

'His best friend from school, Richard, was supposed to be coming down to London to see him. He's at university in Nottingham now.'

He said an old friend was going to visit him …

'What's he studying there?' Singh went off on a tangent.

'Oh. Chemistry, I think. Or is it Physics? I'm not entirely sure.'

'When was Richard supposed to be coming down?' Hal got things back on track.

'This weekend sometime. But he couldn't make it. Girlfriend problems, I believe. Daniel told me all about it but I didn't really take it all in, I'm afraid. Girlfriend threatening to leave and go abroad or something. Love plays such a significant part in your life at that age, wouldn't you agree, Inspector? Even though you should be concentrating on your studies, your love life is still the most important thing in the world to you.' Hal thought back to his time at Exeter with Jackie and silently agreed.

'I'd be grateful if you could let me have Richard's address and phone number. Just so I can rule him out.'

'Of course.'

Hal detected her sadness at the whole situation, but she conducted herself with a quiet dignity, unwilling to be pulled down to a level of unabashed sobbing and wailing.

'When did you last actually *see* Daniel, Mrs Wiseman?'

'I came into town to do some shopping about two months ago. I arranged to meet up with him then. I never tell my husband when I meet up with Daniel.' She corrected herself. 'Never told my husband.'

'What did you do together?'

'We went for lunch. In Leicester Square. I came in by train so I had a couple of glasses of wine. It was a little Italian place – just off Leicester Square. I think I had the carbonara. I don't remember what Daniel had. I seem to remember thinking it was very red.' She ran her fingers through her hair. 'But I fail to remember exactly.'

'Did he say anything or do anything that you might perceive as being out of character?'

She closed her eyes, trying to recall. 'I … don't think so. I can't think of anything.' Suddenly her eyes whipped open and a tiny shaft of vulnerability pierce the unshakeable exterior. 'Who would want to kill Daniel, Inspector? He might have done some bad things, but nothing that warranted this. He was a good boy really. He was very young. Very young.' Her head flopped forwards. 'I don't understand.'

Hal leaned towards her and put his hand on her knee. 'Neither do I, but I promise you that I will do my damned best to figure it out.'

She looked up, her blue eyes wide and warm. 'Thank you.'

At the same moment that Hal put his hand on Susan Wiseman's knee, Freddie Burlock felt a spring go in the sofa he was sitting on.

He didn't say anything. The poor woman had enough to contend with today without needing to be told that she ought to go out and buy a new sofa. Besides which, there was actually less need to buy a new sofa now that the number of residents likely to sit on it had gone down by one. Burlock adjusted his position in the chair and continued.

'I wonder if you could tell me –'

'It was that fuckin' lock-up of his!' The woman's voice was broken and rasped like sandpaper. 'He was always at that fuckin' lock-up working on that stupid sodding car. Stupid bloody idiot!'

'Didn't you wonder where he was when he didn't come home last night?'

Joanna Larby harrumphed. 'No. He's always at that fuckin' lock-up. Sometimes I think that he loves that bloody car more than me. He's spent the night there before, doing something to the engine – stripping it or something. Polishing the bloody thing. Lavishing more care and attention on it than he ever did with me.' Then, sadly, 'Silly sod.'

The room in which Burlock and Green sat was slightly grubby. The décor worn and dated. Along the mantelpiece, at regular intervals, were silly cutesy porcelain teddy bears, each of them too small to make any sort of impression. Burlock could see one holding a big red heart. Another had an old-fashioned flying hat and goggles on, a scarf blowing up around his little furry neck. The one on the very end appeared to be juggling, but Burlock's eyes weren't what they used to be and he couldn't be sure.

The whole room was thick with cigarette smoke as Joanna Larby steadily worked her way through her second pack of the morning. She noticed Burlock staring. 'I'm meant to be giving them up. I was going to start tomorrow, but I don't think I'll bother now.' The PC sitting next to her on a rickety dining chair inched a little closer as she took a prolonged drag of the burning cancer stick.

'Have you any kids?' Burlock didn't smile.

'Oh, God. I'll have to tell them.' She stood up, a gibbering bag of nerves. 'I'll have to call them and let them know. Oh, God.'

'It's all right, love. Sit down.' The PC put her arm over Joanna's shoulder and eased her back into the chair. 'We'll help you with that. PC Standford will help you with that. Don't worry.'

Joanna Larby puffed on her fag. Burlock thought that she looked rather harassed. She looked older than she was (forty-five, apparently), and dressed quite inappropriately (tight black leggings that stopped short of the ankle, white Miss Sixty T-shirt that stopped short of the navel.) Her hair fell greasily towards her shoulders, and was dyed an unnatural black colour. Her hands were old-looking too, nails covered in chipped pink varnish.

'I've got two,' she said. 'Two kids. Jason and Frankie. Jase is a painter and decorator. Works over in Bermondsey. He's twenty-six now. Twenty-six, eh? Time fuckin' flies, don't it? Frankie works in a shop. In Dartford. She's twenty-four. They don't come round very often nowadays. Too busy. That's what life's like, ain't it? We're all too busy to see people. Too busy all the fuckin' time.' She sucked on the fag. 'Fuckin' busy.'

'Joanna, love. Is there anything you think you should tell us about Ray? Was he into anything dodgy? Summat that might have got him into trouble.'

'Hah! Ray was always into something dodgy. That's what got him into trouble up at fuckin' Granton. He was always trying to earn a few quid. Not that I ever saw any of it.' Burlock noticed the empty bottle of wine lying on the floor behind the sofa. 'Used to gamble most of it away. Silly old fucker.'

'Did you ever have any problems with –'

'Hold on.' Joanna's face fell. 'The kid. The black kid. He came around here yesterday looking for Ray.'

'Black kid?' Burlock and Green both seemed to snap to attention. 'What black kid?'

'He's been here before. I've seen him around. Came here asking if Ray was in. I told him he was at the … oh fuckin' hell, he killed him, didn't he? The black kid killed Ray and I told him where he was … Oh, Jesus.'

'How old's this black kid, Joanna? Joanna. Listen to me. How old is he?'

'I dunno. Twenties, perhaps. You can't tell sometimes, can you. But I'd say he was young. In his twenties. Oh, Jesus.'

'What time was this?'

'I dunno. Can't remember. About two-ish. Something like that.'

'You don't know his name? Can't remember his name, can you, love?'

'No. I've only ever seen him a couple of times. Ray never told me his name. Wears one of those funny fuckin' hats.'

'He's Rastafarian?'

'No, no. One of those hats that all the kids wear these days.'

Green chipped in. 'A beanie?'

'That's it. A blue beanie. He wore a blue beanie.'

Burlock gave Green a look. 'Look, Joanna. If I send someone

round, do you think you can help us put together a photofit of the kid?'

Joanna stubbed out the butt of her cigarette. 'Definitely. Definitely. He's the one, I tell you. He's the one that killed my Ray.'

Alexander Judd's wife wasn't talking again. All this morning at breakfast, during the drive to church, throughout the service and now, driving home again, she'd not said a single thing to him. Judd hated this silent criticism. He wanted to reach across and smack her on the face, but he knew that his God would not forgive him. He also knew that he wouldn't forgive himself, and that was much more important. So, as usual, he swallowed down his anger.

Rolling the Bentley onto the gravel drive of his six-bedroom, turn-of-the-last-century mock Tudor house in Shortlands, Judd smiled at his wife. She ignored him completely, got out of the car, and marched straight into the house, leaving him standing there feeling like an idiot. Judd could feel the tears building behind his eyes, his jaw aching with the strain of restraint. He wouldn't cry. He wouldn't let her think she'd won once again. That wouldn't be right. It just wouldn't be right.

Instead of walking into the house, he strolled to the end of the drive and looked up and down the quiet suburban road. Large oaks sprouted sporadically along its length, the pavement slabs buckling upwards at their base. What were little more than dead branches a few weeks ago were now slowly sparking to life – tiny leaves unfurling themselves in the early summer warmth, a few birds chirruping in the Sunday morning silence. Along the road, nothing stirred. It was like something out of *Dawn of the Dead*. There was no sign of human life. Nobody washing their car in the street, nobody taking a dog for a walk, no kids trying to do wheelies off the pavement. An entire street of million-pound houses with their fenced-off drives and gardens, double garages and gazebos, and no sign of who lived in them.

Judd felt unbearably sad. His wife didn't understand his problems, little Danny Wiseman was dead, and, to top it all, he lived in a heartless, lifeless bubble of a place. God could be so cruel sometimes. He tried his best to be a good Christian. Worked hard to provide a decent home for his family. He'd built up the garden centre from scratch, working every minute that God had sent for years before it started to pay for itself. Now he had millions of pounds worth of stock and a comfortable existence. Not that his wife or children appreciated it. They always seemed to want more and more.

He picked up an old twig and threw it into the road. Sometimes he felt his faith being tested. God would throw difficulties in his way, and it was his role to overcome them. Yes, he was a weak man. Like all men, he was weak, but he always begged God's forgiveness and made up for it twice over. Three times over, even. And he believed that God understood – that he and God had come to some sort of agreement. For his weaknesses, Judd would pay his dues.

The day was dry, the sky clear, as Judd turned and slowly shuffled back towards his imposing wooden front door to be further ignored by his wife.

'Give me a bloody chance, will you, Inspector? I've barely started the autopsy. I'm standing here in my office, cradling the phone in my neck because I've still got my gloves on. They're covered in blood. So's my apron thingy. I'll be leaking bodily fluids on the floor if I'm not careful.'

'I just wondered if you'd spotted any similarities between this one and the young boy from the other day. Any first impressions?' Hal scratched his nose as he asked.

Dr Price gave a long silent sigh down the other end of the phone. 'Like I said. Give me a couple more hours and I'll be able to tell you in detail. I've only really examined the head so far.'

'But anything to link them both?'

'Well, I don't believe that any device was inserted into the neck of this one. It looks as though death was due to the multiple cuts inflicted upon the poor man. With an axe, I would say. However, the head was removed with an implement similar to that used with Daniel Wiseman. A large bow saw, or some such thing. That's the only comparison I can think of at this stage. This was a much more frenzied attack. Compared to this one, Wiseman's was positively restrained.'

'Anything else you can tell me?'

'The murderer stabbed the ears and the eyes a number of times – there's practically nothing left of the eyeballs. Used a knife for that. I think this was done once the man had died. I believe the axe wounds to the torso were the cause of death, and the damage to the head was carried out afterwards. The lips had been crudely sewn together with a sort of thick string –'

'You've kept that, haven't you?'

'Look, Inspector, I've been doing this job for eighteen years now. I think I know what I'm doing, don't you?'

'Sorry.'

The pathologist continued. 'Like I said, the lips had been sewn together. I've managed to unpick them, and it appears the murderer left a little something in the mouth.'

Hal's heart fluttered. 'What?'

'A note.'

'A note?'

'It was trapped at the back of the throat. I had to ease it out with tweezers.'

'Have you read it?'

'It was in a little clear plastic bag. One of the ones with a seal at the top. It was folded up neatly to fit into the mouth. Do you want to know what it says?'

'Please.'

'It says ... hold on ... I've scribbled it down on some paper here ... ah, here it is. It says – in big bold letters, printed off on a computer – it says, "THE MAN WHO MURDERED ME WAS CLEAN-SHAVEN. GOD BLESS MY EVIL SOUL." That's all.'

'Evil?'

'Yes. Evil.'

'Fuck.'

'I'll send it over to Johnny Good. See what he makes of it.'

Jason Thickett had just lost another game of chess to Redman. Redman always won at chess. He was a genius or something. Jason never really got to grips with the game. He'd move the pieces around the board, not really planning ahead, in the vague hope that he might stumble across a win, but he never did. Redman was far too tactical.

Jason went up the stairs from the recreation area to the first floor landing and back to the cell that he shared with Desi. Desi was downstairs chatting with a couple of the other inmates so he had the cell to himself for a few minutes. Not that even then he was really on his own. The camera in the corner of the room put paid to that. Leaping onto his lower bunk he stretched himself out, putting his arms behind his head.

The days were long and boring. Being out of contact with the outside world was a pain in the arse and he longed for a grande cappuccino from Starbucks and a family bucket of KFC. The food here was rubbish. Deliberately so, he felt. They were determined to wear you down. Break you for their own amusement. There was no rehabilitation here. Just demoralisation and sadism. That was the nature of the game.

Yawning, Jason shut his eyes and dozed. He imagined himself strolling up Tottenham High Road, munching on a Yorkie, his iPhone pumping some choice tunes into his ears.

The editor was up for it. Stevie had explained the story over the phone and he was happy to run with it. All Stevie needed to do now was write the damn thing (no more than 800 words), get it over to the office by three, make appropriate amendments, and off it goes. Somebody in charge of the library stock was going to check to see if there was a photo of Luchewski on file that they could use, otherwise a photographer would be despatched this afternoon to take a surreptitious shot. Stevie made himself a celebratory cup of tea before settling down at the kitchen table to write the piece. He picked up the battered old dictaphone and pushed the rewind button. High-pitched squeaking emanated from the little black device for a few seconds before he pressed 'play'. The voices that he could hear were slightly muffled – he had to turn the volume up almost to full and rewind it several times to catch what was being said.

'*Then you discovered you were gay and it all fell apart, right?*'

'*I'm not gay.*'

'*What?*'

'*I said, I'm not gay.*'

He clicked the tape to a stop and rewound it further back. Fucking idiot, he thought. Silly self-denying fucking idiot.

Hal had been to the coffee machine when the Good Professor walked into the office, his face flushed and sweaty. He carried some paper files under his arms and his eyes scoured the large communal office trying to find somebody or something. As his eyes fell upon Hal, he mouthed a silent 'Ah' before making his way over to him.

'I've got something for you. The prints from both scenes.'

'That was bloody quick. This morning's, I mean.'

'We could only find one set of internal prints that didn't match Larby's. It was on the inside of the door to the garage. We were lucky to find it really.'

Hal sipped his coffee as he closed his office door behind them. As they both sat in the seats, Good threw a file on the desk between them.

'These are the prints found in Catford. There are eight of them that didn't belong to Wiseman. Not untypical of a bedsit.

However …' he paused slightly for effect, 'one of my team managed to spot it. How she noticed it I'll never know. She's virtually an expert in fingerprints, you see. But she's got damned good eyes too …'

'What? What is it?'

'One of these prints,' he tapped the file on the desk then tapped the file on his lap, 'exactly matches these prints.'

Hal put his coffee down. 'An exact match?'

Good nodded. 'An exact match.'

Hal started getting up again. 'We'll run them through the system.'

'No need. I've already had it done. I assumed your girl wouldn't be in today.' Corrie, being a civilian, didn't really work Sundays. 'So I had it done for you.'

'Have we got a name?'

'Yes. We've got a name.' Another pause. 'Do you want to know what it is?'

Chapter Thirteen

Joanna Larby's photofit slowly pushed itself out of the fax machine. Burlock waited for it impatiently before snapping it up and walking over to Hal, who was busy briefing the handful of uniforms they were taking with them.

'Is that him?' Father Christmas shoved the piece of paper in Hal's direction. 'This your fella?'

'That's him.' He turned it so that everyone could see. 'This is what McKenzie looks like. I've phoned his work and he's not there, so with a bit of luck he's at home.'

One of the uniforms shifted in his seat. 'Sir. If he's connected to these two murders, shouldn't we have some sort of armed back-up?' He looked a tad uncomfortable, as if he could throw up at any minute. 'He's obviously dangerous.'

'I don't believe him to be a murderer. The boy that Sergeant Singh and I talked to yesterday wasn't a murderer. Wouldn't you agree, Sergeant?' Singh, standing to one side with her arms folded, nodded. 'But there's some sort of connection between Wiseman and Larby – other than the fact that both had something to do with Granton ... there's some sort of connection that McKenzie can hopefully shed some light on. We just need to talk to him. Urgently.'

Hal positioned a couple of the uniformed officers at the end of the lane backing onto the house in Hither Green, just in case McKenzie should want to make a run for it. Two more waited in their marked car a little further up the road. The sun was beating down now, with barely a cloud in the sky. Looking up, Hal could see one, two, three, four, five planes in the sky. That was always the case with London. No matter what time of day, or what part of London you were standing in, you always saw planes in the sky. Happy lucky sods flying off on holiday, or resentful miserable bastards off to visit relatives, it didn't matter. There were always plenty of planes to carry them.

Hal knocked the blue door of the 1930s suburban semi, Singh, Green, and Burlock standing behind him. They looked like a bunch of well-dressed, middle-aged carol singers, thought Hal as, through the frosted pane, he watched somebody come out of a room towards the door. Another six months (no make it five or possibly four, these days) and they wouldn't look entirely out of place banging out a few lines of 'God Rest Ye Merry Gentlemen'. The door opened and a short, stocky black woman looked up at him with wide eyes.

'Mrs McKenzie?'

'Yes?' The voice wavered slightly.

'Police. We're here about your son. Denzil.' Hal put his ID card away.

'Oh, thank God for that. Please come on in.' She walked off into a nearby room, expecting the coppers to follow. 'Please.' Being the last through the door, Green closed it, before walking into the chintz-ridden sitting room.

'You were very quick, I have to say. I only telephoned the station about twenty minutes ago. And there are lots of you. This is very good service, I have to say. The police must be getting better. But I've been getting worried, you see. And my ole heart ain't what it used to be. I can't work very much now because of my ole heart. It stops me working. I can't go worrying, you see. And Denzil's such a good boy really. He usually lets me know what he's up to, I have to say.'

'I'm sorry, Mrs McKenzie? Did you say you just called the police?'

Sitting down in her armchair, the puffy little woman stared up. 'Of course I did. That is why you are here. Now, do you want me to give you all of the details? You've got one of those little books you scribble things down in, haven't you? I've seen the telly.'

Singh stepped forward. 'Mrs McKenzie, where's Denzil?'

The woman sighed and shook her head. 'They send four of you and none of you know what's going on.' A quick, short burst of staccato tutting. 'That is why you are here. My son. He didn't come home yesterday. I don't know where he is.'

'He didn't come home?'

'No. Last I saw him he was going off to work in that ruddy car of his. Spends too much money on that car if you ask me. Always buying this for it or that for it.'

'And you haven't heard from him since? He hasn't phoned you or left a message?' Hal queried.

'No, man. Nothing. He's been late back before, so I just went to bed about midnight thinking he'll be home soon, but no. Nothing. I've been up half the night thinking all sorts of things, I have to say.'

'Have you tried phoning his friends?' Green stepped forward. 'He might be with a friend.'

Mrs McKenzie tutted again. 'Hell, man, I don't know his friends any more. He hangs around with funny types. I don't know who they are. They flit in and out of here sometimes, lots of different people. But I don't know who they are. He don't talk about no friends.'

Hal saw Burlock out of the corner of his eye. He was standing with his arms folded and his eyebrows bunched tightly together, his whole face crumpled into a frown.

'Is Denzil a member of a gang, Mrs McKenzie?' Burlock asked roughly.

'A gang?'

'Yes. A gang.'

The woman looked Burlock up and down with a look that seemed to say, *what the fuck are you on about?* 'Hell, man. I said I don't know his friends. How the hell do I know if he's in a gang or not? He don't tell me nothing, Denzil. He might be protecting his old ma but he don't tell me nothing.'

Hal turned to Burlock and sighed. Burlock shook his head back. 'Don't look at me.'

'Mrs McKenzie,' said Hal, twisting back to face the old woman, 'with your permission, I'd like to take a look at Denzil's room. You can give your statement to the sergeants here and we'll pass it on to Missing Persons, but I'd really like to have a quick look at his bedroom. We might find something that will tell us where he's gone.'

'I've already looked and I can't find nothing.'

'Nevertheless, I think a fresh pair of eyes just might stumble across something. Please, Mrs McKenzie.'

She looked doubtful but relented. 'OK then. See if you can find him.'

The stench of old cigarette smoke hit Burlock and Hal as they went through the doorway into the room.

'Bloody smokers,' Burlock coughed. 'I can't stand bloody smokers.'

'How long's it been now?' asked Hal.

'Three months. Nearly four. Those pads work a bloody treat.' He slapped the side of his left arm with his right hand. 'I've not even felt the need for one.'

The room was, at first glance, unexceptional. A bed. A

wardrobe. A chest of drawers. A small bookcase with a smattering of music and film magazines sitting on its shelves. A chair. A poster of Bob Marley taking a drag on a joint. A mouldy coffee cup. A stereo with a tall rack of CDs alongside it. An old portable TV sitting on top of a DVD player. Some DVDs stacked up on the dressing table (*Hostel*, *Cabin Fever*, *Scary Movie 4*). A laptop, folded away on the bedside table. A mobile phone charger. An MP3 player docking port. Everything you would expect in a young man's bedroom.

'I'll have a look in the drawers,' said Burlock. 'Have a quick shufti under the bed. Might be something under there.'

Hal got down on his hands and knees and peered under. It was dark and he couldn't make anything out so he pushed his hand under and tried to feel. His hand hit on something papery and he pulled it out. A couple of pornographic magazines appeared, their covers lurid and glossy. Girls. So McKenzie obviously wasn't gay, judging by the way that some of the pages in the magazines were crisply stuck together. Hal pushed them back under the bed and tried feeling around for something else. After a few seconds, it became clear that there was nothing else of any worth under there. He got up and turned to Burlock.

'Anything?'

'Not a sausage. Plenty of socks, underwear, and Yves St Laurent sweaters, but no sausages.'

'We'd better get the techies to take a look at that,' Hal pointed at the laptop. 'That's probably our best bet here.' He opened the door on the front of the bedside table and looked inside. Again there was nothing. Burlock went into the wardrobe and moved the clothing around.

'Nope. Nowt.'

'We'll seal the bedroom off in any case. Just to be on the safe side. Come on. Let's go down.'

'Hold on.' Burlock stopped in the doorway, staring back into the room. 'Look at that.' He pointed upwards at the ceiling.

Hal hadn't noticed it before, and he felt a bit bloody stupid now that Burlock had drawn his attention to it. In the corner of the room was a hatch up into the attic. It looked wide enough for a man to get through.

'Jesus. There's a light on up there.' Around the rectangular edges of the ill-fitting hatch shone a dim halo of light. Hal looked around the bedroom and found a stick with a hook on the end of it. He picked it up and reached up to the attic door to try and push it open.

'Careful,' warned Burlock. 'He might be up there.'

'He's not a killer.' Hal carried on prodding the hatch cover.

'I don't care. There are a few too many horror films over there –
' Burlock nodded in the direction of the dressing table, 'for my
liking.'

Suddenly the door gave way, falling into the room and landing
on Burlock's foot. The light from the attic filled the bedroom as Hal
positioned himself directly beneath the opening.

'Denzil! Denzil. Are you up there? This is Inspector
Luchewski – I spoke to you at work yesterday.' No reply. 'Denzil!'
Still no reply. Hal grabbed a chair, placed it below the hatch, and
started to step up on it.

'That's it. You'd better have a look,' said Burlock rubbing his
shin. 'You're taller than me. You'll be able to see better. Besides, I
don't fancy having my head caved in by a psychopath today.'

'Shut up, Freddie.' Hal straightened himself up and peered in
through the hole in the ceiling. 'Denzil!' The lights were extremely
bright and Hal's eyes had to adjust themselves for a few seconds
before he could see properly. Shapes. Lots of pointy shapes. No.
Not shapes. Leaves. Plants. Bright lights and plants.

'Ha!'

'What is it?' Burlock asked somewhere near Hal's knees.

'Have a look for yourself.'

Hal climbed down and Burlock clambered up.

'Oh. I see. I see. Cannabis. The little bugger's been growing
cannabis.'

A quick phone call to the Good Professor confirmed that there were
drugs in Larby's lock-up.

'At least, that's what they appear to be – I'll have to run the
tests. They were in an unlocked safe. Some small packets of hash
and a tiny slab of what I assume to be cannabis resin. Not exactly
organised crime levels of supply.'

'But definitely drugs?' Hal shouted into the mobile phone.

'Like I said, Harry, I'll have to run the tests. But, yes. Definitely
drugs.'

'I said it would be about drugs, didn't I? It's usually about drugs
these days, I find.' Burlock had found another packet of peanuts in
his desk and was gobbling them down.

'Do you ever stop eating?' Hal leaned back against the door in Burlock's office.

'Not if I can help it. I sometimes stop to breathe, but that's about it. Gives the jaw a little rest, breathing, you know.'

'So, McKenzie's been growing the stuff,' Singh completely ignored Burlock, 'and Larby processes it and sells it on. Is that the idea?'

'Something like that, I'm sure.' Hal ran his hand over his shaven head. A few bristles scratched at his fingers and tickled his palm. 'Larby would have met McKenzie at Granton. After they had both left – or in the case of Larby, been asked to leave – they teamed up and started working together.'

'Old Ma McKenzie knew he was growing something up there. She just didn't know what. She told me that she thought her electricity bills had shot up in the last year or so.' Burlock scrunched up the packet and threw it in the direction of the wastepaper basket, missing it entirely. 'It's interesting McKenzie works in a garden centre, don't you think? Perhaps someone there knows where you can pick up cannabis plants.' He licked his fingers clean.

'OK. Assuming that McKenzie is the murderer ... where's he gone?' Singh's thinking face looked as scrunched-up as Burlock's nut packet.

'Run to ground. Hiding out with a friend, perhaps?'

'But he's been missing since last night. We didn't find Larby's body until this morning. There was no need to panic.'

'You saw the state of that lock-up. It was a sodding bloodbath. Could easily have been the work of a panicking man.'

'I disagree.' Hal shook his head at Burlock. 'I think the person who killed Larby took his time. Like he did with Wiseman. He would have been covered in blood at both of the crime scenes. If he came away from either one of them – especially up in Catford which is quite a busy residential area – covered in that much blood he would have been spotted. He must have changed his clothing at each of the crime scenes.'

'Why wasn't the neck pump used on Larby?' Singh asked.

'I don't know. Perhaps he abandoned it because it didn't work properly. Found it difficult to use.'

'The pathologist thinks Larby's head was sawn off with a bow saw. You can buy those at garden centres.' Burlock was pushing the garden centre idea again.

'Why did he stab the ears and eyes? And why did he sew up the lips? Was that just a sick way of displaying the note? Or is there something more to it than that?' Everyone had forgotten that Green was sitting on a chair in the corner of the room and they were surprised to hear him speak. 'Why didn't he do that with Wiseman?'

'Are there two different killers? There seem to be two different MOs.'

'I think there's only one killer. Gut feeling, but I think there's only one.' Hal absent-mindedly tapped his stomach. 'But he's got two different ways of killing people, and if we find out why he kills differently, I believe we'll figure out exactly who he is.'

There was a long pause as each of them tried to wrap their heads around the details of the case. Singh was the first to ask the question they all wanted to ask.

'Do you think the killer's taken care of McKenzie?'

Hal sighed heavily before finally shrugging his shoulders.

The afternoon passed slowly. Singh made a few phone calls and confirmed Susan Wiseman's story about Daniel's friend Richard. He'd cancelled a few days before he was due to come down to London.

'You're a woman,' he'd said to Singh over the phone. 'Perhaps you can tell me. Why does she feel that she has to go off to Prague with her friends – some of whom are male, by the way? Why doesn't she want to come and spend the summer with me down in Bournemouth? I don't understand.'

Singh mouthed some rubbish about discovering herself, while secretly thinking that, if it was her decision, Prague would beat Bournemouth hands down every single time.

Meanwhile, Hal filled in some of the mountains of paperwork that needed shifting off his desk. The dreadful, irksome, pen-pushing, paper-exercising nature of the twenty-first century, he thought. Quality. That was the awful word that was currently being bandied about like it was a new drug. Quality. It was 'Quality-this' and 'Quality-that'. Everything had to be qualified, justified and documented. Everything you did had to be followed up with a computer file or hard-copy explanation. Usually both. Doing the things was easy, you just got on with it. Writing it up was a fucking nuisance. Hal wanted to take everyone in the world with the word 'Quality' in their job title – or 'Health and Safety', that was another one – put them all in a room, and set fire to it. Or, like in *The Hitchhiker's Guide to the Galaxy*, put them all on a big spacecraft and tell them they're going to a new planet. Just get rid of the fuckers somehow.

At around four, Woode phoned in to tell him that both Baldwin and himself weren't needed at court until the afternoon, so they'd be coming into the office in the morning.

'You can tell me all about this Larby character then,' Woode said.

'Sure,' replied Hal before putting the phone down. Shit. A morning with fucking Baldwin. Hal looked through his list of the people he needed to speak to and things he had to do. Perhaps he could manage to escape quite quickly tomorrow. That would do. Book something up and get away from the place. It was probably best.

Sunday afternoons in the twenty-four-hour Sainsbury's were never very busy – mostly youngsters hanging around the pick-n-mix or old women on the hunt for cat food. A middle-aged couple pushed a trolley with an ugly whining baby in the seat, and a tall woman in her forties trotted around with a basket hooked over her forearm, picking things up, studying the ingredients and then placing them back on the shelf. Otherwise, it was deathly quiet.

There were only three cashiers on the checkout. Sophie (a brain-dead sixteen-year-old with her hair pulled tightly back into an awful curly ponytail), Sandra (a miserable-looking cow who looked as though the word 'joy' had been erased from her vocabulary) and himself. Thankfully, he was on checkout number eight. Some distance from three and four where Sophie and Sandra were gassing like demented old ducks. This meant he could listen in on their conversation but not be expected to participate. Which suited him just fine. All they ever seemed to talk about was where to get your nails done and which was the best tanning shop in town. He couldn't believe that Sandra had been anywhere near a tanning shop. Her skin was as sickly grey as a pair of his mother's faded bloomers. He imagined the husband going elsewhere for his sex – no one in their right mind could manage to get it up for that maudlin, lifeless old bitch. Perhaps that was why she looked so depressed all time. Her husband had stopped fucking her.

Looking down he found himself tinkering with his name badge. Stupid orange plastic nonsense, but easy to replicate. He'd made himself a couple more at home, and he wore them at work sometimes just to see if anyone noticed. 'Ivor Cnut' one of them read. The other, 'A. Rapist'. Occasionally a customer would glance down at the name tag, and occasionally they would do a double take. He particularly enjoyed it when hot young women noticed – he'd feel a chill go right up his spine. Nobody ever said anything though. Nobody really thought anything of it. By the time they'd handed over their card, tapped in their pin number and been handed their receipt, they'd more or less forgotten all about it. Especially as the man serving them was so nice. So pleasant. After all, perhaps that was really his name. Poor chap.

He always wore the real badge around his work colleagues though. He'd change it as soon as he came off the till. He needed to be seen as normal. There was only one person at work who'd ever seen his alternative name badges – a blonde long-legged middle manager – and she had gone now. Left due to stress. He'd spent months working on her until eventually she went. The thought of it all made his heart thump loudly in his chest. He had control over all things. Over everyone.

The middle-aged couple with the red-faced baby parked their trolley at the end of his checkout. The baby had stopped its screaming and was looking at something in its hands – a rattle or something, brightly coloured and plastic. The dad looked harassed and exhausted, the mother strangely serene.

'Would you like help with your packing?' the Creep asked politely, his face a picture of warmth and decency.

'No. No thank you,' the dad replied, not bothering to make eye contact. 'We're all right.' He started picking items out of the basket and putting them on the conveyer belt.

'Turned into a nice day, hasn't it?'

'What? Oh. Mmm.' The man ignored him and continued unloading the trolley. The woman cooed and patted the little brat's head.

'They say we're going to have a few more days like this. Warm and dry.' The man didn't even bother to respond that time. He didn't even look up.

Right, you fucker, thought the Creep. *Let's have a little race.* As the first of the items smoothly moved along to the end of the conveyer belt, the Creep snatched them up and ran them through the scanner. The dad continued unpacking and the Creep continued scanning. After a few seconds, there was quite a build-up of food down at the packing end of the checkout. The dad looked up and noticed. He twisted back to the wife and said something, before quickly moving down to the other end, fingering some plastic bags off the pole and shoving some of the items into them. The wife picked up where the husband had left off and started to empty the trolley. The Creep didn't let up. He beeped the shopping through as quickly as possible, practically throwing the fruit and veg down towards the dad. The dad couldn't keep up, and a backlog started developing as he hurriedly tried to cope with the oncoming flow. Eventually, the Creep paused to let the dad catch up, but as he did so he sighed audibly – deliberately, just loud enough to let the man know that he was disappointed in his slowness. Once again he was in control.

Just like he was yesterday afternoon …

The wife continued unpacking and, as she leaned over to pick the last few tins out of the trolley, the Creep could see the top of her bosom down her flimsy summery blouse. Just the top of her bosom. The line where the breasts began. Looking at her now, the Creep realised that she was eminently fuckable. Her dark bobbed hair, all clean and straight, swayed back and forth as she reached in and then straightened up. She would have been in her late thirties. The dirty thirties, as the Creep like to call them. Blinking his eyes away from her tits he scanned the last of the food through.

Most of it was organic. Organic and expensive. Stupid hippy twats. Why not just buy ordinary food? Ordinary potatoes and ordinary smoked salmon and ordinary fucking cous-cous. Just like every other poor fucker. There's no fucking difference. Other than the price. Organic's just another word for con. It's all just a big fucking con and stupid twats like you are falling for it all the fucking time.

'That'll be one hundred and twenty nine pounds and fifty-two pence, please,' the Creep smiled at the man, a friendly and sincere-looking smile that showed off his tiny yellowing teeth.

The dad, looking ever so slightly more harassed than he had a couple of minutes ago, reached into his back pocket and fumbled about with his wallet.

'How's school?'

The line crackled.

'S'all right.'

A long pause.

'Still having the piano lessons?'

'Dad,' a big exasperated sigh, 'you know I'm still having piano lessons. You pay for them.'

'Hmm. What grade are you on now?'

'I'm doing grade four next week.'

'Grade four. That's good. Practising every morning, I hope?'

Another long pause. It didn't matter how often he did it, Hal always felt like some stilted stuttering fool talking on the phone to his daughter. A great big, square, embarrassing-dancing, Daddy-o of a fool. Lily would be too ashamed to be seen with him, he had no doubt. If they were out, she'd probably walk a good few steps in front to make sure no one thought they were together.

'Half an hour every morning before school. Mummy always makes me.'

'That's right. Practice makes perfect.' Even as he said it, he felt his entire body wince.

'Don't worry. I'm still practising.'

'When are you going on that school trip? The one to Paris.'

'That's in November, Dad.' He could detect the silent tut in her voice, as if to say, 'For God's sake it's months off, didn't you know that?'

'Looking forward to it?' Still he kept on.

She ignored the question and dropped a bombshell instead.

'Dad, can I come and live with you?'

'Eh? What?'

'Can I come and live with you?'

'Er … why?' He felt himself stumble over the words.

'Mummy can be horrible sometimes. She still thinks I'm about eight.'

'Is this because she didn't let you go to that party last night?' Hal was conscious of his heart twitching away in his chest. 'Is that what it is?'

'No,' defensively, 'not just that.'

'Well, what then?'

Another critical sigh. Lily's mobile crackled and Hal missed the first part of her reply.

'…friends around. The only friend she *will* let stay the night is Hettie, because she knows Hettie's mother. I've asked Mummy for a pyjama party but she always says no. "Maybe next month", she says. She's always saying it.'

'I see.'

'And she's always telling me to go to bed and to stop watching television. *And* we always have to eat vegetables. We're always eating carrots and I don't like carrots.'

'But they're good for you.'

'And I always have to make my bed in the morning. Hettie's mother always makes her bed for her.'

'Then Hettie's mother's a bloody idiot.'

116

'I want to come and live with you, Dad. Can I come and live with you?'

Hal's mind was racing. 'But you'd have to make your bed even if you live with me. I'm not going to be your slave, Lily. And you'd have to move school. You'll lose contact with all of your friends and you'd have to try and fit into a new school and make new friends. It's not easy.' That should take care of it, Hal hoped.

'I don't care. I want to move in with you.'

'Oh, Lily. You're being silly, Lily.'

'I'm not.'

'You are. You're being a silly billy, Lily.' Silly billy Lily was always a running joke between them.

'I'm not! I'm telling the truth.'

Hal desperately tried to cram some levity into the situation, hoping to deflect any further discussion. 'What about your dad's cooking? You know I can't cook anything without it getting burnt. We'll be living off takeaways.' Shit, he thought. Wrong thing to say to a twelve-year-old.

'That's all right. I like takeaways.'

'I'll make sure you do your homework every night, and stop you from watching too much television, and tell you to turn your bloody awful music down, and make you help me with the shopping ...' He tried to think of something else, 'And you'll have to help clean up the house.'

'You've got a woman who comes around and does that for you.'

'Well I won't need her any more then, will I? You can do most of the work at the weekend. Or in the evening. Save myself thirty quid a week.'

'You're not putting me off, you know.' Suddenly his little girl sounded like a grown woman. 'You can keep trying to think of excuses but you're not putting me off. I want to come and live with you.'

Hal sighed inwardly. He felt embarrassed that his daughter should feel – should know – that he was making up excuses. He was behaving like a spoilt little prick again, and the thought that he was doing so in full view of his knowing daughter made him feel like shit. He needed to approach this in a more adult manner and not just have some petrified knee-jerk reaction that revealed him to be the complete tosser that he was. *Adult*, he thought. *You're the adult in this situation, so act like it.*

'I'll talk to Mummy about it.'

'OK.'

'Have you said anything to her yet? Does she know that you want to come here?'

'No. I ... er ... I thought you could tell her.' The phone line made that awful crispy noise again. '... best really.'

Another body had been found. The police weren't saying if it was connected to the one found on Friday, but Laurie Fraser had her suspicions. It was Sunday, and she didn't usually work on a Sunday, but she'd had a phone call earlier that afternoon and she knew she needed to act quickly to break the story. Sitting in the tiny editing booth with Chris, she pieced her piece together. It would be aired in two hours' time.

Looking around the cramped room, she hoped that someone from the BBC would be watching. After spending the last three years covering local stories for this shitty little news channel, she felt that it was time to move on. Time to move up. And the BBC was the ultimate goal. She wouldn't mind being a foreign correspondent for a bit, posted to some god-awful desolate part of the world. She could bear that. A few years doing that and then back to Blighty to be one of the lead reporters covering politics or economics (her PPE degree would be useful for either.) In her mind that was the perfect plan. In her mind that was the only plan. Anything else was second best, and Laurie Fraser never settled for second best.

Never.

'Sir?'

'What?'

Singh had seen him looking a bit befuddled after he'd finished his phone call and something in her heart took pity on him. 'Have you eaten?'

'Eaten?'

'Yeah. You know ...' She mimed putting a fork to her mouth and chewing. 'Eaten. Food. Nyum nyum.'

'Er ... No. Not yet.' His face was pale and far away.

'Would you like to?'

'Like to what?'

She sighed to herself. Sometimes, life could be so tedious. 'Eat.'

He switched his phone off and slid it into his jacket pocket. 'Eat?'

Fucking hell, she thought to herself. Yes, fucking eat.

'Um ... yes. OK. Why not?'

Today's task was to peel some potatoes. Unfortunately, it wasn't just a small bag of potatoes. It was a small mountain of potatoes. Each of them had been given a tump of spuds and they had to peel as many of them as they could in an hour. The winner was entitled to an evening in the TV room and the meal of their choice. The losers would have to eat mashed potato – and only mashed potato – in their cells.

Jason knew exactly what he'd ask for if he won. He'd like to have some chicken chow mein, egg fried rice, and crispy beef, all washed down with a pint glass of ginger beer (no alcohol allowed). He didn't know if he was allowed any pudding (the Chief Warden hadn't made it clear) but if he was he'd ask for a big bowl of spotted dick and custard. He needed to stuff himself up. The small portions were beginning to make his stomach ache continuously, and food was starting to dominate his thoughts.

Casting his eye over the others' efforts, he could see that he wasn't very likely to get his Chinese takeaway tonight. Desi was ploughing mercilessly through the potatoes, his little black peeler slicing through the air like a stiletto. He was easily in the lead. Close on his heels was Thumper. For a man with such big hands, thought Jason, he's very dextrous.

Peel was flying everywhere, and Jason's hands felt wet and gritty. Why didn't he just give it all up? Just walk away. He could go at any time – they made that clear at the start. He didn't need to stay here. Just tell the producer and leave. He could be out of here and into a KFC within the hour. So why didn't he just do it? The reason was the prize money. £50,000. That and the possibility of landing a job presenting a TV show.

After all, you never knew who was watching.

Luchewski had followed Singh in his car. The roads were pretty quiet on this Sunday evening, and as they cut their way across Lewisham the lights were surprisingly in their favour. In the end it took them no more than twenty minutes to get to Singh's fiancé's house. Parking outside, Luchewski whistled to himself. If that's what private dentistry could afford to buy you, he thought, then tooth decay and enamel hypoplasia were the future.

Singh got out of her car and waved back at him as he pulled in behind her.

'This is it,' she said as he slammed the door of the TT behind him. 'Come on in.'

He followed her up the well-tended garden path, past the SLK, to the large front door. She let herself in with a key and they made their way along the dark corridor to the kitchen at the back of the house.

'He's a great cook,' she whispered. 'Much better than I am.'

'Nobody's worse than me. Trust me. I couldn't make an ice cube without it getting badly burnt.'

In the kitchen, Singh's fiancé – Gardener – was bustling about with steaming and bubbling pans. It was as though he was barely containing a small disaster. Lids rattled and shook like an avant-garde percussive orchestra.

'Harry. Good to see you.' Gardener vaguely held his hand out across the kitchen and Luchewski vaguely shook it. 'Pasta alla Genovese okay?'

Luchewski felt as if he should have known what that was, so he nodded anyway.

'Won't be long.'

Ten minutes later, they were all sitting around the extremely large table in the extremely large dining room. The food was served in bulbous metal tureens and Luchewski suddenly realised just how incredibly hungry he was.

'Well, thank you,' he said to Gardener who was grating a block of parmesan on his pasta. 'It all smells delicious.' Luchewski flicked out the napkin and wiped his fingers on it. 'I very rarely cook nowadays.'

'That's right. You live alone, don't you?' Gardener asked. 'I remember Priti saying.'

'Yes. That and … well … I never seem to have time.' Luchewski tried to deflect the conversation away from the concepts of relationships and loneliness. 'The force takes up all of my waking day, to be honest. It's about all I can do to grab a limp sandwich from the station canteen.'

'The station canteen's got a five-star food hygiene rating. Did you know that, sir? God knows how.' Singh had taken off her jacket and had rolled the sleeves of her blouse up. Her hair was down and Luchewski noticed just how relaxed she was here in this house in front of this man. Much more relaxed than she ever was around him. 'I once found a dead ladybird in the chilli con carne. At least, I *think* it was a ladybird. Whatever it was, it was definitely not supposed to be there.'

'"Extra protein". "Don't tell everyone or they'll all want one". "What was it doing in my soup? The backstroke". Loads of old jokes leap to mind, eh, Harry?'

Luchewski smiled and forked a hefty swirl of pasta into his mouth. He might be a good cook, thought Hal, but he's not so hot when it comes to humour. There was a geeky core to Nicholas Gardener. Despite the money and the car and the self-satisfied swagger, there was an awkwardness to the man. Perhaps even a vulnerability. Maybe that was why Singh was marrying him.

Luchewski hadn't really wanted to come in the first place. When Singh had suggested the idea of food, he had just pictured the pair of them getting some fish and chips and sitting on a wall somewhere – but then she phoned Gardener and told him to set a place for another person and it had rather spiralled out of control. Luchewski hadn't wanted to back out then for fear of looking like some sort of unsociable loner (which was, of course, close to the truth), so he'd nodded politely and hopped in his car and followed Singh's Peugeot to this particularly well-heeled part of London, moaning to himself all the way.

After the pasta, Gardener got an enormous vanilla cheesecake out of the fridge.

'I didn't make this one. Harvey Nicks, I'm afraid.'

It was, to be fair, probably the best cheesecake Luchewski had ever tasted. Creamy, crumbly, and not too sweet.

'Good, isn't it?'

Hal couldn't help but nod.

'So,' Gardener started as he pushed his half-finished plate away. 'How's the investigation going? Got a nasty killer on the loose, so I gather.'

'I'm sorry, Nicholas,' Luchewski used his napkin to wipe away the last of the cake, 'I'm sure you know we can't discuss an ongoing case. Not while it's so fresh, anyway. Sorry. I know it sounds stupid but –'

'Of course, of course. Having known Priti for *quite* a while now, I'm used to not asking too many questions. Her work is a world I'm rarely allowed into, and that's fine. I'm kind of getting used to playing the CIA wife. Turning a blind eye and all that. Casting my face to the wall.' He mock-swooned, the back of one hand pinned to his brow.

'Did I ever tell you what a drama queen my future husband can be, sir?' Singh asked Luchewski. 'Give him any excuse and he'll am-dram it all the way.'

Singh and Gardener looked rather too lovingly into each other's eyes and Luchewski suddenly felt like he really shouldn't be there.

'Ah well,' Gardener jumped up from his seat. 'Not to worry. Hope you don't mind, Harry, but I've got a whole load of paperwork that needs doing before tomorrow.' He walked behind Singh's chair and placed both of his hands on her shoulders, squeezing gently. 'Priti, there's a pot of coffee on the go if you want. And some of those cinnamon biscuits you like in the cupboard.'

Her left hand came up and patted one of Gardener's. It was all too sickly-lovely for words.

'Good to see you again, Harry. Best of luck with the investigation. I hope you catch him.'

Gardener closed the door behind him as he went.

'Coffee, sir?'

Luchewski nodded.

Singh got up and filled two coffee cups before plonking one of them down on the table in front of Luchewski.

'How did you two meet?' He didn't really want to know but felt as if he should ask. 'You've got very different jobs, so how did you get together?'

'My second cousin's hen night clashed with The South East of England Endodontic award ceremony.'

'Eh?'

'It's a long story. Singh didn't elaborate. Thank Christ, thought Hal.

'What about you, sir? Hope you don't think I'm prying but are you involved with anyone? At the moment?'

Luchewski twisted the coffee cup on the table. 'No. I'm not. Not at the moment.'

John Rabin looked at his watch. It was nearly nine. Only an hour to go and they could shut up the shop. Thank God. It had been a long, boring day and he couldn't wait to get home and muck about on his Xbox. He'd bought a new game yesterday and hadn't had a chance to give it a go just yet. It was meant to be incredibly violent – you were a serial killer and you earned points by bumping people off in imaginative ways. There were already calls in the press to ban it – there were always calls in the press to ban things – but John had snapped it up before it could be stripped from the shelves.

'Hey, you,' his father shouted at him from behind the counter. 'Stop bloody daydreaming. Put those tins out.'

John sighed and went back to stacking the tins of soup. Cream of

Chicken. Tomato. Oxtail. He found the shop incredibly dull. A couple more years and he was going to leave. To do what, he'd no idea just yet, but he knew that he could only stand a couple more years of it. It was usually all right when his dad wasn't around. His dad was sometimes busy with the Streatham shop and left John in charge of Norwood. When that happened he could listen to his iPod or bring in his Xbox and plug it into the television which was set up above the counter on a wall bracket. It helped the day pass a bit quicker. But when his dad was there, he always had to work hard. He'd wash the floors and straighten the aisles and stack the shelves and do the stock-taking and contact the wholesalers and serve the customers and kick out the kids. It was tiring and it was boring. He hated it.

The television was on at the moment and his dad had the volume up high – he was going deaf in one ear and had recently started shouting without knowing it. He was idly flicking through the channels, trying to find something to watch and moaning at everything he came across. John listened as he dusted off the tops of the tins of kidney beans.

'… come round here with your accusations! As I said to Ashley, I don't want …' *Flick* '… is regarded as one of England's leading figures in contemporary music. In the three years since …' *Flick* '… Don't do it, Terry. It's not right'. 'Why not? What have I got to live for?' 'I've never told you before but –' *Tut, flick* '… leadership has changed hands for the eighth time in as many years. The new regime led by President …' *Flick* '… the workmanship that's gone into that. Beautiful, isn't it. There's nothing like it in the whole world. And we've got fifty to sell. So come on, fellas. If it's your wife's birthday soon, or even your mother's, give us a ring. Make a bid. Remember, we've …' *Flick* '… vote now to kick out the biggest wuss and help us to find Britain's Toughest Jailbird. Dial one for Nigel 'Thumper' Green. Dial two for Gary 'The Nut' Cottlee. Dial three for Jason …' *Flick* '… from backache? Try the new spray from …' *Flick*. Music. 'Good evening. This is the London News Channel. The headlines tonight: Man found murdered in Peckham, the Prime Minister prepares to make a key speech about immigration, and Rory the elephant finally finds love.' More strident music. 'Good evening. I'm Simon Minster. Police are tonight investigating the death of a man believed to have been murdered in Peckham. His body was discovered earlier today in a lock-up garage just off Peckham Rye Lane. So far, investigating officers have not yet ruled out any connection with the discovery on

Friday of a body in Catford – the identity of which has now been revealed as nineteen-year-old Daniel Wiseman. This report by Laurie Fraser …'

The voice changed to a strong female one. 'The man's body was found in the early hours of this morning following an anonymous tip off. Sources close to the police say that he had been brutally beaten and left for dead. Although the identity of the body has not yet been released by police, the London News Channel has discovered that the lock-up was owned by a Raymond Larby who lives nearby in …'

A sharp intake of breath. John turned around and realised that the sound had come out of his father's mouth. He stood in front of the television, his jaw wide open, the colour visibly draining from his face.

'You all right, Dad?'

'Sssh,' came the hard, impatient reply.

Fair enough, thought John as he continued rearranging the processed peas. Be like that then, you silly old tosser, and fuck off.

Mehrzad Rabin wasn't the only one to catch the London news that surprisingly warm evening. Alexander Judd was squatting on the floor in the upstairs study, his arms wrapped around his legs. The TV sound was on low, the Freeview box glowing away alongside it. It was sheer fluke that he happened to turn over the moment that Raymond Larby's name was mentioned. He did a double-take, and stared hard at the woman on the screen.

'Mr Larby's wife was unavailable for comment earlier this evening, but it is believed that the police have already informed her of her husband's death.'

Death? Raymond Larby? Dead? Judd's face crumpled into a confused frown. What was this?

'Police are saying that it's too early to make any connection between Mr Larby's murder and that of nineteen-year-old Daniel Wiseman, whose body was found at home in his flat in Catford earlier this week.'

Murder? Raymond Larby, murdered?

Dear God.

Judd felt bile rushing up his throat and into his mouth. He quickly swallowed it down and steadied himself on the floor. His heart raced and his head spun, and it took all of his strength to keep himself level on the ground.

What was going on? Danny and now Ray. Both dead. Who

could do such a thing? Who the hell would *want* to do such a thing? There must be some reason for it all.

And then he realised.

Chapter Fourteen

Hal shuddered and woke up in a sweat, water beading down his brow. His arms felt wet and the back of his neck was sticky. Reaching out to the bedside table, he grabbed the pint glass half full of water and took several large gulps, swilling the liquid around his bone-dry mouth and over his bone-dry lips.

It had been rather a nasty dream. Danny Wiseman – or rather, what was left of Danny Wiseman – clawing at his feet, his decomposing fingers sticking to Hal's toes. 'Help me,' the body had cried, 'help meeee.' The voice belonged to Wiseman's mother. Then, just as Hal was about to lean down and touch the raggedy corpse beneath him, the dream had cut like a badly edited movie to another scene.

His father was waving at him. His arms outstretched so that you could see the tip of every individual finger. It wasn't a friendly wave. More of a panicked wave. The sort of wave you might expect to see in the distance if you were drifting offshore on a rubber lilo. Definitely panicked. His father was mouthing something at him, but for some reason no sound seemed to come out. It was muffled. Or were there other noises drowning him out? He couldn't tell, or couldn't remember. Whichever. Hal imagined himself to be about ten in the dream. There was no particular reason for it, he simply felt as if he was ten years old and his father was warning him of something. But what?

He hadn't even drunk that much before going to bed, just two glasses of Bell's followed by three paracetamol for his vaguely throbbing head. Perhaps it was the combination of the drink and drugs that had brought it on. Whatever it was, he didn't particularly care. He was wide awake and that was all that mattered. Probably no more sleep now until twenty minutes before his alarm clock went off. That was what usually happened. He'd find himself getting warm, cosy and content just as the clock blared its god-awful foghorn noise thing in his ears.

He turned to see what the time was. Christ, only 1.16. He'd been in bed for just over an hour and a half. That's all. The orange glow haloing around the thick curtains confirmed it. It was bloody ages before dawn. He sighed, swung his legs over the side of the bed, and got up. Picking his cotton dressing-gown off the hook on the back of the door, he yawned and stumbled out onto the upper landing.

The house was deathly quiet. Hal peered over the banister and down the stairway. The lower two floors were bathed in a blackness and his bleary eyes failed to distinguish any of the things that he knew could normally be seen from here. The side table on the first floor landing, the telephone table in the hallway, the wicker hatstand with the brown fedora he'd only ever had the courage to wear once. None of it could be seen in the early morning darkness. He couldn't even make out the outlines of the pictures on the walls. He wrapped his dressing gown around him, pulling the waist cord tight, before opening the door to his father's room.

The Creep's shift had come to an end. In the brightly lit but eerily deserted staff canteen, he popped off his name tag and shoved it roughly into the small holdall that he used for work. He could feel the plaster on his arm scraping against his shirt. It had been working its way off all evening and he'd had to keep pushing it down to keep it in place. He would need to change it when he got home. Apply some more TCP and then put a new one on. Hopefully the gash would heal itself – he didn't want to have to go and get medical help for it. He didn't want some nosy doctor cunt asking too many questions.

Pushing open the fire door, he made his way down the piss-smelling, graffiti-covered stairwell to the car park where his newly acquired car was waiting for him.

Hal sat on the ladder-back chair, directly beneath the bare bulb. It was surprisingly nippy and he adjusted the top of his dressing gown to try and keep the cold air off his pasty body.

The three keys sat in his lap. One for each of the chests. His fingers stroked each key in turn. The tiny, dirtying strips of masking tape wrapped around them ('1', '2', and '3' scribbled in pencil) seemed to be slipping off. Hal made a mental note to renew them at some time, knowing that he probably never would. Sighing, he got up quickly, unlocked chest one and pushed the lid wide open.

His father's equipment. Boxes and boxes of it. Tricks and props going back forty years. Hal started pulling things out and laying them on the floor. There were numerous and humorous hats, capes, and canes, disappearing boxes and magically joining rings. There were cups and saucers, candles and cards, sponge balls and toppits. Books on close-up magic, misdirection and mentalism were stacked against one side of the chest – one of them written and signed by his father. He reached in and levered them out. Once he'd emptied the chest of its contents, he moved on to numbers two and three and did exactly the same thing until the entire floor was covered with routines and memorabilia.

He liked to do this every few months or so. Get it all out, revel in it, remember his dad, before quickly hiding it away again and forgetting all about it. Some of the stuff he was given as a child. It had served its use, the routine was becoming stale or predictable, so Victor Liddle would allow his son to have it. Other items – like the gabardine coat they'd used in the gardening sketch – he'd had to buy himself. Celebrity auctions usually brought up some little thing that had belonged to his father, and Hal was usually the anonymous phone bidder who made off with it.

Hal picked up and flicked through the *Liddle and Moore Annual 1979*, its cover creased and stained. This was his own copy, evidenced by the exceptionally dodgy three-year-old's scribble on one of the first few pages. Hal turned to the comic on page twenty-six entitled 'Liddle and Moore Save the World (Again!)'. Badly drawn versions of Hal's dad and Uncle Barry, dressed in full tuxedos and dickie bows, using tricks and jolly japes to ward off an evil alien army from the planet SpagBoll. The final few cells showed them both receiving knighthoods from the Queen for their services to mankind – Victor looking overly earnest, Barry winking with a 'Ta, Ma'am' speech bubble. He flipped over some of the stiff pages until he got to 'Uncle Barry – Your Caring Sharing Agony Uncle'. A large picture of Barry's head, his hair wild in his trademark manner, sat next to the bubbly title. *Dear Uncle Barry*, one of the mock letters started. *I have very poor skin – spots and all sorts. I find it difficult to go out in public because I fear that people will point at me and say things like 'Ugh! Look at Spotty Robinson there' ... That's if Robinson was my real name, of course ... Which it isn't! It's something quite different to Martin Robinson ... Oops! Anyway, what can I do about it? Signed* Martin Robinson *Worried From Gloucester*. The reply, in bold (obviously), read 'Dear Worried From Gloucester. Don't worry. There are lots of things you could do about your problem. Have you tried popping 'em? The spots, I mean. Squeeze 'em between your nails and see what happens. You'll need to wipe down your bathroom mirror afterwards but it might help. Another thing I recommend you do is join a club. Go along in disguise first of all and see if there are people with worse skin conditions than you. If not try another club until you come across one that has some worse spotty herberts. Then reveal yourself (not in that way) and because your skin will be relatively good in comparison with all the other bumpy-cheeked wonders, you'll feel like some sort of Hollywood love god. Keep yer pus-filled chin up, Uncle Barry.' You'd never be able to get away with that sort of nonsense today. The publishers would have acne support groups calling for Uncle Barry's head on a plate. Hal remembered his dad telling him that they had nothing to do with the annual. That it was banged out by a team of writers and illustrators in an office somewhere, and neither Liddle nor Moore had written a single word of it. It was simply a way of cashing in on the Christmas market.

Hal put the annual aside and dragged himself across the floor to where some of his father's favourite tricks lay. There were dozens of packs of trick cards. Hal opened one up. He felt the red-backed plastic-coated cards in his hands and realised almost immediately that this was a tapered deck. He fanned them out and chose a card at random – the four of hearts. Pushing it back into the pack (the wrong way round, of course), he shuffled them before putting his hands behind his back and effortlessly stripping out the chosen card. He placed it on the top of the deck and brought his hands back in front of him. He tapped the top of the pack with his index finger before turning the top card over with a flourish. The four of hearts. A pathetically simple trick that even a granny with arthritis could perform.

He opened up another of the packs. A rough and smooth deck of Aviators. A blank deck. Let them fall from one hand to another, they look like an ordinary pack of cards. However, fan them open and they appear to be completely blank. An impressive effect, nothing more. Nowadays, such rigged cards could be bought practically anywhere. Most department stores had a magic section, for God's sake. Any old so-and-so could buy them and clumsily perform them in front of family members before happily explaining away how the thing worked. Not so thirty years ago. Thirty years ago there was only a handful of specialised shops that sold such things and the veil of mystery and wonder that surrounded those that performed magic was enough to keep the acts themselves special.

Hal always remembered the trips to Davenports with his father. Coming down the steps from the Strand into Charing Cross tube station, the subterranean little shop always gave the young Harry Luchewski a thrill. Dimly lit, it was like a secret magical cavern. Harry used to wonder if many of the commuters dragging themselves off the tube and up onto the streets of London every day even noticed that they passed a professional magic shop. He doubted many of them did.

Victor Liddle always got a warm and appreciative welcome at Davenports. The assistants behind the counter (all extremely competent magicians themselves) would flutter and fluff at his appearance. 'Good morning, Mr Liddle. Good morning. Loved the show last week. Especially your vanishing lady. A beautiful touch, using the cameraman like that. One of ours, was it?' They were especially proud if he used one of the props that they'd made for him. 'Of course,' he'd say. 'I only use the best on TV.' And they'd coo and chuckle and look embarrassed.

'Mr Liddle. Come over here. I'd like to show you this. A routine developed by our very own Raymonde here.' Raymonde would go slightly red. 'A variation on the three-card monte. We've tried it out on a few unsuspecting customers and they've loved it. Stunningly simple, of course.' And the room would gather around the glass-topped counter to see the trick performed, Hal standing on tiptoe to catch the effect. At the end, everyone would nod appreciatively and say how it could be improved or performed in front of an audience. It was all quite analytical really. Masters of their art unfazed by a display of what seemed to be minor miracles, but the very young Harry always thought it was magic.

'Mr Liddle, sir. The false-floored drinks cabinet that you designed has just been completed. It's out the back, sir. Would you like to take a look at it?'

To the side of the shop was a tiny theatre with a slightly raised platform and a number of chairs positioned in front of it. It was a place that magicians could try out, and perfect, new routines with an audience of professionals before launching the trick on the public at large. Victor Liddle loved to experiment with a trick on the Davenports stage, Harry sitting up on one of the front seats, his legs swinging back and forth. The assistants would usually lock the door to the shop, twisting around the little cardboard notice that read 'Back in Ten' before settling back to watch a truly successful and internationally popular master at work. Those customers lucky enough to have wandered in at just the right time would also be allowed to take a pew.

'A beautiful piece of work. Beautiful,' Hal's dad would say as he admired the equipment that had been specially constructed for him. 'It's just as I imagined it.'

'And if you look at the front,' an excited young assistant would insist, 'notice the detail that's gone into the door panelling. We've tried to make it look as much like a real drinks cabinet as we possibly could. See how the wood's been aged?'

'Incredible. Absolutely incredible.' Victor Liddle was always overly complimentary to the staff at Davenports. 'Absolutely incredible.' Hal never saw his father pay for anything at the shop. 'Now let's see if it works.'

The assistants would sit in the audience and watch as Hal's dad brought the trick to life, expertly using the props even though he had only just been given the thing. He'd already established what his patter for the routine would be and he was trying that out on the audience as much as the apparatus itself.

'... so the man says to the dog, "I only drink whiskey. I never touch anything else ... hic." The dog looks up at him with his big saggy brown eyes and says, "What? You don't drink gin?"' Victor Liddle would whip out a gin bottle from the previously empty cabinet. '"That's a pity because we've got some gin." The man swaggered on his feet, nearly knocking over a couple of porcelain violin players on the mantelpiece. "Hold on," he says. "I never knew that ... hic ... I never knew that dogs could talk." The dog grinned at him. "Of course we can. All dogs can talk. It's just that most of the time we choose to say nothing. We're very good listeners, you know." The man dribbled a bit out of the corner of his mouth.' Victor Liddle pretended to wipe the front of his shirt. '"So," says the dog, "what about a nice drop of rum?"' Out would come a bottle of rum. Nods of appreciation from the audience. '"No, Fido ... hic ... Only whiskey ... I only drink whiskey."' And so on.

At the end of the performance, those sitting on the seats would give a short burst of applause and Hal's dad would give a mock theatrical bow before signing autographs for members of the public.

Hal shifted around on the wooden floor and picked up a rolled-up poster with an elastic band around it. Removing the band he unfurled the thin glossy paper, holding it open on the floor.

LIDDLE & MOORE NATIONWIDE TOUR
1981

it proudly proclaimed, a whole list of placenames and dates beneath. On the sides of the poster, in not-so-little bubbles, were notices from the newspapers:

'A sensation.' *The Times*

'I laughed so hard I needed hospital treatment.' Bernie Redfern, *The Sun*

'Hilarious! A must-see.' *The Guardian*

'If you only see one show this year, make sure it's this one.' Gaz Gascoigne, *The Mirror*

Hal remembered it well. He could recall standing in the wings with his mother at the Fairfield Halls in Croydon, watching the act – his father straight and proper, Uncle Barry being the clown falling on his fat arse a lot. He remembered his dad rushing off stage for a costume change, winking at him as he went. He remembered the bright lights and the applause, the songs and the jokes, the props and the dancers. He remembered how, every night, they would drag some poor unsuspecting member of the audience up on stage and humiliate him or her (usually him), making them participate in some pseudo-disastrous trick. They usually went off with a large bottle of champagne in the end, though, just so they didn't feel too foolish.

The problem was that Hal also remembered the loneliness. The weeks and weeks without his father. His mother's sad resignation to it all. The teasing at school from other kids. 'Your dad's away in Scotland all next week. I bet he's screwing a woman in Glasgow. I bet he's got another family in Edinburgh. I bet your dad's shagging all over the place.' Hal punched a kid on the nose once for suggesting that Liddle and Moore were secretly a gay couple with a big pink tourbus. He'd had to do detention over that one.

He sighed and slowly started putting the articles back into the boxes. There was far too much stuff here. He was going to have to do another run to one of the two rooms he hired at the Big Yellow Self Storage company. That was where most of his father's collection was kept. The wardrobes, the cabinets, the sawing-the-lady-in-half chests – all the big stuff he kept in storage. No, there was no question about it, he was going to have to shift some of it.

Hal grabbed a faded pack of poker-sized Bicycles. An ordinary pack, this time. He picked off the top five cards and started practising his Elmsley count. Holding them in his left hand, he counted them over into his right hand. One. Two. Three. Four. Four cards. Anybody sitting next to him, watching painstakingly carefully, focusing entirely on Hal's hands, would not have noticed the deception. It was such a simple manoeuvre. Disguising five cards as four. A basic tool in the magician's toolbox. He did it again, this time trying to spot the trick himself, but years of practise had made him so good that he could barely detect it. His father had taught him how to do it. His father had taught him to do many things with a pack of cards, starting with a false overhand shuffle. Faking a cut, palming, double lifts, double turnovers, gliding, forcing, Elmsley counts and Duvivier counts. All rudimentary card manipulations that any self-respecting magician could do. The thing that always amazed Hal, even as a young boy clumsily performing tricks in front of his friends, was how easy it was to fool people right in front of their very eyes. They would be watching your hands and seeing you switch things around or peel off too many cards, but their brains wouldn't notice. Wouldn't take it in. They were all too caught up in the magic of it all. Even a novice magician could get away with murder. Misdirection. It was the greatest trick of all. If somebody isn't actively looking for something then they certainly won't find it. That's what made the great magicians great. The ability to mislead. That's what made Victor Liddle great. That along with a decent sense of comic timing and a fuzzy-haired idiot of a partner.

Hal slipped the cards back into the cardboard cover and threw them into box number two. Yawning he got up, leaving the room in a mess, and scuttled across the landing to his bedroom where he thought he'd better get at least a little sleep before dawn.

Before he climbed into bed, the Creep had a quick go at the card trick he'd bought in John Lewis the other day. He was going to use it at his next kiddies' party. Bookings were coming in slowly for Booboo the Clown and he prayed that it wouldn't be too long before he could jack in the Sainsbury's thing. It was far too fucking tedious. It required him to be obsequious and deferential, and he didn't do obsequious and deferential particularly well. 'Hello, sir.' 'Yes, sir.' 'Good morning, madam.' 'Of course, sir.' 'Would you like help with your packing?' 'Terrible weather we're having today.' He was sick to the back fucking teeth with it. If one more customer ignores me, he thought, I'm going to cut out *their* fucking teeth with a smashed-up bottle of ketchup.

Two parties a week and he could survive. He'd worked it out. He didn't pay any mortgage or rent. Didn't have much debt of any kind. He still had a tiny bit of money left over from the Granton – ahem! – *redundancy* package, but he was desperately trying to hold on to that. Two parties a week and he could make it through to the following week. Three parties a week and he could live a little. One party a week and he was fucked.

His stubby fingers pulled the cards out and opened up the instructions. He placed them on his knees as he felt the cards in his hands. *Ask a member of the audience to cut the pack.* He cut the pack. *Have them look at their card then return it to the top of the deck.* He put the three of clubs back on top. *Now let the cards fall from one hand to the next, showing that the pack appears to be perfectly normal.* He let them fall. However, towards the end, a couple of them slipped straight off and onto the floor.

'Oh, fuck!'

Never mind. He continued. *Now cut the pack several times, placing the top cards beneath the bottom selection.* He did so. *When you are ready, tell your audience that you have a feeling that the selected card has now come home and is sitting on top of the deck. Get your victim to turn over the top card. And (ta-dah!) it should be the chosen card.*

The Creep turned over the top card.

The seven of hearts.

'Fuck it!'

He threw the pack of cards across the room. They hit the side of his wardrobe and scattered all over the floor. He stood up, pulled his trousers down, and climbed into bed.

Part Two:
Blue Monday

Chapter Fifteen

Andy Baldwin's early morning cycle ride always started at 6.15. It was something he did nearly every day, whatever the weather. Even in winter, when he could barely see the handlebars in front of him, it was so dark, and he could barely hold them, it was so cold. He'd dig the Raleigh out of the wooden shed at the back of the house, push open the gate, and free-wheel down the hill in Upper Tooting where he lived. Forcing the bike across the twisting network of suburban side streets, he'd cut over Wimbledon Park, skirting the boating lake, and onwards to Wimbledon Common. Baldwin loved crossing the common at such an early hour of the morning. It wasn't that there was nobody else around. In fact, it always surprised him how many other people there were. Dog walkers, joggers, cyclists like himself, late-night revellers straggling back home. No, it was the space that Baldwin always appreciated. The wide open space. At this time of the year, luscious and green and smelling of optimistic freshness. He loved to feel a part of it, slicing over the rough tracks and concrete paths. Pedalling hard over the gritty ground, picking up speed, braking suddenly, pounding the gears. He bloody loved it. Loved the freedom of it all. Even better if he had some good music streaming into his ears from his Nano. Queen or Quo. Perhaps some Bryan Adams. 'Summer of '69' and all that.

This morning, he'd been listening to some UB40. He'd had a good hard session, and felt the sweat trickling down his back as he pushed the bike the last hundred yards or so up the hill, back to the house. His watch read 7.23. Not too bad. About an hour and ten minutes. He'd once done the whole route in fifty-three minutes, but that was a few years ago when the bike was newer and the paths on the common were better laid. He kept meaning to write to the council to complain about the paths, but he never seemed to have the time to get around to it.

'Rat In Mi Kitchen' was stuck in his head and he whistled a few bars as he approached the drive. The paperboy was working his way down the street, his large day-glo orange delivery bag weighing down his tiny eleven-year-old shoulders. They both got to the drive at exactly the same moment.

'Morning, Chris,' Baldwin sullenly acknowledged from under his shiny black cycling helmet.

'Hello, Mr Baldwin. Got your papers here.' He dug out a couple of heavy-looking ones and handed them over. Baldwin snatched them off him and turned to the house, pushing the bike over the cobblestone walkway. The paperboy stood still for a few seconds before continuing on his way. 'Don't thank me or nothing, you ignorant twat,' he muttered under his breath, fishing about for the neighbour's *Daily Express*.

Stevie Denyer had hardly slept. He'd seen his name in print before, of course. Dozens if not hundreds of times. This time, though, it was different. This time people might actually want to read his story. They just might find it interesting, and the thought of that had made him just a little bit excited.

At the crack of dawn, he'd taken a wander down the road to the newsagent's. He was too early, of course. He knew that. He just wanted to be there when the truck arrived. The sun was barely peeping above the horizon, when he heard the rumble of its engine coming from around the corner. The driver hopped out, giving him a bit of a suspicious look, before opening up the back and dropping out large and tightly packed bundles of newspapers on the pavement directly outside the newsagent's. As the van drove off, Stevie peered over the delivery. He could see the copies of the *London Chronicle*, the binding covering up chunks of the main story. However, the headline was easy to see: SECOND BODY FOUND IN SOUTH LONDON. A thrilled little shiver ran up his spine as the newsagent opened the door and told him to come back at six. 'We don't open until six.' He'd looked at Stevie like he was a madman.

So Stevie had wandered around the streets, waiting for the shop to open. The day was beautiful. A still, red screen was filling the sky, and the birds were starting to chatter and tweet. The occasional car fractured the serenity, but Stevie wasn't put off. Today was going to be a wonderful day, no doubt about it. He picked up the papers on the dot of six, and rushed home before spreading them open on his kitchen table.

The alarm had already woken Hal up, so he was quite surprised to hear it go off again, albeit louder and higher pitched. It took about three seconds for him to realise that it wasn't actually the alarm clock that was screeching to his right. It was his mobile, the colour screen flashing brightly up from the bedside table. He shifted his weight onto his elbow and scooped the thing up. 'WOODE' it said in big bold lettering. The time at the bottom of the screen read '7.32'. Hal hit the green button and held it to his ear.

'Hello?' His voice was croaky and he coughed to clear his throat.

'Harry. Is that you?'

'Sir?'

'It's DCI Woode here.'

'Oh. Good morning, sir.'

'Well … yes. Look, Harry,' he sounded like there was something he was trying to avoid saying. 'Er, look. Bit of advice. Do you take the *London Chronicle*?'

'Sorry?'

'The *London Chronicle*. The newspaper. Do you get it delivered?'

'Er, no.' What was he on about now? 'No, I don't have it delivered.'

'Bit of advice, Harry. Might be a good idea to pick one up and have a read before coming into the office this morning. Just so as you know.'

'I'm sorry, sir. I don't know what you're on about. Is it the case? Have they published something we …'

'No, no. Well, yes. The case is in there. But there's something about you with it. Page three, if you need to know.'

'Something about me?' He sat up in his bed now. 'What do you –'

'Buy it. You'll see. I'll see you in the office later.'

Woode hung up. Hal threw the phone on to the duvet. What the hell was all that about? Woode sounded like he couldn't get off the phone fast enough. Why would they be writing about him in the Chronicle? He pushed she sheets down, swung his legs over the side of the bed and headed for the shower.

Baldwin's wife was a good little woman. She worked hard around the house keeping the place spick and span, and took great pride in typically feminine things like kitchen floors and cooking surfaces. Her food, although not brilliantly blessed with tastiness, was always wholesome and filling and on the table at appropriate times. The kids too were always kept clean and presentable, wearing decent clothes and were driven to tennis club on Mondays and ballet lessons on Tuesdays. On Thursdays his wife would have her coffee morning with a smattering of the other middle-class mothers on the cul-de-sac. Baldwin had never met them and never wanted to meet them. There were men's roles and there were women's roles, and the more the roles didn't overlap, the better for everyone, he believed. Marion agreed and was happy to play the role of loving wife and doting mother.

'Cantaloupe or Galia?' Marion asked Baldwin over the kitchen table, a melon held in each hand.

Baldwin lowered the paper he was reading for a second and shrugged. 'Doesn't matter, does it?' He slipped back into the paper again.

'I'll use the cantaloupe. The sell-by date's earlier.'

Baldwin's eyes scoured the paper for the Dawson case. He was up in court again this week, and was keen to see how it was being reported. He'd be giving evidence along with Woode. A rubbish case really. Cut and dried as far as he was concerned. Hubby gets knocked on the head with a hammer. Wife's lover hides hammer (not very well as it turned out). Body gets buried in some woodland. Fake letter sent to workmates saying he'd gone to Australia and that he'd had enough, bye-bye. And then, body found and identified. Houses searched. Hammer found. Two arrests. Rubbish! Old Vulcan features was having a much better time of it, he was sure.

He threw the broadsheet down and picked up the *London Chronicle*. SECOND BODY FOUND IN SOUTH LONDON, the headline ran. Lucky bugger. Bagging himself a serial killer case – not that that was officially what it was yet. Two deaths in virtually as many days, though. That was something to get your teeth into. A proper murder enquiry full of the twisty intrigues that you secretly relished as an AMIP officer. Domestic murder was boring shit. Just going-through-the-motions drudgery. A decent killing (or in this case killings) though – that's what really made the job worthwhile. And Baldwin was good at his job. Much better than that ugly drunken idiot Luchewski. He was beginning to lose it.

He started to read the story. First body – that of a Daniel Wiseman. Found on Friday. Second body – Raymond Larby, found in his lock-up garage. He turned the page to continue skimming through the article. Both men had connections with –

He stopped paying attention to the words when his eyes caught sight of the picture on the right hand page. A badly taken shot of Luchewski. An old one too by the looks of it. Taken before he decided to disguise his alopecia problem by shaving his extraordinarily shaped head. He looked younger and not so past it. Baldwin's interest was piqued, and he abandoned the main story to

139

concentrate on this new article. The headline above the picture read, MURDER COP IS GAY SON OF TELLY STAR.

'Ha!' Baldwin guffawed, his posture correcting itself at the shock.

'What's that, dear?' his wife enquired from over the fruit salad she was preparing.

'Ha! Nothing,' he smiled at her. 'Nothing at all. Absolutely nothing at all.' He flicked the paper straight and carried on reading.

'Oh, fuck.'

Luchewski was standing outside the newsagents on the corner of Penge High Street, the paper open in front of him. 'Oh, for fuck's sake!'

His stomach felt like it had just thrown itself out of a Boeing 737 cruising at twenty thousand feet, and his legs had turned to jelly. He hurriedly shut the paper and tried his best to walk to his car. What the fucking hell was all this about? Why had they singled him out?

In the safe and solitary confines of the TT, he reopened the paper, silently wishing the story had disappeared. Unfortunately for him, it had not. It was still there. The dreadful old picture of him talking on his mobile phone outside a courtroom that he'd seen used somewhere before. Back in the days when his hairline was salvageable. The headline jumped out at him like a bold typographic tiger.

MURDER COP IS GAY SON OF TELLY STAR

Hal sighed, gritted his teeth, and read the whole thing through.

One of the investigating officers involved in the Catford and Peckham murder inquiries is the gay son of 70s TV personality Victor Liddle.

Detective Inspector Harry Luchewski (39) is a regular visitor to the gay clubs and bars of Clapham and Soho, so much so that the staff at Dickie's Bar just off Lavender Hill in Clapham claim to have seen him at the gay pick-up-joint only last week – literally hours before the body of Daniel Wiseman was found. The barman added: 'He comes here a lot. Always on the lookout for men. I don't think I've ever seen him leave Dickie's alone. He buys a drink and watches the talent go by before making his move.'

Luchewski – who was once married and has a twelve-year-old daughter, Lily – lives alone in a large Victorian house in Penge, bought with money left to him by his celebrity father. Victor Liddle (born Victor Luchewski) was part of the magic comedy duo Liddle and Moore. The pair had a number of successful television series on the BBC in the mid-seventies after winning the talent show Stars of The Future. *Tragically, Liddle and his wife died in a car accident in Monte Carlo in 2004*

When asked yesterday about his addiction to promiscuous gay sex, Luchewski replied, 'I am not gay,' and refused to answer any more questions on the subject.

Last year, Luchewski was the Chief Investigating Officer in the case of Arnold Richards - also known as the Headmaster. Richards was given two life sentences for the murder of two prostitutes at his Surrey home.

Hal shook his head in disbelief. He didn't talk to anyone from the papers yesterday. They were making it all up. 'I am not gay' indeed! Hang on, he thought. I did say that recently. His eyes glanced back at the article. Right at the bottom, underneath the story was the writer's name, printed in a slightly smaller font than the words above it.

Story: Steven Denyer

Steven Denyer. Steven Denyer. It rolled around in his head and then clicked. Stevie. That kid he picked up in Dickie's the other night. He said that he worked for the gas board or electricity board or some other board. The lying little prick. He was a journo. Digging around for some dirt on the case. But … his mind raced. Danny's body hadn't been found at that point. So what was he doing? Investigating me. He must have known all the time that I was a copper, thought Hal. But he came back to my house. We had sex. He must be gay himself then, surely. He wasn't just putting up with it for the sake of the story, was he?

Then another dreadful thought hit him. Lily. His daughter didn't know anything of his sexual proclivities. She'd always just assumed that Hal and her mother had split up for more prosaic reasons. No. She'd read this and it would destroy her. Would almost certainly destroy the image she had of her dad. Hal nervously scrambled for the phone in his jacket pocket. It fell out of his twitching fingers onto the floor of the car and he had to fish around under the seat to get it. Holding it in front of him, he hit speed dial number 2 and held it to his ear. Within seconds the voicemail kicked in. The phone was off. Her bloody mobile was off! He cut the call dead and then hit speed dial number 3. This was the landline at the house. It rang and rang until, eventually even that went to voicemail. Neither of them was at home. They'd left for school and work already. Shit! He was going to have to –

Tap-tap-tap.

He was suddenly ripped out of his imagination by a traffic warden knocking on the window. She made a 'wind-your-window-down-please-sir' signal at him, and Hal did as he was told.

'You do know this is a double yellow you're parked on, sir?'

'Is it? Yes, that's right. I did know, yes. Sorry, officer.'

'You're going to have to move your car, I'm afraid.'

'Yes. Of course, officer.' Hal was still shaking as he hooked his seatbelt over his arm and started the car. 'Sorry, officer,' he shouted as he started off, no thought of reaching for his ID card entering his head.

Robbie Green was already sick to death of his flatmates. Sharing a house with two trainee lawyers was getting to be a real nuisance. For a start, they seemed to earn more money than he did. Secondly, they didn't need to work as hard as he did. They always seemed to be out drinking themselves into oblivion and stumbling back in at some awful hour, watching old Kung Fu movies and spewing up semi-digested kebabs. Neither Lee nor Dave seemed to care that Robbie actually needed to sleep sometimes. They'd bang on his door at three in the morning asking if he knew where the sieve was – what they wanted the sieve for at that time, he never understood and never asked. Or they'd put chillout music on really loudly, seemingly unaware that it had the opposite effect on a sleeping detective sergeant. Then there was the kitchen. Lee liked to cook things, Dave liked to eat things, but neither of them seemed keen on washing things up. It was a particular bone of contention with Green, who was fastidious to the point of being obsessive compulsive. Most mornings he would come down to a sink full of dirty plates, cups and cutlery, and most mornings he'd be the one cleaning it up. He would scrub the glasses, wipe the knives, and pick dried-on cornflakes off the sides of the cereal bowls. He'd mop the floor, straighten the cupboards and polish the sink. All before Eric and Ernie stirred from their beds.

Work wasn't much of an improvement either. He was lumbered with DI Burlock. The man was decent enough, he didn't doubt it, but he could be incredibly annoying. All those fishing stories and crosswords. He'd only had a couple of weeks of it and he was already feeling the strain. Give him another six months and he'd probably flip his lid altogether.

Green sat on the velour sofa in the sitting room, one hand lifting a coffee mug to his lips, the other stroking the smooth silky-feeling arm of the chair. He was thinking about the lock-up. The head on the car. The bloody torso in the corner. It was difficult to make a connection in his head between the body parts and Raymond Larby. Raymond Larby was the name of a man. A human being. Somebody who breathed in air and breathed out carbon dioxide. Somebody who laughed and cried and made love and slept and hurt and ate and drank and coughed and sneezed and ... Somebody who did stuff that other living, breathing human beings did. The things in the garage yesterday were little more than doll's parts. All plastic and pulled apart by a stroppy child. It worried Green that he felt so little about this poor individual. This poor man who had been sliced out of existence by a psychopath. It worried him that he didn't feel pity or anger. It was just something in front of him and his brain had accepted it. Without question. In fact, the only thing he had felt – he realised hours after discovering the body – was a combination of annoyance and disgust. That someone could leave even a lock-up garage in such a terrible state. There had been blood all over the place. It was messy.

The thought of it all tickled the back of his neck and he went upstairs to the bathroom to wash his hands for the eighth time that morning.

Chapter Sixteen

Pulling into the car park, Hal could see Baldwin's fat black 4x4 taking up more than its fair share of space. His heart sank at the thought of having to face him today. Any other day, he might be able to put up with his flabby wet lips and his pockmarked cheeks (Baldwin had undoubtedly suffered from a terrible bout of acne during his teenage years). Problem was that today, if the slimy little turd said anything dodgy to him, Hal was liable to give him a punch up the bracket.

Over the course of the twelve-minute drive from Penge to Hartshorn House, Hal's emotions had shifted from nervous confusion, through numbness to his current state of barely suppressed anger. That fucking Stevie kid. Fucking researching him like that. And Hal had encouraged him! Told him to go and use the internet to find out about how he got his money! Hal shook his head, silently calling himself a wanker. How could he be so fucking stupid? How could he leave himself so open like that? He'd spent so many years concentrating on tucking in his personality, protecting himself from emotional pressures, that he'd left a great wide Achilles heel of a door open. The gay clubs, the promiscuity, the drink. All designed to bring him down. Hal felt like a rock at the top of a hill was gently being pressured to roll down and flatten him.

That Stevie prick, he thought. A little journalist tosspot. Well, fuck him!

He got out of the car and slammed the door so hard that the wing mirror needed readjusting.

It was just starting to rain as Alexander Judd turned off the M25 onto the M1. Tiny spits of water were landing on the windscreen and blurring his vision. He flicked the lever up and the wipers swept the droplets away, smudging the window as they went.

He'd been driving for about an hour now, not really knowing where to go. He didn't want to go to work and he didn't want to stay at home. If he stayed at home he was asking for trouble. If he went to work – well, his mind was so distracted, he wouldn't be able to do any work anyway. It was while he was sitting in a parking bay at

144

Clackett Lane services that he realised he would be safest outside London. Head north for a few days. The Lake District or the Peak District. Somewhere like that would be good. He could sleep in the car if he had to. He didn't mind roughing it. He'd quite enjoy it actually. Remind himself of the expeditions he had as a boy scout all those years ago. Carol would have to put up with it, he thought. She wouldn't understand, but she would have to put up with it. The kids too. They would have to manage without him for a few days. It was safest.

He didn't know what he was going to do about it all. Poor Danny. And now Ray. He never really liked Ray all that much – not really a Christian man. Ray sold drugs to kids, which he himself found utterly abhorrent, but they were connected. Bonded, in a sense. Bound together, in a way, by love. Love had brought them together. Alex had so much love to give. So too had Ray …

Judd overtook a caravan choking up the inside lane. He felt hot and he wiped his sweaty brow with the back of his sleeve before switching on the air conditioning. He didn't want to die. He had so much more he wanted to do. So much more love he wanted to give. It wasn't time for him to die yet. And waiting around in London was a sure-fire way of getting himself killed at the moment. That was why he had packed a small rucksack in the early hours and left the house before anyone else was up.

Luchewski. He had his number in his wallet. He'd phone Luchewski soon. That was the right thing to do. Get himself safely out of the way and then phone him. Tell him who killed Danny and Ray and get this whole damned business over with.

Hal could sense it as he walked through the door. To most people it would have been barely perceptible, but he could sense the difference the moment the door locked shut behind him. The chatter was dying down – which it didn't normally do as he walked into the office. A few people snatched glances at him then looked down at their shoes or out of the windows. Some of the uniforms in the coffee area coughed and raised their eyebrows at each other. Even the women. He'd been expecting it, admittedly, but it took him by surprise nevertheless.

He started walking off in the direction of his office. He felt that he just might feel safe there, and as he crossed the floor he could feel the eyes burning into the back of his head.

'Ah, Harry. There you are.' Woode was coming down the stairs from his office, his face beaming. Hal thought that he was trying to make up for his embarrassing behaviour on the phone earlier that morning. 'Caught you.' It seemed a trifle forced to Hal. 'Briefing in fifteen, say? See where we are on this double murder case?'

'Sir,' Hal mumbled and stumbled into his office.

It seemed to Hal that everybody was there this morning. Singh, Burlock, Green, Baldwin, Baldwin's handsome black sergeant, Keegan, and an entire army of DCs and CID. Hal had somehow managed to hold it all together so far, coming across as the eloquent and efficient professional he liked sometimes to pretend he was. Woode sat on a desk to the side, listening and scribbling down notes.

'Anything on Rabin?' Hal turned to a young constable in a mottled brown suit.

'Nothing, sir. Came to Britain with his parents from Iraq in 1958. His father started the shop in Streatham in the late sixties. Rabin inherited it off him and has been involved in business ever since. Bought the house in Norwood a couple of years ago off a doctor. Never been in any sort of trouble with the law. Nor have any of the current residents in any of his houses.'

'What about the black lad?' Woode didn't even look up from his notepad. 'Any idea on him?'

'We've got a missing persons out on him, sir,' Singh piped up. 'Every station in the south-east is on the lookout.'

'But no word so far?'

'No, sir.'

'Think he's victim number three? Or two, even, depending on the order of things?' Woode directed the question at Hal.

Hal shrugged. 'I really couldn't tell you, sir. At this stage –'

'I can tell you,' Baldwin was leaning against a wall with his arms folded defensively, 'I can tell you that that boy is dead. Obviously. That makes three murders in as many days, Harry boy. That's pretty good going.'

'Andy,' Woode chided gently, but Baldwin ignored him and carried on.

'Need to get to grips with it pretty bloody sharpish I'd say. Before you've got more poor buggers dropping like flies.'

'Shut up, Andy.' Woode was a little more stern this time.

'Aye. Shut up, yer daft pillock.' Burlock rubbed his swollen nose and shook his head.

'Granton?' Woode pulled things back around to the investigation. 'Have you spoken to everyone from Granton?'

'We've still got our people out talking to them at the moment. The reports I've had back so far suggest that nobody knows anything more than we do. Is that right?' Hal turned the question back onto the crowd of DCs and CID in front of him. Most nodded.

'Everyone I've talked to so far knows that Larby pushed drugs at Granton. Some of them knew Wiseman. Knew what he was in for. That's about it,' one of the more forthcoming constables ventured. 'Not much more being said.'

'So where do we go from here?'

'The Granton interviews should be completed sometime today. There was no information coming from Blossom Hill – the garden centre Wiseman worked at, so I'd like to take another run out there. Likewise Granton itself. I've an appointment with the psychological profiler this morning. We're waiting on DNA samples from both crime scenes, but I'm not holding my breath on those. Might take up to ten days. We'll widen the door-to-doors at both major scenes and put a team together to check out CCTVs in the areas. We're releasing McKenzie's details to the press, asking for any info on him. Corrie's put out a call to other forces. See if they are aware of anything similar in terms of MO.'

'Right.' Woode slid off the desk. 'I'll get on the phone to the Chief Super. Let him know what's happening.' Then turning his attention to the team, 'And you lot need to get to work. Find out what this weirdo's up to and stop him before he does it again. Any questions for DI Luchewski before we kick-start the day?' Lots of shaking of heads. 'OK. Get going, then.' He tapped the photograph of Denzil McKenzie sellotaped to the board behind Luchewski's head. 'And find this one if you can.' The crowd started to loosen slightly.

'You never told us you were related to the late great Victor Liddle, Harry.' The crowd stopped loosening. The voice belonged to Baldwin. A little nasal, high-pitched and bitterly acerbic squeak. Hal pretended not to hear him.

'I said you never told us that Victor Liddle was your dad, Harry.'

'Er, no.' Some of the more sensible members of the team had continued their way out of the firing line. 'No.' Hal nervously collected his notes together.

'I never knew that. I used to love Liddle and Moore when I was a kid. Hilarious stuff. That sketch in the restaurant. What was it…? 'Potato, potato, potato!' That's the one. Classic stuff. Proper television that was. Better than the nonsense you get these days. Just not funny these days, is it? Full of swearing or crap jokes about politicians. That's what you get nowadays. A load of old crap. No, I used to love Liddle and Moore. Decent Sunday night telly that was. Oh, and they were good magicians as well, weren't they?' Harry saw Baldwin wink at one of the DCs who was still milling around. Woode was watching closely. 'Pretty good magicians they were. Did some clever stuff if I remember rightly. Hey, Harry,' he stopped leaning against the wall and straightened up, his arms still crossed. 'Did your dad teach you any magic tricks? I mean, did you learn anything off him?'

'Er …' Hal wasn't sure how to react.

'Only I've heard that you're very good at making a cock disappear up your arse!'

Some of the younger officers burst out laughing.

'Aw, fuck you, you pock-faced wanker!'

'Oooooooo! Who rattled your cage, ducky?' Baldwin strutted about with his wrist limp. 'Backs against the walls boys, Harry Arsebandit's around.'

'Baldwin! Shut your mouth!' Woode raged.

'I never knew you were queer, Harry.'

'I said shut it! Now!'

'Sorry, sir.' Baldwin winked again at the silly little puppy-dog DC. 'Just having a bit of fun.'

'Well you can stop having a bit of fun.' A moment of silence passed, convincing Woode that he'd got the situation under control. 'This is a bloody police force, for God's sake. Not a kindergarten.'

'Sorry, sir.' Baldwin didn't look all that sorry. 'Just trying to cheer some of the boys up.'

'Well don't.'

'Only they seem a bit depressed since I've been away.'

'Bloody delirious, more like,' Burlock muttered under his breath, but if Baldwin had heard him, he didn't let on.

'Just trying to cheer them up. Everyone seems a bit down to me. Miserable, like. Stress of the case must be getting to them.' He turned to go back to his office. 'Either that or it's sexual harassment by Harry Queero there.'

Hal didn't know what came over him. His anger swelled up too quickly and he lurched at Baldwin, swinging his fist as he went. It connected with the side of Baldwin's head, and both of them went sprawling over somebody's desk, knocking pens, files, and boxes of paperclips as they went. Baldwin went down on his side, and Hal landed on top. Hal managed to throw another punch, smashing

Baldwin on the cheek, before he felt the hands of other officers on his shoulder lifting him out of the way.

'You fucking twat!' Hal screamed as Burlock and Keegan held him back. 'I'll fucking break your fucking head open, you fucking twat!'

'Calm it down Harry. Leave it.' Burlock whispered in his ear.

'Easy, Harry.' Woode stepped into the area between the two men, his arms outstretched in a bid to hold them at bay.

Baldwin picked himself up off the ground. His lip was bleeding. He pulled out a handkerchief and held it in place.

'Jesus Christ! What was all that about?'

'What was all that about? What was all that about? Fuck, you're a stupid fucking –'

'GBH that was. Bloody GBH.' He examined the blood on the tissue. 'Bloody GBH that was. You all saw it. You saw him attack me. The man's deranged.'

'You're the one who's fucking deranged.' Hal was getting himself back under control. Burlock and Keegan released their grip on him. 'Snipey little turdwipe!'

'You all saw it. He attacked me. Bloody disciplinary action that is. You'll lose your job over this, Luchewski. I'll make sure of it. You all saw him.'

Woode looked pitifully at Baldwin. 'The only thing I saw this morning was you behaving like a complete idiot, Baldwin. I saw nothing else. And I'm pretty certain nobody else saw anything either.' He frowned at the entire room before pointing his finger at Baldwin. 'Now, *you*. Get to your office and get ready for this afternoon.' He twisted and pointed his finger at Hal. 'And *you*. My office. Now.' Without saying anything else Woode headed off up the stairs, with Hal following close behind.

Baldwin started to shuffle towards his office door.

'You really are a tosser,' Burlock sighed as he passed him.

'Shove it, Santa!' Baldwin muttered as he dropped a chunk of tissue paper on the floor.

'Good morning, Inspector Luchewski.'

Trudy smiled as they cut across the room to Woode's office. It was a pleasant smile, but it wasn't the sort of smile he was used to from Trudy. There was absolutely no hint of flirtation in it. If anything, Hal rather detected a smidgeon of resentment. Perhaps she felt that she'd wasted her flirtatious time all along. Pouring out her sexuality on a middle-aged gay man who had misled her all the way.

The door closed behind them both and Woode pounced a millisecond later.

'What the hell do you think you are doing? I mean, downstairs. What are you doing? You've not been drinking, have you?'

'Drinking? Oh, for Christ's sake. I've not been drinking, no.'

'Because we know it's a problem of yours, don't we?'

'Not this time it's not. Jesus! I can't believe you think I've been drinking. It's not even ten o'clock yet. And you think I've been drinking.'

Woode sighed. 'Look, Harry.' Hal could sense the sympathy bubbling up in Woode's chest once again. 'I don't give a flying fig what floats your boat. Sexually, I mean. It doesn't bother me in the least. Each man to his own, I say. But ...' and this was going to be a fairly big 'but', thought Hal, 'but you know what the force is like. People in the force. You know how homophobic they can be. It's still difficult to be a gay man in the Met, even today. Jesus Kid Jensen, it's difficult enough being a woman in the force, never mind being gay.'

'I'm not gay.'

Woode ignored him and carried on. 'What I'm saying is that I can't protect you, Harry. In this world – in this job – there are always going to be the Andy Baldwin's who'll try to kick you in the teeth. And they'll kick hard, believe you me. Kick hard and drag you down. That doesn't mean you can thump them any time you feel aggrieved. You have to be better than that.'

Suddenly, and for no discernible reason, Hal felt like crying. He gritted his teeth and held it off, but Woode had already noticed. Hal squinted and spotted that Woode *did* have a counselling certificate on the wall, after all.

'What's wrong, Harry?'

'Hmm?' Hal choked it all back, his throat feeling tense and strained.

'Tell me.'

Hal sighed, releasing the stress. His eyes watered and his nose seemed to start running. 'I tried to phone my daughter. Lily. This morning. I tried to phone her to warn her. But I couldn't ...' Pause. 'I couldn't get hold of her. Her phone was off. Her mother wasn't home.'

'Lily doesn't know, I take it? About you.'

Hal slumped in the chair and shook his head. 'She probably does now. Be all around the school by now, I'm sure.'

'You don't know that.'

Hal looked up and rolled his eyes at Woode.

'Well, yes. All right,' Woode conceded. 'Things do tend to go like wildfire around schools. Perhaps you'd better go and tell her. Go to her school and talk to her, I mean. Right now.'

Hal shook his head again. 'You heard Baldwin down there. Three bodies in as many days. I can't spare the time. I need to find the bastard who's doing these things and I need to find him fast.'

'An hour of your time isn't going to affect anything. Besides, don't pay too much attention to Baldwin. He's still worked up over the Dawson case.'

'No.' Hal sniffed. 'No, I can't. I've got a killer to find.'

'Well, promise me one thing,' Woode picked out a tissue from a man-sized box sitting on the edge of his desk and handed it to Hal. 'Promise you'll speak to her sometime today. She needs an explanation.'

The zombie threat was keeping Paul Norris awake at night.

He would wake when Levi stirred in the very early hours and then found it hard to go back to sleep. Tracey didn't seem to have too much difficulty – she would be snoring away within minutes – but Paul always found it impossible. And in those quiet dark hours Paul had started putting together his zombie survival plan. It was probably a sign that he was clinically depressed or something, he thought, but the zombies in his head just wouldn't rest.

The first question he always asked himself was, where would he be when the zombie plague took hold? He would either be at the garden centre or at home. He'd hear it over the tannoy at work, or he'd see it on the telly. Assuming the fucking *Wiggles* DVD wasn't on at the time. If he was at work, what would he do? He didn't own a car (nor have a licence, come to think of it) and catching the bus would be hopeless. The drivers would all panic and the buses would be abandoned. No, he'd have to steal someone's car. He'd done it before and it wasn't a big deal. A big fucking gas-guzzler was probably best – a BMW or Range Rover. Something that could do serious damage to a group of oncoming zombies, and was strong enough to protect him should he get surrounded by a crowd of the fuckers.

He'd also plotted the route he would take back to the flat. Main roads were out of the question. There would be too many people desperately trying to get out of the city clogging up the main roads. He would use back roads. Little residential streets and avenues people wouldn't think about in their moment of panic. He would cut

151

across Beckenham, down past the Royal Bethlem hospital, and over to Spring Park. From there it was simply a case of getting onto the Shirley Church Road and down to New Addington. Hopefully Tracey and Levi would be there and together they could embark on Phase Two of the survival plan.

Phase Two consisted of finding some guns. And some ammo. Some sort of protection against the flesh-eating hordes. Luckily Paul knew of a guy who lived nearby and who had all sorts of guns – some hand grenades, too. Paul had been there a couple of times and seen it all. He kept them in the back bedroom, in a suitcase under the bed. If the zombies started attacking, Paul knew it would be a good place to go. Admittedly, the man might not want to give up his stash of firearms, in which case Paul would have to kill him with a baseball bat or something. There was no time for other people in a zombie-dominated world.

Once equipped, Phase Three would kick in. Supermarkets were good places because they were stocked up with food and were excellent places to hide. The big ones, however, tended to have big glass windows from ceiling to floor. Zombies could easily crash in, they didn't care if they got cut if there was human flesh inside the store. Paul had done his research and had realised that smaller supermarkets were actually more secure. Especially if they were out in the sticks somewhere. The plan was to drive out of London into Surrey or Kent, find a small supermarket, get in, and take it over, making it as secure as possible. Trolleys stacked against the doors, shelving units moved to cover any windows, barbed wire over and around fire exits.

And then wait.

Paul pictured Danny Wiseman as one of the living dead. Stumping along, his clothes rotting tatters. Face gaunt and green, like in all those Romero movies.

'Buhb! Buhb! Buhb a Beehar!'

Paul snapped out of it. The zombie plan had started to infiltrate his daytime thoughts now too. Looking around he found himself in the Whitgift Centre, just behind WHSmith, next to the lifts. They must have drifted in from the North End pedestrianised area while he was daydreaming. Levi was jumping up and down and pointing at a yellow Bob the Builder digger ride. The kid looked like a denim-clad rubber ball. With hair.

'Buhb! Daheee! Buhb a Beehar!'

Levi started clambering on, his little legs struggling to reach up to the step. Before the muscles in his arms kicked in and pulled him up, he shook and wobbled like he was about to fall. Paul rushed over to catch him.

'For fuck's sake, be careful.' He pushed the boy's bottom up and Levi pulled himself into the driver's seat.

'Soup! Soup a Buhb a Beehar!' the boy laughed.

'Scoop! Not soup. Scoop!' Paul tried to correct him on the name of the digger. 'Fucking Scoop!' It was driving him slowly mad. All of it. The Bob the Builder Wiggles Fireman Sam shit. The dirty nappies. The lack of sleep. The fact that it was sometimes impossible to work out what the little git was trying to say. The tantrums too – that was a new one. Lying on the floor and kicking his legs in the air. The flicking food on the wall. The crying. All of it seemed designed to send him mental.

'Muneee! Muneee, Daheee!' Levi held his hand out like a beggar. Paul sighed and rubbed his brow. He could feel a headache coming on. Monday was his day off and in the morning Tracey did a stint at the florists. It was just for a few hours, but it meant that Paul had to look after his son for a bit. So today they'd hopped onto the tram and taken a ride in to Croydon. Levi loved the tram. Skipping off onto the platform on George Street he'd shouted 'MUHR! MUHR!' and seemed on the verge of tears before his daddy had managed to convince him that he would go back on the tram again later. 'Beh-ter!' the boy had said, wiping his eyes with his forearm.

'Muneee, Daheee!' Levi started clawing at Paul's trouser pocket. 'Muneee!'

'Get off!' Paul pulled the boy's hand away and looked around to make sure that nobody noticed. It might come across as pervy, and some people could get the wrong impression and think he was some sort of fucking sicko. It gave Paul the shivers to think that people might think that.

'Muneee, Daheee! Pweees!' Levi tried to be a little more subtle. He lowered his voice and used the virtually-guaranteed-to-work word he'd recently learned to say. 'Pweees!'

Paul smiled at the youngster and dug his hand into his jacket pocket to try and find some change. He pulled out everything that he had, only to discover some two pence pieces, three ten pence pieces, two twenty pences, and an old bus ticket. He was certain that he had more. He checked his other pockets but to no avail. He also pulled out his wallet, opening it up to find that not a single note was currently gracing its lining. Paul shook his head. He wasn't paid until Thursday and all he appeared to have in the world right now was 78p and a tram ticket.

'Muneee?' More of a questioning tone now. 'Muneee, Daheee?'

'Sorry, Le. Daddy hasn't got any money. Go on Bob the Builder next week. OK?' He held out his hand to help the boy down, but Levi was going nowhere.

'Buhb! Soup! Pweees, Daheee!' The tears were welling again.

'Not now.'

'Pweees!' The first tear started to roll down his left cheek. 'Pweees, Daheee!'

'Oh, for fuck's sake!' Paul pulled seventy pence out of his pocket and shoved it into the machine. 'Now press the fucking green button!'

''Ank ooo, Dahee.' Levi hit the button and the digger started rocking gently back and forth, the *Bob the Builder* theme tune playing out of a muffled speaker somewhere on the ride. 'Ank ooo.'

Paul got his wallet out of his trousers once again. In the back section he found two slithers of paper, one more rigid than the other. The rigid rectangle was the card that copper had given him the other day. Luciano or something. Tall cunt. He slipped that back in. The second was the roughly ripped edge of an envelope with a mobile number on. The number that Danny had given him. The number for The Club. He gritted his teeth and pushed that back too, shaking his head to himself.

Within a minute, Scoop had eased to a halt, the music abruptly snapping off. Levi looked up and grinned at his daddy. 'Muhr!' he said, his nose wrinkling. 'Muhr, Dahee! Pweees!'

Chief Manager Hurley's secretary Simon Thurston was sitting behind his desk at Granton looking through the list of names he'd sent to the police. Probably not very much information for them to go on, he thought, playing with the tip of his collar. Just names and crimes and reasons for leaving. He toyed with the idea of sending more details on each of the people listed, but Chief Manager Hurley had made it clear that she didn't want some of the staff notes going into the public domain. 'Keep as much of it in-house as is sensible, Simon,' she had said, and so he had tried.

He had missed it the first time around though. He just listed the names without truly thinking of them or acknowledging who these people were, but now that he was reading over the list again, one name leapt out at him. A name that before a couple of weeks ago he wouldn't have paid any attention to at all. He logged on to his computer and typed the name in. A couple of seconds later, the screen was filled with that person's file. The mugshot at the top of the page confirmed Thurston's suspicions. Lifting up the receiver, he tapped in Luchewski's number and waited for him to pick up. He did so surprisingly quickly.

'Luchewski.'

'Oh, hello, Inspector Luchewski. This is Simon Thurston – Chief Manager Hurley's secretary at Granton.'

'Hi.'

'Hi. Just phoning to let you know that Robert Francombe – the last of the guards from Daniel Wiseman's time at Granton – is here today, if you'd like to come in and speak with him.'

'Oh, thank you, Mr Thurston. Yes I would. I'll come in sometime later if that's all right? Well, either myself or my sergeant.'

'Yes, of course.' Thurston turned to the picture filling his computer screen. 'And there's one other thing, Inspector. One of the people on the list I sent you: Jason Thickett. Well, I think I've recently seen him on television.'

Chapter Seventeen

Detective Constable Mark James was steadily working his way through his designated list. After interviewing people, he would fastidiously put thick ticks next to their names with his red Bic biro and write the word 'Done' alongside them. So far this morning he had already 'Done' two previous Granton employees – one of whom seemed pleasant enough, making him coffee and digging out a packet of Penguins to mark the occasion. They had joked together about the changeable weather and the state of English cricket, and Mark had felt the sort of connection you always hoped for as a young and aspiring copper. The other interviewee, though, had been a bit rude. He'd stood in the doorway in his pyjamas scratching and yawning while DC James had asked him questions. The man barely answered in grunts and coughs, and Mark had come away with little more information than he had had before knocking on the door.

Mark consulted his list as he walked along the street. *Keith Humphreys. 31 Oakfield Avenue.* Unusual spelling, he thought to himself. Humphreys. Surely it should have been spelt *Humphries*. Humphrey – spelt H-U-M-P-H-R-E-Y – was a Christian name, wasn't it? Humphries – now *that* was a surname. He made a mental note to triple-check the spelling when he got back to the office later.

Arriving at the right address, DC James pushed the rusting gate open and walked up the path. The house had obviously seen better times. The paintwork was grubby and the patch of earth in front of the uPVC bay window was bumpy with bricks and chunks of cement from some building work undertaken at some point many moons ago. A scruffy lean-to garage to the left of the house was shielding a worn old car from the elements, and a piece of guttering had been displaced resulting in a long brown stain from the top of the house down to the ground floor window. A small concrete ramp had been built up to the front door and Mark walked up this before pushing the seventies looking doorbell. He waited for one minute before pushing the bell again. He whistled softly to himself and fidgeted with his list once more. *Keith Humphreys. Humphreys!*

He was just about to turn on his heel when the door opened. Not much. Just slightly. Just enough for a face to appear through.

'What is it? Who's there?' The face belonged to a very short, very fat, very aged man wearing glasses.

'Oh. Hello. Are you Mr Humphreys?'

'*Mrs* Humphreys!' The wrinkled old face scowled at him. '*Mrs* Humphreys! Are you blind?'

'Oh.' Detective Constable Mark James started to blush. 'I'm terribly sorry.' He tried to move things on as quickly as possible. 'Is your husband in?'

'Husband? Husband?' The face contorted painfully, the mouth set in disgust. 'Husband! What are you talking about? My husband's been dead for nigh on twenty years. What is this? Who are you?'

'I'm looking for a Mr Keith Humphreys. Does he live here? According to my list he lives here.' Mark's face was getting more crimson by the second. Nothing had prepared him for this onslaught, not even his encounter with Mr Yawning Man earlier that morning.

'Of course he lives here. He's my son. Who are you? What do you want him for?'

Mark swallowed hard. 'I'm Detective Constable Mark James of the Metropolitan Police.' He nervously fished his card out of his jacket pocket and showed her. 'I just need to ask him a few questions.'

The woman had a look of disbelief on her leathery old face, but after a few moments spent chewing her dentures and mulling it over she said: 'What do you want to talk to my Keithy for? He's a good boy.'

'I just need to ask him a few questions about his time at Granton. That's all. Just a few questions.'

'Pah!' The old sow in front of him spat a green gobbet out onto the garden path. 'Granton! Don't mention that name in my house. Bunch of crooks there. Selling people out to save their skins, that's what they do there. It's immoral.' Her face seemed to turn in on itself like a runner-up in a gurning competition. 'What is it? More money being nicked, is it? Doesn't surprise me. All the bosses are on the take.'

'Is Keith in?' Mark felt his lips moving. 'I really would like to speak to him.'

The woman opened the door a tiny bit more, and Mark could see that she wasn't short, but sitting in a wheelchair. Suddenly the ramp he was standing on made sense.

'He's in, but he's in bed. And I don't want him disturbed. He's working nights and he needs all the sleep he can get. He works hard – very hard – my Keithy, and I won't have him disturbed. Not even by the police. You'll have to come back later.' And with that the wrinkly old witch slammed the door.

Mark stood there for a couple of seconds, his nose just inches from the door. He really was getting a lesson in rudeness today. Stepping up the path he tutted and put a big red tick (but no 'Done') next to Keith Humphreys' name.

On the way back to his car, Mark passed a red, old shape Ford Fiesta – the ones before they started to look like miniature, budget versions of Ford Focuses. One of the things they were all told to look out for that morning was a red, old shape Ford Fiesta. A W-reg, red, old shape Ford Fiesta. Mark's eyes shot down to the plate. It wasn't a W-reg. He shrugged to himself as he walked on, instantly forgetting about it, preferring instead to ponder the dreadful state of manners in society today and how nasty and crude some old women could be.

Hal was pleased to be away from the office. The sniggers and titters behind his back; the winks and nudges that he wasn't meant to see (or was he?); Baldwin and his socially dysfunctional ways of dealing with things (ha-fucking-ha!); the shuffling sergeants; the lack of eye contact, it pissed him off no end. It pissed him off and angered him that, today, his life had changed. And that change hadn't been down to him. Hadn't been something of his own choice and making. He'd been stuck in the stocks, and everybody else had been armed with a rotten tomato and it was down to them as to whether or not they threw it. Baldwin had thrown it (of course), so had the shuffling sergeants and nudging knobheads. Pelted him for all they were worth. Spineless bastards. To her credit, though, Singh hadn't reacted. Hadn't mentioned it in any way. She had carried on filing reports, reading through statements, double-checking forensics with him all morning without mentioning any of it. So it came as something of a surprise when she finally broached the subject during the traffic-jammed drive over to Granton YOI.

'So, your father was on TV, sir?'

Hal's head momentarily whipped to the left to look at Singh.

'Mmm.' His eyes stared back at the number plate of the car sitting in front of him. He didn't really want to talk about it. Winding his window down he focused on the awning of a roadside café, his hands tapping out some imaginary tune on the driver's wheel.

'What was his name again?'

Hal sighed. 'Victor Liddle.' A man was coming out of the café holding a sugar-coated Danish pastry and a polystyrene cup of coffee. Hal thought that the trousers the man was wearing were very green. Too green, in fact.

'Liddle and Moore, was it?'

'Mmm.'

'I can't remember them myself. I remember the Two Ronnies. And Little and Large. They were rubbish. The big one kept doing a Deputy Dawg impersonation and the thin one looked like a mentally retarded pipe cleaner. Talked like he was deaf. I must have been too young for Liddle and Moore. Were they on the BBC?'

'Yes. BBC One.' The tortoise head of pride peeped out for a second.

'When were they on? I mean, what years?'

'Why, Singh? Are you really all that interested?' He found it difficult to keep the annoyance out of his voice. Looking up, Hal saw that the man in green trousers was gone.

'Well. Yes I am, actually, sir. I am quite interested.'

Hal rubbed his nose as the traffic started moving again.

'Liddle. That must have been his stage name, was it?' She wasn't letting this dog lie down and die.

'Mmm.' Hal shook his head. He was going to have to go along with it for a bit. 'He felt that Luchewski was far too difficult a surname to make it on the comedy circuit. Besides, those were less enlightened times. The name Luchewski would have conjured up images of the Communist red peril. Thoughts of KGB spies and mushroom clouds. He would never have got taken on if he'd kept his real surname.'

'So, was he Russian? I mean, are you Russian, sir?'

'Polish originally – going way way back. One strain of the family moved to Russia at some point, then my great-grandfather came to Britain just before the Revolution. Thought he was in New York, so hopped off the boat. Turns out he was in Swansea. Married a local girl and settled down.'

'So where were you born?' Singh smiled with her eyes but her mouth did not.

'Swansea. Just before my father hit the big time. Want to know my birth weight or my first word while you're at it, Singh?'

'Sorry, sir. I don't mean to pry. Just interested.'

The traffic grumbled to a halt once again. Hal punched the wheel and looked at his watch. 'Fucking roadworks,' he muttered under his breath.

They sat in silence for a short while, Hal squinting against the sun that had suddenly decided to pop out from behind a cloud, Singh dusting some invisible dirt off her trousers. Then, without warning, Singh started again.

'I never knew you had a daughter, sir?'

'What?'

'Lily, isn't it? Your daughter's name? I didn't know –'

'No, you didn't!' Hal's voice teetered on violent, the words spilling out at a hundred miles an hour. 'You didn't know I had a daughter! You didn't know because I didn't tell you! And I'll bet you didn't know I was gay, did you?! Not that I'm gay anyway but, whatever I am, I bet you didn't know about it, did you? And do you know why you didn't know? You didn't know because I didn't fucking tell you! I didn't fucking tell you, Singh. Because in this life, it is possible for someone to have a working relationship with someone else, without revealing the tiniest, most insignificant details of their life! For Christ's sake, I don't really know anything about you, Singh and, to be frank, I don't particularly *want* to know anything about you. All I need is for you to do your job. Do it well and shut the fuck up!' Hal tried to prise his fingernails out of the steering wheel.

For the remainder of the journey, Singh didn't utter a single word.

'Robert Francombe,' the tallish man in front of Hal held out his hand. He wore a navy blue jumper with a shirt and tie tucked underneath. 'Let me show you around.' He smiled at Singh, then returned his gaze to Hal. 'Is she coming with us?'

Singh stepped forward and frowned. 'Yes *she* is! Is that a problem, Mr Francombe?'

The man shrugged his shoulders. 'Sorry to sound so off-colour, Miss –'

'I prefer Sergeant. Sergeant Singh'

The corners of Hal's mouth turned up in amusement. He'd pissed her off in the car and now here she was taking it out on this poor unsuspecting sod. Life's dreadful pecking order.

'Sorry to sound so off-colour, Sergeant Singh, but we don't tend to take many ladies into the main holding area. Some of the boys inside might make some quite unpleasant comments.'

'That's all right, Mr Francombe. I'm a big girl. I can handle it.'

Hal nodded in agreement. 'She's a big girl.'

'Very well. Follow me.'

The white metal gates to D wing were pulled back and the three

160

of them stepped into the main hall. Five or six young lads were crowded around a pool table, laughing at something on the floor. Some others were sat on a brown stained sofa watching Phil and Holly on a television set fifteen feet above the ground. A thin weedy-looking boy in glasses was studiously reading a book on a chair in the corner of the hall. Francombe pointed over to him.

'That's Luke. Doing his GCSE English with us. Last exam's tomorrow. How's the revision going, Luke?' The boy wrinkled up his nose. Hal thought that he looked about fourteen. Francombe dropped his voice to a whisper. 'Stabbed a man in the head.'

Beyond an idle ping-pong table, Hal could see the stairs leading to the cells above. Sorry, not cells, Hal corrected himself. Rooms. The boys here stayed in 'rooms'. The whole area was painted grey with the occasional splash of vibrant reds or soothing blues – an attempt to de-dehumanise the place. Hal felt that it didn't really work. An institution was an institution and no amount of jazzed-up modern art decoration could detract from that fact. Hell was always going to be hell, even with a couple of aspidistras dotted around the joint.

'The recreation areas are all exactly the same. Each of the wings has one. They haven't changed very much either – apart from a little bit of paintwork. C wing would have looked just like this when Danny Wiseman was here.'

'Fackin' 'ell!' One of the pool players had detected the presence of a woman. 'Look at 'er! 'Ello, darlin'!' Some of the others started wolf-whistling.

'Right! Keep it calm, you lot. You've seen a woman before.'

'Not like her we haven't, Franny.'

'Wanna come and stare at the patch of ceiling above my bed, sweetheart?' Some of the others laughed. 'I've got a nice little package for you to unwrap. Just here!' The boy grabbed his crotch.

'Yeah, little's about it,' another boy poked the crotch-grabber with his cue.

'Fuck off, fish feet.'

'I said shut it, or you'll be consigned to your rooms for the rest of the afternoon.'

'All right, all right, Franny. Keep it fucking real.' The boys went back to their game. Hal couldn't help feeling that he'd walked into a youth club, not a prison for the young. They seemed so normal, so typical of teenage boys that it was difficult for him to come to terms with the fact that some of them had attacked, raped, or killed people.

161

Francombe led Hal and Singh to a table. Hal recognised it as one from IKEA. 'Take a seat, please. They're good boys really. Most of them. Just made a few mistakes and now they're paying the price. A lot of them learn their lesson and we never see them again.'

Hal cut to the chase. 'Mr Francombe, tell me about Daniel Wiseman and the time he spent here.'

'Nothing much to tell, I don't think. Kept his head down, kept clean, didn't stir up too much trouble. A nice lad really. Mum used to visit him. Don't recall ever seeing much of his dad. Like I said, not much to tell really.'

'Did you know he was gay?'

'To be honest, I assumed. You just know sometimes, don't you?'

Hal coughed. 'It's quite a difficult thing to be gay, I'd've thought, in a place like this. A lot of macho posturing and anti-queer sentiment.'

'You'd be surprised, Inspector. Our youngsters can be more accepting than you would imagine.'

They listened to the *click-clack* of the pool balls for a moment before Singh started to speak.

'Did you work with Raymond Larby, sir?'

'Mmm.' His eyes momentarily darted down to the ground. 'I did.'

'Did you get on well with him?'

Francombe looked as though Singh had just insulted his gran. 'No, I did not. I didn't like Raymond Larby one little bit, Sergeant.'

'Why not, sir?'

'He was a horrible man. I know we shouldn't speak ill of the dead but … Let's just say we should make an exception for Raymond Larby.'

'Why didn't you like him, sir?' Singh pushed.

'He was corrupt. Supplied drugs to the boys. Not that I knew that while I was working with him. He was doing it behind everyone's back. I don't think many people did know, but all the staff were aware of the complaint.'

'Complaint?' Hal pulled his chair a little closer to Francombe's. 'What complaint?'

'One of the boys made a complaint against him.'

'What sort of a complaint?'

'Said that Raymond Larby had tried to feel him up. In the treatment room.'

'The treatment room?'

'Yes. The doctor's treatment room. Old Dr Saunders – died a

162

few years back – had his own treatment room in the main annexe.'

'What did this boy say exactly? What did he say Mr Larby had done to him?'

'I don't really know the details, Inspector. All I know is that one of the boys – I can't even remember his name now – had claimed that Raymond Larby made an inappropriate … suggestion … contact – I don't know really – in the treatment room. You'd have to consult his record if you want to know any more. This was during Governor Burgess's time though, so I very much doubt there'll be any record of it. There was a lot of corruption under Governor Burgess. He ignored most of the things that went on.'

'Too busy embezzling to do his job properly, it would appear,' Hal smirked at Francombe, who gently nodded in agreement.

'It would seem so.'

The *This Morning* theme tune blared out from across the other side of the room. Hal waited for it to subside before continuing.

'Does Granton still have its own treatment room, Mr Francombe? What I really mean to say is, does it have its own doctor?'

Francombe shook his head. 'Not any more. All medical provision is contracted out to private companies now. If one of the boys is sick, we have to call someone in to have a look at him. Same thing goes for dental and psychiatric help. The current gov –' he pulled himself up, 'the current Chief Manager think it's probably cheaper in the long run not to have a doctor on the premises.'

'FUCKIN' ACE, FUCKIN' BOLLOCKS!' One of the pool players screamed at the top of his lungs. 'BEAT YA INTA THE FUCKIN' GRAHND, YA PUSSY!'

'You jammy fucker!' another boy shouted back.

'Right, you lot,' Francombe got up from his chair and started to make his way over to them. 'What did I just say about keeping the noise down?'

'Keep it calm, Franny. Just havin' a laff.'

'Well shut up then!'

Hal smiled at Singh but she didn't smile back.

Hal dropped Singh back at the station before pushing on to Greenwich. He was sick of the cold shoulder treatment she was giving him. 'Check the Granton interviews, chase up any missing ones – check the garden centre statements too – put them all together, see if you can spot anything odd. You're good at that.' Even before he said it he realised it would sound condescending. He

163

didn't mean it to be, but it was how it came out and it was how Singh had taken it.

'Sir,' she had grimaced through tight lips and he knew instantly that she wanted to punch his lights out. She had slammed the door shut and strolled steadily towards the stairs at Hartshorn without once turning to look back at him. Before driving away, he'd speed-dialled Lily but the ring tone just cut straight through to her answerphone. 'If you want to leave a message ...' Hal had hung up and restarted the engine.

Using back streets to bypass the centre of Lewisham, Hal found his brain trying to mentally beat him up. He was bitter and angry, tired and desperate. And it was all the fault of that fucking journalist. 'Listen to yourself,' his brain was telling him. 'Always blaming others. Always in the right. Everybody else is wrong. Listen to you. You're always so fucking certain of yourself. Well you're not. Don't deny it. All of this is your fault. All of this is because you can't keep Mr Donger in your pants. Face up to it. It's all because of you.' Hal quickly pulled the car over and dug about in the glove compartment. He pulled out *OK Computer* and put in on full blast. 'Airbag' kicked in and the dashboard seemed to rattle with the noise.

Dr A. D. Potterton
BSc (Edin)
MPhil (Cantab)
PhD (London)

The bronze plaque on the door had read like a Japanese tourist's itinerary. 'He's at the gym,' the stuffy grey-haired old harridan of a secretary had almost spat at him over the tops of her heavy-rimmed specs. Her cheeks were sunken and her hands covered in liver spots. 'Boxing.'

'But I've arranged to see him,' Hal protested. 'I booked an appointment. It's a murder enquiry.' He patted the files he held by his side.

'I'm well aware of that, Inspector. And so is he. He said to tell you he'd see you there.'

'What? At the gym?'

'Three doors down. In the basement. "Bazzer's Gym".' She agonised over the name Bazzer as though having to merely say the word made her tongue burn. 'He's expecting you.'

Bazzer's Gym was not the seedy, run-down, blood-spattered place that Hal had pictured. He had expected to see chunky toothless men, with puffy cauliflower ears and sweat pouring down their faces, bashing seven shades of shit out of each other. Instead it turned out to be a rather more posh affair than that. Middle-aged, middle-class, upper income-bracketed men poncing about in their fancy sweat togs, tapping spotless punchbags, and skipping with ropes. One especially weedy character – wearing spectacles and a far too big black Adidas vest – stood in a corner punching thin air. Hal thought that he looked a little like Mr Muscle trying to swat flies. His ungloved hands snatched furiously at the space in front of him, his mouth making small 'phww' noises with each impotent knock. The owner had obviously called the place Bazzer's Gym in a bid to make the lawyers, accountants, managing directors and stockbrokers feel as if they were doing something gritty. Something real. Something where, for a couple of hours of the week, they could pretend to be Robert de Niro or Sylvester Stallone. They probably all secretly wished for a gnarly old man with a woolly hat on his head to stand in the corner shouting encouraging abuse at them.

Mr Muscle pulled his guard in tight against his imaginary opponent and jogged about a bit on the spot.

A boxing ring dominated the centre of the room, and Hal turned to watch the fight that was currently taking place. A short stumpy man in a blue headguard was landing the occasional punch on the torso of a tall wiry man wearing a red headguard. The dull slap, followed by the sound of involuntary exhalation, made Hal nervous. The tall man was undoubtedly Dr Potterton, and he wasn't very good. Hal wondered how much a month in membership fees he was paying to be bashed about like that. Far too much, he thought to himself. Suddenly Stumpy Man stepped in quickly and swung a powerful blow to the side of Potterton's head. His head jerked to the side, legs stumbling slightly, but Potterton recovered himself surprisingly well. He corrected his position and straightened up, only to receive another knock to the head. This time, stumpy man wasn't holding back. He pushed forward and continued pounding Potterton's face. One, two, three decent hits and Potterton tripped backwards and fell on his backside. Stumpy Man strolled back to his corner while Potterton crawled up and rubbed the back of his neck with his clumsy gloved hand.

'Call it a day?' Stumpy Man shouted over at Potterton.

'OK. If you like, Tone.'

Hal tried waving up to Potterton, the files clasped in his hands, but it was Stumpy Man who spoke first, causing Hal to switch his eyes quickly to the opposite side of the ring.

'Inspector Luchewski. I won't be long. Quick shower and I'll be with you. Good fight, eh?' he asked pulling the blue headguard over his bulbous little brow.

'There are three really effective ways of getting rid of anger. The first is to shout. Shout and scream until your lungs have squeezed it out of you.'

'Primal scream,' Hal interjected, shifting his buttocks on the changing room bench. Potterton was in the process of looping his silk tie over itself, his shirt still hanging outside of his trousers waiting to be tucked back in.

'Primal scream. Exactly. If you scream and scream and scream you feel as though you've let the anger out of your body. Which, let's face it, is where it should be. The longer it stays in the body, the more harm it can do. Secondly,' he bent over to slip on his tan suede shoes, 'exercising. And exercising hard. No gentle jog or stroll with Fifi the poodle around the park. I mean full-on aggressive cycling or running or working out. Really going for it. Pushing yourself to the extreme. Forcing yourself on when you feel you've given your all. Breaking the pain barrier.'

Hal unwittingly patted his stomach and thought about the gym. He kept meaning to get back, but recently he just felt like drinking. Drinking and shagging – not pumping iron. The thought of a strenuous workout made his whole body sigh with dull resignation.

'Number three,' Potterton continued, 'The next best thing to do after shouting and exercising is to punch someone. Someone or something. Some people punch walls, some people punch their spouses.' Some people punch fellow DIs, thought Hal. 'Whatever and whoever, it still gets anger out.' Potterton pushed the bottom of his shirt into his trousers and readjusted his belt. 'That's why I like boxing. It incorporates all three. You shout a bit – admittedly through a gum shield – you put your body through a surprisingly physical exertion, and you get to hit someone smack in the face. It's the perfect solution to anger control.'

'Your opponent didn't seem too good,' said Hal, his fingers impatiently flicking over the files on his lap. 'He didn't seem to hit you once.' Potterton looked Hal straight in the eyes. It was obvious that he wasn't certain whether Hal was paying him a compliment or criticising him. Hal wasn't too sure himself.

'No. Dave's very good actually. He's a professional sparring partner. I pay him forty quid a week to stand there and let me knock him about a bit. I mean, for goodness' sake, I enjoy boxing but I don't want to get hurt doing it.' Potterton pulled his suit jacket over his arms and shrugged it into place over his shoulders. 'There. Now, let's have a look at these files.'

Potterton sat down on the bench next to Hal and started reading through the reports. He hunched over the pictures and documents, reading silently to himself for a few minutes. Other sweaty men flitted in and out, paying them no attention. Doing business in the locker room was obviously quite a common occurrence, and to see a criminal psychologist helping a member of the constabulary was probably no different to seeing two lawyers discussing the finer points of shipping law.

After a while, the silence started to make Hal feel uncomfortable. 'If there's anything you can say that would help us. Anything you can pick –'

'Shhh,' Potterton interjected, his head not shifting from its position. Hal recoiled slightly with embarrassment, before turning to look at the room in which they were sitting. The floors were marble – or, at least, marble effect. The lockers, rows upon rows of them, were shiny and spotless and Hal realised that Bazzer's Gym was a fairly new establishment. Even the showers looked as though Jasper Conran had had a hand in designing them.

'This one …' Potterton eventually pipped. 'The boy. He was found in his bed, yes? The body had been moved after death and placed in the bed, yes?' Hal didn't have a chance to answer. 'And a pump had been used. On the neck. Whereas … this one …' he lifted up the photograph of Larby's head on top of the roof of the car, 'This one had been killed with an axe or some sort of weapon. No pump had been used, and the body was left as it was. Dumped in the corner. In fact, he didn't even just leave it where it fell. He went further than that. He removed the head and placed it on top of a car. An act that …' He seemed to search desperately for the right word, but never found it.

'Why the change in MO?' Hal asked, a little quieter this time.

Potterton sat up. 'I'd've thought that was obvious, Inspector.' He pulled two of the photographs off the pile. One of Wiseman, one of Larby. 'The notes left at the scenes as good as tell you why he changed his modus operandi. This one,' he pointed to Larby's picture, 'was killed out of anger or hatred. The murderer obviously hated him. The removal of the head was the final act intended to demean his memory. Whereas this one,' he pushed the photo of

Wiseman forward, 'this one was killed out of love.'

'Love?' Hal asked incredulously.

'Mmm. The pump in the neck. It was used to gently ease him out of this world. To let him die slowly and without much pain.'

'But the bump on the head? Surely that was painful?'

Potterton nodded and considered the point. 'Probably something the killer regrets. He needed to do something to restrain the boy. Perhaps that was all he could think of. But everything else is consistent. Even the fact that the blood was neatly collected in a bucket suggests that the killer respected the boy's space. The placing of the body in the bed, the pump – all of it points to the fact that the killer loved – or, if not loved, then at the very least highly regarded – Daniel Wiseman.'

They sat in silence for a few seconds while Hal digested this information.

'Then why remove a piece of the body and take it away with him?' Hal eventually enquired. 'And why cut off the hand?'

'The hand was obviously left deliberately so that you would find him. Again, an act of love of a sort. As for the midriff,' Potterton thought a little, his fingers gently rubbing the bridge of his nose, 'I don't know. But I would hazard a guess at ...' His eyes stared off to a point somewhere in the distance. 'He was trying to remove evidence. Getting rid of something incriminating.'

'Evidence? You mean sexual evidence?'

Potterton suddenly sat up dead straight and turned to face Hal. 'Have you ever thought about boxing? Big man like you. Could do some damage with those fists.'

The coffee in the plastic cup on his desk had gone cold. Not that it was especially tasty in the first place – vending machine coffee never seemed to taste anything like coffee to Stevie. Always far too watery and bland, like the machine had forgotten to add any actual coffee to the mix. They'd even put the prices up recently. Eighty pee for something with absolutely no nutritional value whatsoever. Eighty pee! And the machine constantly ran out of change. He'd pop a pound in and press the button for his change and nothing would come out, just a scrolling message saying 'NO CHANGE AVAILABLE ... SORRY ...' It was a rip-off. A bloody awful rip-off. He'd toyed with the idea of bringing in his own kettle. The problem was that his desk was right in the middle of the office, and the only plug sockets ran straight into the floor and were required for his computer and printer. He would have to put one of those three-plug adapter thingies in the ground to accommodate his kettle, and even then someone in the office would kick up a fuss saying it contravened health and safety or something.

Stevie picked up the cup and dropped it in the wastepaper bucket that sat to the side of his desk. He was starting to feel a little sick. He had read his story twenty-three times that morning and each time he read it his confidence and pride had dipped a tiny bit more. He felt a traitor. He felt as though he'd betrayed the kind of person that he was. He had made someone's sexuality a story – something to talk about. Something to be ashamed about. He'd gone and shone a torch at Luchewski and shouted, 'Here he is. Here's the freak. Come and have a laugh at the big old gay – the pervert!' What right did he have to do that? What right did he have to point the finger at someone just doing their job? And the daughter – his stomach churned. The twelve-year-old daughter, Lily. She probably didn't know Luchewski was gay. It's not the kind of thing fathers talk about with their daughters. And now she was probably having a hell of a time of it at school because of him. Stevie remembered his own schooldays. It was bad enough being gay yourself, struggling to get through the day – the finger-pointing, the punches, the kicks. How hard must it be if your *dad* is gay? Being ridiculed because of somebody else's choices. It just didn't bear thinking about.

He stared at the computer screen in front of him, the page completely bare. The editor wanted a follow-up. Something meaty. Something scandalous. Something that readers could really get their teeth into. Stevie shook his head. He knew exactly what he should write, but he was finding it difficult. He was beginning to feel guilty – not the best emotion for the hard-nosed journalist he sometimes day-dreamed he was. Luchewski didn't really deserve it. He was just a public servant doing a public service in a very public forum. He didn't need all the bad attention he was likely to be getting currently. He probably didn't need it at all.

Stevie sighed hard before starting to type.

Killing people was incredibly easy – he'd forgotten that. All you had to do was get yourself physically close to them and the rest was child's play. As soon as they turn away, BANG on the head and off you go. Simple. Not exactly rocket science. Something a child could do. In fact, it was something children regularly did in this black and tarnished society.

The next one was going to be a little trickier though. He'd never killed in such an exposed place before. There would be dozens, if not hundreds of people floating around. There would also be cameras – lots of them – filming everything. They would film him going in, and they would film him going out again, but he knew how to deal with the cameras. Never look up, keep your face down, put an extra little limp in your step and keep frowning – he knew that people found it difficult to recall the details of a face if that face was frowning. He also had his disguise. He checked out the beard in the mirror. Although it felt strange, it looked quite natural. Anyone not looking too closely would never suspect that it was false. The glasses helped too. Big heavy black-rimmed ones that left a dent on the bridge of his nose every time he put them on. The disguise was certainly good enough.

He squatted on the floor and checked the holdalls. He'd put the pump in even though he knew that it was going to be virtually impossible to use it in such an environment. Much more importantly though was the bow saw. After Danny – poor young Danny – he'd cleaned it up, scrubbing each individual tooth. It had soaked in a bucket overnight and the following morning he had polished it with wax. Now it sat crammed awkwardly into the bottom of the second holdall with his change of clothing on top.

The saw was important. It enabled him to do the one thing he desperately needed to do. It was vital to him. Vital for his well-being. In a sense it was the whole point of today's little visit.

And nothing – absolutely nothing – was going to stand in his way.

Chapter Eighteen

Luchewski was turning into one of the office turds. He had become grumpy and snappy recently, stamping on her for the smallest little thing. Well screw him again, she thought as she pushed down hard on the staple gun. He could dig his own grave if that was what he wanted. She was just going to stand back, impassively take all his bullshit, and watch him throw his career away. So what if he had just been outed in the press. He didn't have to take it out on her. She'd only been polite in the car, trying to make conversation about his daughter, and he'd crushed her like an empty Coke can. There really was no need for it.

Singh laid the freshly printed document on top of a brand new blue file on the side of her desk. She evened up the paper edges with the tips of her fingers, her pink nails scraping over the cardboard.

She understood the pressure he was under though. Three dead in three days (because, let's face it, she told herself, McKenzie was long dead). Three dead and no clues. And not only that. To be suddenly unveiled as a homosexual in what must be one of the most bigoted, racist, and homophobic institutions in the country must be rather daunting. She believed that he must be feeling exactly the way she'd felt when she first walked in through the doors of Hartshorn House three years ago. A tiny Indian girl with a funny name, in a business suit. She'd taken all the jibes, all the racist, sexist comments, and buried them deep inside herself. It fuelled the anger she knew she needed to succeed in this environment. No one knew how angry she could get, because no one had been allowed to see it. She utilised it and never let it break her public façade. She wanted to yell 'Fuck you!' at all the fat men in silly ties, but knew that a more effective 'Fuck you!' would be to do something better than them. Beat them at something professional. She wasn't going to lash out at Baldwin like Luchewski had done that morning. That was a car crash.

She dusted up some white papery confetti that had fallen out of the hole punch and dropped it into the recycle box against the wall. No doubt about it, Luchewski was losing her respect. Which was a pity, because she desperately wanted to respect him.

No answer from Lily's phone again, but a short and very acerbic message from Jackie.

'Oh well done, dickhead. You've done it again. Made a complete balls-up of everything as usual. Hope you're happy it's all out in the air now. Oh and, by the way, I don't know if you've given it that much thought, but you need to have a word with your daughter. I told her you'd phone so you'd better fucking phone and have a word. Right? She's in school so phone her tonight. Or even better, come and see her. Talk to her face to face. I might let you into the house if you're lucky!'

Hal deleted the message immediately. The pit of his stomach always seemed to drop away whenever he heard his ex-wife get angry. It reminded him of the bad old days. The days when they were bumpily splitting up because of his sexuality, their love for their young daughter pulling them even further apart. Jackie would shout and scream, and Hal would shout right back. Only Jackie always seemed to be shouting sense and Hal would be screaming indefensible nonsense back. He'd be spouting some load of old crap that nobody in their right mind could justify, while good old rational Jackie would be coming out with things that were difficult to undermine. Things that Hal really didn't want to hear. It was a time of his life that he tried hard to forget, but never completely succeeded.

Hal lifted the mobile in front of his face and scrolled through his contact list. Finding the name he was after he punched the 'Call' button and waited. After a couple of seconds it started ringing. Hal waited, looking at his watch as if that would help speed things up.

'I'm not available right now ...' the familiar voice dully intoned.

Bastard just turned his phone off, thought Hal. Saw that it was me calling and turned his phone off.

'... but if you leave a message and your number I'll get back to you later.'

BEEEP!

'Thanks a lot. That's really what I need right now. Some sneaky little git publishing crap stories about my sexuality. Cheers! I'm trying to find a murderer here, and all you've done is make me the butt of a load of queer jokes! Great. Exactly what I need, you ...' he tried to find the right word, 'you tit! Do you know what it's like being a copper? Well, no, you wouldn't because you're a journalist. A sneaky little journalist. I found out to my cost. Now I've got to talk to my daughter because of you. Bloody selfish idiot! I hope you go and die of –' Hal managed to stop himself. Even he felt that that was going too far. 'I hope you fucking fall off a ladder or something!'

He hung up.

Unfortunately the shouting didn't make him feel better.

In fact, it never had done.

The security guard saw the car coming and leaned out of his window to see who it was. He didn't recognise the car – an extremely muddy black Vauxhall Astra – so thought that he'd better lower the volume on Jeremy Vine. He was halfway through a discussion on British foreign policy and would like to have heard what the Governor of the Bank of England sounded like. But work was work and he had to be polite, so he twiddled the knob on his decaying old radio and smiled.

'Good afternoon, sir.'

A miserable-looking man with a fluffy beard wound the car window down. He fidgeted about with something on the passenger seat before thrusting his arm out at the security guard.

'Police,' said the man, flicking open and quickly shutting the ID card he was holding. 'I'm here to speak to Jason Thickett. I'm afraid there's been a terrible accident.'

The producer of *Britain's Toughest Jailbird* was in a flap. The ratings had taken a severe dive in the last few days, one of the contestants was threatening to walk if he didn't start getting decent food, two of the camera team were down with a stomach bug and now there was a policeman wanting to speak to Jason Thickett. It just wasn't his week. To top it all he was certain he could feel his male pattern baldness getting worse. Stress could do that to you. Give it a few more days and it would be coming out in clumps. There would be nothing for it but to bite the bullet and go back to that awful trichologist with the bad breath and the sticky fingers. She had fingered his scalp, advised applying shampoo number three ('For ex-*treeeeem* hair loss. I only use it in the most ex-*treeeeem* cases') and recommended having an electric net strapped to his head to stimulate 'follicular activity'. All for seventy pounds a session. Rubbing his hand over his thinning pate, he shook his head and stepped into the ramshackle makeshift office. He desperately needed a coffee. Or a couple of lines of coke.

'Daniel Ferris,' he said marching up to the bearded man in front of him, hand outstretched. 'Producer.'

The detective reached out and clasped his hand. 'Inspector Luchewski,' he growled. 'Inspector Harry Luchewski of the Metropolitan Police.

Thumper was sulking. He was lying on the floor, staring upwards, flicking the Vs at the cameras hidden behind the mirrors. The other inmates were doing their best to ignore him.

'I wan' soom proper fookin' food. I carn manage if I doan get soom proper fookin' food. Yer bastards. I'll fookin' leave if I doan get fed proper.'

Jason was sitting on the sofas with Desi and Redman. Every time Thumper moaned, they shook their heads and tutted loud enough for him to hear.

'Yous lot can shut up too. Buncha fookin' queers. Yous doan need food like I does. I'm protesting for me stumach.'

'Oh stop fuckin' going on, yer twat.' Desi was starting to get pissed off. 'Yer starting to piss me off.'

'I'll fookin' land one on yous if yous doan shoot yous fookin' mouth.'

'Fuck off! We're all hungry, you idiot. Just shut up about it or fuck off. Give the rest of us some fuckin' peace!'

Jason smiled. He wondered how this exchange was coming across on televisions out in the real world. Were people even watching? It was difficult for him to believe sometimes and, every now and then, he found himself doing something that he shouldn't be – the thought that he was being constantly watched slipping his mind. It was strange that even here, in such an intensely focussed situation, you could forget all about the thousands of pairs of eyes scrutinising everything that you did. Had Thumper forgotten, or was he simply playing to the camera? Perhaps that was what Desi was doing too. Playing to the gallery. Once you started to think about it, it became a total headfuck. You couldn't trust anyone. Not even yourself. Things you thought were true about yourself became things you just had to question. Things you took for granted about the way you behaved became things that you could no longer rely on.

'I'm desperate. Give me soom fookin' food. Now!'

Suddenly the door leading out of the studio swung open, and one of the studio hands peered around. Thumper heard the swoosh of the door and twisted his thick neck to try and see.

'Wahey! Aboot fookin' time. Give us soom proper food, or I'm goanna deck soom cont.'

The boy looked about nervously and scurried up to the sofas where Jason, Desi, and Redman were sitting. Jason thought that he looked like a sickly little mouse and a laugh started bubbling down in his chest. It was soon squashed, however, when the boy leaned in close to Jason and whispered something that seemed to tickle his ear.

'Come with me.'

'Eh?'

'I said come with me. It's important.' The boy nodded his head in the direction of the door and jerkily started moving.

'What's going on?' Jason seemed to automatically straighten up off the couch. 'Where am I going?' He trailed slowly behind the studio hand who looked faintly ridiculous in his oversized trousers and baggy basketball top.

'What's all this about?' Jason could hear Desi behind him. 'Is he being evicted?'

'Whada yous dooin'?' Thumper started to wail. 'Where's me groob? I wan' me fookin' groob!'

'I don't know how the poor girl puts up with you.'

'She grins and bears it and keeps one eye on her lovely career. That's how. Anyway, I don't know how your sergeants put up with you. Poor old Green. What is he now? Fifth in two years, is he?'

'Sixth.'

'Sixth? Oh, sorry. I obviously forgot one.'

'I boost them on to better things. That's what I do. Give them the benefit of my vast experience –'

'And waistline!'

'Like I said, I give them the benefit of my vast experience, and then *pwff,*' Burlock did a strange movement with his fingers, 'Off they go. Fluttering their little wings to peck up the seed of a greener and better pasture.'

'You do not! You scare the shit out of them.'

'I don't!'

'You do. You worry them into believing that they're going to have to spend the rest of their career putting up with your fishing anecdotes and they run away. Every time.'

'What exactly have you got against my fishing stories? You've brought them up before.'

Hal turned and smiled at Burlock. 'Nothing,' he said his tone softer. 'I've got nothing against your fishing stories. They're the highlight of my week.'

'What's going on?' Jason frowned at the producer who looked seriously more frazzled than the last time he'd seen him. 'Where am I going? Is this a task?'

The producer shook his head and tried to flatten down a chunk of his irregularly spiky hair.

'No. No. This is no task, Jason. There's someone to see you. A policeman. In here.' He opened the door with what seemed to Jason to be an over-dramatic flourish. In the sparsely furnished room stood a tallish man with a beard wearing thick-rimmed NHS specs. He stood with his arms folded, his face cold and impassive.

'You'd better go in,' the producer suggested. 'He needs to have a word with you.'

Jason shuffled in shaking his head. 'This better not be some kind of set up. You'd better not be trying to get me kicked out.'

The producer pushed the door shut behind the boy, before turning to the studio hand.

'Come on. We'd better leave them to it.' They walked down the corridor back to the control room.

A dreadful business, thought the producer. Dreadful. Finding out your father had just lost both legs in a car accident, not knowing whether or not he would make it through the night. Horrible. Could work in the show's favour, though. Bit of publicity. Might bring back a few viewers. Sympathy voters and that. Yes. Could be just what the doctor ordered.

He smiled as he turned a corner, and totally forgot to ask himself why the policeman had been carrying two large canvas bags.

The rain had started to fall. Gently at first, then a tad heavier. Not light enough for the lowest setting on the windscreen wipers to be sufficient, but then again not heavy enough to warrant switching the lever up to the second position. Hal flicked back and forth between the two, alternating between not being able to see where he was going and hearing the wiper scrape dryly across the glass.

'You've got to keep your mind on the job. Focus for a while. Find this murdering bastard and *then* analyse your private life.' Burlock shoved a finger into the back of his mouth to try and pick some food out from between his teeth. He hooked his arm around and fished something out. 'You have to focus. Be professional.' He looked at it before flicking it onto the floor.

'I know,' replied Hal, glaring down at the area in front of Burlock's feet. 'Do you know how much it costs to have this car cleaned?'

Burlock ignored him. 'Punching Baldwin doesn't help. I mean, I know he's a right shitty little tosspot, but –'

'I know, I know.'

'Do you though?'

'Eh?'

'I mean, you say "I know. I know", but do you know? I mean, *really*?'

'What are you on about?'

'Well if you keep taking it out on Singh, the poor girl's going to hate you. And if the poor girl's going to hate you, you're going to have one more enemy waiting to see you fall. An enemy that stands at your side and sees everything that you do – all the good, all the bad. But it'll be the bad that she makes a note of and will use against you when the moment is ripe.'

'*"The moment is ripe"*?'

'Aye. The girl's ambitious. You know that. She's going to want to be made DI any day soon. And rather than moving on to get that, she just might stay put and drag you down so that she can take your place. See what I'm saying?'

'Oh, shut up.' Hal chuckled. 'You do talk some bollocks!'

'Well,' Burlock winked. 'I may do. But keep it professional. That's all I'm saying.' He stared out of the window for a moment before breaking the silence once again. 'Where are we going did you say?'

'Not far now. Couple of miles on. Granton kid. Taking part in a reality show – *Britain's Toughest Jailbird*.'

'Never heard of it.'

'Me neither, but it's been some years since I've been in a TV studio. Thought I'd take a look.'

'You enjoying your time on television, Jason?'

Jason was sitting on a chair in front of a small desk in the middle of the room. The copper kept walking in circles, around and around the table so that Jason had to continually turn his head to see him. After a while, Jason gave up and concentrated on a clock that was fixed to the wall opposite. The red second hand rotated smoothly – not jerkily like other clocks – and gave the impression that time was moving more swiftly than it should have been.

'Having fun appearing on television, are you? Good fun, is it?'

'What's going on?' Jason folded his arms and slouched down into the chair. 'I wanna speak to my lawyer. I'm not saying anything without my lawyer.'

'Don't worry.' The copper's hand touched him on the shoulder. Jason recoiled automatically. 'You won't need your lawyer. I just want to ask you a few questions. That's all. Just a couple of questions.'

'What about?'

'About where you were on certain dates.'

'What dates? What are you on about?'

'June 3rd last year? September 8th? November 11th?'

'What? I don't know what you mean.'

The copper stopped at the opposite end of the table. Jason took his eyes off the clock and stared at the man's face for a few seconds. He looked sad, as if he was on the verge of tears, the sides of his mouth drooping downwards into his beard.

'I don't know what you're on about,' Jason repeated. 'I really don't.'

The copper carried on walking around the table to the spot behind Jason's chair.

'Perhaps you do. Perhaps you don't. It doesn't really matter any more. It really doesn't matter. *I* know where you were. *I* know what you were doing. I also know who you were with.'

Suddenly a piece of the jigsaw slotted into place somewhere in Jason's brain.

'Hold on. I know you, don't I? I recognise your face.'

'I'm sorry, Jason. I really, *truly* am.' With that the copper released the heavy cudgel he had been concealing up his sleeve and lashed out at the back of Jason Thickett's head.

'How is Lily, anyway? What is she now, eleven? Twelve? I haven't seen her in years.'

'She's twelve. Year … eight, is it? You know, the second year. Says she wants to move in with me.'

'Haaah!' Burlock spat a loud laugh out of his wide mouth.

'What's so funny?'

'Nothing. Nothing. Only …'

'Yes?'

'It's not really a very good idea, is it?'

'Why not?' Hal felt rankled. 'What's wrong with living with me?'

'Listen, Harry. I've known you for years now. I know how much you love your own space. You hate any sort of intrusion. For Christ's sake, you can't stand it if someone walks into your office without knocking. Never mind having a teenage girl with PMT storming in and out of the house looking for her Justin Timberlake albums, giving you filthy looks, and spitting in yer porridge when you're not looking. Remember, I've been there. I've had to put up with four of the little witches!'

'I don't hate intrusion.'

'You do, you daft bugger. You love your own space. I remember when you had those plumbers around, putting in your new boiler. Hated every minute they were there, if I remember rightly.'

'Yeah, only because they were rubbish. Left bits of pipe and plasterboard all over the floor. Stubbed my toe on a box of pipe joint crimpers one morning. Bloody hopeless they were.'

'Aye, aye.' Burlock didn't sound convinced. 'Whatever.' There was a pause as Burlock scratched the tip of his nose. 'You're practically misanthropic, man.'

He didn't have long.

Jason's body was twitching on the floor next to the table, spittle dribbling out of the side of his mouth. He hadn't made a noise, which was good. Danny had given a sharp yelp before collapsing, and he was pleased that this time it had been silent. So far.

He quickly unzipped the first of the holdalls and pulled out the pump with the extension, the saw, a kitchen knife, and a roll of duct tape. Reaching into his jacket pocket, he removed a digital voice recorder and the laminated piece of card. He looked around for a plug socket and found one. Hurriedly he pushed the end of the extension into it. The pump was set and ready to go.

The boy shook violently on the floor and he was suddenly overcome with a strong desire to comfort him. Crouching beside him, he stroked the smooth youthful face.

'Shhh. There, there, Jason. It's all right. It's all going to be all right. I'm going to take all the pain away. I'm going to make you feel better.'

'I used to love Liddle and Moore. Cracking telly. Proper telly. Not all this *Britain's Toughest Bugger* bloody nonsense. Total crap that is.'

Hal put the car in neutral and waited behind the large white van in front of him, the chassis humming softly beneath the two men.

'Don't know why you never told me before that Victor Liddle was your dad. I wouldn't have told anyone – you know me.' Burlock sounded a little hurt. 'I'd've kept it to myself.'

'I know.' Hal found himself wanting to explain, even though a tiny part of him said that there was absolutely no reason for him to explain *anything*. 'I think I just didn't want people to see me as just Victor Liddle's son. Didn't want them saying "There goes Victor Liddle's son. He's been given everything on a plate". Do you know what I mean? I just wanted the world to see me as Harry Luchewski. Just wanted my own identity.'

'I know.' Burlock smiled warmly at Hal.

'It's like when I was at school. Everyone knew who my dad was. The kids, the teachers. They all knew. They always referred to me as the Liddle boy. I never really got to use my proper surname for the whole of my school career. So, once I got to university, I totally blanked it out. Never really told anybody – except for Jackie, of course.'

'Of course.'

'She understood.' An ice-cold sensation ran down his spine as he thought back to the awful phone message she'd left him earlier. 'She knew how I felt.'

The van was still sitting still in front of the TT. They were trapped in a narrow one-way road just outside Hounslow, the rain continuing to spot itself over the windscreen.

'Well, it explains how you've got such a nice house and are always driving classy cars. I did always wonder. Thought you might've won the lottery or summat. Or robbed a bank. I did once think that you might be on the take.'

'What?'

'That was before I got to know you better.'

'I should hope so.'

The driver in front climbed out of the van and skipped quickly away, disappearing in front of his vehicle, his door wide open.

'Something's going on here.' Hal lowered his window and craned his neck out to try and see.

'I'll go and have a look.' Burlock unclipped his seatbelt and heaved his mass out of the passenger door.

The pump was too loud.

'Shit!'

He'd tried it out before making the insertion with the knife and the fucking thing was too loud! It echoed around the flimsy walled

180

room. He stood up and tried to compose himself. He felt lost. This wasn't supposed to happen. If he turned the pump on somebody walking past the room was going to hear it and wonder what was going on. He couldn't be caught. Not now. Not now that things were going so well. The pump had worked brilliantly in Danny's bedsit. The soft furnishings had smothered any sound it made. But here ... here was going to be impossible.

'Shit! Think, think!' He tried to push down the panic in his chest.

'Nnggn.'

Jason grunted. Grabbing the voice recorder and laminate, the bearded man squatted over the still twitching body.

'Read this, Jason. Read this. Then I'll cover your mouth with duct tape and we'll finish the job.'

'Cyclist. Knocked off his bike. Fiesta, a few cars up.' Burlock climbed back into the car. 'Woman driver. He's a bit shaken up. She's on her phone.' He snapped the seatbelt back into place. 'Clearing the way in a minute. Should be all right then.'

'I think I'm destined to spend the rest of my life in traffic jams,' said Hal moments before the van driver hopped back into his vehicle and eased off his handbrake.

He wasn't responding. The boy just wasn't responding. He wasn't reading any of the words on the card at all. The man tried holding the boy's head up so that he could see more clearly, but it didn't seem to make a difference. All the boy did was moan. At one point it sounded like he was asking for help, but that was all. The man put the laminate and the voice recorder back into the holdall and strapped a piece of duct tape across the boy's mouth.

He'd been thinking about his predicament, and he came to the realisation that there were three possible options. Firstly, he could carry on and use the pump regardless. He could risk being caught and finish things off the way he had planned them – using the pump and the saw, before changing his clothes and getting out of there. This seemed far too dangerous a solution and he needed to consider another of his options.

Secondly, he could walk away now. Leave everything as it was and just go. Although the safest of the three choices, his head refused to believe that it was possible to do such a thing. He'd come so far and done so well in the last few days. The police were nowhere near him – he knew that for a fact. They didn't have a clue.

Why waste the opportunity now? Why do something now that would hurt his obsessive brain forever? Walking away was impossible.

The last option was a compromise and the one that he already realised he was going to take. Forget the pump. Use the metal bar and kill the boy. Try to saw and take the evidence of sin. Try. At least try.

His hand was reaching out to the table where the slightly bloodied metal pipe was sitting, when a tiny knock on the door froze him to the spot.

'Hello?' It was a woman's voice. 'How are things in there?'

Suddenly he could see the handle start to turn, twisting slowly around in an anti-clockwise direction. The man caught his breath and rushed to the door catching it as it began to open. He grasped it firmly in his hands and poked his head outside, desperate to stop whoever it was from seeing in.

'Oh!' The woman was taken aback by the speed of it all. 'Sorry!'

He smiled. 'That's OK.'

'How is he taking it?' she whispered, nodding knowingly.

'Not too well. As you'd expect.'

'Do you need someone to –'

'No. No. That's fine. I'll stay here with him for a few minutes.' He smiled awkwardly, secretly wishing she'd disappear.

'OK,' she replied. He could see that she was young and hip. A bright and beautiful young thing with a smooth and soft complexion. Media-savvy, no doubt, and longing for a job in television where she could make controversial and thought-provoking, award-winning documentaries. A bit of a keenie. 'Well, I'll just be outside if you want me. OK? I'll just be out here.' She turned and he pulled the door shut behind him.

His heart and stomach churned. Why was this happening to him? Why couldn't they just leave him alone? Why was she sitting outside the fucking office waiting for him? What was the point in that? He started to get angry.

There was no way he could do anything now. Not with the girl just a matter of feet away. No way he could start sawing. It would take too long. His brain ticked and ticked. It always did that when it started obsessing about something. Ticked and ticked. Ticky, ticky, tick tick. Ticky fucking tick tick.

'Stop it!' he muttered to himself. 'Fucking stop it!'

He had to get out of there. No plan was going to work. Not now.

It was impossible. Utterly fucking impossible. There was only one thing for it. He picked up the metal bar and walked around to Jason Thickett's dying body. The spasms were fading now and the boy only occasionally twitched.

'I'm sorry, Jason. I didn't want to have to do it this way. God go with you, young one.'

Something had been bothering Hal for the last couple of days. It had come up and niggled him now and then, but he'd not been able to put his finger on it. It was something to do with one of the crime scenes. Something that just didn't sit right. Something out of place. Thirty yards from the Ashfield Studio gate his brain did an extraordinary leap and he knew exactly what it was he'd been agitated by.

'Bloody hell. Of course.'

'Eh?' Burlock snorted. 'What's up?'

'Nothing. Go back to sleep.'

Hal turned the wheel to the left.

He could see the studio beyond the security gate. It didn't look much like the studios he used to visit as a child. They were usually solid buildings made of brick, built to withstand anything – the Blitz included. BBC Television Centre, the Thames building. Made of brick. This one looked as though it had been cobbled together by a couple of NVQ Level One Construction students from some leftover corrugated iron and bits of old drainpipe. It looked like the sort of thing that wouldn't survive a bloody good blast from an easterly wind. John Kettley could knock it over in a trice, thought Hal, as the security guard let a dirty-looking Vauxhall Astra out from the car park. Hal backed up a little to give the driver some room. The Astra turned left and shot off in the opposite direction from where Hal and Burlock had just come.

'Miserable git,' Burlock mouthed.

'What's that?'

'Didn't thank you.'

'Didn't he?'

Hal pulled up to the security guard's window. The guard seemed to sigh and lowered the volume on his radio.

'Detective Inspector Luchewski. We're here to speak to Jason Thickett.'

The guard frowned.

'He's just been seen.'

'I'm sorry?'

'The police. They've just been here. To see him. Well, when I say "they", I mean "he". That was him then. It was just a copper on his own. He said there'd been an accident.'

'Accident?'

'Yeah. That's what he said. Said there'd been an accident.'

'Could you let me through, please.' Hal pointed impatiently at the barrier.

'Well, I've got to speak to –'

'LET ME THROUGH! NOW!'

By the time they were out of the car, a tetchy-looking man had come out of the building and was marching towards them.

'What on earth is all this about?'

'DI Luchewski,' Hal said as he jumped out of the driver's seat. 'I'm here to see Jason Thickett. And you are?'

'Daniel Ferris. I'm the producer. But that's not possible.'

'What's not?' Burlock had hauled his tubby body around to where Hal was standing.

'Detective Luchewski was here just a minute ago. He only just left. He'd been in with Jason consoling him.'

'Consoling him?' Hal felt his stomach drop for the second time that day.

'Yes.'

'What for, man?' Burlock looked stunned.

'His father's accident.'

'Where the hell is Jason Thickett now?' Hal leant forwards.

'Er ...'

'I SAID WHERE IS HE?'

'There's no need to shout. He's in the spare office. Follow me.'

Ferris pushed open the door to the studio complex and led them in. They walked down a long corridor until they came to a closed door. A young woman was leaning against the wall a little further down.

'Inspector Luchewski said we should leave him for –'

'For fuck's sake, *I'm* DI Luchewski!' Hal pulled the door wide open and walked in. 'Oh, Jesus!'

'Oh bloody Nora!' Burlock raced around Hal to where the boy lay on the floor.

'Aaarghmigod!' The producer squealed like a girl behind them. 'What's *happened*? Ohmigod!'

Burlock knelt on the bloody floor beside Thickett and placed his fingers on his neck.

'He's still alive, Hal. It's really faint but he's still alive.'

Hal turned to the producer. 'What did the other Luchewski look like?' He felt ridiculous asking the question but it was the first thing that leapt into his head. The producer stood there in shock. Hal grabbed him by the lapels and shook him gently. 'WHAT DID THE OTHER COPPER LOOK LIKE?'

'Er … beard. He had a beard.'

'Freddie. Get an ambulance and tell them to get units looking for a dirty black Astra.'

'What are you going to do?' Burlock was gently stroking the brow of the boy on the floor, his other hand fishing in his pocket for his mobile.

'I'm going to try and catch the fucker!'

Hal had run along the corridor, scrambled into the TT and shot out under the skyward pointing yellow barrier onto the road, turning left. He didn't have a clue what he was doing. His whole body had just shot into action without first asking permission of his brain. Now he was driving far too fast down a residential street in south west London.

He felt that there was a decent chance of finding the Astra. It had been no more than about three minutes since they'd passed the car coming out of the studio and, knowing south west London, it shouldn't have managed to get very far in that time. Hal quickly caught up with an old Rover, and overtook it, much to the dismay of the old timer driving it who did a double take as Hal passed by.

After about a minute, the road came to a T-junction. The road to the left was signposted:

Hounslow Town Centre 1
Hanworth 4½

The road to the right was signposted:

Brentford 3
London (West End) 8

Hal thought for a second or two before flipping a coin in his head and turning right. He had no idea if he'd made the right decision. Had no idea whether or not the car was still on the road. The driver might have stuck it in a garage a hundred yards from the studio as far as he was aware, but he kept going, something within him making him feel that there was a chance he could find the car. Find it and stop the driver from doing the thing he'd spent so much time doing of late. Murdering people.

This new road was much, much busier though. Buses blocked lanes, cyclists blocked buses, and pedestrian crossings blocked everyone. Hal wished he had one of those blue lights you could stick on top of your roof to show everyone he was a copper. But he didn't have one and, as he zoomed in and out of the traffic, he was treated with the same contempt, horn blasts, and middle fingers as any other boy racer. He came off the accelerator slightly as a woman with a fag hanging out of her mouth finished pushing a pram across the road, before applying more pressure and cutting up a Mini.

There were a million different roads coming off this one, and Hal knew that the Astra could have gone down any of them. In a way, what he was doing was madness. A real life goose chase. Still he kept driving.

Up ahead he could see a green light turn to amber turn to red.

'Shit!' He dropped to second, before dropping to first and rolling to a stop in neutral. He wound down his window and looked up the road. A spasm of doubt shot up his spinal column. What the hell did he think he was doing? Chasing an imaginary car across London like this. He should be back at the crime scene – keeping the area pure, checking out CCTV, interviewing the staff. Not racing across suburbia like a middle-aged Lewis Hamilton. It would make sense to turn the car around and get –

Then he saw it.

Four cars up ahead. Waiting at the lights with him. A dirty, black Astra.

'Holy shit!'

As soon as he had said the words, the Astra's wheels started squealing. Hal realised immediately that the driver had spotted him. The Astra pulled out across the centre of the road into the oncoming line of traffic, forcing its way onwards. The cars coming the other way beeped and honked, swooping out of the way of the madman in a muddy car.

Hal quickly twisted the gear stick into first and edged out. He waved his hand at the cars as he tried to push his way forward.

'GET OUT OF THE FUCKING WAY!' he shouted. 'I'M A POLICEMAN! GET OUT OF THE FUCKING WAY!' He crept slowly forward through the traffic. He looked across and noticed that the Astra had already cleared the crossing and was zooming off along the road ahead. 'GET OUT OF THE FUCKING WAY!' One driver stopped his car directly in front of Hal and was mouthing obscenities at him through the windscreen. 'I'm a policeman!' Hal protested, backing up before squeezing past the angry man.

Eventually he shot past the lights and onto the other side of the crossing. He got into third as quickly as he could and tried to make up the speed. He could see the Astra about two hundred yards ahead of him, dangerously swerving and mounting the pavement in a bid to get away. Hal fumbled about in his jacket pocket for his mobile, but he found that he needed both hands on the wheel to control the car.

Suddenly the Astra screeched sharply left around a corner, its back end smashing into the side of a lamppost as it went.

'Holy shit!' As he approached the turning himself, Hal dropped down into second, the engine roaring. Hal managed to control the turn a damn sight better than the driver of the Astra, and he nodded in appreciation of his own driving skills.

The new road was a back street, as residential as they came. Terraced houses with pretty window boxes and bay trees in pots on the tiny front patios. Hal slowed down automatically. The Astra was nowhere to be seen. Streets seemed to lead off streets here, and cars lined all the roads. It was a suburban rabbit warren.

Hal drove up a few of the roads, but couldn't find a single sign of the Astra. It was a maze. Too many back streets to check. Eventually, on the other side of the estate, Hal found an exit onto the A4. He knew then that the Astra was gone for good.

'Bollocks!'

He pulled over and switched the engine off. It was only then that he realised his hands were shaking.

187

Chapter Nineteen

The car was found abandoned an hour later in Hammersmith. The rear bumper had been ripped off on the driver's side and was barely attached to the car. The near side was badly smashed and two of the front lights were also damaged. A sticker in the back window showed it to be a hire vehicle from a place in Wandsworth. Singh had run it through the system, only to find the card used to pay for it had been reported stolen earlier that morning.

'Bastard covered it in mud to hide the numberplate.' Hal shook his head as he wandered around the car now being lovingly looked after by one of the forensics teams. 'Got it dirty so we couldn't see the bloody numberplate.'

'Why would he want to do that?' Singh stood at his side. 'If it was a hire car that had been paid for with some stolen plastic?'

'Extra level of security, I suppose. Keep us off the scent for as long as possible.'

'Well, he's doing a good job of it.' Singh gently chided.

Hal found himself frowning.

'Get a team up to Hammersmith. Check out all the CCTV cameras you can find between where the car was found and all the possible tube stations. There are about four he could have got to – Hammersmith, Kensington Olympia Overground, Shepherd's Bush, and the Goldhawk Road. Check them all. He disappeared somewhere and I need to know where he went.'

'What are we looking for exactly?' Green's tie looked particularly crisp today thought Hal. 'I mean, what does he look like?'

'This,' said Hal, his hand pointing to the screen in one of the back rooms of the studio. A piece of footage from one of the CCTV cameras in the complex was continuously looped to show the man walking along a corridor with the producer. As soon as they reached the door to the makeshift office, the film jumped back to show them repeating the same short journey.

'It's the best shot we've got of him. Bugger doesn't look up very often, I'm afraid. What is he? Five nine? Five ten?'

'Could be five eleven or six even. You can't tell exactly from this.'

'The producer's not that tall. Five eight, say. And our man is definitely bigger than that. Techies'll take a look at it and give us a better picture of it all, I'm sure. Until then, we'll have to use the sketch that the artist is putting together with the producer and his assistant. She's in there with them now. Soon as it's ready, I'll fax it over to you. OK?'

'Sure.' Green turned and left.

'I could have done that,' Singh complained. 'I would have checked out the CCTV if you'd asked me.'

'No. I want you with me. There's something I want to check out later. And I'm probably going to need you there.'

'Talking about the technical team, nothing suspicious was found on McKenzie's hard drive. It was quite a new laptop so there wasn't much of the usual rubbish clogging it all up. Bit of porn but nothing to concern ourselves with.'

'Nobody you recognised in the porn?' Hal asked Singh as they walked along a brightly lit corridor to the room where Jason Thickett had been found.

'No. Nobody. Just good old fashioned boy-girl or boy-girl-girl or – in one case – boy-girl-girl-girl-girl-girl business. Nothing iffy.'

'Boy-girl-girl-girl-whatever sounds iffy enough to me.' Singh gave him a funny look. 'Anything else turn up back at the office?'

'Dr Potterton had sent through his preliminary report for you to read. It arrived just as we were on our way out here, so I didn't have time to look at it myself. Sorry.'

'That's all right.'

They arrived at the door to the room. Inside Hal could see John Good and a couple of assistants busy dusting and photographing.

'Keeping me busy, Harry?' John Good shook his head and picked something up off the table. 'He left another note for you.' Hal could see that the thing he was holding up was another poly pocket with a sheet of paper inside. 'Want to know what it says?'

'What does it say?'

'It says, "THE MAN WHO MURDERED ME HAS AN A LEVEL IN GEOGRAPHY. GOD BLESS MY POOR SULLIED SOUL."'

'What?'

'"AN A LEVEL IN GEOGRAPHY. GOD BLESS –"'

'He's taking the piss! Bastard's getting cocky and taking the piss! '

Hal turned away and stormed off down the corridor leaving Singh in his wake.

'Billions of prints!' Good shouted as Hal made his way back to the main entrance. 'Billions and billions of the buggers.'

The note was wrong, though. Wrong about one thing, at least. Jason Thickett hadn't been murdered. Not yet, anyway. He was clutching the thin straw of a life support system in a quiet room in the Middlesex Hospital, Freddie Burlock waiting by his bedside until the distraught parents arrived.

The murderer had panicked, Hal realised. Thrown into confusion at having to attempt such a dangerous act in such an open place. It was sheer bloody madness. The man was obviously completely bloody mad. Hal felt a terrible desire to throw up at the thought of the last few days. Two dead, one nearly dead, one missing. In four days! It didn't make for particularly inspiring reading. The unwanted phone call with Woode didn't help things.

'The Chief Super wants me to pull you off the case. Reckons you're not... er...' Hal could sense him feeling around for the most suitable word or phrase. 'He thinks that now you've been brought up in the press, that you're not able to ... give it your all.' *Give it your all*? Was that the best he could do? 'Thinks that your mind's not on the job.'

'Oh come off it, sir!'

'I know, I know. Don't blame me. I'm just relaying information here. Thinks you're being distracted. I mean, three definite murder attempts in four days. Come on man, he's losing confidence.'

'I can find him, sir. You know I can. Just give me some time.'

'I already have.' Woode paused for effect. 'You've got forty-eight hours. I've bought you two days. Come first thing Thursday morning, I'm handing it over to Baldwin.'

'Thank you, sir.' Hal felt a sigh of relief blow out of his nostrils.

'Two days, Harry. Catch this evil sod in two days. That's all I ask.'

'Thank you, sir. I won't let you down.'

'You'd better not. Now,' Woode changed his tone, 'have you talked to your daughter, yet?'

'So ... What's wrong with this picture?'

'Sir?'

They stood in the middle of Wiseman's flat, the carpet still damp with blood.

'What's wrong with this picture, Sergeant?'

'You mean apart from the big puddle of blood on the bed and the stink of rotting flesh?' Singh felt her gag reflex start to tickle once again.

Hal got out his mobile and started scanning through his contacts list.

'It niggled away at me. I don't know why. To be honest it should have smacked me in the face right away. But ...' he hit the green dial button on the phone, 'for some reason it didn't. It simply didn't register. Stupid of me to thi – Oh hello, John,' Hal directed his attention to the phone. 'We're back at Wiseman's flat, Singh and me ... Look John, it's not for me to tell you your job or anything, but are you sure you and your team checked everything? ... Absolutely everything?' A pause as The Good Professor defended his role. 'OK. No, no. That's fine. Just wanted to check ... Cheers.' Hal flipped the phone back into his jacket pocket before continuing with Singh. 'It should have registered but it didn't. Obvious really when you think about it.'

'What is?'

Hal pointed at the part of the wall directly above the fireplace.

'That.'

'The poster?'

'Yep. The poster.'

Singh shook her head. 'I don't get it.'

'How old was Wiseman? Eighteen? Nineteen? Why would a nineteen-year-old gay man have a Beatles poster on his wall?'

'Perhaps his Dad liked them and got him into them.'

'From what I can tell, Wiseman had barely spoken with his father over the last six years. It doesn't make sense.'

'He could still have been a fan, though. No reason why not. Surely not every gay man is into Hi-NRG and Tammy Wynette, are they?' She realised that, given recent revelations, her question might not come across as the rhetorical statement she meant it to be, so she quickly added, 'Perhaps a friend bought it for him.'

'Perhaps.' Hal moved towards the poster and started to sniff it. 'It's new. Look, you can see it's still slightly curling.'

'What does that mean?'

'I think it was bought in a hurry.' Hal began unpicking the Blu-Tack at the corners. 'I think it was bought to cover something up.' With a theatrical movement, Hal pulled the poster away from the

191

wall.

There was nothing there.

'There's nothing there,' Singh sighed. 'Looks like you were wrong. Wait –' She came closer. 'What's that?' Halfway up the wall, slightly on the left of the area that had been covered by the *Abbey Road* poster was a crack in the plaster. Barely more than a couple of millimetres wide and a few centimetres long, Hal had to squint to see it. Standing on the hearth, he ran his fingers along its length. Singh looked at Hal and Hal looked at Singh, and for the tiniest, briefest of moments they stood there in silence. Then –

'I'll find a knife,' Singh headed to the kitchen area.

'There's something in here, I just know it.' He fingered the crack, picking off some of the flaking paint along its edge. 'I just bloody know it.'

'Here. Try this.'

Hal took the stainless steel knife from Singh and started digging about in the slit. The plaster crumbled away and fell onto the mantelpiece and dusted down onto his shoes. Hal squatted a little and tried to peer inside.

'There is. There's something in there.' He slid the knife along the gap, trying to hook the thing out. 'Come on. Bloody thing.' The knife slipped and fell to the ground. 'Shit.' Hal scooped it up and tried again. 'If I could … just …' He flicked the knife and something tiny flew out of the crack and landed on the bloodied carpet in front of the fire. 'There! What is it? What the hell is it?'

Singh bent over it, looking down at whatever it was. It took a few seconds before she could make out its shape, and a second or two more before her synapses managed to complete the puzzle forming in her head.

'It's a memory card,' she ventured staring up at Hal. 'One of those small ones you get in mobile phones. A *micro* memory card.'

The Creep was busily trying to avoid the zealous glances of the young (and far too keen) sales assistant. The hair-gelled little fucker was watching him work his way along the TV aisle. The screens got larger and larger as he went along it. Nineteen inches, then twenty-two inches, then twenty-six, then thirty-two. The second aisle was dedicated to the even larger TVs. A couple of ridiculously massive fifty-inchers stood on the wall at the end, and the Creep had a sense that the commission-hungry hedgehog was about to swoop. He couldn't stand sales assistants. They were the lowest of the low in his book. They didn't seem to understand that sometimes you just wanted to be left alone to browse. Browsing seemed to be frowned upon these days. People who worked in large electrical retailers like this worked on the assumption that as soon as you walked through the door, a trigger went off in your head and you suddenly realised exactly what it was that you were looking for. No time needed to think things over or compare the possibilities. On your own. Oh no. What you needed was the dubious expertise and opinion of a gap year student with a name tag and a tooth brace.

The Creep stared down the aisles of TVs, all of them showing the same programme – a man with no hair growling at a builder with a trowel in his hand. Some of the screens were crisper and clearer than the others, but they were all far too expensive. He closed in on the price of a slim-looking Samsung, before backing off shaking his head. How could people afford to spend so much money on a telly? Some of them cost more than he earned in a month. Unbelievable. And as for the 3D ones! The Creep hated the idea of a 3D telly, mostly because he didn't want to feel like a tit wearing those stupid fucking glasses while he watched it. Although the thought of his mother wheeling herself around the room with monstrous bloody specs on, complaining about the man on the TV trying to poke her with a stick, did make him smile for a second.

But only a second.

His mind had been racing the last few days – he had found it difficult to stop it. He'd tried to keep everything at bay by doing all that arrogant 'I am a God' bullshit that normally got him through the week, but even that wasn't helping. He knew that, this time, he'd gone too far.

The police were too close to him. Asking too many questions. Mostly about Wiseman and Larby, not that he knew anything about those two. Whoever it was who had killed them had the police on the run. Some moron with a grudge from Granton, no doubt. But the copper that had come to the door and had sat in the sitting room asking the questions while his mother sulked in her wheelchair like a thundercloud in the corner – that copper had mentioned McKenzie, the black lad. Said he'd gone missing, did you know him, have you seen him, would you recognise him? The Creep had said no, he didn't know him, hadn't seen him, and probably wouldn't ever recognise him. All lies, of course. He knew precisely who and where McKenzie was.

The car was another worry. He was going to have to dump it soon. A stupid idea. Stupid. Trying to keep it like that, after everything. What was he bloody thinking? Just an open invitation to get arrested, that was. Stupid. It all comes down to money again, the Creep thought as the boy with the badge finally came in for the kill. It's all about money.

'Hello,' the boy fake-beamed at him. 'Can I help you? Is there anything in particular you're looking for?'

The Creep stared down at the floor to avoid his gaze. 'No,' he said. 'Fuck off.'

'Detective Inspector George?'

'Aye?' The voice was stereotypically Scottish.

'DI Luchewski. Metropolitan Police. I hear you have some information on a –'

'That was quick. I only left a message with your lass a few minutes back.'

Hal chuckled to think of Corrie as a 'lass'. He didn't think she'd be very pleased. 'You've some information on a case –'

'As soon as we got wind of the details of the South London murder,' DI George bumbled on regardless of Hal's professional niceties, 'I thought back to the Brown case. 1991, it was. Poor girl. Still unsolved. Parents were ripped to shreds over it. Tore them apart, it did. I was a sergeant back then. Detective Inspector Kingston's Sergeant – Kingston retired a few years ago now. But as soon as I saw the details, my mind thought back to poor little Emily Brown.'

Hal found himself struggling to keep up with the broad Edinburgh accent on the crackly landline. For some reason he imagined DI Ian George as a slightly redder-haired version of Freddie Burlock. All tartan and tam o'shanters but soft as a Teletubby.

'Tell me everything.'

George sighed before continuing. 'It was January 1991. We were stationed at Edinburgh Central when we were called out to a house in Morningside. Landlady was worried about one of her residents. She hadn't been seen for over a week and there was no answer from her flat. Emily Brown. Emily Brown was a twenty-year-old secretary at a local solicitor's office. A pleasant, pretty girl. Wide circle of friends. Everybody liked her. The sort of girl my old dad would have referred to as having the DIL factor, meaning she'd make a good daughter-in-law. Worked hard and enjoyed life. Her whole life in front of her. When she didn't turn up at work four days on the trot, someone at the office called around to see if she was OK. When they didn't get an answer they phoned the landlady who ended up calling us.

'We broke in and found her lying on the bed, a single bloody sheet draped over her. Just like *your* boy. And just like your boy, the bastard that had killed her had mutilated her after death. The whole of the stomach to genital area had gone. She was left in pieces. The two legs and the upper half of the body were still there, but the genitals had gone … Bastard!' A twenty-year-old anger momentarily spat itself out of the Scottish copper, and Hal's mind flashed back to the seconds after John Good had pulled back the sheet to reveal what was left of Danny Wiseman. The shock, the confusion, the revulsion, and the rage, all rolled into one.

'We never found it, of course. Whatever he did with it, we never found it.'

'Did you question her friends? Her colleagues?'

'Christ, man, it was a murder enquiry! Of course we questioned everyone who knew her. We're not all Rob Roys and Rab C. Nesbitts up here you know.'

Hal felt a pang of guilt. 'Sorry.'

'That's all right. You're keen to catch your fella. I understand.' George suddenly sounded sad. 'I understand only too well. I've lost count of the sleepless nights I've had because of Emily Brown's killer. Feelings that I've let that poor girl down. I know Kingston felt them too. But there was nothing. Absolutely nothing to go on.'

'Boyfriend?'

'A couple of her friends said that they thought she might have been seeing someone, but none of them were sure of anything. Nothing concrete. We put out an appeal at the time, but nothing surfaced.'

'Exes?'

'There was one, but he had a cast-iron alibi and, to be perfectly honest with you, I wouldn't have thought he'd have had it in him. Lived with his grandma and grandpa. Kept pigeons. Worked in a fishmongers. It's all in the file. I'll send it down to you.'

'What about at her work?'

'Like I said, nobody had a bad word to say about her. Everyone at her work was devastated when we found the body. There were hundreds at the funeral – I mean literally hundreds. Family, friends, colleagues. Hundreds of them. She was well-loved.'

Hal thought the voice was starting to crack up, so he quickly filled the gap with a banality. 'Must have been difficult. For you, I mean.'

George sighed again. 'Whatever you do, Inspector Luchewski,' he croaked, 'make sure you catch your fella. Don't make the mistake we made and let him go free. It'll eat you up for the rest of your life. Trust me. It'll eat you up.'

'Ages him, I s'pose.' Burlock was leaning back on a desk in the main office, the tops of his fat legs squashing tightly against his grey trousers. 'Means he must be at least ...' his eyes rolled up into his head as he tried to make a quick calculation, 'Er ... er ... hold on ...'

'Assuming the killer of Emily Brown wasn't younger than sixteen in 1991, we can safely say that he must be at least into his early forties by now,' Hal finished the mental arithmetic for Burlock. 'Of course, that's assuming –'

'That's assuming it's the same person.' Singh joined in the finishing-other-people's-sentences game that they seemed to be playing. 'It's a pretty big assumption, isn't it?' She spun slightly in the chair behind her desk. 'Can we really go making that assumption?'

'Of course not.' Hal's fingers scratched at an itch on the top of his scalp. 'Not officially, anyway. But we need to bear it in mind. Get a couple of constables to run a check on staff at Granton during Wiseman's and Thickett's time. See if any of them could be traced back to Edinburgh in '91. If the cases are connected then we can forget about it being one of the Granton inmates because none of them would have been born then. How's Thickett?'

'Stable. Mum and Dad are with him.' Burlock felt his bum going numb and shifted his weight against the desk. 'Won't be up to answering any questions for a while though, I can tell you. Not until he wakes up, anyroads.'

'Well, looking on the internet,' Singh pointed to her computer screen, 'It seems the producers of *Britain's Toughest Jailbird* have, in their infinite wisdom, decided to ship in a substitute housemate – housemate? Prisonmate! – to replace Thickett. Nothing stops the show, it seems.'

'Not even attempted murder,' Hal agreed. 'If anything they'll be rubbing their hands in glee. There's no such thing as bad publicity in the TV world, and the ratings were taking a dive from what I can gather. It's the best thing that could have happened to them.'

'Evil bastards, these media types. Sell their own grandmothers for a two-minute slot on *Loose Women*, they would.' Burlock gave up with leaning against the desk and started to rub the pins and needles out of his left leg. A beep came from Singh's computer. She pulled her chair closer to the screen, her eyes narrowing as she read something to herself. 'It's all Ferraris, underage sex, and cereal bowls full of cocaine with these TV people,' Burlock continued.

'Message from the technical division, sir,' Singh turned to Hal. 'They've analysed the memory card and there appears to be a single jpeg on it.'

Hal grabbed the back of Singh's chair and leaned in closer. 'And? Do they say what it is?'

'It's just here, sir.' Singh double clicked a paperclip and a second or so later an image filled the whole of the screen. Hal and Singh stared at it while Burlock lumbered around behind them.

The picture was dark, slightly blurred. Taken inside in a gloomy room. On the left was part of a bulky, naked back – too close to make out its owner. On the right was a white triangle, as though somebody's elbow had accidentally bent into shot. But in the centre ... In the centre of the photo was a man, naked or partially so – it was difficult to tell which – wiping himself down with a blue towel, his head twisted to one side. A goatee beard. Something glinting around his neck. Both Hal and Singh recognised him immediately.

'Is that who I think it is?' Hal queried, his heart beginning to thump hard in his chest.

'I ... think so,' Singh answered slowly, hypnotised by the image on the screen. 'I think so.'

'Who is it?' Burlock looked from Hal to Singh and back again.

'The garden centre man,' Hal eventually responded. 'Alexander Judd.'

Judd was gone. The wife had explained. Driven off first thing in the morning leaving a handwritten note saying sorry but that he had to get away for a few days – he'd explain everything when he came back. He would make it all *perfectly* clear when he came back in a few days, so kiss the kids an apology and tell them to be good.

He'd done it before, apparently. Several times. 'He just doesn't handle stress very well,' the wife had explained. 'Anything stressful and he's off like a shot. I'm used to it now. After twenty years of marriage, I'm used to it now. I think this boy who worked for him – the one who was murdered, I can't remember his name – this business with the boy who was murdered has given him a bout of the heebie-jeebies. Drives me mad, of course. He clams up, shuts down. There's no getting through to him, trust me. I've tried the shouting and throwing stuff, the being sympathetic, the reasoning.

But it's no good. He clams up and then bolts through the door like a rabbit. Goes to the pub and drinks himself silly or drives around for a day or two, before stumbling back home full of apologies. It's what he does. It's his way of dealing with all the stress.'

Hal had put out the call to all mainland police forces to keep a look out for Judd's car and faxed them all a photograph of the man himself. It was late in the afternoon and Hal was beginning to feel like he'd been through the day from hell, the conversation he needed to have with Lily still hanging heavily upon him.

Green phoned in with bad news. CCTV at the underground stations had shown nothing of Thickett's attacker. Admittedly it was early days but so far there was nothing obvious to latch on to. Then Good had phoned in with more bad news. No prints on the drawing pins, and the notes were all printed on generic printer paper available in at least seven hundred different outlets in the UK alone. A dead end of an enquiry.

'Thanks to you, I've had a slap on the wrist.' Good sounded a tad pissed. 'We should have spotted the crack in the wall. It was unforgivable.'

'I don't blame you, John. We're all up against it here. This bastard's going around bumping off people at a rate of knots. Thinks he's bloody Usain Bolt or someone. Of course we're going to miss things. Impossible not to.'

'Well …' Good didn't sound convinced. 'Whatever. We missed it and you found it. It pains me to say it but, good job, Luchewski.'

Hal felt a tiny twinge of pride for the first time that day.

'Hi, Dad.'

Hal had gone for it as soon as he'd got in through the front door. He'd fished the mobile out of his pocket and called Lily before he could even get his jacket off.

'Hi, Lily. Sorry, should have called you earlier than this. Busy at work, you know. Lots to do. Meetings and paperwork. Stuff.' He was flannelling. 'You know what my work's like.'

'Yeah, I know. Another murderer, isn't it? That one killing the ex-prisoners, yeah? Cool.'

'Murder isn't cool, Lil. No matter what they tell you on television.' He flung his jacket over a dining chair and dumped himself down on the sofa. 'All those beautifully shot beautiful people in designer suits and expensive sports cars, solving crimes in hour-long segments on Channel Five – murder's nothing like that at all.' He was still flannelling. 'It's dirtier than that.'

'But *you* wear designer suits and drive an expensive sports car, Dad,' Lily came back.

'Er ...' She'd thrown him off guard. 'Yes. I suppose I do. Er ... I suppose you're right.' A short pause. Hal tried tossing something else into the silence to distract his daughter from the task at hand. 'School OK, is it?'

A sigh. 'Dad,' she started. 'Isn't there some other thing you are meant to be talking to me about? I mean, Mum's been going on about it all day – to be honest, she's really been getting on my tits.'

'Lily!'

'Sorry, Dad, but she has. Been on at me all day to talk to you. Moaning about you not having called me. She even phoned me at school to see if you'd been in touch. Honestly, she's been sending me bloody boggle all day.'

'Did she tell you what it was all about?' Hal's heart began to jitter. 'Did she say anything ...?'

'What? About you being gay?' Hal breathed a slight sigh of relief. 'Of course she didn't. Mum still thinks I'm five and need protecting from the big, bad world ... *woooo*.' She put on a deep, scary voice and Hal could imagine her wriggling her fingers like a ghost as she said it. 'She doesn't seem to realise that I'm capable of reading the newspapers or of discussing the state of the world with other people, or in some way engaging with the modern status quo on an emotional and intellectual level.' Jesus, thought Hal, my little girl is growing up. 'Mum thinks I should stay at home and play with my dolls and dream of the day that I meet a nice wholesome doctor or a vicar and I can become a dutiful wife and cook. Organising playgroups and mothers' meetings. That sort of shit.'

'Lily! Don't swear.' Hal found himself smiling nevertheless.

'Sorry, Dad, she just gets me so angry. Sometimes I could scream.'

'You're wrong about your mother,' Hal found himself unexpectedly defending his ex-wife. 'She only wants the best for you. It's natural for a parent to want to protect their children, you understand that, don't you?'

Lily sighed again. 'Of course I do, Dad. She just goes about it in such a dreadful, clumsy way. I still want to move in with you, you know. You haven't talked to Mum about it yet, have you?'

'You still want to move in?' Hal sounded a little disbelieving.

'Yeah. I still want to move in. Why wouldn't I still want to move in?'

'Well ... today. You know ... Finding out ...'

'What? The gay thing? Doesn't change anything. If anything, it makes me want to move in more. It's cool, you know. Having a gay dad. Romilly Barrington's dad is gay, and Romilly Barrington's the coolest girl in the lower school.'

'Is she now?'

'Romilly Barrington's dad runs nightclubs all over the world. She's always jetting off with her dad and his husband during the holidays.'

'And what does Romilly Barrington's mother think of all this?'

'Dunno. Never met her. Obviously the gay thing was why you and Mum split up in the first place, wasn't it?'

Hal was finding it surprisingly easy to open up to his daughter. 'Yes. Yes, it was. I don't think I'd ever really got to grips with it, and meeting your mother … well … it confused issues, I think. Of course, the one good thing about meeting your mother was that it led to you being brought into the world.'

'So you didn't split up because of me then?' Suddenly she was vulnerable, a little girl once again.

'Jesus, no! God, no. We didn't split up because of you sweetheart. Is that what you think? No, no, no. Is that what you've always believed?'

'It's always been something I wondered about. You going so soon after I was born and everything. I just thought it might have had something to do with it – that *I* had something to do with it.'

'Oh God, no, Lily darling. You had nothing to do with any of that. It was just two people coming together who didn't … fit together as perfectly as they should have done. There was nothing you could have done or not done about it, sweetheart. It's just how it was.' Hal felt sick to the pit of his stomach to think that he'd made his daughter feel so shitty in the formative years of her existence. *What sort of a man makes his own daughter feel like that?* he thought to himself, and *What sort of a man doesn't even realise he's made her feel that way?* A double whammy of guilt. 'Christ, no, Lily. It had nothing to do with you. I'm sorry if I ever made you think that it did.'

'S'all right, Dad.' Back to the tough young woman that she liked to pretend to be. 'It's all cool now. Like I said, I get extra cool credentials at school with a gay dad. All my friends think it's great.'

'Ha! That's OK then. I was a bit worried about talking to you. Thought you might have been upset by the whole thing. A bit of a shock, so to speak.'

'Nah. Not really. To be honest, Dad –'

'Yes?'

'I think I've known for years.'

Thirty-seven seconds after Lily had hung up, Hal's mobile rang again. Looking at the screen, he could see that it wasn't a number he recognised. He clicked the answer button before getting up off the sofa and heading for the kitchen. He suddenly realised that he was starving.

'Hello. Harry Luchewski.'

'Inspector Luchewski …'

It was a voice he vaguely recognised.

'Hello?'

'Inspector Luchewski … erm … I don't know if you remember me…'

'Yes?'

'You came to the garden centre last week to tell me about Danny Wiseman, poor boy …'

Hal stopped in his tracks.

'Mr Judd?'

'Yes. Look, I –'

'Mr Judd, I need you to go to the nearest police station and hand yourself in now, do you understand? There is a warrant out for your arrest and –'

'What? My arrest? What?'

Hal slowed himself down. The last thing he needed now was Judd bolting. He was going to have to take this more slowly.

'Mr Judd. I think you have some information regarding Danny's death. I really do need you to come back home so that you can fill in gaps in my enquiry. We have a murderer that needs catching, and I don't believe even for one second that that murderer is you, but I *do* desperately need your help, sir.'

'I can't, Inspector Luchewski.'

'I'm sorry?'

'He'll kill me too.'

'Who will?'

There was a long silence as Judd summoned up the strength to say the name.

'The Creep.'

'The Creep?'

'Yes.'

Hal felt himself slip into a puzzled smile. 'Who's the Creep?'

Judd paused again. 'Inspector, there are creatures on this earth

201

not of God's making. The Creep is one of them.'

'Come on, Judd, tell me. Who the hell is the Creep?'

'The Creep is a monster, Inspector. A demon from the very bowels of –'

'For Christ's sake spare me the fire and brimstone claptrap and tell who this Creep is, will you!'

'I DON'T KNOW!' The anger with which Judd screamed down the line made Hal jump. 'I don't know! I never knew his real name. He never used his real name, just wanted to be called the Creep.'

Hal slowed down once again. 'How did you know him?' A long, long pause. 'Mr Judd? Sir? How did you know the Creep?'

Judd sighed. When he spoke, he sounded much calmer. 'Inspector Luchewski. Time is precious. I realise that you've probably got some fancy device triangulating, or whatever it is, trying to locate my position from this phone call. The longer I stay on the line, the likelier you are to find me. And for a few days it's probably best that I'm not around.'

'No! That's rubbish. Go to a police station right now and –'

'So at the end of this call,' Judd continued, 'I'm going to drop my phone into this dustbin I happen to be standing next to. I just can't risk it. The Creep's deranged and he's obviously out to kill us all.'

'Who's *us*? Please, Mr Judd, give me something to go on.'

'He's already killed Ray and Danny. Poor Danny. Wouldn't harm a fly. He won't rest until the rest of us are dead, I'm sure of that, as God is my witness.'

'Please, Mr Judd. Tell me who they are. We can save them. Save you all. Just give me their names.'

'Please give my family police protection, Inspector,' Judd sounded as though he were in a trance. 'I doubt the Creep'll target them if I'm not home, but it will give me peace of mind.'

'For fuck's sake, man, I couldn't give a shit about your peace of mind.' Hal finally lost it. 'Look, Danny Wiseman had taken a photograph of you semi-naked on his mobile phone. Tell me, was he blackmailing you? Was Danny Wiseman blackmailing you? Were you having an affair?'

'Like I said, INSPECTOR,' angry again, 'Danny Wiseman wouldn't hurt a fly. NOT A FLY!'

'What's Larby got to do with it? Was Wiseman blackmailing him too?'

'"Let HE who is without SIN cast the FIRST STONE", INSPECTOR!'

'Cut the bollocks, Judd, and tell me something about the Creep. I need something to go on. What was the point of this call if you weren't going to tell me things? Eh?'

'This phone call is over, Luchewski –'

'WAIT! Tell me something about the Creep. What age is he? What does he look like? For God's sake, anything!'

Hal could hear Judd sucking in air at the other end.

'You take the Lord's name in vain as readily as you take sugar in your tea, Inspector.'

'Anything, man!'

'He's in his forties. Mid to late forties, I'd say. And he's very, very fat.'

The phone went dead.

Hal tried call back a few times before throwing the mobile across the room and onto the sofa.

'Fuckety fuck!'

Then Wiseman's photograph of Judd flashed into his head, and the bulky, naked back of the man on the left seemed to lodge itself into his mind.

It was all falling apart. He could feel it all falling apart. Jason Thickett was still alive and Luchewski was on his tail. He could feel it. Could feel it hanging over his shoulders like a wet coat, dragging him down.

It wasn't meant to be like this. In his mind's eye it was all going to flow beautifully, seamlessly, with each execution being ultra-slick and ultra-efficient. In reality it had been very different. The pump had been a stupid idea, he could see that now. The knocks on the back of their heads had been difficult to judge. Larby had been a struggle. The TV studio had been too busy. The police were closer than they realised.

He stood in the hallway staring up at his favourite picture in the whole house. A framed print of Goya's *Atropos*. The Fates. A beautifully ugly picture painted on a wall in the artist's house near Madrid during a bout of mental despair. In a bleak Mediterranean landscape, the three female Fates float, suspended in the air: Clotho, spinning the thread of human life, deciding when a person should be born; Lachesis, who takes the cloth and measures it, deciding when a person is to die; and then Atropos herself, the goddess of death, the carrier of the scissors, who slices across the fabric of life and brings that life to a close. A male figure bound in the foreground representing the futility of fighting that which has already been determined by the gods.

He had tried to fight the Fates. Tried to twist everything to his own advantage – tried to control everything that had happened. The destruction of his disease – the cleansing of his mind and body – had been central to the fight, and he couldn't stop now. So close and yet so far. Close but, as yet, no cigar. Corners were going to have to be cut. The whole process speeded up. He needed to bring it all to an end as quickly as possible so that, like Atropos, he could cut the dead weights that had pulled him down.

The grandmother clock read 9.44pm. He was going to Streatham – a worrying place to be driving late at night in a car like his, but he was going to have to risk it. The job needed finishing. He didn't need the holdalls any more, so he'd packed the essentials – the bar, the axe, the knife, the needle, the thread, the note, and the dictaphone – in one of his old rucksacks he'd found in the box room.

Looking ahead he could see an old postcard he'd once bought at an art gallery tucked under the bottom edge of the painting. He reached up and slid it gently out. It read:

The fates lead the willing
And drag the unwilling.

Seneca the Younger

He smiled and put it into his trouser pocket before switching off the hall light and opening the front door.

Chapter Twenty

A beautiful day in London – one that would prove to be the hottest of the year so far – slaps into life with a jolt. Two jolts to be precise.

A little before dawn, the Marine Support Unit of the Metropolitan Police based at Wapping, received a call from a cleaner at the London River Services stop at Greenland Pier. Within minutes a Targa fast response boat was deployed, and soon after, a bobbing body – limbs twisted through mooring cable – was being picked off the dock wall as the sun stretched up setting fire to the cold, mirrored buildings in the distance.

Meanwhile, six miles to the south, a milkman was prodding another body with the tip of his boot.

'Hello. You all right?'

The man on the ground didn't move or make any sort of sound.

'Is he OK?' The boy in the van shouted out at the milkman who was standing on the path with a pint of full fat in each hand. 'Is he drunk?'

'Don't really know.' He pushed at the man once again. Still no movement or noise. 'Hello? Are,' he started speaking in loud syllables, 'you ... feel ... ing ... O/... K ...?'

Nothing.

'Isn't that the house where they found that hand last week?' The boy shifted in the passenger seat to try and get a better view without getting too near. 'That hand on the doorstep just there?'

The milkman looked around to get his bearings.

'You're right. I think he's dead.'

'What?'

'I said I think he's dead.'

'Really?'

A flash of light from across the road – the glint of a window or a reflection of a car – momentarily distracts them both before the milkman turns and walks back to the van.

'Yes, really. You'd better get your mobile out and call the police, I think.'

'Déjà vu, Harry.' The Good Professor smiled as Luchewski

approached the white tent covering the entire patch of front lawn of 33 Chester Row.

'This is taking the piss,' was all Hal could think of saying in return.

'I don't think I've ever had to examine the same scene on two separate occasions over four days. It's certainly a first for me. Remind me to scribble a note of it on my list of professional firsts.'

'Who is it?'

'Pop these on and come and take a look.' He handed Luchewski a pair of forensic shoe covers. Hal slipped them on quickly and, holding open the flap of the tent, went in.

On the doorstep of the house, in exactly the same spot where just a few days earlier Danny Wiseman's left hand had been left in a brown McDonald's bag, a dead body lay on its side crouched in an almost foetal position, the legs pulled up loosely toward the chest. Hal immediately identified the body by the way the smart shirt had been neatly tucked into the black trousers. Was *still* neatly tucked into the black trousers.

'Rabin.'

'The house owner,' Good confirmed. 'Come over here and take a look.' He gestured to Luchewski to step around the body. 'Come look at this.'

Hal picked his way carefully over the grass, accidentally nudging the arm of an assistant (*Sprout*, was it? thought Hal) on the way. He squatted over the face and involuntarily jerked away in shock.

'Stabbed the eyes out again,' Good continued unfazed. 'Like Larby. Also like Larby, the killer has sewn the lips together with what appears to be the same thick thread. I'll bet my petrol money for the month that there's another stupid note in there.'

'Not so much stitching this time,' Luchewski observed. 'Looks a little more hurried to me.'

'Hmm. Didn't behead this one like he beheaded Larby. Didn't use an axe like he did on Larby. No obvious signs of blood being pumped, and the body's still intact – unlike Wiseman. And Thickett, of course. How is Thickett, by the way?'

'Still in a coma.' Hal tried to peer over the back of the head. 'Cause of death? Just a crack on the skull this time, was it? Nothing fancy?'

'Obviously can't be certain yet, but it looks like a knock on the nut, like you said. You're right, it looks more rushed.'

'He's losing his cool. At last. Finding this whole thing a bit more difficult than he imagined.' He straightened himself up, a pang of impending middle-age pain skittering up his spine.

'Heard you've been having funny late night phone calls from suspects.'

Hal smiled, rubbing his back. After Judd's phone call, he'd had some of the techie boys on duty come and take his phone away. He didn't know what they could do exactly, but it was the correct thing to do. Proper procedure. The only trouble was that he now didn't have a mobile phone, and was feeling surprisingly bereft without its weight swinging about in his jacket pocket. They'd promised to return it later that morning and, secretly, Hal couldn't wait.

'This Creep guy,' Good stood up, 'he the killer?'

'No. Judd says he's fat. The man who tried to kill Thickett wasn't fat. The CCTV images are definitely not of a fat man. If anything he was more on the slender side.'

'When did Judd last see him? He might have lost a lot of weight in that time?'

Hal squinted in thought. 'No. Doesn't feel right. I don't know what the Creep's got to do with all this, but I don't think he's our killer.'

They both pushed through the other side of the tent, into the hallway of the house. Hal smelt the terrible musty smell, the dusty damp and greasy uncared for scent that had hit his nostrils for the first time last Friday morning. The Friday morning he'd met Mehrzad Rabin for the first and last time. Now Rabin lay twisted and folded on the doorstep like an origami swan and Hal was feeling as frustrated as he had that first day.

Woode was in the hallway chatting to a couple of officers. When he saw Luchewski he broke off and went up to him.

'You know the river police pulled McKenzie out of the Thames this morning, don't you?'

'I'd heard.' Luchewski was pulling off the paper shoes and slipping them into one of the clear plastic bags. 'Do we know how he died yet? Is he … intact?'

'He's all there. First reports say strangulation.'

'Strangulation? Doesn't sound like the work of our killer.'

'Must be. Surely,' Woode snorted. 'Anyway, I've lost count of how many bodies we've got. So has the Chief Super. Just called me to remind you you've got twenty-four hours before he pulls you off the case.'

'Charming.'

'He might have the grace and manners of an untrained terrier, but his back's against the wall too.' Woode wasn't smiling. 'You've really got to get somewhere today, Harry.'

'Don't you think I know that already? Where's Singh?'

'Singh, Green, and Burlock have been interviewing the residents. Again.' Woode gave him a *tut-tut* of a look.

'What? The residents are still here?'

'Most of them. These are lonely people. They haven't actually got anywhere else to go. So we're allowing them to use the rear door through the garden and up the side lane for now.' Woode pointed to an open door at the end of a corridor. 'I think Singh's out there now.'

'We're just waiting for Rabin to be removed,' Good aimed his statement at both Woode and Luchewski. 'Then we'll give the area a good going over. See what there is. If anything.'

'Garden' was far too generous a term for the scrappy and untouched patch of land that was stuck on to the rear of the house. Years and years of uncut grass had turned what was once a lawn into a pale green hazard zone: lumpy, uneven, somewhere you would more than likely twist your ankle or fracture a metatarsal. The grass had edged out over a flagstone path that was now barely distinguishable from the lawn itself. Dandelions and brambles choked up the sides of the garden, and broken plastic pots sat on the cracked patio next to something wooden that was rotting and alive with woodlice. To top it all, Hal was certain he could detect faint traces of cat shit. The flies were starting to make their yearly bid for world domination, and he swatted a couple away as he approached Singh and the old woman with the dog.

'Morning, Sergeant. Good morning, Mrs Thompson.'

'Oh. Good morning, Inspector.' The old dear turned around.

'How is little … er … hmm …?' Hal looked at the mutt on the lead. He could tell the dog didn't like him.

'Archie.'

'That's right. Archie. How's little Archie this morning?' Archie gave him what he thought to be a bit of a snooty look.

'Rather unsettled, I'm afraid. All this commotion is making him a tad twitchy, isn't it, my little darling?' She bent herself over slightly to tap the dog on the head. 'When he gets nervous he gets a terrible, terrible tummy. I mean absolutely terrible.'

Hal wondered if the smell in the garden wasn't cat shit after all.

'Yes, well. Sorry about all this fuss. Not much fun having police swarming all over the place, I'm sure.'

'Well. It's a bit of excitement at least.' She suddenly seemed to lean in closer, the look in her eyes sharp and keen. 'Tell me Inspector ... Is it a body this time? A *whole* body?' Her tongue darted out and swept over her dry lips.

Hal saw no reason not to let her have that one piece of salacious information. 'Yes. I'm afraid it is, Mrs Thompson.'

'Oh dear. How terrible.' She recoiled in pretend shock. 'Terrible. Oh, poor man – it *is* a man, isn't it?' Eyes keen once again.

He held back on this one. 'I'm afraid I'm not at liberty –'

'Of course, of course. I understand, Inspector. Too early in the investigation and all that. I just hope you catch him – the one doing it all I mean. A ghastly business. I've been following it all in the newspapers.' She gave Luchewski a little wink. 'Now, if you'll excuse me, I need to take Archie for his morning stroll around the block. Poor little chap needs to go poo-poos again.'

'Bye, Doris,' Singh smirked at Luchewski as the old woman slowly and deliberately – watching her footing – made her way around the side of the house through a wooden gate, a tiny bundle of fluff strutting alongside her.

'Bet you ten quid she's off to try and get a quick gander into the forensics tent up front,' Luchewski sighed, his hands playing with bits of old receipts and biscuit crumbs in his jacket pockets. 'Made her year, this has, I tell you.'

'McKenzie's been found, then.'

'Strangled, according to Woode,' Hal flicked some of the old biscuit crumbs out onto the lawn. 'I really don't think it's our killer.'

'No?' Singh's forehead dropped into a frown.

'No. I don't think so.'

'So who killed McKenzie then?' She was still frowning. 'It's too much of a coincidence, isn't it?'

'You're starting to sound like Woode. McKenzie was involved in a spot of small-time skunk production. Perhaps he and Raymond Larby were starting to tread on other people's toes. Who knows? Perhaps the Creep killed McKenzie. Judd seemed to think he was easily capable of it. I don't know. All I know – all I believe – is that there is more than one thing going on here, and somehow we've got to pick them apart.'

Burlock limped out from the house and joined them in the garden.

'Bugger all from those buggers,' he nodded his head towards the house. 'None of them have got anything to do with this, I can tell yer. A more hopeless bunch of individuals I've never met. Living in a place like that. Frankly I'm glad their landlord's got killed. Should

209

have been lynched years ago, the state of some of them rooms.'

'Why Rabin?' Hal leaned back upon what, in a previous life, must have been a wooden fence, but he jumped quickly when he felt the whole structure starting to give under his weight.

'Sir?'

'What have Wiseman, Thickett, Larby, and Rabin got in common? What connects them? And where do Judd and the Creep fit into all this? And now McKenzie?'

'Wiseman, Thickett, and McKenzie all did a stint at Granton. Larby worked at Granton –'

'Until he got the sack,' Burlock added.

'Until he got the sack,' she continued. 'Judd employed ex-inmates and Rabin –,' she stumbled. 'Did he ever work at Granton? Do you think the *Creep* is something to do with Granton?'

'Dunno. Possibly. I need to talk to that guard again. What was his name?'

'Francombe. Robert Francombe,' Singh replied.

'Yes. Francombe. I need to talk to him again.' Hal turned to Burlock. 'Where's Green?'

'Last I saw of him he was washing his hands in the bathroom on the first floor there.'

'He does that a lot, doesn't he?'

'Mmm.' Burlock gave Luchewski a knowing look. 'He does.'

They stared in silence for a few minutes – Hal picking at the thick rug of moss under his feet with the tip of his shoe, Burlock picking his nose. Singh, with the traces of a migraine, closed her eyes and rubbed at her forehead. Eventually –

'Body's off,' Woode leaned out of the door and shouted at them before disappearing back inside.

'I'll go see where Green's got to,' Burlock moved away from the rickety fence and shuffled his way to the house.

Hal and Singh slowly clambered over the tufts of grass.

'It's a lovely old house, really,' Hal noticed for the first time. 'Edwardian. But they've let it go to pot. Some of the stonework's crumbling there, look. And that's original, the piping – but it's calling out for a lick of Hammerite. It's rusting towards the top.'

'It smells of mould inside,' Singh wrinkled up her face. 'Looks like it hasn't been cleaned in years.'

'Terrible waste. Do it up you could probably put it on the market for – why's that window look different to the others?'

'Sir?'

Hal had stopped and was looking up to the top of the house.

'That window. The one on the right. On the top floor. It's got different glass to all the others, hasn't it? Or are my eyes playing tricks on me?'

Singh shaded the sun from her eyes and squinted upwards.

'The one on the right?'

'Yes.' Suddenly an image of Singh's Peugeot jumped into Hal's mind. 'It's tinted. The glass in that window is tinted. Who lives in that room? What do they want with tinted glass?'

'Erm,' Singh thought for a moment. 'There's only one room on the top floor. It's unoccupied at the moment.'

'Have we got the keys? Can we get in?' Hal was speeding into the house now.

'Er ...' Singh trailed behind. 'Graham Parke in Flat 1 has some. Rabin entrusted him with spare keys in case –'

'Get them.'

'What?'

'The keys. Get them.' Hal raced up the stairs leaving Singh standing in the hallway a little dumbfounded as other officers milled about pretending to help the forensics team.

Up the first flight of stairs he flew, past Doris Thompson's door, then up the second flight. At the top he stopped. Two doors faced him; the one on the right had a greasy-looking brass '6' screwed onto it. He tried the handle. Locked.

'Dammit!'

He looked up at the ceiling. Dirty polystyrene tiles – outlawed years ago due to the fact that, in a fire, they would melt and drip scalding liquid onto the skin – were stuck gracelessly all over it. A hurried, unprofessional job undertaken by someone who really didn't give a shit. The wallpaper was peeling with damp and the carpet was thin and without any distinguishable colour, as if something had come along and sucked out of it any joy and beauty that it might once have had.

He twisted and tried the other door. It too was locked, but he could hear the keys Singh was holding rattling as she rushed up the stairs behind him.

'Here. Try these.'

Luchewski took the keys, all looped onto a big ring, and started flicking through them. A small tag of masking tape had been rolled around each of them and Hal quickly found the one with '6' scribbled in pencil on it. He slotted it into the lock and turned.

The room was almost bare – it contained a bed, a chair, a table, a small wardrobe, and a tabletop hob. Hal walked over to the window and looked down at the garden below. He nudged his forehead against the pane, cupping his hand over his eyes to block out the brightness of the blazing sun.

'This isn't right. There's only the one window.' He unlatched the window and stuck his head out before whipping it back in. 'The tinted glass is on the window next door.'

'There isn't a room next door.'

'Hmm?' Hal was busy trying to pull the badly fitting window to.

'There isn't a room. It's just a broom cupboard.'

'Show me.'

They shut the door to flat 6 behind them before Singh jangled with the keys and unlocked the second door on the top landing. Hal grabbed the handle and pushed it open.

'See.'

Singh was correct. The door opened onto a small broom cupboard no more than five feet wide and three feet back. Shelving with pots of half-used paint and sprays and rags covered the rear wall. Long-handled brushes and a couple of old-fashioned Hoovers sat on the floor, and a rusty ironing board was propped up against the side.

'Doesn't make sense,' Hal griped. 'Doesn't make sense.'

Burlock, Green, and Woode came up behind them.

'What is it?' Woode puffed.

'Hold on.' Hal pulled the brushes, the vacuum cleaners and the ironing board out of the cupboard and onto the landing, before turning his attention to the shelves. He lifted the bottles and sprays off the top shelf and started moving the rags off the middle shelf when he came across a small wooden handle hidden on the wall. 'Look at this.' Luchewski rapped the wall with his knuckles. It sounded hollow. In fact the whole wall, along with the shelves, seemed to rattle slightly. 'It's a door.' He lifted one of the wooden shelves and it came straight up.

'They haven't been screwed down,' Burlock said. 'Quickly, get them all up.'

Hal sped up now, his heart pounding like a jackhammer, lifting and throwing the shelves out onto the floor until the cupboard was clear, shelving brackets attached to the door itself. Hal twisted the handle and pulled, but it was locked.

'The keys. The keys.' He snapped his fingers at Singh who jabbed them towards his hand. He tried a few at random, before –

Click.

'That's it.' Green looked more animated than ever. 'You've

done it.'

Hal twisted the handle once again and pushed, the door opening into a room beyond, and all five of them stepped through.

Hal knew that this was the room with the tinted glass for, even though the curtains were wide apart, the light coming into the room was dimmer than in the room next door, giving it a kind of mistiness. It was larger than the one next door too, with alcoves either side of the chimney breast. A fat, comfortable sofa sat facing a wall with a large TV fixed onto it. A double bed – no, a kingsize bed – took up most of the space nearest the window. Silk sheets and pillowcases and plush velvet cushions made it look and feel out of place in the run-down house. A camcorder on a tripod stood facing the bed, and half-empty bottles of whiskey and gin sat on a side table with some crystal glasses.

Hal went over to one of the alcoves. On the shelving unit built into it stood dozens of DVD cases, filed neatly, with the occasional gap where one was missing. Hal angled his head so that he could see the handwritten entries along their spines.

22/03
17/04
25/04
Then a gap …
14/05
19/05
Another gap …
16/07
And so on.

Woode twitched. 'We need to secure this room and get Good and his team up here asap.' He pronounced *asap* as if it were a word.

Hal slid one of the DVDs out from the shelf.

'Should you be touching that, Inspector?' Woode glared at Hal. 'Shouldn't we leave that for Forensics?'

'Afraid we don't have the luxury of time, sir,' Hal moved back to the door then turned to Singh. 'Doris. Does she have a DVD player?'

'I think so, yes.'

'Good.' He slid a couple more of the DVDs off the shelf and made for the door.

Detective Constable Mark James was feeling a little used. Overtaking a double-parked Fiat, he slipped the car into third gear and tried to concentrate on the road ahead.

He felt as though he'd drawn the short straw that morning. Ordered to pick up Luchewski's phone from the technical team and to return it to him. He didn't join the police force to be a messenger boy. He joined because he thought that he had a lot to give – that he had a lot of skills that would make him a good copper. He was precise and observant, keen and sharp. He wasn't a ruddy courier.

He flipped down the sunshade and turned right. At least he was visiting a crime scene. That was one good thing about the expedition. A visit to the crime scene. It was something he didn't do enough of. Far too lowly to be allowed too much access to a crime scene, but he was going to walk straight into this one – and what a crime scene it was. The hand on the doorstep just the other day, and now a body. Two crimes in a week. Even though he wouldn't dream of admitting it to anyone, Mark James was secretly looking forward to it.

Hal kneeled on the floor in front of Doris Thompson's TV set and popped open the DVD player. Singh, Burlock and Woode were standing behind the scruffy worn sofa – Singh clutching the headrest, Woode with his bear-like arms crossed and Burlock flipping Minstrels into his mouth. Hal ripped open one of the cases and pushed the disc into the player. He straightened up before falling back onto the sofa.

'Here we go,' Burlock mumbled through a mouthful of chocolate. 'The main feature.'

The black screen flickered and then …

OK, it's on. Say hello, Danny.

Danny Wiseman was sitting on the plush bed in the hidden room upstairs.

Hello, Danny. He waved to the camera.

Very funny.

Suddenly Judd walked into shot and sat on the bed next to Wiseman.

Oh look, it's your boss, said the man operating the camera. *Fancy earning some overtime today, Danny?*

Wiseman smiled at the camera and said something unintelligible. Judd laughed and muttered something back before reaching out and unbuttoning Wiseman's shirt.

'Jesus,' Burlock stopped chomping for a second. Wiseman leaned forward and kissed Judd full on the mouth.

That's right. Best way to get a pay rise. Fucking the boss.

Pack it in with the stupid comments, would you, Ray? Judd grimaced in the direction of the camera before turning back to kiss Wiseman.

'Ray,' Singh interrupted. 'Raymond Larby. Larby's behind the camera.'

'Mmm,' Luchewski was concentrating on the scene being played out in front of them. 'We need to speed this up.' He hit the fast-forward button and everything started zooming. Within seconds Wiseman was naked and on his knees fellating Judd.

'Jesus Kid Jensen.' Woode watched, eyes agape, as Judd quickly whipped off his shirt and trousers.

'I'm not sure I really want to see this through to the bitter end,' Burlock had given up on his packet of Minstrels.

Then, in high speed, another naked man walked into shot and joined the two men on the bed. Hal slapped the 'play' button and the action slowed down to its real speed.

'Rabin.'

That's it, Mez. Larby's voice was too near the microphone on the camera and sounded like a rattle, *Get in there and fuck the boy's brains out.*

Rabin said something unintelligible before grabbing Wiseman by the hair and forcing him to lick his testicles.

'It's not exactly Pinter, is it,' Burlock nervously coughed into the silence of the room. Nobody paid him any attention.

Hal leaned down and pressed the fast forward button once again. The action suddenly took a comedic turn as the writhing on the bed became blurred and began to look a little like something from a lurid Benny Hill sketch. After a couple of minutes of high-speed bouncing about and jerky writhing, the DVD came to an end and stopped itself.

'Larby, Rabin, Judd, and Wiseman.' Hal took out the DVD and put another in its place. 'Who else is there?'

A slightly different angle this time, as though the camera was positioned right next to the bed, with nobody in shot. The room, a touch darker. Then a muffled voice:

OK? If you're ready. Don't worry.

'Larby again.'

'Seems to be the cameraman for this little set up.'

I'm still not sure. I've never actually done this sort of thing before.

You'll be fine. Larby's was trying to be soothing but his voice betrayed a hint of impatience. Then, from the right, Jason Thickett walked awkwardly into view, wearing nothing but a pair of boxers.

And you promise to give me the other half of the money afterwards? You swear? He sounded like a lost little schoolboy.

Fuckin' hell, Thickett. Of course we fuckin' swear. A different voice. An angry, coarse-sounding voice that made the four officers in the room sit up and take notice. *We keep our fuckin' promises. We're not thieves. We're not like you, you piece of shit. Just get on and do your fuckin' best. Jesus!*

OK. OK. Keep your fucking shirt on.

Then the owner of the voice walked into shot. An overweight man with thinning hair and heavy bags under the eyes, dressed in a red jumper and cheap blue jeans. He stood next to Thickett, glaring, before turning to the camera.

You got the fuckin' thing turned on this time, Larby? Remember what happened last time, you dozy cunt?

Yeah, yeah.

Don't 'yeah, yeah' me. Just fuckin' film it, will you. Then to Thickett, *Bend over.*

Hal hit the pause button.

'The Creep?' ventured Singh.

'The Creep,' nodded Hal. 'Give me your phone, will you?'

DC Mark James was ushered through the garden and into the house, narrowly avoiding stepping in some fresh doggy doings and a crooked paving stone on the way. Across the hallway, Forensics were finishing up around the front door. The body had been left on the doorstep, and James tried to peer over to see if it was still there. It wasn't. It had already been taken away. He felt slightly deflated, as though he'd missed an opportunity.

'They've found a hidden room upstairs,' a constable with googly eyes told him as he started to ascend the first flight. 'Hidden behind a storage cupboard it was.'

'Really?' That perked James up. 'What was in it?'

'Video cameras. Pervy shit. Guys sucking each other off and all that. They're watching some of the films now. Luchewski's watching it too. He's a poof, did you know? Probably getting off on it.'

They reached the door to the flat and the googly-eyed copper knocked the door, giving James a little conspiratorial wink.

'Constable here needs Inspector Luchewski to sign for his phone, sir.'

Woode nodded at the policeman with bulging eyes and the fresh-faced constable was allowed into the room.

Luchewski barely noted the newcomer. He had finally got put through to Robert Francombe at Granton and he needed a few answers.

'How can I help you, Inspector?' The voice was crisp and tight. Singh's mobile network was obviously better than his own.

'The Creep, Mr Francombe.'

'I'm sorry, Inspector?'

'Does "The Creep" mean anything to you?'

'Ha!' A sharp stab of a laugh. 'The Creep doesn't exist, Inspector.'

'What?'

'The Creep's a mythical figure.'

'What do you mean, a mythical figure?' Hal looked around the room. Old-womanly doilies and white lace curtains seemed to swamp the place. The pictures of the unsmiling man reverentially positioned on the mantelpiece, a long line of tiny china teddy bears sitting upon a shelf – everything dainty and chintzy, with a distinct stink of dog.

'The boys who come to Granton have always talked about the Creep. The Creep is meant to be the cruellest, most sadistic of the guards. Black-hearted. Evil. Corrupt in the extreme. He's been a figure of fear ever since Granton was opened. In a strange way, he's a part of the history of the place. But, as far as I'm aware, he never ever existed.'

'Well there's somebody going around calling himself the Creep.' Hal turned back towards the muted TV screen where the fat man, now naked and sweating, moved in a grunting animalistic way behind a shocked-looking Jason Thickett. 'Any idea who that might be?'

'Afraid I can't help you there Inspector.'

The constable who had just walked into the room thrust a clipboard into Luchewski's face, along with a small plastic wrapper through which Luchewski could see his own mobile phone. A small wave of relief washed over him, as he signed the document on the clipboard. Peering up, he could see the look of horror on the young officer's face as he caught sight of the action on the TV.

'What if I told you the Creep was a very fat man in his late forties? Balding. Rubbery puffy lips. Obviously sweats a lot. Is there anyone you know from Granton who satisfies that description?'

217

'Very fat? Puffy lips, you said? Sounds like Keith Humphreys to me.'

'That's Keith Humphreys.'

Hal jerked his head upwards again to hear the constable standing beside him. 'That man ... behind. He's Keith Humphreys. I interviewed him yesterday.' The young officer was pointing at the screen. 'He lives with his mother. She's in a wheelchair. I had to go back and interview him yesterday.'

'Hold on,' Hal pulled the phone away from his ear. 'You're telling me you interviewed *that* man –' Hal nodded his head towards the flatscreen TV. 'The fat one. Yesterday.'

'Yes.' The constable looked at Luchewski with a deadly serious face. 'His name's Keith Humphreys.'

Hal put Singh's phone back to his ear. 'Mr Francombe. Tell me about Keith Humphreys.'

'Not much to tell really. Not a very nice guy. Didn't care much for his job, I don't think. Got kicked out when Chief Manager Hurley took over. There was some fuss. Never knew why. Wouldn't surprise me if he was calling himself the Creep. Bit of a loner. Never really got on with many of the staff.' He paused. 'A bit of a creep, in fact.'

An early lunch with Marianne at a pavement café on Denmark Street. The sun was blazing down and Stevie Denyer was pleased that he was sitting under the canopy with his back to it. Marianne had her massive shades on, so it wouldn't have bothered her too much. Her hair was wild and she was in one of her pretend foul moods.

'Honestly, Stevie darling, if I have to sit through one more fucking meeting with the typesetters, I'm going to do a protest piss all over the floor. See how they like that, the filthy-fingered little fuckers.' She took an enormous suck on the butt end of her cigarette before tossing it across the pavement into the gutter. 'See how they like a woman on the blob dropping her trouser suit and pissing all over their carpet, the ugly little troggs!' She pulled another of the Marlboro Lights from out of the packet on the table and lit up.

'Bad morning?' Stevie lifted the cappuccino to his lips.

'The worst, darling. The worst. Ever since the editorial team decided – in their infinite wisdom, ha! – on a new layout it's been sheer unadulterated fucking hell. The left hand doesn't know what the right hand's doing and the right hand doesn't even know there's a fucking left hand. It's all over the bollocks I'm afraid.'

Stevie had known Marianne for some years now, since she was Rachel with an English degree and two pairs of jeans to her name. She'd lived on Pot Noodles and week-old Asti Spumante. She wouldn't say boo to a goose and had started smoking as a way of hiding the nervousness in her hands. Nowadays she was Marianne, Assistant Fashion Editor at a well-known women's glossy. She travelled the world and had breakfast meetings in Madrid, business lunches in Milan, and lakeside dinners in Mali. But every now and then – every month or so – she would slum it and come back down to earth for a greasy spoon lunch with her old mate Stevie.

The teenage waitress dropped two plates of pig fat and beans onto their table.

'I'm *sooooo* fucking stressed out, I simply cannot believe it.'

'You love it. You know you do.'

She pulled the fag out of her mouth and thought for a second.

'Mmm. I suppose I do. Good point well made, Denyer!' She shovelled some beans onto her fork. 'So how's life at the *Chronicle*?'

'Oh.' He paused. 'Shit.'

'Good as that, eh?' In went the beans. 'You want to get a job on a magazine. Not mine, obviously. But one of those cheaper, weekly ones. You know – the gossipy, white trash sexual abuse ones. Easy money. Just get some undernourished ex-smack addict traveller who's never heard of shampoo to tell you about how her own dad used to beat her, and how the father of her children turned out to be a two-timing miserable criminal cock of a man, and you're well away.'

'Oh, careers advice now, is it? I thought we were just going to have a bitch and a moan and a coffee. I wasn't expecting careers advice.'

'You know me,' she replied eyeing up a passer-by in tight jeans and a white T-shirt. 'I'm like the Citizen's Advice Bureau of the fashion editing world. Just come to me with your problems and I'll straighten them up with my razor-sharp insights and encyclopaedic knowledge.'

Stevie smiled as he tore a piece of toast in two and dipped it into his fried egg. 'How's Jean?'

'Who?'

'Jean?'

'Jean's gone, baby. Jean's long, long gone. He spent longer in the bathroom than I did, and that's just not on. When I caught him plucking his eyebrows ... Well, let's say it was the last straw. It would only have been a matter of time before I found him prancing around the flat with my Louis Vuitton and in my Jimmy Choos. What about you? Anyone new on the horizon?'

Stevie felt himself start to blush. It seemed to come from nowhere but Marianne picked up on it.

'There is, isn't there?' she squealed. 'You've gone and bagged yourself a new bloke, haven't you, you randy little sod? I knew it!'

Stevie put down his fork and swallowed his toast.

'Well …'

'I knew it! I just bloody knew it! So …' She leant in a little nearer. More intimate. 'Spill the beans – so to speak. Tell me all about him.'

Stevie shook his head. 'No. No. It's more complicated than that.'

'"Complicated"? You're talking to the queen of complicated here, sweetheart. Tell me all about your "complicated" new man.'

'It's not … I …' He struggled to find the right words. He hadn't paid much attention to his feelings over the last few days, but here they were, bubbling up out of nowhere, making his tongue do somersaults and cartwheels, while his head seemed to empty of all rational thought. 'He's a policeman,' he eventually spat out.

'A copper? No, no. Avoid like the plague, honeybun. Avoid like the plague. I used to shag a copper. Anal as fuck. Would give scores out of ten every time we made love. No, no. Keep well away, that's all I'm saying. Keep well away.'

'This one's nice.'

'"Nice"! Nice? Nice don't cut the mustard, sweetmeat. You need more than just nice to survive this wicked world. Get yourself a biker boy with big muscles, a bigger dick, and a very tiny brain. Someone who fucks hard, can punch hard, and who doesn't give a shit about opera. It'll pay off in the end, you'll see.'

Stevie sighed as he drained the last of the froth from his cup.

Keith Humphreys plugged his phone into the wall socket. It was a shitty old Ericsson that literally did weigh and look like a house brick, but apart from him having to replace the battery once, in 2003, it had served its purpose. Humphreys didn't have the need for Bluetooth or an internet connection, so replacing it with a smartphone was pointless. Besides, contracts were expensive for those phones and he couldn't bear the thought of shelling out thirty-odd quid a month for something that he wouldn't really use. Or want.

I must remember to take the phone, he thought to himself as he got up from the floor and started getting ready. *I must remember to take the phone in case I can't find the place.*

He felt the scar on his arm where the boy had scratched him. That fuckin' boy. He shivered at the thought of it. Luckily his mother had been asleep during it all. She didn't have a clue. Nasty little fucker. Trying to blackmail him. Coming out with those lies. Saying he knew about the Club and what went on. Accusing him of killing Danny Wiseman. He'd only just found out about Wiseman a couple of hours before the boy had arrived, so how could he have done it? But the boy … what was his name? McKenzie. Derek McKenzie or some such shit name. One of the kids from Granton he used to try and scare the crap out of. Doped-up little prick. But the boy … He hadn't believed him. Started raising his voice and jabbing his stumpy finger. Started ranting and raving saying how he wanted two hundred quid a week to keep quiet and that he'd better give him his first payment now or he'd go the pigs. It was the thought of his mother being woken up that had made him grab the boy around the neck, and the thought of the two hundred quid a week that made him squeeze as hard as he could. The boy had thrashed out and scraped skin from Humphreys' bare arm, causing him to bleed, but still he'd held on. Crushing. After a few seconds the boy's body had gone limp, the legs buckling under the weight, but he'd kept on squeezing until his fingers got cramp and he was certain McKenzie was dead.

He'd carried the body through to the lean-to garage at the side of the house where his dead duck car was rusting away. His mother never went in there because of the steps, so it would be safe until he'd planned what to do next.

He hadn't meant to do it. It was all a lightning flash in his head. Like someone shining a torch into his eyes. A moment of blindness. He'd always had a problem with anger, and this time his anger had slashed across his life – may actually have ruined his life. All he could do was minimise the damage. So, once his mother had taken her pills and gone up to bed, he'd searched the body and found McKenzie's car keys. In the middle of the night, he'd found McKenzie's little boy racer parked on a road round the corner. He'd got in and driven to the front of the house, parking the boot level with the lean-to door. Quickly he'd popped the boot and carried the body out from his ramshackle garage, checking all the time that no one was watching. No one was. He'd dropped McKenzie into the boot before gently pushing it shut and driving off as quietly as he could.

He hadn't known where he was going. His mind had flitted

about, wondering what to do with the body. He'd thought about driving out to the countryside, finding a secluded wood, and burying it there, but he hadn't had a spade on him and, anyway, the whole thing would have taken too long and his mother would have woken up before he was back. He hadn't wanted to have to face the question of where he had been. He'd thought about leaving the car on a patch of wasteland somewhere before setting fire to it, but that would have drawn attention to the car – and the fire brigade might have put the fire out before all incriminating evidence had been destroyed. He would also have had to walk home. It was too much of a risk. He'd even toyed with the idea of going to the police and confessing, but he'd quickly put such a ridiculous notion out of his mind. All the time he was thinking, he kept driving the car north towards the river. Suddenly noticing a signpost for Bermondsey, he'd swerved off the main road and down a side street. *Of course, the river.* He remembered stories about weighted-down bodies. The Richardsons and the Krays and all those other fuckers. Stick a body in the Thames, put rocks in the pockets, and it wouldn't be found for years, if ever. Dropping a gear, he'd headed for the dockside streets of Rotherhithe.

Booboo the Clown. The Creep. They were all acts really. He fished out the pack of trick cards from the drawer nearest the wall. It was all just pretence. Parading around like a monster. Putting the fear of God into people. Trying to conjure up an aura of dominance and malevolence. Truthfully, he was as shit-scared as everybody else. Life had a way of undermining you. Pushing and pushing and prodding away until it found a weak spot and then … BANG! In for the kill. No mercy shown. That's what this McKenzie thing had been. A stab through an Achilles heel. An elaborate joke devised by a God who shouldn't exist. Ha ha fuckin' ha, God. Very fuckin' funny.

He'd cruised about looking for an ideal spot. The whole area was gentrified beyond being gentrified. Warehouses and dock buildings all sucked empty of any soul, now refurbished to within an inch of their foundations to accommodate the yappy yuppie fuckers doing jobs that paid too well. It made him mad to think that the people who used to walk those streets were hardworking and dedicated with blisters on their hands, and that the people who now walked those streets didn't actually walk those streets any more, just drove over them in their Porsches on their way to the City or the gym or Waitrose. Hiding away in their sterile little boxes, only interested in their savings accounts and property portfolios.

After a while, he'd spotted a gap in a fence – a blind spot hidden from the viewing eyes of a poncy block of flats. By this time, it had been half past three and the streets were as black and silent as they ever got in London. He'd pulled over, turned off the engine, and killed the lights. The air inside the car was chilly, and he'd sat there for a few minutes just waiting and watching. Waiting and watching. Everything was peaceful, almost dead in its nothingness. He'd seen nobody, so he'd got out and walked over to the gap in the fence, ducking his head as he pushed through. A tiny stretch of scrubland led to a short wall and, peering over it, he could see the Thames, flickering with reflected light, lapping gently at the base of the wall below. The tide was well up. Throw the body in now and it might get carried a little, but soon it would settle, sinking down to the bottom of this giant of a river. Looking around the ground, he'd found some broken bricks and a couple of largish smooth pebbles which he'd stacked next to the wall before going back to the car. As quietly as he could, he'd opened the boot and lifted out McKenzie. The boy was only small but the dead weight had made him stagger a little as he forced his way through the fence, over the scrub, and towards the wall. He'd lowered the body next to the bricks and stones and started stuffing them into McKenzie's pockets. He'd pushed some down the arms of the sweatshirt, tying the ends of the arms over the boy's cold, stiff fingers. Once they were all in place he'd grabbed the body and dragged it up the side of the wall, the extra weight making him work even harder, before he'd heaved it over the top of the wall and let it roll off the cold stone and splash into the river below. He'd looked down but could see nothing of the body. For a passing second, he'd felt like saying a prayer, but the noise of a nearby car had made him start and he'd hurried back to the car where he slammed the boot shut and speedily shot off. The next morning he'd unscrewed the plates from his own car and put them on McKenzie's.

It all seemed to him now like a lifetime ago. Was it really only three … four days? He shook his head, partly out of disbelief and partly to get rid of the memory. He found himself hooking his clown costume out of the wardrobe and packing it away in his case, along with the props and tricks he was going to use.

'Keith. Keith. Where are you? Keith!'

'I'm up here, Mum,' Humphreys sighed.

'I need my pills. You've forgotten about my pills again, you selfish boy.' The voice seemed to scrape up the stairs like fingers on a blackboard. 'What are you doing up there, you selfish, selfish boy? Leaving me on my own down here like this. Leaving me to sit here talking to myself all morning. What sort of a way is that to treat your sick old mother, eh? You're not at work today. You should be down here looking after me.'

'I'm getting ready for a party.' Anger started to rise in his chest.

'Party! Pah! You and your stupid parties. Dressing up like a stupid clown. What sort of a man goes around dressing like a stupid clown? You should be down here getting me my pills is what you should be doing. Not putting make-up on your face like a stupid queer.'

'I'm coming.' He tried swallowing the anger back down his throat.

'Going around looking a stupid fat fool. Is that what you want for the rest of your life? Is that what you want people to think of you? I don't know what your father –'

'I SAID I'M COMING!' he shouted towards his bedroom door. 'I'M BLOODY COMING. You poisonous old cow.'

He clipped the case together, threw it on the floor, and stormed out of the room, banging the door hard behind him and forgetting all about his mobile phone.

Woode flicked his phone shut.

'Judd's handed himself in.'

'What?' Hal jumped around and nearly knocked Singh down the stairs.

'Greyfriars Police Station, Bedford. Handed himself in about half an hour ago. Said he wanted protection.'

'Fantastic.' Hal felt as though the pieces of the jigsaw were at last sliding into position. 'Abso-bloody-lutely fantastic.'

'Do you want Bedfordshire Police to bring him down here?'

'Yes, bring him down … No, wait.' Hal turned to face Woode. 'I want someone from the team to go up there and bring him down. Leave it to the local yokels and it'll take ages before we get him in an interview room. Probably not before it's gone dark. At least with someone who knows the case, the journey back might be an opportunity to see what Judd knows.'

'I'll go,' Green put his hand in the air like an overkeen schoolboy. Hal ignored him.

'Singh. I want you to go.'

'Me?' They all reached the bottom of the stairs.

'Squeeze him for information on this sex club. How he joined it. Who introduced him to it. How well he knows – or knew –

everybody else. Try to find out the names of all the kids they involved. Were they all from Granton? Did they pick up young boys at random? That sort of thing. But –' he stopped in his tracks and stared Singh hard in the face, 'most importantly, I want to know about the fifth man.'

'The fifth man?'

'What do you mean, "the fifth man"?' Burlock growled.

'It suddenly struck me. This whole thing. It's an Elmsley count.'

'An Elmsley what? What are you on about, Harry?' Woode shook his chimney-shaped head and frowned.

'An Elmsley count is a card trick. Well, not really a trick, more of a manoeuvre – a move to use in more elaborate card tricks. It's kind of a shuffle where five cards are disguised as four. It's used quite a lot by magicians.'

'Well, you would know.'

'We've got Larby, Rabin, Judd, and now Humphreys. But there's a fifth man – our killer. I just know it.'

'You don't think it's one of the boys? The Granton boys?' Burlock fiddled with his beard. 'Getting his own back?'

'No. It's not one of the boys. It's somebody better-placed than that, I'm absolutely certain of it. The CCTV images from the studio showed someone older. Someone more in control. The fifth member of the group. Humphreys and Judd know who he is.'

'The DVDs –'

'Some were missing. Taken by the fifth man, whoever he is. Took all the ones in which he makes an appearance, I'm sure.'

'He might've missed one,' Burlock mumbled.

'True. Sergeant Green?'

'Sir?'

'Once Forensics have cleared the DVDs, I need you to wade through them – speed through. Try and see if there *is* another man in this group.'

'Sir.' Green didn't sound particularly enthusiastic about the prospect of fast-forwarding through a mass of homemade gay porn.

Hal turned back to Singh. 'Get Judd to tell you everything he knows about our missing man. I want a name, job, address, shoe size. Anything. Judd never knew the Creep's real name, so it's not impossible he doesn't know the killer's. Just do your best.' He smiled at Singh. 'Come on. You'd better get going.'

'Sergeant Singh. Priti. Hold on.' Singh stopped, standing in the road holding her car door open. Luchewski was walking along the pavement towards her, his hand outstretched. 'Wait a minute.'

Behind Luchewski, Singh could see the forensics team busying themselves and Burlock shambling along like a lethargic toilet brush on legs. *What is it now?* she thought impatiently to herself.

'Priti. Look I just want to apologise for the way I've been behaving the past couple of days. If I've come across as a twat, then I'm really, really sorry.'

'Er ... OK.'

'What with all this,' he waved his hand in the direction of the activity, 'and the newspaper nonsense. My daughter. Everything really. I've been a bit distracted ... ha! ... to say the least. So ... I just want to say sorry.'

'That's all right.' She wasn't too sure about all this. She felt a bit uncomfortable with Luchewski going on, almost pleading. 'Doesn't matter.'

'No, but it does matter. It really does. You're a good copper and you don't deserve me on your back.'

'Don't worry.'

'I've had a difficult couple of days – no excuse, of course – but I understand why you talked to Woode about my drinking. It was the right thing to do, so in a way, I thank you for it.'

'I'm sorry?' Suddenly she didn't know what on earth he was going on about. 'Drinking? I don't understand.'

'You raised some concerns over my drinking. Baldwin did too, I think.'

'I've never talked to Chief Inspector Woode about your drinking.'

'Hmm?'

'You daft sod, Luchewski,' Burlock came alongside them. 'Stop harassing the poor girl. It wasn't her. It was me.'

'You?'

'Me.'

Luchewski spun on his heels to confront Burlock. '*You* talked to Woode about my drinking?'

'Yep.'

'What did you want to do that for? Why didn't you just talk to *me* about it?'

'You don't listen to a ruddy word I say, man. I've *tried* talking to you about it but you never seem to catch on. Seemed like the logical thing to do, to let Woode in on it. Turns out, Baldwin's been on at him too, but then he would, wouldn't he? And for different reasons to me. Slithery, shit-climbing little snake.'

'Ahem.' Singh coughed and Luchewski looked over his shoulder at her. 'Shall I be getting on, sir? It's a long drive to Bedford.'

'Er … yes. Yes, Sergeant. You'd best be going. Er …' he looked slightly red in the face. 'Sorry about all that.'

Singh gave a little grimace and climbed into the seat before firing the engine and driving off. A glance in her rear view mirror showed the two men still standing on the pavement, talking. *What the hell was all that about?* she thought to herself as she turned the satnav on. As the screen lit up, she realised that it was going to be a very long day. She would have to call Nicky to let him know what was going on. They were meant to be meeting for dinner tonight. Thrashing out the guest list and the seating arrangements. Settling on the venue and the floral displays. That was going to have to be put on ice for a day or two, dammit.

Oh yes, it was going to be a very long day indeed.

'I would have listened if you'd spoken directly to me about it.'

'Would you bollocks.'

Hal shaded his eyes from the sunlight that seemed to be trying its hardest to burn out his retinas. They were both back outside the house where a couple of dog walkers were nattering on to one another and pointing at the white-suited forensics team.

'I'd listen to you, Freddie. You're one of the few people I probably would listen to.'

'Don't give me all that flattery shite. You know as well as I do that Harry Luchewski doesn't listen to any bugger, least of all me. No, hang on. Change that. Least of all *himself*.' Burlock turned to the two old gasbags with dogs. 'Would you mind moving along, ladies? The forensics team are trying to get on with their work here.' He smiled a large generous smile and the two women giggled and shuffled off, dogs in tow. 'What is it with old women and dogs around these parts? Aren't old women meant to have cats or canaries or summat?'

Luchewski ignored him. 'Generally, you don't give a shit. All the bullshit of work, you just let it go. So when you do actually give a shit –'

'That's a lot of shit.'

'– then it's obviously something worth listening to. If you'd come to me and said "Look, I'm a bit worried about your drinking", I'd've listened. I might not have liked what it was you were saying, but I'd certainly have heard you out.'

'Arse.'

'You really didn't have to go behind my back and grass me up like some fucking little schoolboy. Honestly.'

'OK, OK. I get the message. Jesus. Next time I'll come straight out with it. It'll save me the bloody earache.'

, 'Thank you.' Hal turned to go back into the house, but Burlock stood stock still.

'So?'

'So what?'

'The drinking. Under control, is it?'

'Of course it's under control. It's always been under control. At no point has it ever been *over* control. Christ, Freddie. You can put it away too, you know.'

'Ah yes, but not every single night. And I'm a very, very old man, you know. My daughters have all … well, *nearly* all flown the nest. The only person depending on me now is the wife and, to be perfectly honest with you, she probably sometimes wishes I'd drink myself into an early grave so she can get a bit of bloody peace.'

'Your fishing stories aren't as interesting as you think, I keep telling you.'

'Don't try to distract me from telling you your own business.' Burlock wiped the sweat from his forehead with a rotten-looking handkerchief that he managed to find in his trouser pocket. 'Whereas you … You, Detective Inspector Harold Luchewski Liddle or whatever your name is. You have a young daughter that doesn't see enough of her dad. You have a young daughter who needs a decent, respectable male role model so that one day, when the juices start flowing, and she finds herself staring at the gibbons in tight T-shirts and jeans – and she will, you mark my words – she'll have a good enough yardstick to measure them by. Do you see what I mean?'

Luchewski repositioned himself so that the sun was to his right. He looked hard at Burlock, who grinned back somewhere beneath his scruffy beard.

'Lily?'

'Yes, Lily. She's at the age now where a strong male character is essential. If she doesn't get it from her dad, she might go elsewhere to get it. Capiche, el capitan?'

Luchewski swallowed hard enough to hurt his throat.

'It's not about you, you daft bugger. It's about your daughter.'

Suddenly Luchewski's eyes were hit by a bright flash from across the street.

'What was that?'

'I said don't distract me –'

'No. Just then. Across the road. From that house there. One of the upstairs windows. There was a flash.'

'What are you on about?' Burlock twisted his head just in time to catch a second flash.

'There!'

'I saw it. Some sod's taking photos of us.'

'Come on.' Luchewski started crossing the road.

'It's probably some tabloid hack renting out a bedroom,' Burlock shouted before shaking his head and following. 'Shouldn't we be concentrating on this Creep idiot?'

'We will be. As soon as the ARVs are ready.' Hal reached the front door and banged on it with a succession of angry, heavy thumps. 'Police! Open up!' He looked at the peeling black paint and the green brass '30' that had been screwed in at a very dodgy angle. The stonework around the door was crumbling and old, fat moss was forcing its way up between the paving stones. Once again, the whole impression was one of seen-better-times. Hal slammed the door. 'Police! Open up!'

'Be another bloody journo. You'll see.' Burlock puffed alongside him. 'Can't believe their luck a second body –'

A low click and swivel sound from within, followed by a chain sliding out of its clasp. The door eased open frustratingly slowly, Hal dug his ID out of his jacket pocket and, after what seemed like a minute, a man's head wedged itself in the crack between the door and its frame.

'Yes?' The face twitched, the gaze darting from Luchewski to Burlock then back again before shifting towards the ground. 'Can … can … can …' The man gulped. 'Can … can –'

'Detective Inspector Luchewski, Metropolitan Police. This is my colleague Detective Inspector Burlock.' Burlock did a little salute to the man. 'I'm sorry but I was standing across the road just now and I saw a flash from your window, as if somebody had been taking photographs?' Hal's face was stern and unfriendly, and he let the statement hang in the air.

'I … I … I … ah … I … I …' The man gulped again. Hal guessed him to be in his early fifties. His eyes were wet, the skin creased. The hair on his head just brittle wisps of brown. 'I was … I … I … I was … I …'

'I realise that it's all very interesting having dead bodies appear on your neighbour's doorstep but I would be grateful if you didn't take pictures of the forensics … team as they … Are you all right?'

The man looked as though he were having a heart attack, his face spasming and jerking as beads of sweat began to amass at the edge of his forehead. His jaw shuddered as if his mouth were desperately trying to gasp for air. All the time his eyes were focussed on the stone step in front of him.

'I ... I ... Could you ... I ... er ... ah ... um ... I, er ... oh.'

Suddenly the face withdrew from the gap quickly followed by soft, racing footsteps up some stairs. A comedic beat, before Hal turned to Burlock.

'Am I right ...' he started, 'Am I right in thinking he's run away? Run off upstairs?'

'Looks that way,' Burlock shrugged.

'Run off and just left us standing here like idiots?'

'Speak for yerself. As I believe the youth of today would say – the common parlance of the day, if you like – WTF.'

'Jesus,' Hal sighed. 'Come on.'

He pushed the door wider and walked into the hallway, Burlock close behind. For the second time that day, the stink of damp and dust attacked his nostrils like a rabid dog. The hallway was dark and fusty, the air hot and still. Towards the stairs, some crumpled, smelly old coats were hung on pegs. A broken umbrella had fallen over on its side onto some boots covered in flaking, dry mud.

Hal stood at the bottom of the stairs and called up. 'Hello? Sir? Are you OK?' A slight whimper came from one of the upper floors. 'Sir? Is everything all right?' There was no answer. Hal looked back at Burlock who shook his head in a 'don't-look-at-me' sort of way. Grabbing onto the handrail, Hal began to slowly make his way up.

'That's it, you go first,' Burlock whispered. 'I've seen *Psycho*. If he comes rushing out at you dressed as his own mother, wielding a carving knife, don't say I didn't warn you.'

'I'll try to remember that when I'm lying on the slab,' Hal whispered straight back.

At the top of the stairs, Hal could see the man crouching in front of a closed door. He held his head in his hands and was sobbing uncontrollably. Alongside the man, stacked against the wall, were hundreds and hundreds of little boxes covered with a rainbow design.

'Sir?' Hal sounded as sympathetic as he could given the circumstances. 'Is everything OK?' He moved gently towards the man.

'Careful,' Burlock muttered under his breath.

'Sir? Is everything OK? Can I help?'

'Please,' the man raised his head 'P ... Please.' Hal could see spittle dribbling down the man's chin. 'P ... Please. Don't ... don't take it all away. Please.'

'Take what away?' Hal edged closer.

'My ... my ...' the man stuttered. 'My ... collection.'

'Your collection?'

'In there. Please don't take it away.' He motioned to the door behind him.

Hal came alongside and squatted next to the man. 'I don't understand. What do you mean "collection"?' He could now see that the hundreds of small boxes had 'Polaroid' written on their sides.

'Nobody's ever seen it before.' The sobbing was coming under control now. 'It's my own ... little ... thing.' He shuffled out of the doorway and looked Hal straight in the face. 'Please ... don't take it all away. Nobody's ever seen it before.'

Hal stood up and turned the handle to the door.

'Are you sure?' Burlock's face was more serious than Hal could ever recall. 'You don't know what's in there.'

Luchewski ignored Burlock and pushed the door open.

The light coming in through the solitary window was exceptionally bright, catching the midday sun in all its glory, and it took Luchewski a couple of moments to adjust his vision. Then he turned and looked at the walls.

'Jesus!'

'What is it?' Burlock pounded along the landing and into the room. 'What is – bloody hell.' He stopped when he saw what Luchewski had seen. 'Look at that.'

The walls of the room were covered in Polaroid photographs. From where the skirting board started to where the ceiling began. From corner to corner and around the window, not a single inch of wall space had been left uncovered. Hal looked back and saw that even the door had been plastered with prints, along with the alcove in which the window was set. Only the wooden floor and cracked plaster ceiling were free of glossy, white-framed shots. He moved to the wall and noticed the thousands and thousands of little plastic-tipped pins that held the pictures in place, before pushing his finger at one of the photos. It felt spongy. He pushed again. It didn't feel like hard wall or solid corkboard behind. It felt like ...

'There are layers of them.'

'Eh?'

Hal saw that beside the doorframe, the photos stood at least a quarter of an inch out from the wall. 'There are layers of photos.

Three or four deep by the look of it. He's been building this up for years.'

'They all look the same to me.'

Hal zoomed in and inspected what was actually on the photos. Houses. People walking past houses. Cars parked in front of houses. Shots of windows on houses – curtains open, curtains closed. A dog pissing against a garden wall. Crows tugging away at a broken black bin liner on the path of a house. A recycling van. A cyclist. All taken in front of the same few houses with the same front doors.

'It's this street.'

The man came into the room looking more composed.

'We're up to here.' He was carrying another photo and he pointed to a particular position on the left-hand wall. 'I take them round and round.' He pulled a couple of pins out of the wall and, using one hand to hold the shots underneath in place, he positioned the new photograph on top and stuck the pins back in. 'There.' He stood back to admire his handiwork. Hal could see that it was the photograph of himself and Burlock talking on the pavement opposite. Burlock was looking serene and Hal was mid-twitch, his arms waving around the air. He thought that he looked rather comical.

'You won't take it away, will you?'

'Hmm?'

'It broke, you see. My camera.' The man's face dropped into a nervous frown. 'And I didn't get it fixed. My wife kept telling me to get it fixed, and I kept putting it off. Always other things to spend money on. Food to buy, shoes for the boy, a bike for the boy, bills to pay. All the usual. So I never got it fixed. She told me I should, but I never got it fixed. It just sat in the drawer getting dusty. Sat there for years. I could have bought another one, I suppose, but again, I couldn't afford it. Useless at earning money, me, you see.'

'I can't get –'

'Useless. Could never do it very well.' The man continued. He had a story to tell and he was going to tell it. It was spilling out of him like someone had de-stoppered an overfull bottle. 'Hopeless, you see. Not much of a husband or father. Managing like that. Making do. Never really gave them anything much. Never had much to give.' Hal could see the man's eyes moistening again. 'No luxuries. Nothing like that. Not like a real dad should.' He swallowed hard. 'So it sat in the drawer. For ages. Never getting fixed. Then it happened.' A tear rolled down the man's ashen cheek. 'It was after school. Just after school. Susan had picked him up.

232

Loved school he did. Brilliant. Brilliant boy, he was. Always trying out his times tables and all that. Always looking at the books and asking questions. Brilliant boy. It was on the bend – on the corner. The driver of the van that was parked there said afterwards that there was nowhere else he could go. It was busy, you see. People picking up their kids. They always go in their cars these days. But Susan didn't – no second car, you see. She walked. Always walked. Said it did her good anyway. Said a second car would be a waste. No need for it. It was only just over half a mile. Said it did her good.' He wiped the tear away with the back of his hand. 'Anyway. The boy in the 4x4 said afterwards that he didn't see them. Said he couldn't have seen them. The van was in the way, you see,' he tried to smile at the two policemen and the compression of his eyelids made two more tears run down his face. 'Couldn't have seen them. Anyway. Ashley was killed instantly, that's what the policeman said at the inquest. Would have been killed – pop – like that. Wouldn't have felt a thing. Which is good, isn't it? That's a good thing that he didn't feel anything. Just gone like that. Susan lived – for a few days anyway. Life support but her brain had gone. Had to turn it off. The doctor said there wasn't any point. That all they were doing was keeping her organs alive. No point.'

Burlock walked up to the man and laid a hand on his shoulder. The man didn't protest. 'I'm sorry. I'm really sorry about that. When did it happen?'

The man shrugged. 'I don't know. I can't remember. In the past. I lose track nowadays. The months and years just pass me by.' He coughed to stop his voice from breaking. 'So, we bury them together. Ashley on top of Susan. A terrible month for rain, I remember, but the sun shone that day. Came out and shone down on us all as we said our goodbyes. A beautiful day. Beautiful. Birds singing and that. But then, over the weeks, I get to looking around the house – digging out all the old stuff that Susan had and in Ashley's room – and I realise that, because I hadn't fixed the camera, because I'd left it sitting in the drawer for over two years, there were no recent pictures of them both. No pictures. I didn't have any pictures. Ashley was eight. The last picture I had of him was at his sixth birthday party. Have you got children? You know there's an enormous difference between six and eight. An eight-year-old is nothing like a six-year-old. They're more grown up, more on the ball. Turning into proper little human beings, they are.' He tried smiling again. 'Almost human they are. On their way. So all I was left with was out-of-date photographs. Nothing to show what they were like on the day that it all happened … Nothing to remind me … Nothing …'

'So you've been photographing ever since, haven't you?' Hal's voice was soft. 'You've been trying to fill the gaps with everything else. Taking photographs, not missing a moment, because you never know which moments might be the important ones, isn't that right?' Images of a Monte Carlo dash – his mother and father lying side by side in the hospital mortuary – ran through his head. Their faces, cold and grey. Their hair, oddly perfect. Not being allowed to see below their necks. Then the thought of Lily being ripped out of the world made the back of his eyes tingle and he felt nothing but sympathy for this wreck of a man.

'That's it. That's it exactly.' Teary snot poked out of the man's nose and he wiped it with his sleeve. 'I'm capturing everything. That's right. Isn't it the Aborigines who say that every time you have a picture taken you lose a tiny piece of your soul? It *is* the Aborigines, isn't it? Well, I don't agree. I think that every time you take a picture you hold on to moments – hold on to seconds that will never exist again. It's like keeping butterflies in a glass jar. Preserving them. You actually give the seconds a soul by keeping them forever.'

Hal couldn't really see the logic but nodded as if he did. 'So how long has it taken you to build up this … collection?' He waved his hand around the room.

'Oh this isn't the *entire* collection,' the man now stood proudly. 'These are just current. I keep the majority of the photographs in boxes in the attic and in the spare bedroom.' He grinned through the tears. 'There's rather a lot of it, you know.'

'Do you document it all? What I mean is do you keep records of days and dates?' Hal saw his chance.

'No …' The man was obviously pleased to have someone show an interest in what had become the main focus of his life. 'No, I don't keep a record – I'm not *that* anal – but it's not impossible to track back and find photographs taken on a particular date – I keep them all in order. Why?'

Hal looked at Burlock. 'This morning a body was dumped on the doorstep opposite. It might have been too early for you, but I was wondering if you'd taken any snaps of it happening? I realise it's really unlikely but –'

'Let's see.' The man wasn't crying now. 'This is the last photograph I took – of you both – sorry.' He placed his finger on the image, then started to walk alongside the wall, his finger trailing over pictures that had been taken before the one with the two detectives. Hal noticed shots of the forensic team going about their business, one of Singh walking along the pavement, Dr John Good yawning, some passers-by watching the proceedings. All the while, the man's finger traced a line back in time. Eventually, after walking two complete circuits of the room, the photos spiralling upwards, Hal saw some pictures of the two milkmen discovering the body, the light slightly dimmer than the ones before (*Or was it after?* thought Luchewski). Then the man stopped. 'There.'

'What is it?'

'Now I remember. It woke me up. A car's engine running – it was left running. Normally, traffic down this road doesn't stop – well, not at three in the morning it doesn't. Or if it does – somebody local getting home late or something – then the engine dies quickly. But this one woke me up. Was just turning over for a couple of minutes, I'd say. So I got a shot of it.'

Hal leaned forward to get a look at the picture. It was dark. Very dark. Slightly blurred, too. Yet he could make out the shape of the car, behind which a figure seemed to be crouching.

'An SLK. A Mercedes SLK. Silver. I think. Could be black, it's hard to tell. Come have a look, Freddie.'

Burlock sidled up and squinted. 'Aye. Looks posh. Could be an SLK. Probably silver, you're right. Is that him?' He pointed at the smudged shape. 'Do yer think that's him? It's not a very good picture of him.'

Hal smiled gently at the man. 'I'm sorry, sir. I don't know your name.'

'Trevor,' the man extended a hand. 'Trevor Phillips.'

Mr Phillips. Collects crisp packets, Doris Thompson had said. Hal took the hand and shook it firmly. 'Mr Phillips. Last Thursday night or early Friday morning, we believe that this same person left a severed hand on exactly the same front doorstep. I wonder if you got a shot of that. Do you think you got a shot of that?'

Phillips shook his head. 'No. I didn't. The first I knew about it was when the police arrived. I must've slept through that one. The police kept knocking.' His eyes suddenly flicked down to the ground again, as though he were embarrassed about something. 'I don't usually answer.'

'Did you know Mr Rabin well – the owner of the house?'

'Not really. I might've said hello to him a couple of times. I don't really know which one he is. Lots of people go in and out of there.'

'Lots of people? Do you have shots of them all?'

Phillips shrugged. 'Dunno. I've probably got shots of most of them at some time or other. Like I said, I do a lot of photographing nowadays.'

'Do you think we could have a really good look through your collection, Mr Phillips?'

The man looked panicked. 'You're not going to take it all away, are you? Please don't take it all away.'

'Of course not. No. Don't worry. We'll keep it here – in this room, if you like – but I think you might have some vital evidence. Something that can help put this killer away for good.' Hal's phoned bleeped and he glanced at the screen. 'Do you think you can help us, Mr Phillips?'

The man face began to crack open into a wide grin. 'Shall I get a box down? From the attic? One of the recent ones?'

'Please. I would be very grateful.'

Phillips seemed to leap through the door.

Hal turned to Burlock. 'What is it with people and their little secret rooms? McKenzie grows skunk in his attic. Wiseman keeps a memory card in a gap behind a poster. Rabin has his little secret sex den. Now this. What is it with people and their secrets?'

'You're a fine bugger talking,' Burlock muttered through his beard.

Hal coughed and straightened his jacket. 'I'm putting you in charge of going through these photos. See if you recognise anybody.'

'Oh joy of joys.' Burlock winked. 'Given me and the Green the best jobs today, I see. Well, I suppose it's not as bad as having to wade through hours of hardcore amateur gay pornography. Or driving through the badlands of Bedfordshire.'

'See if you can spot Judd, Larby, or Humphreys. See if someone else comes along with them.'

'Will do, boss. What about you?'

Hal wiggled his phone at Burlock. 'Woode's got the ARVs together – Christ knows why – so we're off to see Mr Humphreys. Leave you here with Mr Phillips and his boxes of fun.'

'Thanks.'

'My pleasure. Consider it my little gift for the concern you showed for my drinking … ahem … problem.'

Burlock looked around the room. 'Great.'

The door swung open and in bundled Trevor Phillips with a large wooden casket. He was having some difficulty carrying it.

'This is about two weeks' worth. Probably about a month ago. All in order, forward to back, left to right and top to bottom. Might be something in here.'

Burlock stared at Hal. 'Great,' he said once again, this time through gritted teeth.

Paul Norris tapped his fingers on the screen of his mobile, his body resting back on the green gazebo with the zig-zaggy 'NOW ONLY £850' sign on it. He'd shoved the brush behind the 'Gravel and Wood Chippings' fence and was enjoying the feel of the hot sun on his face. It was a quiet morning. Not too many customers to piss him off. Only a couple of coppers pestering the staff with some questions about Mr Judd. Everyone was beginning to wonder if Mr Judd had had something to do with Danny Wiseman's death. After all, he'd taken the last couple of days off sick, and it wasn't really like Mr Judd to take time off. Then again, everyone knew how religious Mr Judd was. It obviously wasn't him. Nah, the police were just covering their arses as per fucking usual. Some other cunt had gone and killed Wiseman and all those others. Must've done.

Scrunched into the fleshy folds of his right hand was the torn piece of paper that Wiseman had written on a couple of weeks back. Before he'd been murdered, of course. The piece of paper with the number for The Club on it. It was a mobile number, not a landline, and he started to roll the paper open into the palm of his hand, the fingers of the left hand still nervously tapping his own phone's screen.

The night before, he'd had an argument with Tracey. About money. Again. There was fuck all in the cupboard for them to eat, and they'd ended up having cheesy pasta for the third time that week. Tracey had a go at him after that. Kept saying how cheesy pasta wasn't good enough for a growing boy of two years old. Said how he needed good quality proteins and all that nutritional shit or his bones and his teeth weren't going to develop properly. She said that he'd probably end up stunted if they didn't find some more money from somewhere. Paul had shouted back something along the lines of how he was trying his best and that he couldn't do any more than he was doing already. And yet there was a digging sensation in his heart that there probably was more that he could be doing.

He shuddered at the thought of it but, in a funny way, it was easy money. They paid pretty well, that's what Danny had said. It couldn't be that difficult, could it? Wanking off a bunch of old farts? There were definitely things he wasn't going to be able to do. He wasn't going anywhere near anyone's arse, for a start. And he wasn't going to let anyone near his. He might, he thought, allow someone to suck him off, but he drew the line at putting some other bloke's cock in his mouth. Just the thought of it made him want to puke. He wasn't bent like Danny. He wasn't going to get any thrill out of it. He'd just have to swallow his pride and get it done and hope that no one he knew would find out.

It felt funny looking at Danny's spidery writing – swirling all over the crumpled stub of paper – knowing he was dead. A bit weird. His sevens had rounded tops and the fours looked as if they were trying to be nines, but his zeros were definitely zeros. Danny murdered. Fucking hell.

The number belonged to one of the pervy guards at Granton. Not somebody Paul had ever met, but somebody he had heard of. The one that called himself the Creep. Funny fucker by all accounts. Fat fucker. He kind of ran The Club. Got boys for them. Told them where to go and when. They'd go to a house in Norwood usually. That's what Danny had said. A room at the top of a scruffy DSS house where they'd film you touching yourself. He didn't mind that as long as it didn't end up on Redtube or something. As long as they just kept it for themselves.

Now. It was now or fucking never. Paul flicked the phone into life and the screen lit up in his hand. He brushed the 'Number Pad' button and started to tap the mobile number in with his thumb. He didn't pause to give himself time to think. It needed doing. He could feel his heart thumping gently in his chest as he finished inputting the number and hit the 'Call' button.

A quiet ringing as he held the phone to his ear, then a few seconds later –

'*Welcome to the Orange answerphone. The person you are trying –*'

'Ah, fuck.'

Paul tucked his phone into his trouser pocket before flicking the wrinkled piece of paper into a nearby plant pot. He'd have to try again later.

Chapter Twenty-one

He knew he'd forget his damned phone. Bloody woman. Because of her and her stupid bloody pills he'd left the phone still charging in the socket in his room. It would probably overheat and start a house fire from which there'd be no escape. The old witch would be stuck in her fucking chair and roasted to death like one of those chickens on the rotisserie at Sainsbury's. They'd probably find her with her tongue lolling out, clutching the latest edition of *Woman's Own* or *Bella* or whatever it was she was reading that day.

Ah, well, I can dream, he thought to himself as he yanked the wheel hard left and struggled to keep the car from mounting the pavement and killing a couple of well-heeled pedestrians.

Blackheath. A part of London he didn't really know. One of the posh pockets that didn't really seem to fit in with the rest of the squalor that was London. Pockets of posh houses and posh people that stood out like warts on a baby's arse. It always amazed him how close to the shitholes these rich little clusters could be found. Only a minute and a half ago he was driving through Lewisham – one of the greatest concentrations of drug addicts, whores, thieves, and gangsters in the whole of South London. Now he was passing two-million-pound houses with their own drives, all smothered with expensive cars. Two totally different worlds. A universe apart, yet a mile apart. How could people so different live so near each other? *Why* would they live so near each other? He could never understand it. The only conclusion he could come to was that everyone was a fucking crook, but that some crooks were more successful than others.

Something else he could never understand was the appeal of Blackheath. It always struck him as barren. Flat. Far too open. In a way it looked wrong in the hubbub of shitty city life. Like a building site just waiting for planning permission. It seemed to him to be little more than a field for people with fat wallets to walk their fat dogs on. Too exposed. He knew of better places further south, along the Kent and Surrey borders, where there were plenty of places to lie in wait.

The car was starting to wind him up too. The stupid kid had put flash tyres on it and it made turning the wheel a lot harder than it should have been. It felt like they were sticking to the road half of the time and his arms were getting knackered just steering the fucking thing. Either that or the power steering was kaput. That was another good reason to dump the sodding thing as soon as he could. Probably tomorrow, after this job. Yes, definitely tomorrow.

He found the road quickly enough. A row of brightly painted pointy things with Grade II Listed written all over them. Victorian black railings and traditional sash windows. All la-di-dah and toffee-nosed. Still, if rich idiots wanted to pay him good money for entertaining their chinless offspring for an hour, he'd happily take their cash and leave piss on their toilet seat. Number nineteen was yellow and white with a green regency canopy over the sitting room window. He stopped the car and turned off the engine. Cars zipped past him on the road and he had to wait a few seconds for a gap in the traffic before getting out and running round to the passenger's side. Opening the door, he lifted out the two carrier bags with his costume and tricks in and, after locking the car, made his way through the gate.

He couldn't remember the kid's name – he hadn't bothered to write it down. It was one of those mental names that posh people give their kids. 'Beautiful' or 'Glorious' or some such idiotic fucking thing. Something that would give the kid a lifetime of hell. Something hippyish.

He trudged along the stylish flagstone path and climbed the steps to the imposing front door. Pressing the doorbell, he stood back and waited. The front lawn looked perfect – not a weed or fallen leaf to be seen. It was evenly green – not patchy or overgrown like his own tiny yard – and he was certain he could catch the pale scent of jasmine on the air. A minute passed before he pressed the bell again. It was then that he noticed the door was ajar. He left it for another minute before pushing the door open.

'Hello?' He peered into the hallway. There was nobody to be seen 'Hello? Anyone at home?' He edged into the hallway. The house looked dark, as if all of the curtains were closed. On the wall, Humphreys noticed a monstrous painting of some ugly looking women floating up above a mountain. Drab smears of brown that nobody in their right mind would spend money on. 'Too much fucking money,' he mumbled to himself before once again shouting, 'Hello. I'm here for the party. You left your door open.'

There was still no answer, so he walked further in and dumped his bags on the floor. The house felt hot and stuffy and he pulled his shirt out of his trousers and flapped the bottom edge up and down in a feeble attempt to get some air. It didn't work. He could feel the sweat running down his body. He waited a few seconds before calling out again. Louder this time. 'HELLO. ANYONE HOME?'

Nothing.

Idiots had gone and left the door open and forgotten all about the party they were throwing for their spoilt brat. He sighed to himself and decided he'd take a good look around the joint. Even if they found him wandering around he had the perfect excuse for being there. He was, after all, *supposed* to be there. They'd booked Booboo the Clown, and there he was, trying to find someone to tell him what was going on. He twisted the knob on a door and went in.

It was in those few seconds between putting his hand on the handle and stepping into the room that two things came rushing into his head. The first was that two o'clock on a weekday afternoon was a very strange time to be holding a party for a six-year-old. The second was the name of the six-year-old in question.

Pretty. *That was it*. The girl's name was Pretty.

'I said he's not here. Get out! Go on, get out!' She spat at Woode and a blob of grey spittle landed on his trousers.

'Oh … Madam! Please keep yourself under control.'

'Get out. You've got no right to be here. This is my home. We don't want no police here, do you hear? Get out.' She twisted the wheelchair around weakly and tried to block the way. 'You've got no right.'

'We've got every right, madam,' Woode dabbed at the spit with the corner of a rather flowery-looking handkerchief. 'We have a warrant for the arrest of your son.'

'A warrant? Pah! Not worth the paper it's written on. My Keithy's a good boy. You ask anyone. They'll tell you. Anyone around here,' her head nudged towards the door that was still wide open, 'Ask anyone. They'll tell you what a good boy he is.'

Hal leaned in close to the old woman's ear and whispered very calmly. 'Don't you want to know what we want to arrest him for? Or do you already know?'

'What are you saying? This is harassment. This is police harassment. That's what this is.'

'We want to interview him in connection with the recent murders. You know the ones. The Granton murders.' The old hag went quiet and still. 'That's right,' Hal continued whispering. 'The murders. We want to have a little chat with your Keithy about the murders.' Hal stood up straight and went back to speaking at his normal volume. 'Shocked? You *look* a little bit shocked.' The junior officers pushed past them and spread themselves around the house. 'So, where is he?'

'No, no. Not my Keith. You've got it all wrong.' She was less aggressive now and her eyes seemed to dart about as if trying to spot something in which she could find some comfort. 'He's … he's not like that. He's a good boy. He wouldn't have anything to do with those murders.'

'Shall we ask him and find out? Where is he?'

'He's not here. I told you, he's not here.'

'So where *is* he?'

'He's out.' She looked shifty. 'On a job.'

'On a job?' Woode had finished wiping down his trousers. 'What sort of a job? Works at Sainsbury's, doesn't he? He's not down to do a shift today.'

'No. Not Sainsbury's. He does … something … else.'

'Yes?' Hal was started to lose patience with this terrible sour-faced old sow.

'Booboo the Clown.'

Hal found himself snorting out loud. 'Booboo the Clown?'

'He does children's parties.'

'*Children's*? Jesus Kid Jensen.'

'Does stuff with balloons and cards. Says he wants to do it. Says that he wants to give up Sainsbury's and be Booboo the Clown all the time. I've told him it'd be silly. Sainsbury's is a steady job. He can take good care of me properly with a steady job. Be taken seriously. But a clown? People laughing at you all the time and poking fun at you all the time? It's not a job for a man, is it?'

'Where is this party, Mrs Humphreys? We need to find Keith as quickly as possible.'

She looked up at Luchewski with large sad eyes and for a split second Hal felt sorry for the selfish old harridan in a wheelchair.

'I don't know. He never tells me nothing. Comes and goes all the time. Does his work, comes home, goes out, comes back home again. I lose track. All I have is the telly for company, my medicine, the occasional bit of food, and a poor night's rest. That's all my life consists of now. Nothing much.'

One of the junior officers with a dodgy haircut walked up to Hal and interrupted the woman's speech. 'He's not here, sir. We've searched the house. Top to bottom. Not a dickie bird.'

'OK.' At Luchewski's insistence, the Armed Response Officers that Woode was keen to bring were kept on standby a hundred yards up the road, twiddling their thumbs and comparing the size of their weapons. Instead, Hal had drafted in some of the CID constables and a handful of uniforms to swamp the Humphreys residence. Surrounding an ordinary suburban house with a bunch of guns wasn't going to bring them much luck and Woode had grumbled and grudgingly gone along with it all. Eventually. 'We're after an address. Try and find a piece of paper or a diary or an address book or something like that,' Hal ordered the young officer. 'I need to know exactly where he is right this minute.' The officer turned to go. 'And, Constable ...' Hal continued, stopping the detective in his tracks. 'Every second counts, OK?'

'Sir.'

Hal wandered slowly over to the window overlooking the road in front of the house and watched as a fat spider in a formidable web scuttled along to deal with a fly that had managed to get itself ensnared in the silky threads.

'How old is your son, Mrs Humphreys?'

'What?'

'Your son. How old is he?'

'Forty-nine. He'll be fifty next year. Why?'

'Always lived at home with you, has he?'

'What?'

'Has he ever been married? Had a family?'

'What is this?'

'Or has he spent his entire life running around like a servant to you? A slave to a domineering mother –'

'Harry,' Woode warned.

'– who would rather have her only son spend his days wiping her arse and fetching her Cup-a-Soups than trying to live his life in the big bad world.'

'Harry!' Woode was more forcible now. 'This isn't going to help.'

'What are you saying? You can't talk to me like this. I have rights, you know.'

'Oh, that's right.' Hal turned back to face her. 'People like you always know their rights. Covering your arses from every angle. It's all a game to you, isn't it? Life. A game where you only feel happy when you're centre stage and pulling all the strings.'

'She's in a wheelchair, for Christ's sake.' Woode looked red in the face.

'I don't need you to defend me.' She seemed to spit at Woode once again. 'I can speak for myself.' She twisted back to Hal. 'What's your name? I want to know your name. I'll make sure that you get strung up for the way that you're talking to me. You're a disgrace. Picking on a wheelchair-bound old woman. Makes you feel big, does it? Going on at an old woman who can't do anything for herself. What a big man you are! Oh so big, ain't ya? Well, let me tell you –'

'Oh, shut up.' Hal flicked his hand dismissively towards the bubbling old boiler and walked straight out of the room, back into the hallway in time to catch the constable with the severe Number One cut jumping down the last few stairs.

'Got it, sir. On the bedside table.' He handed Hal a scrappy piece of paper on which was scrawled in spidery blue pen, 19 POINTER'S HILL RD, BLACKHEATH.

It was a few moments – Hal's blood still steaming from the argument with Mrs Humphreys – before the address slipped into Hal's consciousness, swilled around his synapses, sorted through the filing cabinets of his mind, cross-referenced and double-checked itself and, eventually, flicked the switch. In the days that followed, he would describe those first few seconds as like waking in the morning, blissfully unaware of some dreadful job needing to be done, and then … WHAM … a slap in the face with realisation, a jolt into the cold and complete harsh light of day, and a sinking sensation down through the chest to the pit of the stomach. Random thoughts and ideas pulled together and stuck themselves like jigsaw pieces.

A house in Blackheath … A silver SLK … Tall … Some degree of medical knowledge … 'All medical provision is contracted out'…

'Blackheath? Did you say Blackheath? Are you sure?' The constable answered something but Hal drowned him out with the blood rushing through his ears and the sound of the mobile buzzing in his pocket.

He knew. Knew who it was. Not why or how, but certainly who. None of it made sense. But he knew who it was.

Flustering with his jacket, he clumsily fumbled out the mobile and flipped it up to his ear.

'Yes?'

'Got a couple of pictures here –' it was Burlock. He sighed before continuing. 'You'll never guess who's going in and out of the house.'

'I can … I know … I've worked it out.'

Burlock sighed again. 'What are we going to tell her?'

Hal found himself shaking his head. 'I don't know. I really don't know.'

'You don't think she knows already, do you?'

'No. God, no. She hasn't got a clue.'

'Thank Christ for that. I mean … poor bloody girl.'

'I know.'

'Her whole life's about to be ripped apart.'

'Yeah.' Hal rubbed his hand over the top of his head. 'I know.'

Suddenly the door to the sitting room sprang open and Woode lurched towards Hal.

'What the bloody hell do you think you're up to?'

'What?'

'In there. You can't go around behaving like that to members of the public.' Then in a slight whisper, 'She's going on about the IPCC in there. Seriously too. You'd better get your arse back in there and apologise. Pronto.'

'We know who he is?'

'Eh?' Woode was nonplussed for a second. 'Who? What're you on about?'

'Our murderer. Remember? We're investigating a murder?'

'Don't be a smart-arse, Harry.'

'Sorry.'

The constable coughed his excuses before running back up the stairs.

'Well?' Woode straightened himself up. 'Who is it? Do we know him?'

'I'm afraid we do, sir. I'm afraid we do.' Hal pressed the red telephone button on the mobile before sliding it back into his pocket.

'Well?'

'His name is Gardener. Nicholas Gardener.'

'Gardener?'

Hal nodded. 'He's Singh's fiancé.'

Part Three:
Ruined in a Day

Chapter Twenty-two

The TT squealed to a stop at the side of the road. Luchewski leapt out while Woode tried to extract himself from the passenger seat.

'Jesus … You need a bigger car.'

Hal ignored him. The entry sergeant, spotting Luchewski, flipped up his visor and waved towards him.

'He's gone, sir.'

'His car? A silver SLK?'

'Gone, sir.'

Hal's eyes turned back to the road and instantly spotted the Fiesta directly in front of the house.

'Erm …'

'We saw that too, sir. Got a team coming to check it out.'

'Hmm. Good. Good work. Is Humphreys here, or has he gone too?'

'No. He's here. In the basement. Bloody mess I'm afraid, but he's still breathing. Should be an ambulance here any minute.'

'What happened?' They walked up the path towards the door. 'What did he –'

'Head injury. Don't know if he got disturbed or what but –'

'You had people around the back?'

'Of course, sir. Standard procedure. But he'd gone by the time we got in. Front and back doors were wide open.' Woode caught up with them as they walked into the hallway. 'There's something else you need to see, sir. In the basement.'

Officers in helmets and body armour shuffled out of the way. The entry sergeant led Luchewski and Woode to a door under the stairs. Ducking, they eased themselves down the rickety staircase to the dimly lit basement below. Two officers were crouched over the body of a largish man, a raincoat covering colourful clothes underneath. Humphreys. The Creep. Blood seeping from the back of his head.

'Bloody hell. He's in a bad way,' Woode muttered under his breath. 'His mum won't be pleased.'

'Over there.' The entry sergeant pointed to a corner of the small room where an enormous glass tank sat.

'What is it?' As he spoke the words, Hal became aware of the sharp, acid stench that filled the air. 'What's that smell? Shit.' He stopped dead in his tracks.

'Vinegar, sir. It's vinegar.'

'Jesus Kid Jensen.'

At the bottom of the tank, in the cloudy liquid, was a bloody mass.

'Wiseman. Wiseman's remains. Shit.'

'Christ.'

Hal walked up to the tank and stroked the glass gently before turning around and addressing Woode directly.

'Big. It's big, isn't it? Plenty of room for others.'

'Jesus Kid ...' Woode looked pretty shocked.

The ambulance arrived just minutes later, the paramedics rushing into the house. Woode and Luchewski watched them from the pavement out front as passing cars slowed to a crawl to see what was going on.

'I still don't understand what's going on,' Woode scratched himself under his jacket. 'I mean, what's he got to do with Wiseman and Larby?'

'Granton.' Luchewski was starting to get very pissed off with the hot weather. 'The guard at Granton – Francombe – said something about how all the medical and dental treatment was contracted out to private companies. I'd bet my liver that if you looked into it you'd find Gardener's dental practice was, or is, one of them. He gets caught up in this Club shit and ...' Hal stopped, realising he knew little more than Woode.

'You think he's involved in this Club? You think he's one of the men on the DVDs? But he's engaged to Singh. He's straight, isn't he? I mean, why would he ...' Woode's voice tailed off as it dawned on him that Luchewski wasn't necessarily the best person to be having this conversation with.

Luchewski smiled. 'It's a funny old world and there are some very funny people clinging onto it.'

Hal's phone cut in before the silence could venture into embarrassment territory. He pulled it out and shoved it up to his ear.

'Hello?'

'I suppose this means it's all over.'

'I'm sorry?'

'Sorry, Harry. I took your number from Priti's phone. Thought I might need it at some point.'

'Gardener?'

'Hmm.'

'Where are you?' Hal pointed at the phone and mouthed *It's him* at Woode.

'Not that far away. Thankfully I've very good instincts. I could virtually sense you all coming. So I took my chances and got out fast. Only just in time too by the look of it.' Hal looked up and down the road. Traffic and nosy neighbours cluttered the view. Hal watched Woode tapping on the screen of his own cell phone. 'Don't worry. I'm not *that* near. Let's just say I'm out of Blackheath now.' Hal could hear the roar of cars on the other end of the phone.

'You know you've got to give yourself up. There's nothing else you can do now.'

'I know, I know. I realise that. I'm not stupid.'

'No.'

'But there's one more thing I need to do – one more person I need to see – before I hand myself in ...'

'What? Priti?'

'No,' Gardener sighed sadly. 'Not Priti.'

'What? No. No more murders. The killing stops now. Just turn yourself in, for God's sake.'

Gardener ignored him. 'I'm going back to where this all began. I'll see you there, Harry.' The phone went dead.

'What do you think he means?' Burlock seemed to have lost at least three stone today through sweating. Even his beard seemed to be dripping with his own body fat. '*Where it all began*?' Green straightened his tie as he strolled up from where Burlock had parked the car.

'Edinburgh. He's heading up to Edinburgh. I've put all forces along the M1 on standby and notified Lothian and Borders of what to expect.' Woode puffed out with authority. 'He's making his way back up there for some unknown reason. Something to do with Emily Brown.'

'I'm not so sure.' Hal spoke quietly. 'It doesn't really make sense. Why would he go back to Edinburgh? Who would he want to see?'

'Well that's where it all began, surely?'

'Priti?' Burlock suggested. 'Is he trying to see Priti?'

Hal shook his head. 'I'm going to take a run over to Granton. In a way, that's where all this began.'

'I'll come with you,' Burlock shuffled.

'No. Stay here. Get all this –' he waved his arm up at Gardener's Georgian house, 'sorted. Get it searched. Make sure this Creep guy stays alive. There's enough shit back here to keep you occupied. I just want to go and get a few points clarified.'

'Sir.' They all turned back towards the house where the entry sergeant – minus his helmet – was running from. 'We found this. In the study.' He waved an unopened envelope at Luchewski. 'There were others, but this one is addressed to you.'

Green came alongside them. 'Have I missed much?' he said with a deadpan smile.

Hurley, Thurston, and Francombe were sitting around Hurley's desk looking glum. Hal was positioned in front of the desk on a chair that was far too small for him.

'It's true,' Hurley ventured. 'Pieterson, Gardener, and Handley have been our contract dentists for a number of years now. Have been since 2007, I believe.'

Thurston flicked through a file and started nodding vigorously. 'Yes. Yes. February 2007. We switched contracts from –'

'Would Gardener have access to the guards?' Hal wanted to force this whole thing on. He already knew the answer. 'I mean, Larby and Humphreys. Would he have known them?'

'Possibly.'

'Possibly?'

Hurley shifted in her seat. 'Quite probably. A guard would have escorted the patient to the treatment room. There's no reason to think it might not have been either of Mr Humphreys or Mr Larby.'

'Why were Larby and Humphreys sacked?' Hal leaned in closer. 'Larby was supplying – which, by the way, he continued to do with a business partner – another of your boys, Denzil McKenzie, whose body we pulled out of the Thames this morning …' Sharp intakes of breath. 'But there's something more. Something you're not telling me. Mr Francombe mentioned something about a complaint made by one of your inmates.' Hurley shot Francombe a look. 'What sort of a complaint?'

'Inspector Luchewski,' Thurston started. 'We really do need –'

'Oh, tell him, Simon.' Hurley shrugged. 'Tell him'

'Er …'

'The reason they were both sacked, Inspector, is that a number of boys made complaints that they behaved inappropriately towards them.'

'They were touching them up?'

Hurley winced. 'Perhaps … a little more than that.'

'Obviously, you can understand why we tried to keep a lid on it all, Inspector. Having inherited an institution that was shot to pieces and under fire from the press, we desperately needed to straighten things out in-house. Damage limitation if you like.' Thurston was starting to sound as though he ran the place and not Hurley. 'And it has turned around. Granton is now a success. Over the last few years great leaps have been made in terms of –'

'I don't think Inspector Luchewski is all that interested in our strategic plan, Simon.' Hurley half rolled her eyes at Luchewski and for the first time since meeting her, Luchewski found himself warming to her. 'I think he's got more to be doing than listening to revenue predictions for the next five years. Robert,' she turned to Francombe, 'is there anything else you think Inspector Luchewski should know about Mr Humphreys and Mr Larby?'

Francombe shuffled in his chair. 'No. Not really. Not that I can think of. Both Raymond Larby and Keith Humphreys were horrible men. It's no surprise that someone would want to kill them.'

Luchewski saw Hurley cast a look towards Thurston. 'What?'

'Hmm?'

'What is it? What are you thinking?'

Hurley grimaced. 'One of the boys who made a complaint against Mr Humphreys …'

'Yes?'

'His name was Denzil McKenzie.'

'Really?'

'Yes. Really, Inspector.'

Luchewski's mind shot off like a greyhound. *McKenzie knew Humphreys. Humphreys killed McKenzie. The car. The car was parked outside the house in Blackheath, not because of Gardener, but because Humphreys was using it to get around. Humphreys killed McKenzie. Perhaps McKenzie was blackmailing Humphreys, but Humphreys killed McKenzie. Humphreys killed McKenzie …*

'Probably confuses matters,' Hurley popped the top of a pen in and out. 'Apologies, Inspector, but life under the previous Chief Manager was a very messy affair by all accounts.'

Hal looked up at the row of photographs on the wall behind the desk. A succession of stern old, unsmiling faces, one after the other – Frederick Masterton OBE 1984-1987, Lionel Numan 1987-1991, Sir Randolph Peach 1991-1996, Neal O'Donnelly 1996-1997 – ending in the troublesome visage of the previous governor, Peter Burgess 1997-2012.

Peter Burgess 1997-2012.

A familiar face …

'Holy fucking shit.'

'I'm sorry, Inspector?' Hurley didn't entirely trust her ears.

'Er … Sorry. I … er … need to…' He stood up from his chair and pulled his phone out of his jacket pocket. 'I need to … er …' He waggled his phone at the three stunned faces in front of him.

'Of course.'

Hal made his way across the room to the door, unaware of exactly how his legs were able to carry him. Slipping through the door into the secretary's office, he swished his thumb over the screen of his phone and suddenly realised that he didn't know who to call.

The dead governor's face flooded his thoughts, only this time the face was squinting in the sun and the man was resting his elbow on a water butt. A tough-looking man in a wedding photo, arm in arm with a pretty girl. Why hadn't it struck him before?

Of course, none of that would have happened had the governor at the time been doing his job properly (in many ways I blame him most of all for all of this).

Luchewski knew what Gardener meant when he said he was going back to where it all began. The man would be walking into the lion's den, of course, but at this point he wouldn't really care, and a man who didn't really care could be a dangerous creature indeed.

He tapped the screen and called up what he thought would be the most appropriate number. It took a couple of seconds for John Good to answer.

Hal didn't waste time. 'Look, John, I know where Nicholas Gardener is –'

But Good cut him short. 'Harry. He's here. He's got a gun and he's gone straight up.'

Luchewski's heart dropped like a dead tree.

Chapter Twenty-three

Corrie had it all worked out for Hal during the drive back to Gypsy Hill. Doris Thompson had reverted back to her maiden name after the death of her husband – the late and not so great ex-governor Peter Burgess. As the accusations had started to fly, Doris had stood by her man like the trusty wife that she was, denying that her husband had done anything wrong. The expensive house in Shortlands, the cars that could each have stood in as a mortgage for most people, the foreign holidays twice a year – all of it had been duly and dutifully earned, according to Mrs Burgess. She clung to the idea that somebody was trying to discredit her husband for the sin of being handsomely paid. So it had come as a massive shock when her husband took his own life, knocking the poor cow for six. Confused and depressed, it hadn't helped when the police and Her Majesty's Government waded in, stripping everything apart until nothing was left. Then, broke and practically homeless, it was Rabin who had come to her rescue. Having given rooms to some of the Granton boys over the years – he had known Peter Burgess and Alexander Judd through their roles as governors of a local primary school – Rabin offered Doris one of his empty flats in his house on Gypsy Hill. With little other option and no children to help her out, she had accepted.

'Perhaps I should come back here tomorrow and the day after that. And the day after that. See if I can't add to this ever-increasing record.' John Good approached Hal as he walked up to the crowd. 'Twice in the same day. Three times in the same week. It's got to be something of a record, eh?'

The police had evacuated the entire street and set up road blocks at either end. Crowds of residents and passers-by were chattering and teetering on tiptoe to see if they could see anything, and Hal thought that he caught a glimpse of Trevor Phillips amongst them, Polaroid camera in hand. Along the edge of the road, at various positions, were a number of Special Firearms Officers.

'He's armed?' Luchewski asked, his eyes scanning the street.

'Came here waving a revolver about. Ordered us all out but took the old woman up to her room. Looked a bit manic to me.'

'Negotiator here yet?'

Good pointed beyond the cordon. 'On the phone already by the looks of it.' Hal could see a weaselly-looking man standing at the back of a police car with its boot open. 'Hasn't been here long.'

Hal pushed forward through the crowd before flashing his ID at a uniformed officer that he vaguely recognised. Nodding, the officer lifted up the cordon and let Luchewski through.

'... not the end of the world, Nicholas ... I can call you Nicholas, can't I? ... OK ... Nicholas,' the negotiator saw Luchewski coming and deliberately turned away from him, shoving a finger into his other ear to block out all noise. Hal stopped and waited. 'Nicholas, I realise that at the moment it doesn't look too good for you. You're probably starting to feel as if everything has gone too far. That if only you could have kept everything in, you wouldn't be in this mess now,' Jesus, thought Hal, Roy bloody Chubby Brown would have more tact and sensitivity than this particular negotiator, 'but what you need to get to grips with is the idea that the vast majority of your life will probably be the same as it was before all this began. The people you love will all be there, you will still be able to enjoy at least some of the things you enjoyed before, the sun will still rise in the morning and set in the evening. None of that will alter ... What? OK ... But killing an old woman will not help anything. It can only make things more difficult for you ... Doris is an old woman ... What? OK. I'll see.' He cut the call dead and turned to face Luchewski.

'DI Luchewski,' Hal lifted the card up but the negotiator ignored it.

'He wants you.' He didn't make eye contact.

'Hmm?'

'Says he'll let the woman go if you go up. Says he'll swap her for you.'

'Oh.'

The negotiator looked at Luchewski. 'Waste of time in my opinion. What usually happens in situations like this is that we end up with two dead bodies instead of one – don't tell anyone I told you that.' A slight twinkle in the eye. 'But, you know him best –'

'I don't really know him at all, actually.'

'Ah. Well. It's down to you of course. If you think you're up to it. You've done a negotiating course before, I'd've thought?'

Hal had a vague idea that he might have done a number of years ago, but it was *very* vague. 'Er ...'

'You going up?'

'I … er … I supposed I'd better. Hadn't I?'

'Don't worry. Just keep him talking. Keep listening. You'll be fine. Like my old gran used to say to me, she'd say "Tommy. You've been given two ears and one mouth for a reason. Use them in the correct proportions."' The negotiator pulled up his phone and hit a button before speaking again. 'Inspector Luchewski is going up. Let him pass.' He flicked his thumb back in the direction of the cordon and stared at Luchewski. 'You might want to go and get yourself fitted with a Kevlar vest under your jacket. Just in case.'

'No.' Hal found himself walking away from the car towards the house. 'It's all right.' He wasn't quite sure if he was pretending to be brave or just being fucking foolish. 'I don't need one.'

As he got nearer the front door, John Good shouted at him. 'Be careful with my crime scene. I haven't finished with it yet.'

The SFO situated just inside the front door gave Luchewski a curt nod as he came into the hallway, but he was far too nervous to notice. At the bottom of the flight of stairs, two other officers were stationed, and along the stairs themselves, another two. As Hal made his way up the stairs he could see one more SFO positioned on the next flight up. All of them helmeted, covered in body armour and carrying MP5s. It suddenly struck Luchewski that the Kevlar vest might have been a sensible choice after all.

At the top of the stairs, he turned right and knocked on the door.

'What is it?' Gardener's voice came from somewhere beyond.

'It's me. Luchewski. You wanted to see me.'

'Are you alone? You'd better be alone.'

'It's just me.'

A few second later the door cracked open and Doris' face peered out.

'Hello, Inspector,' she grinned a fake, strained grin. 'You come to join us. We were just having a nice little chat … Yes, a nice little chat.' She looked completely out of it.

Hal pushed his way into the room. 'Are you all right, Doris?'

'Hmm? Oh yes. I'm fine. Like I said, we've been having a nice little chat.' She was clinging to the tiny dog with all her strength. Realising that something wasn't quite right, it hadn't even bothered to yap at Hal as the door shut behind him.

Hal looked up to see Gardener pointing a gun straight at him. The Kevlar vest leapt to mind once again.

'Come on. Get in.' He waggled the gun towards the threadbare sofa. Hal grabbed the old woman gently by the arm and led her

255

towards the chair.

'What's all this about, Gardener?' Hal asked as they both sat down.

'What?'

'All this shit. It's over. What's the point of coming here and scaring an old age pensioner half to death?' Hal could see that Doris was bent over, with the dog on her lap, stroking the top of its head like crazy. 'I mean, she hasn't even got anything to do with all this.'

'What?' Gardener became suddenly angry. '"She hasn't got anything to do with all this"? If anything, she's the main cause of all of this! If it wasn't for her and her expensive lifestyle, her husband wouldn't have stolen and turned a blind eye to all the corruption at Granton. Corruption that led to Humphreys and Larby forming their little group with Rabin and Judd. A group that eventually sucked me in and –'

Sucked you off, more like, thought Hal. 'Look, Gardener. I've already had a bitter old woman in a wheelchair spit at me today. The last thing I want to do now is sit here and listen to the solipsistic rantings of a self-deluded idiot who thinks that the whole world has been designed around his ego. The fact is that *you* decided to join the fucking Fucking Club upstairs. *You* decided to kill people. Horribly. End of. Now you need to man up and take what's coming to you.'

Gardener looked stunned. Hal pushed on before he could react.

'But before you blast my head off with that thing, bear in mind you made a deal.'

'A deal?'

Hal inclined his head towards Doris, who was sitting seemingly oblivious to all that was happening, still patting the dog. 'You said that you'd let her go. If I came up to replace her, you said you'd let her go.'

'So?'

'So let her go. I mean, look at her. She shouldn't be here. She's frightened. I don't know about you but frightening old women isn't really my cup of tea. I mean, dealing with those others – the men – I can *kind of* understand, but scaring old women? I wouldn't have thought even you would have time for that.'

'Don't pander to my vanity.'

'No. No. I won't. But,' Hal turned to look at Doris, who was now muttering gently into the dog's ear, 'let her go. I mean, look at this place. Spending your final years in a dump like this. I think she's suffered as much as anyone, don't you? Anyway, you've got *me* now.'

Gardener sighed, his eyes flickering back to the old woman, and he gave a small nervous shuffle.

'OK. OK. She can go. I don't need her anyway. She's not worth my time.' He walked to the other end of the room and, once again, levelled the gun at Luchewski. 'But no funny business. You understand?'

'No. Don't worry.' Hal got up and grabbed Doris by the shoulder again. 'Doris, love. Come on. The gentleman says you can go.'

'Eh?'

'You can go. He's letting you go.'

'What about Archie?'

'Him too. Now come on before he changes his mind.' The old woman got up from the sofa and, clutching the little dog as if her life depended on it, started hobbling towards the door. 'Go down the stairs. There are some policemen there who'll lead you to safety. They'll look after you.' Hal twisted the handle on the door and pulled it open. 'Go on.'

Doris made her way through it and onto the landing, but before disappearing, she looked back at Luchewski and whispered: 'You know, Inspector, my husband was a good man. A good, hard-working man.'

'Yes, Doris,' he lied. 'I know.'

The door shut with a soft click.

'You are aware, aren't you, that there are men with guns bigger than yours just outside this room?' Luchewski said, turning to find Gardener pointing the gun directly at his head. 'Much, much bigger. All of them trained at this door.'

'I don't understand. Have you got a death wish, Luchewski? Is that it? Do you actually *want* me to put a bullet through your brain? You want to feel hot metal tearing through your hippocampus, do you? Because you're going about it the right way.'

'Actually,' Luchewski was trying to keep as calm as he could despite the fact that he was more petrified than he'd ever been before in his life, 'I've had a pretty crappy week. You'd probably be doing me a favour.'

'I'd be doing the *world* a favour. I mean, look at you.' Gardener spat the words out like rotting pips. 'You're a mess. An uncontrollable mess. Even though, according to the papers, you are a very rich man, you've got no style, you've got no culture. I mean, look at that awful car you drive – the estate agents' choice! You're just a tasteless little chav at heart, aren't you? A tasteless little chav with no idea of art and beauty. Your beloved father never taught you that, did he? Never taught you how to have class. *Real* class. Possibly because he didn't have any himself. You're just rich scum – that's all. Whereas *I* had to work my fingers to the bone and I *learnt* how to be me. You were just *born* into it. A stroke of luck. A toss of the dice. Nothing more. You've no idea what it's like to really make something of yourself.'

I *do* fucking know, Luchewski thought to himself. I know a fucksight more than you imagine.

Gardener waved the gun slightly to one side. 'And *sooo* selfish too. A spoilt little rich kid who rips his family apart so that he can go to bed with whoever he likes.'

'You're a fine one talking.'

'What?'

Oh, shit, thought Luchewski. Still, he decided to front it out. 'You heard.'

'All that … stuff … in this house,' Gardener could hardly control his temper. 'All that stuff … it was all … a mistake. A terrible, terrible mistake. But *you* …' he was almost growling, so Luchewski stood very, very still. '*You* are a catastrophe by design.'

Even though he had a gun pointed at him, Luchewski couldn't help but admire the phrase that Gardener had invented to describe him. *A catastrophe by design*. He found himself half-nodding in agreement.

'You place yourself in front of everyone, *Inspector* Luchewski. And you let them all down."

'What about your fiancée?' Hal asked. 'What about Priti?'

'Don't you mention her. Don't you *dare* say her name!"

'Haven't you let *her* down?'

'Shut up!'

'Haven't you put yourself in front of her?'

'SHUT … UP!'

They stood there in awkward silence, the blood in Luchewski's head racing around making him feel numb. He needed to regain some sort of control.

'Look, Nicholas. We need to bring all of this to an end. One way or another.' He walked across the room to the window and stared out, Gardener's revolver still aimed at his head. In the garden, two SFOs looked as though they were playing *Rock, Paper, Scissors* to while away the boredom. It was a moment of ridiculousness that almost made Luchewski smile. 'Only you can decide which way this goes.'

When Hal turned back, Gardener looked a very different man indeed. It was as though all the anger and strength had drained out of him, and his eyes seemed tired and defeated. Resigned. He lowered the gun and slumped back, sitting on the single bed in the corner of the grubby flat.

Still trying to look as cool and collected as possible, Hal found himself standing with his arm resting on the mantelpiece covered with silly little porcelain teddy bears and ducks. He thought back to earlier that day when he, Woode, Burlock, Green, and Singh had stood in this very room, watching the homemade pornography that they'd found in the hidden flat above. Bizarre, he thought, to think that that was just a few hours ago.

'You took some of the DVDs from upstairs, didn't you?' Hal asked. 'The ones in which you made an appearance. You were trying to wipe it all out.'

'Yes, yes,' Gardener didn't seem remotely interested. 'They're at the house. You'll find them at the house. You'll find *everything* at the house.'

'And it wasn't you who killed McKenzie, was it?'

'What? Who?' He looked genuinely confused. 'I don't know what you mean. Who's McKenzie?'

'Denzil McKenzie. He was a boy at Granton. We found his bo –'

'Have you ever been in love, Luchewski?' Gardener was staring at the floor again. 'I mean *really* in love?

Hal was about to speak but stopped when it dawned on him that, no, he didn't believe he'd ever truly been in love. Not with Jackie. Not with anyone. Ever, if he was being honest. And that thought disturbed him somewhat. He loved his daughter, of course, but that was a different sort of love. Not love as in 'I Love You'. He suddenly felt as though this man in front of him had stripped a layer away, peeling him like an apple, leaving him exposed. His mind danced back to that Stevie kid. Typical bastard journalist, putting the story about him in the papers – he'd had no right to do it. But … it had all been fine with Lily. Yes, he'd come to blows with Baldwin over it, which in all honesty was no bad thing anyway, but overall it had been oddly liberating. Being outed. It had been less traumatic than he had told himself it would be.

'I … er …' He tried to say something, to kill the embarrassing gap, but Gardener had stopped listening anyway.

'It's a weird thing, love. If you hunt it out, try and catch it in a net, you'll never get it. It will always elude you. It is as though it senses you coming. Watches your every, deliberate footstep as you try to creep closer. Easing closer and closer, softly until – whoosh. Up it goes, out of reach. A twitching, nervous butterfly.'

Hal sighed. This man in front of him was a murderer, plain and simple. He had to keep that in mind. And yet Gardener looked broken. Visibly crumbling in front of Hal. His molecules dissolving in the air of the stuffy room. He was slipping away.

'But when you don't look for it, when you're busy, distracted by the world and its terrible ways, that's when it swoops. It comes at you from nowhere. Like a brick through a window. And it hits hard. So hard you can't prepare yourself for it.'

'Priti.'

Gardener fell silent, his fingers massaging his temple, his eyes shut. Luchewski shifted his weight from one foot to the other. There was no need for the Kevlar vest after all. He suddenly knew that this man wasn't going to hurt him.

'A strange thing, love,' Gardener began. 'I'd resigned myself to never having it. It wouldn't be fair on somebody else. I just couldn't manage it. When your head keeps telling you you've got AIDS … Well. It just wouldn't work.'

'Look, Nicholas,' Luchewski's voice was more soothing now, 'I can't pretend I understand, because I don't. I really don't. But I *do* know it's time for all this to stop. You need to bring it all to an end, and bring it all to an end *properly*. Leave the gun on the bed and come downstairs with me. I'll make sure the officers downstairs take you gently. We'll bring a van right up to the front gate. Get you away from here quickly. Yes?' Hal pointed at the gun. 'Just leave it here. We'll take you away. Somewhere safe where you can speak to Priti. Yes?'

Silence seemed to fill the room like a balloon, but somewhere in the distance Hal could hear a crow caw and the dull buzz of traffic.

Suddenly, Gardener sat up straight.

'Harry.'

'Nicholas?'

'Afterwards, when you inspect this gun, you'll find that there was only ever one bullet in it. Tell her that I loved her very much.'

'NO!' Hal made a slight jerk forward, his hand extending to the gun, but the frighteningly loud bang froze him to the spot.

There was some shouting on the stairs outside before the door burst open and the SFOs ran in, weapons raised. One of them pushed Luchewski back behind him, keeping his semi-automatic pointed towards the bed where, slumped on the bed, was the dreadful, bloody mess that had once been Nicholas Gardener.

Part Four:
The Perfect Kiss

Chapter Twenty-four

FAO Inspector Harry Luchewski, Metropolitan Police.

Harry,

At the moment you are sitting downstairs in my kitchen having eaten the pasta alla Genovese that I made and a slice of the Harvey Nicks cheesecake that I bought. You are probably, right now, swallowing my coffee and stuffing cinnamon biscuits down your neck as you discuss the case – my case – with my wife-to-be. Oh the irony. Such beautiful, flawless irony. How perfectly neat.

Anyway, I am hoping that you will never read this note. With a bit of luck it will just sit on the top shelf of my study gathering dust until, one day, I remember that I left it there along with all the others. How I shall smile when I realise that I pulled the wool over your eyes – the Metropolitan Police's eyes, that is. That I managed to get away with some of the most daring murders ever committed in this stinking city of ours. Apologies for the devastating effect this will have had on your career, by the way.

On the other hand, if you *are* reading this then it means that something has gone disastrously wrong with my plans. Two things might have occurred should you be reading this note. Number one – you have caught me. Ensnared me in your net. Tracked me down with your sense of smell and pounced on me like a tiger. Unlikely given what I've seen over the last few days (I am writing this just before eight o'clock on Sunday, June 7th). To be honest, Harry, I've not been impressed. Perhaps they should put Priti in charge of the investigation. She'd probably do a much better job. I'll rephrase that – she'd *definitely* do a better job of it.

The second thing that might have happened is that – BANG – you've discovered that it is … yes, *moi* committing these (quite frankly) appalling murders, but that – BANG – I've disappeared. Done a bunk. Bolted. Ha! If this is the case, just so you know, I'm keeping my options open. I'm sure I'm miles away by now – there's a nice young man who lives on the New Addington estate who does a quality line in fake passports and stolen credit cards (guns too) –

so there's little point in chasing me. Get Interpol on the blower, if you like, but chances are I'm gone for good. Like that Monty Python parrot or the Scarlet Pimpernel. (I could just as easily be living around the corner. Imagine if we bump into each other in Costcutters one day! Would you even recognise me?)

Should I have gone then there are probably about a billion questions that are running through your head right now that you can't find any answers to. I don't have to answer any of them, of course. There's no real need. But I feel that should my ... ahem ... *exploits* (not the right word, I know, but it'll do) come undone, then, for my own piece of mind if nothing else, I would like to fill in a couple of gaps. For me, you realise. Not for you or your investigation. Satisfy the twitch in my own peculiar little soul.

To begin at the beginning as they say. Well, there's probably an awful lot that can be skipped over – stuff that, fundamentally, you've very little interest in. Born in 1970 to a loving mother and a hopeless father. An only child. Got a bump on the head from an accident at a birthday party when I was eleven. All of which one of your psychologists will have a field day with, I am sure, but which, in my mind is totally irrelevant. In truth, I think it all starts around 1988.

Do you remember those AIDS adverts, Harry? The ones with the John Hurt voiceovers? Slabs of stone being dramatically chiselled and pneumatically drilled? I was in the sixth form at the time. (I think you know that I got an A Level in Geography, don't you?) I was never the most popular of students – a couple of friends here, acquaintances there. Never really the life and soul. But one thing I did – and still do – have is a strong mind. A mind that is stronger than my own common sense. If my mind tells me something is true, then there's no other part of my body or spirit or soul – call it what you like – that can tell me otherwise.

Those adverts. I was impressionable. A young man with a brain that ticks too loudly. My mind started to latch on to the idea of AIDS. That I might even have it. Now bear in mind the fact that I hadn't even had sex with anyone and that I'd never taken any sort of drug intravenously, and you get the idea of how powerful my mind can be. Overwhelmingly so. Unbearable.

So, off to university I toddle with this mental timebomb. Tick, tick all the time.

I didn't bother getting to know the other students on my corridor. I was there to study dentistry. I'd spent years avoiding people, not interacting, burying my head in books and generally hiding from my peers, and I was not going to stop (or should that be 'start'?) now. So it came as an enormous surprise when, one wet afternoon, at a bus stop just off Queen Street, I struck up a conversation with a pretty young girl called Emily Brown.

–Rain.
–I'm sorry?
–Looks like rain.
(I can remember the conversation as if it were yesterday)
–Doesn't surprise me. Always rains round here. Never stops. You a student?
–Hmm.
–You look like a student. Got a sort of … studenty look about you. What're you studying?
–Dentistry.
To make the point I opened my mouth wide and pulled down my upper lip before pushing a finger towards my teeth. The girl laughed.
–You're funny.
–Am I?
–Yeah. What's your name?
–Nick. What's yours?
–Em. Emily, but everyone just calls me Em.

A bus ride, some flirting, a hastily arranged date. I found it all surprisingly easy. The only problem was the irritating tick, tick in my brain. A tick, tick that built up over the course of three seemingly successful dates. At the end of the last night of Emily Brown's life, the tick, tick was nigh on unbearable.

–D'you want to come up? she asked. You've not come up yet. Don't you want to see my little flat?'
–Of course I do. You know I do. (I could feel the strain in my brain.) But I don't think I should. I really don't think I should.
–Oh, don't be daft …
In a flash the key was in the lock, the door open and she was leading me up the stairs by the hand.
–It really is a nice flat, you know.

It was a nice flat. The coffee tasted good and the bed was warm and soft, but afterwards, as she rolled off me and into the fug of sleep, the ticking felt more like thudding. Thudding and banging, as my mind latched on to the thing that kept washing back up like a dirty tide for the rest of my life.

AIDS.

You remember surely, Harry. It was the late eighties, and the fear and paranoia of such a devastating, bewildering disease was at its peak. Rumours and whispers in playgrounds and offices, factories and shops, all blurred any facts and fanned the flames of anxiety. *Can you get it from kissing? How much saliva do you have to swallow before you get it? Can you get it from a toilet seat? If you breathe in the breath of somebody who has it, can you get it too?* Even the government and scientists – people who ought to know best and do the right thing – were caught off guard, unsure how to deal with a potential epidemic. In their haste to protect the general public from such a profligate disease they managed to produce clumsy literature and films that could only ever add to the panic. Adverts of bleak landscapes, with drills and chisels, a doom-laden John Hurt monotone, the toppling of a towering black monolith. White lilies. Nothing reassuring. Nothing sympathetic. Nothing informed. Just pure fear.

And in Emily Brown's bed, fear and frustration pounded away in my newly deflowered head. AIDS, I thought. I have AIDS. And even though somewhere in my heart and in my brain I knew that I didn't have AIDS – that the whole idea was ridiculous – the tick tick, thump thump, bang bang did its best to knock sense into a corner and beat it to a quivering pulp. No matter how much I tried that night to tell myself that Emily Brown was not the type of girl to carry the HIV virus, the obsessive dictator who lives in my brain forced me to believe that she could, that she might, that she did.

After hours of restlessness and turmoil, I went to the bathroom to wash my face before returning and placing a pillow over the pretty sleeping face of Emily Brown. Pushing down hard and avoiding her thrashing arms, I told myself that the disease had to die. That it wasn't a real disease but that it would grow to become a real disease if I let the girl live. It would grow inside me like a cancer, eating away at my mind and my body and my soul. If she died, my head kept telling me, I would live. Be free of it. Be cleansed.

I spent the rest of the night and most of the next day crying in the corner of the room, huddled on the floor against a dusty wicker chair. Then my brain started to tell me that I needed to get rid of the evidence. That the police would be able to trace me if I left everything as it was.

That was why I removed the sex organs. I didn't enjoy doing it, but I felt, or thought, that it needed to be done. I wrapped it all up well and, after catching two buses (yes, I took it on the bus!) I pushed it into the Firth of Forth. I tidied the room wiping everything down, and tried to leave the whole sordid incident behind me. I vowed to keep myself to myself forever. Never to touch another living soul for the rest of my life.

Fast forward nearly twenty years (sorry for the corny phraseology, Harry) and there I am, a partner in a highly successful dental practice. Don't think for a second that I just happened to land such a position. Those twenty years were filled with hard work and determination. When it finally came it was well deserved, I can tell you. One of the first things I helped to do upon becoming a partner was to win the bid for dental provision at Granton YOI. That meant that for one afternoon a week I was to be based at Granton and deal with all of the fillings and abscesses and rotten teeth of those boys.

That was where I met the Creep. Keith Humphreys, but likes to be known as the Creep. Laughable in a way. Ridiculous. But he saw something in me that I hadn't even seen in myself.

He was the guard who escorted the boys one by one down to the little room used as a surgery. He'd bring them down, watch me as I did the work, then take them back to their areas. This went on for months and then, one afternoon, he brought Danny Wiseman down for a check-up.

Danny Wiseman was a pretty young boy who'd managed to slip down the wrong track in life. Tragic, really. Such a terrible, terrible waste. When I met him I saw the spark in his eyes, a fire almost. If I wore tie-dyed tops and lit incense sticks, I'd say he had an aura about him. An aura of beauty and purity. I think I probably gasped. Whatever I did, Humphreys picked up on it. At the end of the session, instead of just ushering Wiseman out of the surgery and back to the main hall, Humphreys came up to me and whispered in my ear.

–Good-looking young lad, ain't he? Suck your cock for a pack of fags.

(That's the way Humphreys speaks, I'm afraid. Not my choice of words.)

I think I was horrified, but Humphreys just winked at me before taking the boy off. Over the months, every Wednesday afternoon, he'd bring down boys and, over the months, every Wednesday afternoon, his language would get cruder and cruder, proffering up particular boys for sex. They all seemed to be aware he was doing it. Some even seemed to enjoy it. Of course, none of that would have happened had the governor at the time been doing his job properly (in many ways I blame him most of all for all of this), but I did my best to ignore it – or at least that's what I thought I was doing until, one day, Humphreys handed me his telephone number on a card.

–We've a little club. Me and some people I know. You might like to come along.

Obviously, if you are reading this then you know what happened next. Yes, I made the phone call. Yes, I went along. The others seemed happy to welcome me. They all seemed to have a connection with Granton. Judd – the garden centre manager (and a pious idiot in my opinion) would give some of the newly released boys jobs. Rabin – the owner of the house where the club met (have you found the secret room yet?) would let some of his rooms to the boys. Humphreys (who always insisted on being called 'The Creep' during the sessions) and Larby both worked at Granton. And then there was me – the dentist.

At first I simply filmed them. Yes, I'll admit I got off on it all. Having restrained myself for the best part of twenty years, it all seemed rather titillating and twistedly exciting. And, after a while, I started to let myself go. It was all consensual. The boys willingly took part. They were paid well and many of them seemed more than happy to indulge the fantasies of a band of middle-aged men.

And so it went on.

But then I met Priti. I never believed in love at first sight. In fact, I still don't. But love at second or third sight didn't seem unreasonable. And that was how it was with Priti. Anyway, the manner of our meeting and of our getting together isn't relevant to this – all you need is the story, so I'll get back on track.

I fell in love with her and she fell in love with me (she's only human after all!) and all of a sudden The Club seemed to become a terrible taste in my mouth. Then the AIDS thing started to pound away in my head once again. Having controlled it so well for so long, I found myself struggling to keep it contained. If Priti and I were to have any sort of a future, if we were to get married and have children and lead a happy family life, then I was going to have to put a stop to the ticking and banging that went on in my head, of that I was certain. And the only way I could do that was to wipe it all out.

It seems weird writing this all down. All this stuff I have known so intimately for the last few years. I'm sure one of your psychologists would say that if only I'd written it all down a lot earlier I could have avoided having to murder however many people I needed to murder (twelve altogether – Humphreys, Larby, Judd, and Rabin, and then eight boys). They would say that writing everything down would be catharsis enough. But I don't think I would agree. Words are one thing. Actions are another.

And so I started planning. Planning the destruction of my disease. Humphreys, Larby, Judd, and Rabin I couldn't care less about – they were largely responsible for it all anyway. I don't care how the rest of *them* die. The more violent, the better, I suppose. The boys, though. They are different. At some point they were innocent before Humphreys et al (myself included) corrupted them. They deserve some degree of respect. That was why I put together the pump. An attempt to take them slowly. Let them slip out of the world as gently as they entered it. To be honest, it didn't work particularly well on Danny Wiseman – I may have to rethink things a little but, hey, necessity is the mother of invention and all that!

Sorry, Harry, but I'm getting a tad bored of this now (there's only so much confession a man can stand, you know). Besides, I've got a busy few days ahead of me and I need my sleep. Lots of people to kill and an entire police force to befuddle. Hey ho.

Bonne chance (not!)
Nicholas Gardener.

P.S. I suppose I'd better spell it all out because I know just how thick you rozzers can be: Priti knows absolutely nothing of any of this. She's 100% oblivious to it all. The poor girl thinks me completely spotless and, boy, do I love her for it. (I shall unfortunately have to 'borrow' her ID card for one of my little trips, but hey-ho, needs must and all that.)

A wonderful thing, true love, Harry. You should try it some day.

Epilogue

270

Fifteen minutes after disconnecting the call to the Creep that never was, Paul Norris found an advert for a job in The Codfather, a fish and chip shop not two hundred yards from his own front door. The manager, a jovial puffy-cheeked man called Lionel ('Lionel Gulliver, but you can call me Lionel. Everyone does'), invited him around for a chat at opening time. By ten past opening time, Paul had served customers saveloys, cod, haddock, pies, sausages in batter, and chips. Four hours later, as Lionel twisted around the silly little 'Closed' sign in the shape of a grinning fish, Paul felt exhausted and covered in grease, but he also felt oddly elated. The people had been a distraction. Some he knew, some he didn't. The chatter had been friendly and fun, and for brief moments, Paul had felt as though he was doing something important. Not just serving chips. He was lending an ear, being a straight man in a long-winded joke, cheering people up, calming people down. He was listening and talking, and other people were listening and talking back. He wasn't just a broom-pushing ghost like he was at Blossom Hill. He had suddenly become more than that. He felt as though he had some sort of purpose.

'So, what do you think? Job's yours if you want it.' Lionel gave an enormous warm smile that made Paul think of his dad. 'You did well tonight. Very well. I'd be more than happy to have you on board.'

The money was better than at the garden centre, and he didn't have to catch any stupid buses. He could walk to work in less than five minutes. The hours would be good too – he could lie in until lunchtime if Levi had been playing up the night before – but it was the thought of the interaction, the people, that did it for him. For the first time in months, he felt wanted. Not just tolerated. Wanted. An integral part of a system. An important part.

'Why not?' Paul said. 'Go on then.'

Singh's mum was a pretty woman in her late fifties with her hair pulled back in a tightish bun and her eyes lightly made up.

'Inspector. It is good to meet with you at last,' she said as she waved him through the door. The house smelled of turmeric and… Hal struggled to make it out… Rosemary, was it? 'Priti has told us everything about you.'

'Oh, not everything I hope.'

'Yes. Everything.'

'Oh dear.'

'No, no. It is all good. Can I take your coat?'

'No. Thanks. I'll be all right.'

A short man bumbled down the stairs, his eyes glaring at Luchewski.

'It is Inspector Luchewski,' the woman said to him. 'Come to see Priti.'

'Inspector Luchewski.' The man took Hal's hand and shook it like it he was trying to make it come off. 'Priti has told us everything about you.'

'So I've heard.'

'What?'

The woman gave her husband a weird sort of tap on the head. 'Don't worry yourself about it, Ash, he already knows it.'

Singh's dad just looked confused.

'Is she in?' Luchewski asked.

The mum beckoned him into a room.

Singh was sitting cross-legged on the sofa, remote control banging away towards the television. A split second of a TV programme, then another, then another. She looked up at him as he came through the door.

'Oh!' The legs came down and the TV went off. 'Hello, sir.' It was like a teacher had caught her smoking. 'Er ... how are you?'

'OK. I'm ... OK.'

'Some tea, Detective Inspector?' Singh's mum peered around the door.

'Yes. Thank you, Mrs Singh. That would be very nice.'

The woman disappeared from view, closing the door behind her.

'So ... er ... what are *you* doing here?'

Luchewski sat down on the sofa next to her. 'I'd've thought that would have been obvious. I'm here for your mum's amazing cooking.' Singh smiled. 'I heard she does a mean egg and chips.'

'Second to none.'

'No, seriously. How are you? How are things ... going?'

Singh was on long-term leave and had temporarily moved back in with her parents, taking comfort in the things and people she knew best. Luchewski understood. It was the easiest and most obvious thing to do. Pull the comfort blanket over yourself.

'Well, you know. Pretty shitty really. Given everything.' A grimace crossed her face. 'How's the case going?'

'You don't really want to know about the case?'

'No, I do. Honestly. Well ... certain parts of it. Not necessarily the things about ... him.' She didn't so much spit the word out as dribble it.

'OK.' Luchewski thought for a moment. 'Jason Thickett's making a good recovery. Managed to open one of his eyes last week, apparently. Not much longer and I think he'll be winking it at the pretty nurses if the stories I've heard about him are true.'

'Not gay then?'

'God no. Little bugger for the girls according to his mum. Oh, and Alexander Judd's wife has now taken full legal control of the garden centre. I don't think he's too popular with his family now. Probably has to sleep with the dog in the kennel. Got himself a perverting the course of justice slap on the wrist.'

'What an idiot.'

'And I assume you know all about Humphreys from the news? He's still in a coma. Forensics found some of his skin tissue under McKenzie's nails. Turns out he's also the Tonbridge Rapist. Kent police have been after him for over twenty years now. With any luck, when he wakes, he'll be going down for the best part of forever. No more Booboo the bloody Clown for him.'

'Or anyone else.'

Singh's mother came into the room with a tray heavy with cups and pots and milk and biscuits. She edged towards the coffee table and put it down as the dad peered around the door smiling.

'The best news of all, though,' Luchewski suddenly remembered, 'is that Baldwin – the git – is currently on gardening leave.'

'He's not?'

'Yep.' Luchewski grinned. 'Woode's orders, while they investigate the enquiry.'

'What for?'

'"The dubious methods of DI Baldwin and his team in soliciting a confession from the accused". That's what the judge kept referring to. "Dubious methods".'

'Good. I'm pleased.'

'So am I.'

'I take it,' Singh's mum asked, lifting the empty tray away from the table, 'you don't like this Baldwin man?'

'No, Mrs Singh. Not really.'

'No, Mum. He's a twat.'

Luchewski did a double-take, expecting the nice, respectable Indian lady to be shocked. Instead she just shook her head and said, 'Too many twats in the world these days. Far too many twats.' Still shaking her head, she went back out of the room.

Luchewski and Singh roared with laughter.

'To be fair to her,' Singh eventually managed to say, 'I don't think she really understands what a twat is. I think she thinks she's saying twit or something.'

'And you've never disabused her of that?'

'God, no. Why should I? It makes life more interesting.'

They laughed some more until the tricky silence crept slowly over the situation and Luchewski found himself picking a chocolate digestive off the plate as some sort of distraction.

'You know the worst thing?' Singh eventually said, her voice quiet and low. 'The worst thing of it all?'

'What?'

She paused as if she was unsure whether she should continue. 'It's like my judgement is all wrong. I couldn't even tell that he was a murderer. The man I loved. The man I was going to marry. I was standing right next to him and all the while he was doing these terrible things.' She swallowed hard. 'I mean, what sort of a fucking useless copper does that make me?'

Luchewski placed the biscuit back down on the plate. 'Just because you're a copper doesn't mean you have magic eyes that can see inside everyone's soul, you know.'

'But you'd think I would know, wouldn't you? Isn't that our job? To know.'

Luchewski shook his head. 'No, Priti. We don't know. Like I said, we're not fucking magicians. We're not fucking wizards. All that rubbish about copper's intuition … it's bullshit. Sometimes we see things and sometimes we don't. Sometimes there aren't even things to see. We're only bloody human. For God's sake, I had pasta-alla-whatever with you both the other night and *I* couldn't see it. Jesus. Nobody would have done. He kept it buried well.'

They sat there in silence for a while, the distant *whoosh, whoosh* of cars passing the only sound.

'So, what happens now?' Luchewski leaned in closer to her. 'Where do you go from here?'

She shrugged. 'I don't know. To be honest I don't know.'

'Look, Priti … You are a fucking brilliant copper – no, no, don't say anything. You are. And the force needs you back – *I* need you back. At some point. But at the moment you need to let it all go.' He sighed. 'I know this sounds really cheesy and like I've no idea what I'm on about, but, give it time. Time will sort it. It always fucking does. It may seem like an impossible wall to climb right now but in due course, it'll bloody crumble right in front of your eyes. It'll become easy. Trust me.'

'Yeah, but –'

'No buts. Just sit it out. That's all you have to do. Just give it some space. The truth is that no amount of counselling can do what time does. It squashes everything down and whittles away at the things that seem big. It's true when they say that time heals. It really is.'

Singh nodded and sipped some of her tea, but couldn't help thinking that Luchewski was talking about something other than her own problems.

On the way out, Mr and Mrs Singh shook his hand again.

'Very very nice to have met you, Detective Inspector,' said Mr Singh. 'Very very nice.'

'You too.'

'Very very nice.'

Singh stood in the doorway to the sitting room and smiled at Luchewski.

'Inspector,' the mum asked, 'you have been giving her good advice?'

'I hope I have.'

'Good. That is good.' She turned and looked back at her daughter behind her. 'She needs good advice.'

'She will get over it,' the dad looked thoughtful. 'Of course she will.'

'She will.'

'I *am* here, you know?' Singh tutted at them all.

'Yes, yes, of course,' dismissed Mr Singh.

'Anyway,' Mrs Singh frowned, 'I never liked him.'

'You did, Mum!'

'No. Not really.'

'You did.'

'No. I thought he was a cock.'

'Yes,' Mr Singh agreed with his wife. 'He was a cock. A complete cock.'

Luchewski burst out laughing and Singh quickly joined him.

'What is so funny?' asked her mum.

It had been a spur of the moment thing. Luchewski had woken up one morning and thought it would be fun. He didn't even consult Jackie over it. Just a quick call to the school beforehand and then, once he and Lily had hit the road and had stopped off for coffee and doughnuts at Leigh Delamere, he rang her and left a message on her answerphone, before switching his phone off.

The sun was obliterating the horizon as they drove over the Severn Bridge, and even though Luchewski had never really lived in Wales there was a tiny part of him that felt as though he was coming home.

They had lunch in Swansea before walking up out of the city towards the house where Victor and Mary Luchewski had lived in the days before fame had mutated their surname. Lily clapped her hands in delight to see the blue plaque that was stuck to the wall above the door.

Victor Liddle
Comedian and Magician
lived here between
1969 and 1970

'I wish I'd been old enough to meet Grandpa and Grandma. I mean, I know I was born and everything ... but I wish I'd met them properly.'

Hal found himself with a slight lump in his throat. 'They were good people,' he muttered before coughing himself together again and suggesting they drive to the Mumbles and have ice cream.

After the Raspberry Ripple and Caramel Fudge and laughing at seagulls fighting on the mudflats, they drove along the A48 towards the Vale of Glamorgan. The place they were going was down a lane, near the sea and not on any map. Several times they had to reverse when aggressive tractors barged their way up the single track roads, forcing the TT into sunken ditches alongside.

Luchewski tried to remember where it was – it had been some years since he'd been here – but in the end it was Lily who recognised a turning and got them going in the right direction. It was late afternoon by this time, but the sun was still blazing.

Eventually, they found it. Hal slammed on the brakes just as they were about to pass the gates, sending Lily jerking forward in the passenger seat.

'Sorry, love.' He pulled the car over to the side before stepping out.

The gates were ridiculous. Tall, black, wrought iron things at least thirteen feet high with spikes on top, built into a solid looking brick wall. Lily shut the door behind her and joined him, rubbing her neck.

'Do you think he's even in?' she wondered. 'What if he's on holiday?'

Hal pressed the button on the intercom and waited. After about a minute he pressed it again.

A crackle before… 'Yes. Yes. I heard you the first time. What is it?' A woman's voice.

'Er… I was just wondering if Barry Moore was in? I'm Harry. His godson. Victor Liddle's son. I'm here with my daughter.'

'Have you made an appointment?' A sharp Welsh lilt to her voice. 'Only he won't see anyone without an appointment.'

'No. No we haven't. We were just –'

'Hold on a minute.' The line went dead.

Hal looked at Lily who just shrugged her shoulders back at him.

'I knew you should have called ahead, Dad.'

'No. It'll be all right. He'll be –'

Crackle. 'Harry, boy! Come on in, Harry. Come. On. In.' Barry's voice sounded old and round like mucus. 'I'll open the gates for you. Drive on up. It's good to see you.'

Hal smiled at Lily as a buzz and a clank from the electric gates filled the lazily warm afternoon.

'Good-looking woman, eh?' Luchewski's Uncle Barry nodded towards the woman playing with Lily and the dog on the massive expanse of lawn in front of the house. The dog had snatched a ball they were throwing, refusing to give it up while Lily and the woman were laughing and chasing the boisterous collie. 'Thinking of making her wife number four.'

Luchewski nearly choked on his champagne. 'Haven't you learned your lesson yet? Surely three failed marriages is enough for one lifetime?'

Barry leaned back on the white seat far too delicate for his bulky frame. 'I keep on looking. Haven't given up yet. As soon as you've given up, that's it. Kaput! You might as well be dead. Anyway, you know me. I'm just a hopeless romantic at heart. Bedazzled by the glitz and flowers, I am. Just a sucker for the icing on a wedding cake.'

'How old is she? Fifty?'

'Forty-nine.'

'Exactly half your age then.'

'Cheeky sod.'

Luchewski sipped at the champagne, pleased to be out of the sun under the veranda. 'Retirement suits you.'

'Retirement? Don't give me that retirement rubbish.'

'No?'

277

'No. I'm in talks with Channel Four at this very moment.' He leaned in conspiratorially close and lowered his voice to a whisper. 'One of these reality TV thingies again. *At Home With Barry Moore* sort of thing. Cameras following me around all day. Funny incidents at Waitrose and all that. People love that stuff. Christmas special and everything, they're saying. Nice six-figure fee too.' He winked at Luchewski and topped up his glass with more fizzing pink bubbly. 'She's growing up.' Hal looked at his daughter racing about on the immaculate lawn, the dog slobbering all over her. 'Got a look of her grandfather about her, I'd say.'

'Would you?' He'd never thought about it before, but Uncle Barry was right. There was something about the eyes, the fall of the mouth. The gracefulness. The posture. All of it was screaming Victor Liddle at him and it was only now, sitting here on the patio of a house far too large for a single man in his seventies, that he noticed it. The thought that he hadn't realised before suddenly saddened him and he felt himself slumping a little in his seat.

'I read the papers, you know.' Uncle Barry's voice took on a more soothing tone. 'About this fella you were after. This killer. A terrible business. Terrible. Got him in the end though, didn't you? A good job. Well done.' Barry looked him straight in the eyes. 'Your dad would have been proud of you.'

Luchewski sighed. 'I'm not so sure.'

Barry harrumphed slightly. 'Well I am. Remember, I shared a dressing room with the man for thirty-five years. You don't get to see a man in his underwear every night for thirty-five years without having some idea of the sort of things he would or wouldn't be proud of.'

Luchewski smiled. 'I don't know. In the end – just before the end – I let him down. Let them both down. They died not talking to me. Did you know that? We'd argued and they died a couple of days later.'

Barry nodded. 'I knew you'd argued. But they weren't angry with you.' He put his champagne flute on the patio table. 'I spoke to your father the morning he and your mother died. Did you know *that*?'

'No. No, I didn't.'

'Well, I did. He phoned me from the hotel they were staying at. Told me all about it. Told me everything. There were no secrets between me and Victor. We talked about everything.' A seagull screeched overhead and in the distance a plane's tail was scratching the perfect blue of the sky. 'And I mean everything.'

Luchewski looked at the old man beside him. 'So you knew the reasons why Jackie and I split up?'

'The gay stuff? Of course I did. We all did. We'd known for years before you even announced it. It came as no surprise to any of us, I can tell you. In fact your mum and dad and I were probably more surprised when you said you were going to marry whatsername. That was something that Victor and Mary didn't imagine, I can tell you. They'd always just assumed you were gay. We all did. And then little Lily came along and –'

'They'd always known?'

'Of course they did. Parents just do, I suppose.'

'They never said that to me.'

'No, well, they didn't get much of a chance to, did they, what with them getting themselves killed like that.'

Luchewski watched as the woman and his daughter strolled along the lawn back to where the two men were sitting.

'But we argued.'

'Stuff and nonsense. They were sad for Lily, that's all. They weren't angry at you. You were finally making decisions that were right for you. If anything they were pleased about it. You were facing up to who you obviously were. At last.' Barry wiped his brow with the back of his hand. 'But you should never think that they weren't proud of you. Never. One of the last things your dad said to me that morning when he phoned – and I can remember it like it was yesterday, it's burned into my memory that last conversation with your dad – he said that you were making your way in the world, on your own terms. Not as the son of Victor Liddle but as yourself. Harold Luchewski. Detective whatever Harry Luchewski. It would have been easy to just sit back and ride along on your dad's coat tails, but you weren't doing that. You were doing things for yourself and, my God, he was proud of that. Looked like you were having fun there,' he smiled at the two women coming towards him. 'You'd better watch Tebbit there though. His teeth will rip your fingers out given half a chance.'

'You two catching up on things?' The woman was puffing as she slugged back her champagne. 'Reminiscing?'

Barry gave Luchewski one of the widest smiles that Luchewski had ever seen. 'Oh, you know. Setting a few things straight, eh, Harry?'

'Teaching? What do you want to go into teaching for?'

Stevie Denyer grinned at Luchewski as they walked along Old

Compton Street, past the crowds spilling out of the Admiral Duncan. Luchewski's mind leapt momentarily back to 1999, when David Copeland's home-made nail bomb ripped the gay community apart in a matter of seconds, leaving straight people dead in its wake too. The world was packed with such witless baboons, he knew, but as long as everybody else came back fighting stronger and harder and faster than the idiots, the world would keep being a decent place. It was the role of good men and women to drown out the voices of the sick and evil. People like Nicholas Gardener. People who put their own feelings and ideas above everyone else's. People who would take what they wanted for their own piteous beliefs. Good men and women should just smother them.

'It's an honourable profession,' Denyer said. 'More honourable than journalism anyway. Or,' he turned to look at Luchewski, 'the police force. Bunch of crooks, journalists and the police.'

Luchewski nodded his head. 'Hmm. True. Nothing worse than a rubbish policeman or the journalist that tries to expose him. Leeches, the lot of them. Throw them on the fire, the wankers.'

Denyer laughed and his hand seemed to instinctively reach out for Luchewski's arm. For a second, Luchewski seemed to freeze before relaxing and allowing Denyer to feed his arm through.

'What about Lily?'

'Lily?'

'Yes.'

'Lily's fine. Nothing wrong with Lily.' Luchewski peered into the Stockpot restaurant before carrying on. 'One of the most up together people I know. Nothing fazes her. Not even this.' He nodded down at their interlinked arms.

'I'm sorry,' Denyer started to withdraw his arm. 'I didn't –'

'No. No. Don't. I like it.' He clamped Denyer's forearm to him with his own. 'It's good.'

Denyer nuzzled up close to him. It felt like rain. Again. The last few days it hadn't stopped, and the clouds above them were black and thunderous-looking, thick and heavy, as they made their way across Charing Cross Road.

'It's going to rain again,' Denyer pointed upwards to the sky.

'Oh I don't know about that.' Luchewski smiled before pulling Denyer in through a restaurant door.

Arnold Richards sat at the Governor's computer. Having been a good boy since his arrival in Ashmoor Prison, the Governor – Mr Trevillick – had granted him certain privileges. One of those privileges was to clean the Governor's office twice a week. Not that Richards considered emptying out the wastepaper basket of a pompous geriatric prig a privilege, but it did at least get him away from the cells and all those mindless baboons who inhabited them. Honestly, putting someone like himself in a wing with that sort of scum – he was so much better than that. The people he was banged up with had no brains, no imagination. They were mere thugs. Not one of them had any style or panache about their work. Stabbings and shootings. Hopeless. He felt a king among such detritus.

The best thing about cleaning the Governor's office though was the fact that the Governor would leave him to it. On his own. Nobody else around. And he always left his computer logged on, the fool. Every time. In his bunk at night, Arnold Richards would find himself looking forward to Mondays and Thursdays.

Ten minutes. He checked the clock on the wall. He usually had around ten minutes. It would take him around seven minutes to clean the office if he really hurried and that would give him two or three minutes on the computer. After hoovering the floor he would keep the vacuum cleaner running so that the secretaries outside would not get too suspicious. So far it had worked, he had never been caught.

During one of last week's sessions, he had been horrified to find out that Luchewski, who'd been in charge of his own investigation, had put an end to those South London killings. That annoyed Richards more than he thought it would. There was at least something a bit sophisticated about those murders – a little like his own. The sheer speed of them. The audacity. A pity the killer couldn't have been allowed to continue a little while longer, keep the suspense going, but *no*. Somebody was going to have to teach that Luchewski a lesson. He had it coming. He *really* had it coming.

Three minutes. He quickly checked his secret email account. It took a couple of seconds before the screen filled.

'*1 New Message.*'

Richards clicked on it and started reading.

Hi there TheHeadMan.

Just to keep you informed of how things are panning out here. We're nearly there with the holiday plans. Everything's slotting into place and soon we can get moving on it. Hopefully it won't be long before you're out of the house and breathing wonderful fresh air. Details of the flight will follow shortly.

Hang on in there,
NO1FAN.

Richards sat back in the chair and smiled. Fresh air. It would be good to taste fresh air again. Real fresh air. The sweet fresh air of freedom. Not long now, he thought. Not much longer now. Weeks, months. Not long.

Checking the clock, he leaned in and started typing a reply.

For more information about **Mark Lock**

and other **Accent Press** titles

please visit

www.accentpress.co.uk